THE ICE KISS

L. STEELE

FOR THE GOOD GIRLS
WHO LOVE
MORALLY GREY HOCKEY PLAYERS
WHO READ YOUR SP!CIEST BOOKS
THEN OUTDO
THE DETAILED SCENES
IN REAL LIFE...

I SEE YOU!

PS. Because you asked:
F w0rd count: 225
C w0rd count: 77
D w0rd count: 50
P w0rd count: 47

SPOTIFY PLAYLIST

Drunk in Love – Beyoncé
You Belong with Me – Taylor Swift
About You – The 1975
Loe Race – Machine Gun Kelly, Kellin Quinn
Wanna Be – jxdn, Machine Gun Kelly
Summertime Sadness – Lana Del Ray
Bigger Than The Whole Sky – Taylor Swift
What Was I Made For? – Billie Eilish
We're Not in Love Anymore – Knox, Charlotte Sands
ceilings – Lizzy McAlpine
Faulty Wiring – Sam Short
Matilda – Harry Styles
My Mind & Me – Selina Gomez
MEAN! – Madeline The Person
How Do I Say Goodbye – Dean Lewis
Chaotic – Tatte McRae
One More Shot – CIL
this is what sadness feels like – JVKE
In The Stars – Benson Boone
Take My Breath Away – Berlin

STAR SIGNS

Rick: Taurus - The Challenger

- You are confident, ambitious, intelligent, and very, very passionate, though you like to hide that behind your easy-going nature.
- You're obstinate and want to get your own way.
- You're possessive, yet also sensitive.
- You are materialistic but also sensual, loyal, and generous.
- You like to hold a grudge.
- You are a romantic at heart.
- You have a taste for the finer things in life.
- You love to spoil your woman with the best restaurants or make her a delicious meal at home and provide her with the silkiest sheets and the bubbliest champagne.
- You are strong and powerful and stand up for what you believe in.
- Your greatest fear is to be powerless, so you focus on controlling your environment.

Giorgina: Scorpio - The Achiever

- You are energetic and emotional.
- You secretly crave intimacy and romance.
- You can be very vengeful when someone does you wrong.

- You don't handle betrayal well.
- You can be defensive and you fear being vulnerable.
- You have a jealous streak.
- You want to be successful and admired by other people.
- You're very conscious of your public image.
- You fear failure and not being seen as valuable by others.

1

Giorgina

"You're such a good girl." *He wraps his fingers around my throat and leans in until his breath raises the fine hair on my forehead.* *"You take everything I give you so beautifully."*

My toes curl. When Shane East says, 'good girl', I'd do anything he wants, even if it causes pain. Especially if it causes pain. A-n-d... Don't tell my friends I'm listening to *The Billionaire's Fake Wife* by L. Steele, instead of *How to Win Friends and Influence People* by Dale Carnegie. Everyone knows I only listen to motivational speakers and only read self-help books. Oh, I also have my life organized by the minute — the only way to stay in control. Which reminds me, I have precisely thirty minutes to get in and out of this shindig. The only reason I'm here is because my friend, Abby, invited me, and I couldn't say no. I flounce into the room, hitch my Hermès bag over my shoulder and declare, "Hello, everyone. Sorry I'm late."

Silence descends, broken only by Shane's baritone in my ear which growls, *"Come for me. Right now."* Oopsie, best to shut off my audiobook for the time I'm here.

I'm addicted to the voices of my growly audio narrators. There's nothing like listening to them to drown out the thoughts in my head. The ones where I worry about everything that can go wrong with my life. The ones where I work myself into a tizzy and end up talking to myself—a sight that draws strange looks from people near me. One of the last things I want my friends to witness.

I slide my phone from my handbag, stop the audio, then pull out my earphones and drop them into my bag. When I look up, my gaze arrows in on the man hulking by the bar.

He's six-foot-six—no kidding, the tallest, biggest man I've ever met outside of my spicy novels, though I'll never tell him that— with shoulders that fill my vision, and that chest of his clad in a black T-shirt, which is threadbare and outlines every single ridge and divot of his pecs. And that throat—OMG, that gorgeous, sinewed throat with veins that pop in relief when he's pissed.

Of course he's pissed, as evinced by the set of his jaw, the nerve that flexes at his temple, and those dark brows drawn down over his eyes. Blue eyes. Icy, frosted, and glacial. They chill me to the bone, even as the sight of his luscious, pouty, lower lip makes me want to dig my teeth in and draw blood. *Argh.*

These conflicting emotions where Rick Mitchell is concerned always give me whiplash. How can you hate a man and yet be attracted to him so much? His gaze intensifies. He brings the bottle of water to his mouth and his biceps bulge. The veins on his forearms stand out in relief, my toes curl. Ugh, why does he have the most deliciously sculpted arms? And that narrow waist, lean hips, and thick, powerful thighs, which contract as he walks. And between them that bulge —which indicates he's packing something mean and big and— he widens his stance. I jerk my head up. His lips curl and oh, my word, that smirk. It's hot and mean and so very annoying.

So, he caught the staring—big deal. It's a free country, last time I checked. So what if this city is dull and grey, and the rain gets on my nerves. I'm not one to complain. I'm going to work with the cards I've been dealt. Everything in my life so far has prepared me to meet challenges head on. It doesn't stop heat from flushing my cheeks, though.

His frown deepens, then he wraps those succulent lips around the bottle of water and guzzles from it.

I will not stare at his throat as he swallows. Will not allow myself to salivate at the thought of licking my way up that hard column and tasting the salt on my skin. Will not.

He raises the bottle in my direction. Caught again. Twice in two minutes. What a disaster. I toss my hair over my shoulder, pop out my hip—clad in the latest Max-Mara creation, by the way—and tip up my chin, then force myself to tear my gaze away from that gorgeous, irritating hunk of a man.

"Hope I'm not disturbing?" I arch an eyebrow at the room in general and spot the bottle of champagne Cade—my friend Abby's husband—holds in his hand.

"Aha, so you're the guardian of the bubbles?" I say brightly. Guardian of the bubbles? Clearly, I've been spending too much time in the company of Hollywood personalities. Couldn't come up with anything better? Whatever. I'm funny, charming, and I have a larger-than-life personality. *Stay positive. Fake it till you make it, remember?* I strut toward him, snatch up a flute from the bar, and taking the bottle from him, check out the label. "Dom Pérignon, excellent. I think I might have found my tribe, I—"

Suddenly, a pony—no, it's a dog, a massive mutt, a Great Dane, by the looks of it—leaps up to his feet. He must have been crouched down by Rick's legs, and I didn't notice him because, of course, I was focused on the man to the exclusion of everything else.

Seriously though, am I that taken in by this man that I missed this... this... Enormous beast who now prowls toward me? There's a glint in his eyes, as he takes me in—like I'm his next meal. The hair on the nape of my neck rises. His jowls shiver. He opens his jaws, and drool drips from them. His teeth are so sharp. I swallow. He's moving toward me with such intent. Is he going to bite off my head, or maybe, a hand? Doesn't anybody else see this? Why isn't anyone stopping him?

My pulse rate spikes. Ohmigod. I should cry out for help. I should. I open my mouth, but nothing comes out. He draws closer, and every cell in my body seems to freeze. He gathers speed as he nears, then rears up, and believe me when I say, he's taller than I am.

I whimper. That's right—brave, confident, takes-no-prisoners Giorgina whimpers. My heart fights to escape my ribcage. The blood pounds at my temples. He snatches the bottle of champagne from my hands, upturns it so the contents empty down his gullet, then plants his paws back on the floor, drops the bottle, and pushes past me to the sound of several voices yelling in unison, "Tiny!"

Seriously? Tiny?

I stumble back. The six-inch high heels of my Louboutin's catch in a crack in the wooden floors. *Oh, no, no, no.* I begin to tip over.

I throw up my hands to try to find my balance, and my handbag goes flying. *This is it. Death by Great Dane. Ugh! That's not the kind of headline I want to make.* I squeeze my eyes shut and brace for impact, only something strong and hard bands around my waist. The breath whooshes out of me. The next second, I'm hauled to an upright position. I know who it is before I sense the heat that leaps off of him and lassoes around me. I know who it is before that scent of fresh snow and cut grass teases my nostrils. I know who it is because I'm plastered from back to hip to thigh against his front and his sizable thickness stabs into the curve of my butt. I know who it is because no one but he could sport an arousal so big, it feels like a hockey stick has slapped me in the rear.

Jesus. Of course, my brain goes to hockey sticks. He's likely to be the new Captain of the London Ice Kings, so he'd better know how to wield a hockey stick. I mean, not the one between his legs—nope, not going there in my head. Obviously, I'm sure he plays with that one, too—the one between his legs, I mean. And ohmigod, the image of his big, fat fingers squeezing his monster cock is something I'm not going to forget in a hurry.

His grasp around my waist tightens, and he pulls me so close, said hockey stick—is it curved at the end, too?—throbs against me. It seems to grow longer, thicker, larger... *Gah, that's your imagination. It has to be.* No one has such a big dick, except maybe, porn stars. And Rick's not a porn star. He's a freakin' ex-NHL player, who did a stint with the Royal Marines, did some moonlighting as a bodyguard, and is now back to playing hockey. That's all he is. He's human.

He may look like a god, avenging angel and devil, all rolled into one, but he's a man. A man who's larger-than-life and built, given no inch of him gives while I'm plastered to him, including his dick, which is now happily nestled in the cleavage between my butt-cheeks, and... *OMG!* My flush deepens and spreads down my chest to my extremities. A thousand little fires spark across my skin.

Someone clears their throat, and I glance around the room to find every single gaze is on me. *Oh no, no, no. Nice way to make an impression on your new employer.*

"Let me go." I pull free from Rick, who, thankfully, releases me, then spin around. "How dare you touch me, you oaf?"

2

Rick

She raises her hand, and I sense she's going to slap me, but I don't stop her. Instead, I welcome her palm connecting with my cheek. I welcome the sting of pain that zips out from her touch and down my spine. I welcome the throb in my balls, the twitch of my dick, which has only grown harder thanks to the contact of her skin with mine. I welcome the flash of anger in her golden eyes, the red stain of her cheeks, the pulse that beats at the base of her throat. When I don't react, her gaze grows stricken, and she firms her lips. "I don't need your help," she hisses at me.

"What *you* need and what you *need*, are two very different things," I drawl.

Her gaze flicks to my cheek where her palm-print is, no doubt, in evidence. "I'm not sorry I slapped you," she huffs.

I angle my face. "I'm not sorry I caught you."

"Good."

"Good." I feel my lips twitch but manage to keep a straight face.

She tips up her chin, then turns to leave and promptly stumbles on the same crack in the wooden floor. If I were a bastard, I'd let her fall. If I were the asshole she thinks I am, I'd allow her to hit the floor on her knees and hurt herself, but the thought does funny things to my guts, so I catch her around her waist—again—because that's going to piss her off to no end. I righten her. Before she can turn and tell me off again, I step back. "Looks like you can't do without me." I brush past her and snap my finger at Tiny, who, having emptied the champagne bottle down his gullet—don't ask— jumps to his feet, retrieves the bottle, and prances over to hand it over to me.

I stare into the bottle—nope, not a drop left in it—then back at Tiny who pants up at me with a happy smile on his face. The mutt has what must be the biggest and most satisfied smile in the doggy world on his face. He belongs to my friend, Liam and his wife Isla who are currently on their island off Venice. Isla is pregnant, and they've decided to stay there until she feels strong enough to travel.

They'd asked our mutual friend, Knight to dog sit when Knight was going through a rough patch. A bit of an understatement, considering the man was an ex-Royal Marine who'd been held behind enemy lines for six months. When he returned, he was a changed man. Someone who shunned his friends, until he met his future wife, Penny, who transformed him. She and Tiny softened the man's heart until he re-engaged with life. To look at him now, you'd never guess how much he's been through. That's what the love of a good woman does to you. And the unquestioning devotion of a mutt.

"Can't take you anywhere, eh?" I scratch behind Tiny's ears.

In response, Tiny thumps his tail on the floor and the ground seems to shake a little. Or maybe, that's from the gnashing of teeth that I hear coming from Giorgina's direction.

I ignore Little Miss Spoiled Brat and walk toward Knight, who's also my new boss. Not only does he have Penny, but they've adopted his friend Adam's little girl Bianca, since Adam was killed in action. Now, Bianca jumps to her feet and races toward us. "He's sooo cute." She throws her arm about Tiny's neck. The Great Dane stays still and lets her fuss over him.

"He also polished off a $4000 bottle of champagne," I say in a low voice to her parents.

Knight chuckles. "Doesn't seem to affect him at all. Besides, Cade, the bastard, can afford it."

As if hearing his name, Cade Kingston, captain of the English cricket team prowls over to us. "What are you ladies whispering about?" He smirks.

"Just that you're going to have competition for rabid fans now that the London Ice Hawks have him as their captain." Knight nods in my direction.

Cade does a double take. "You're accepting the offer?"

"I haven't said yes… yet," I admit.

Knight's wife Penny rises to her feet. "You going to make that a habit?" She jerks her chin toward the palm-print I wear on my cheek.

I shrug. "It was worth it."

I'm sure she suppresses a smile before scowling at me. "Gio has a good heart. I know she can come across as all up herself, but she's a loyal friend."

"So am I."

"Go easy on her, okay?" She pats my shoulder.

"I don't plan on having anything to do with her," I murmur.

"Hmm." She turns to Knight; a look passes between them, then she bends and kisses his cheek. "Time I get Bianca to say goodbye to everyone."

"I'll be right behind you, baby." He wraps his hand about the nape of her neck, and pulls her back for a thorough kiss. By the time Penny straightens, she's flushed, blushing, and her eyes are sparkling. With a giggle, she bends and puts her arm about Bianca's shoulder. "Come along honey, let's say our goodbyes to everyone."

Baby? Honey? I throw up little in my mouth. Why is it that married couples think it's their right to inflict their sickly-sweet PDAs on the rest of us? If I ever reduce myself to mouthing off such gooey words, feel free to kick my legs out from under me. I school my features into a mask of polite disinterest — something I'm good at. Keeping my feelings to myself. That's the first lesson I learned after being forced to leave the NHL for showing my emotions too freely on the ice.

"Do I also have to say goodbye to Tiny?" Knight and Penny's little girl pouts.

"You'll see him again soon," I point out.

"Promise?" She holds our her palm.

"Promise." I place my much larger palm over hers and squeeze gently. She seems satisfied. Enough to pull her hand from mine, and with a last hug for Tiny, she allows her ma to lead her toward the others.

Knight turns to me, and says, "Right, then. I do need to go, as well. But first, I need to point out that hockey is your first love. Not a day went by in the military when you didn't follow news of the sport from around the world. You're the only man I know who tunes in regardless of who is playing."

"So?" I raise a shoulder.

"So, I don't know of anyone else who lives and breathes the game as much as you. You're perfect to lead the team into the League."

The League is the European equivalent of the Cup in the U.S. Competition is fierce. The very fact that he thinks the man who hasn't competed professionally in well over five years stands a chance of playing well, let alone leading the team to victory, shows how deluded he man is.

I open my mouth to tell him so, but he shakes his head. "You know that's the only reason you were on the military's ice hockey team."

"It was the best way of working out." I raise a shoulder.

"Bull-fucking-shit," both Knight and Cade say at the same time.

I chuckle. "Fine, so it's because I love playing on the ice. That doesn't mean I want to compete on a professional level."

Knight scans my features. "Think about it. Think about what you want, mofo. After all these years of doing what's expected of you, do the thing you want to do, in here—" He slaps his palm into the space over my heart, and I hesitate.

"Where is this coming from?" I crack my neck. "And how do you know I'm not doing exactly what I want right now?"

"You mean babysitting Hollywood stars—"

"It's called being a bodyguard," I snap.

"And not that I don't love our resident silver screen icons"—he nods to where my principals, aka Solene, the biggest pop star since Taylor Swift, and her fiancé Declan, the leading superstar of Hollywood, are currently sucking face in an armchair across the room—"but even you have to admit it doesn't hold a candle to the feeling you get when you mow down the opposition and you swing the puck home."

I'm bombarded by images of the last time I was on ice at the final of the Cup as the centerman of my team—controlling the pace of the game, impacting both the offensive and defensive positions, assisting the players on my team, winning face-offs, leading breakouts, throwing that final puck toward the goal... Then walking off the ice and never looking back. What happened that day is something I don't like to revisit. It's the reason I've avoided playing professionally since. Am I ready to go back and finally face the ghost of what happened that day? I'm not sure, to be honest.

I open my mouth, but Knight claps my shoulder. "Don't answer yet. There's one more thing you should know—" He breaks off to look over my shoulder. "Giorgina, you're just in time."

3

Giorgina

"In time for what?" I strut over to them—because that's the only way I can walk in these heels. I spent half a month's salary on them, so might as well as make the most of them, right? "What are you gentleman conspiring about?"

Cade flashes me a smile. "I've heard so much about you from Abby, but we've never been formally introduced. I'm Cade."

"Giorgina." I hold out my hand. "You can call me—"

"—Giorgina," Rick snaps.

I shoot him a shocked glance. What's wrong with this man? He's even angrier than the other times I've seen him.

"Gio, is it?" Cade's grin widens. He reaches for my hand, but Rick snaps his fingers, and the Great Dane lumbers to his feet and steps between me and Cade.

"What the—?" I gape.

Cade laughs. "Sending a mutt to do your dirty work, hmm?" He shoots Rick an amused glance. "I'm off to kiss my wife. I haven't done so in nearly ten minutes, so I need to remedy that." He tips his head in my direction. "Nice to meet you Giorgina. Don't let Rick's bad attitude color your opinion about the rest of us."

Rick glowers.

Knight chuckles.

Cade swaggers off, and I follow his progress. He reaches Abby, draws her in, then bends her over in a theatrical move and kisses her. By the time he straightens, Abby's laughing.

Michael Sovrano and his wife Karma approach them. Michael's a scary mofo, with that scar around his throat and dark, penetrating eyes that seem to follow you wherever you are in the room. He's earned his reputation as the ex-head of the *Cosa Nostra* and now claims to have turned legit. "Claims" being the operative word. I tend to believe him, given he did so to ensure the safety of his wife and child—not to mention, the second one they have on the way. He's a reformed man, and while you wouldn't know it from his looks, it comes through in how his features soften when he takes in his wife.

Abby and Karma begin an earnest conversation.

There's an ease among this group of people, one that hints at shared experiences. One I'm not part of and might never be. But I've never had the time to focus on building friendships. I've been too focused on my career. And the one time I did let my guard down and trust someone... Nope, those warm, fuzzy feelings are not for me. Besides, I don't need friends. I'm here to focus on building my new career and developing a relationship with my new boss. I turn to Knight, the owner of the London Ice Hawks. "I can't wait to start work on the marketing and PR for the team."

Knight smiles. "We're very lucky to have you on board, Giorgina."

Rick mutters something under his breath that sounds suspiciously like, "That makes one of us."

I shoot him a glance. "What was that?"

"Who, me?" He stabs a thumb into his chest. "I didn't say anything."

"Hmm." I firm my lips.

"I'm glad the two of you are building a relationship; you'll be working closely."

"We will?" Rick scowls.

"He's indicated he's not interested in the captaincy of the team," I remind Knight.

"You're right." Knight slowly nods. "Since he's shown no inclination in accepting the position, you'll work in *close proximity* with whoever else is the Captain." He emphasizes the words "close proximity." I think nothing of it, but it draws a low growl from Rick.

"Something you want to say, Mitchell?" Knight murmurs.

Rick scowls at him. "I know what you're doing."

Knight chuckles. "Is it working?"

Something passes between the two men.

"What am I missing? Someone care to fill me in?" I interject.

"Just that you'll also be reporting to the Captain. This being a new team, a lot of the attention will fall on him, so you'll need to not only work closely with him, but also take your cues from him in terms of building up his image," Knight explains in a smooth voice.

"O-k-a-y," I nod. It's unusual but not unheard of.

"Also, Priest has agreed to take on the role of the General Manager—"

"Edward has?" Rick arches an eyebrow.

"Given his background and the challenges he's overcome, he's the perfect choice for the role. I have to admit, I was surprised when he accepted, but he has his reasons." Knight cuts the air with his hand. "All in all, things are shaping up well. But it's going to require a lot of effort on the part of everyone involved to pull things together. This means the Captain will need to not only get the team working together as a unit, but he'll also have to pull his share when it comes to the marketing and publicity."

"Makes sense." I nod.

"As the PR manager, you'll have daily meetings with the General Manager crafting the details of the publicity strategy for the team."

"That's what I do best." I square my shoulders. "In no time at all, I'll have the image of the Captain and the team whipped into shape."

Rick looks at me with interest. "Interesting word choice. You like the sound of whipping?"

Heat squeezes a lasso around my lower belly. Of course, he'd misconstrue the meaning of what I said. And of course, I find it a turn on. But I'm not going to let on how much his words affected me. I tip up my chin and attempt a bored tone. "As much as the next person," I say slowly.

"Is that a yes?" he rumbles.

I shake my head.

"Liar," he says without heat.

My cheeks flush. He notices it, and his gaze widens. The air between us charges. I open my mouth to tell him off, but the words stick in my throat.

Knight clears his throat and shakes his head at Rick before directing his comment at me. "In the initial days, you'll have to work closely with the Captain."

I frown, bringing my complete attention back to the conversation at hand. "I understand. I'm not one to shirk from hard work, and since Rick is not the Captain"—*thank god*—"things should run smoothly and—"

"I accept the role," Rick interrupts.

"What?" I slingshot my head in his direction. "You're saying that to get on my nerves."

"I'm doing it because Knight needs me."

I slap my hand on my hip. "Until a few seconds ago, you were positive the role wasn't for you."

"That was then."

"So, what changed?"

"I realized Knight was right all along. I'm the man for the job."

"You are." Knight nods.

"I don't want to work with you," I counter.

"Are you saying you're not accepting the role?" Knight frowns.

"Umm…" I turn to him. "That's not what I'm saying." I need this job. I ran out of L.A., breaking the lease on my place, and without any savings. Stupid move, but facing a personal crisis, followed by a professional crisis, meant it was time for a new start.

Oh, I don't regret spending all my money on my designer outfits and shoes, but it means my cashflow is rather lean—closer to non-existent, if I'm being honest. And the Ice Kings' salary is more than generous. To be frank, I don't have an option. But if it means I'm going to be working closely with this asshole, well… Do I have a choice?

"Good, so you're on board as the PR and Marketing Manager, and you"— he turns his gaze on Rick—"are the Captain." Knight's face breaks into a smile. "About fucking time." He claps Rick on the shoulder. "I'll leave you two to get acquainted and come up with a plan."

With a nod that encompasses both of us, he heads off.

"Shit." I curl my fingers around the strap of my bag.

"Fuck." Rick rakes his fingers through his hair.

"This is all your fault." I stab a finger at him. "Why couldn't you have said no to the role?"

4

Giorgina's To Do List

1. ~~Wake up at 5 a.m. & meditate for fifteen minutes.~~
2. ~~Go to the gym by 6 a.m. = half-hour workout.~~
3. ~~Healthy breakfast = oats?~~
4. ~~Get to the office by 8 a.m. & get through all emails by 9 a.m.~~
5. Arrange press-conference for the team.
6. Avoid douchebag Rick/Prick/Dick…whatever his name is. (His prick does look big!)
7. Catch up with new physical therapist for team.
8. Healthy lunch – salad, no dressing.
9. Arrange new PR pictures for Captain Monster Dickface. It's his face that looks like a monster, not his dick. Not that I would know. Moving on…
10. Search for new apartment.
11. Learn a language. Time is running out. Do it now!
12. Start that grapefruit diet?
13. Check work emails one more time on the way home.
14. Prepare clothes & tasks for tomorrow.

15. Make time for Steely Dan. Why does the Dickhole's dick seem bigger than the Dan?

16. Wind down with spicy novel. (Goal is to read/listen to 110 spicy books this year. 51 down, 59 to go.)

17. Make list for tomorrow.

18. Put this down for the satisfaction of crossing it off the list.

5

Rick

"You said 'yes' to the role?" Sinclair Sterling, also known as one of the Seven who run one of the leading financial companies in the country, and one of my oldest friends, holds the punching bag steady as I take my stance.

"I was played into taking it." I slam my fist into the boxing bag. The vibrations from the impact shudder up my arm, down to my ribcage. The dull pain sharpens my nerve-endings. It's a familiar ache, one my body is used to from all the beatings I took while in the Royal Marines and before that, from the NHL games. The latter is something I've worked hard to forget, and now I've agreed to take on a position that's going to take me straight into the eye of the storm. Fuck.

"You and played?" He scoffs. "I'm assuming it wasn't Knight's persuasive powers that convinced you to accept the role."

"That, too, but not only." I follow up with a second hit, and a third, alternating fists and keeping the hits going for another fifty before I finally stop, heart pumping, blood racing, pulse spiking as I bounce on the balls of my feet. Sweat pours down my temples and drips onto my T-shirt. I shake my head and droplets fly to the ground.

"You're not in too bad shape for a senior," Sinclair murmurs.

"I'm the same age as you." I frown.

"I'm not taking on the captaincy of a hockey team and competing with men a decade younger."

"Thanks, *Captain* Obvious." I wince, then snatch the bottle he tosses at me. I glug down the water and slide it to the side. The task of pulling together the team is something I've yet to come to grips with. Knight and I will be scouting the country in search of the most hopeful candidates. It's a pipe-dream he has of taking this team to the finals of the League, but I'm someone who's yet to back down from a challenge.

"Why are you putting yourself through this?" His eyebrows knit. "Not that I don't understand the lure of leading a team to victory, but do you want the attention it brings with it? Not to mention, the torture you're going to put your body through."

My biceps twitch and my triceps ache. My shoulders and legs are already leaden, and I've only been working out for the past three hours. I'm in excellent physical shape, having worked out every single day since I left the Royal Marines, but that doesn't mean anything. Not when I'll need to hit speeds of twenty to twenty-five miles per hour on the ice and hit the puck at more than double that speed, all while on skates. My entire body aches at the thought, my guts churn, and I haven't even begun the season. I roll my shoulders, then begin to unwind the tape from around my fingers. "It's a question I've been asking myself since I agreed," I admit.

"What made you agree?"

"You mean *who* made him agree?" a new voice asks.

I turn to find the former Father Edward Chase, now simply Priest, as he prefers to be called, prowling over to us. He's not often in town, but when he is, he can be found at this gym in the basement of the 7A Club.

I chin jerk in greeting. "As always, nothing skips your powers of observation."

One side of his lips twitches. "Whoever it is, I hope you don't waste too much time dancing around the obvious."

I pull off the tape and glare at him. "Going straight for the jugular?"

"You don't get too many chances in life."

"Not all of us want the girl," I shoot back.

He winces. "Nice shot, and I probably deserve it—not."

"You didn't get the girl and never got over it." I pop a shoulder. "But I'm not in the running for the girl at all, and don't intend to be."

"If you say so," Edward says in a tone that he thinks I'll interpret as agreeable, but instead, ends up sounding condescending.

I roll the tape and throw it in the basket against the wall. "Fuck, Priest, I can do without you getting on my balls."

"I'd rather not be acquainted with that part of your anatomy. And you trying to convince us or yourself?"

"Hear, hear," Sinclair murmurs.

"And the lot of you call yourself my friends?"

"Oh, we're barely getting started," a new voice sounds, then JJ Kane draws abreast. He slaps me on the back, and I stumble. Asshole's a giant of a man, almost as tall as me, "almost" being the operative word. He's built, and the silver at his temples only adds to his charm. It's no wonder his son's ex-girlfriend fell for him.

"The fuck you doing here?" I growl.

"Heard you were going to take on men half your age; thought you could do with some advice."

"Fuck no. This is hockey we're talking about. Not affairs of the heart."

"You sure?" He stabs his thumb over his shoulder.

I glance over to find Giorgina gliding in. Next to her is Finn Ashford. Finn was my partner on the last security assignment we undertook. He's an ex-NHL player who left in disgrace a year ago. It's no secret he wants to make a comeback. He's also my first pick for the team.

Finn says something, Giorgina places her hand on his arm, and he laughs. Her mouth is parted, her skin flushed. Today, she's dressed in a dark-blue colored skirt that comes to mid-thigh, with a jacket that nips in at her tiny waist, and her usual six-inch-high heels, this time in a scarlet-red. With her blonde hair piled high on her head, and the specs she has on, she looks like sexy-librarian Barbie.

They stop midway across the floor. She thrusts out her hip and tips up her head, and the gesture is so confident, so fucking sexy, my dick instantly stands to attention. Then she rises up on tiptoe and kisses him on his cheek. *What the fuck? Why are his hands on her hips?* A hot sensation stabs my chest. My gaze narrows. All of my senses hone in on the man with her. In that moment, I don't care that he's a friend. That he's someone I've trusted in the past like a brother. Or that he's known to prefer men. All I know is that he has his hands all over her.

I take a step forward, but someone grips my shoulder. "Easy, Tiger, you don't want to nip this relationship before it even starts," Edward murmurs.

I shake off his hand. "There is no relationship, so I have nothing to lose."

I close the distance between them, then grab Finn by his collar and haul him to the balls of his feet. "Welcome to the team, motherfucker."

6

Giorgina

One second, I'm talking to Finn; the next, a big growly presence looms over us. He grabs Finn by his collar and hauls him up to his toes. Finn's no weakling. He's at least six feet three inches, and all hulking shoulders and barrel chest, but in front of Rick's thick muscular—and rage-consumed—body, he seems slender.

"Hello, douchebag. Clearly, your mood hasn't improved since we last saw each other. Have you been getting any?" Finn shakes his head. "No? No wonder, you look like you have a stick stuck up your ass, you—"

"Shut the fuck up, man." In contrast to his body language, Rick's voice is mild. He drags Finn to the side and away from me.

"Remember that fight you owe me?" He half hauls-half pulls Finn to the boxing ring in the center of the gym. "Now's the time; I'm collecting."

He releases Finn and hauls himself up on the platform and under the ropes.

Finn looks up at him and smirks. "All you had to do was tell me to keep my hands off."

Rick scowls. "I don't know what you're talking about."

"Me either." I walk toward them. The soles of my Jimmy Choo's stick to the floor, and I try not to wince.

Before I can draw abreast with Finn, Rick holds out his arm. "Unless you're chicken, Kilmer?"

Finn scoffs, "You know the answer to that." He grabs Rick's hand and allows him to haul him up and onto the platform.

They pull on their gloves, and protective gear, then step into the ring. Rick throws up his fists.

"Wait, what the hell is happening?" I stare up at the men who're circling each other.

"I believe lover-boy here went into a tizzy because Finn dared touch you," Priest drawls as he draws abreast.

I huff. "More like, he had a prior score to settle with Finn."

"More like, he's clearly sweet on you." Sinclair joins us.

"More like, he needed to act out his frustration, since he's not going to act on what he wants." JJ walks over to the boxing ring and hauls himself up. "I do believe you gentlemen are going to need a referee."

"No referee needed. I'm winning." With that declaration, Rick throws the first punch. He catches Finn in the side of the head. Finn stumbles back, recovers himself and attacks, and the two begin to trade blows so quickly their motions blur.

"The first round of tryouts start this afternoon and the two of you need to be there, you—" I gasp, for Finn gets in a good punch at Rick. Blood drips from his forehead. "Oh, my god—" I close the distance to the ring and grab the edge of the platform. "Stop it. You're going to be the two most seasoned members of the team. Is this the example you want to set for the new recruits? Shouldn't you be talking out your differences or whatever?" Rick lands the next punch, then Finn, and so on, they keep trading punches, until their movements slow.

JJ whistles, and the two break apart. Rick's chest rises and falls. His already sweat-stained, cut-off T is now sodden. His cheekbones stand out in relief; the blood slides down his temple. He looks like a soldier who's been to battle. He looks magnificent.

My thighs quiver, I grip the edge of the platform with nerveless fingers. He's a beast. I should not find him so attractive. He's too similar to my ex. Exactly the kind of man I've sworn to stay away from. He continues to glare at Finn, who scowls back. Then, as if they've exchanged a silent message, they move toward each other.

"Stop! Don't fight. This is no way to resolve an argument, this—" I gape, for the two do that weird man hug routine, where they slap each other's shoulder then bump fists, "Huh?"

"Sometimes, the best way to resolve a disagreement is with your fists." JJ joins me.

"Sounds stupid, if you ask me," I grumble.

"They needed to blow off steam. A bit like puppies fighting," Sinclair drawls from behind me.

"More like full grown Dobermans," I murmur.

Priest laughs. "Once they get cleaned up, you won't notice their bruises."

"Hmm." I watch as Rick and Finn exchange words in low voices. Then, my mouth falls open again as Rick pulls off his T-shirt. Jesus H. Christ, the man is ripped. Massive shoulders roped with muscles that could be carved from steel, deep ridges between his eight-, or is that a twelve-pack abs? Narrow waist with that panty-melting 'V' arrowing down to disappear under his sweats. Oh, and the tent at his crotch is impressive. My mouth dries. My throat feels like every bit of moisture from it has been sucked down to between my thighs. He's more delectable than the latest design by Louboutin, and that's high praise coming from me.

Next to him, Finn, too, yanks off his T-shirt. The two converse for a few more seconds. Then, Finn nods and jumps off the ring. "I'll see you at the play-offs." He raises a hand in farewell, winks at me, then prowls off toward the dressing room.

"I gotta go, too. See ya later?" Priest murmurs.

"Oh, the wife's calling, can't keep her waiting." Sinclair turns and walks off, followed by JJ, who flashes me a grin.

"Meeting Lena for lunch. She said to call her if you need anything and that you're not alone in this city."

A warmth steals up my chest. I had colleagues and people I knew through my work in L.A., but it was such a cut-throat world, you never trusted anyone. I've been in London mere days, and it feels like I have more of a support network here.

"I will and tell her I said thank you." I nod as he stalks off. In the ensuing silence, I realize I've been left alone with that overbearing, too-hot, over-the-top, sexy bastard. Rick thrusts his arm over the ropes on the perimeter of the ring. I glance at his hand, then up at his face. "You're joking."

He merely looks at me with an expression that implies he never jokes. Which, to be fair, he doesn't. When he doesn't speak for a few more seconds, I huff, then thrust my hand in his.

He lowers his other hand, grabs the wrist of my free hand, and the next second, I'm rising in the air. My heels slip off. Before I can protest, he lifts me over the ropes and parks me on the platform. It's as if I weigh nothing, which, in comparison to him, I suppose I don't, but I'm not that slim either. Sadly, the way his muscles bunched as he lifted me, and the way his shoulders flexed and the veins on his forearms popped as he hauled me up sent a flurry of sensations swirling in my lower belly. I resist the urge to squeeze my thighs together. Resist the urge to look away, either.

He holds my hips until he's sure I'm steady on my feet, all the while holding my gaze in that unblinking fashion that zips an electric current up my spine. Neither of us look away. The air between us flares. The blue in his eyes grows more azure, more penetrating. Then his jaw tics. His left eyelid twitches. It's the only give that he feels this weird whatever-it-is that sparks between us. I pull away from him, and he releases me. Of course, I stumble but manage to find my balance.

"You planning to say something, or are we going to stare at each other all day?"

Does he reply? Of course not. There's no change of expression on his features. He seems to have turned to stone, except for the rise and fall of his chest, which confirms to me he's breathing.

I toss my head. "Why do I bother trying to have a conversation with you?" The heat of his body rolls across my spine, and I gasp. I glance about the now empty gym and take a step forward. He moves with me, blocking my path, and the fine hairs on the nape of my neck rise. I swallow. "So, you want to do the planning session here, I take it?"

His gaze intensifies. Those cerulean orbs slice through the barriers I've thrown up against the world, sharp-edged sapphires as mesmerizing as the depths of a frozen lake—once you've cut through the ice. No wonder, this man plays ice hockey. His body could be carved out of the frosted surface he plays on. Not to mention, the glacial frigidness of his gaze. He draws that gaze slowly, leisurely, down my face and to my lips. Where he stays. Without apology. He continues to stare at my mouth, and heat zips under my skin. My pulse rate soars.

I shuffle my feet, then laugh lightly. "If I didn't know you better, I'd think you were trying to seduce me."

"Am I succeeding?" His voice is hard, low, a dark chocolate that coats my nerve-endings and slides into those parts of me I didn't know existed. I shiver, take a step back, and this time, he doesn't follow me, thank god. I put a little more distance between us, then do a slow turn, pretending to take in the entirety of the gym. "So, this is your hang out? I'd have thought you'd prefer the local butcher where you get to chop up the meat and gut little animals."

I look up at him in time to spot the crease between his eyebrows. "Have I made that bad of an impression on you?"

"Worse," I say with false cheer. "If it weren't for the fact that I need this job —" I pop a shoulder.

"I'm not normally this—"

"Grumpy?"

"—this—"

"Growly—"

"—this—"

"Bad-tempered? Crotchety? Crabby? Prickly? Surly? Stripy? Churlish?"

"—this silent," he drawls.

"That, too." I hitch my bag over my shoulder, then pull out my phone and navigate to the planning app on it. "I've set up a joint calendar for the two of us so we each have access to the other's appointments. I've also updated the information on our daily meetings." I open the app to the meeting details and hold up the phone, "This is where you were supposed to be."

"Where I was supposed to be?" He blinks without looking at the screen.

"Our daily meetings take place in the conference room at the offices of the London Ice Kings, above the rink. When I didn't find you there, I was informed that the gym at the 7A Club was the next best option. Good thing I tracked you down because we need to finalize the PR plan for the team."

"PR plan?"

I stifle the urge to roll my eyes. What is wrong with him? This shouldn't be news. "That's what I'm here to do... The publicity for the London Ice Kings, and that includes the publicity for—"

He glances over my shoulder and his gaze widens. A flashbulb goes off. And before I can react, he's moved to plant his body in front of mine and throw out his arm to protect me from whoever is there. I turn and peek around his bulk, and more flashbulbs go off.

"Stay behind me," he growls and shoves at me. I stumble and have to throw my arms about his waist to right myself. There's the sound of running feet as whoever is taking the pictures moves to the side and continues to film.

"What the—? How did he get past security?" And we haven't even announced the line-up for the team. If this is the level of attention we're getting at this stage, it makes my job both easier and more challenging, at the same time.

"Guys, how about a kiss?" The pap calls out.

"Eh? No, there's nothing like that between us." I release him, and he races to the edge of the platform, jumps down and pounds toward the pap. "Stop, don't—" I begin to say, but it's too late. Rick grabs the camera from his hand and, throwing it on the ground, he brings his foot down on it.

There's a crunching sound and the journalist yelps, "That's my camera!"

"You'll be reimbursed." He stabs his chin in the direction of the exit. "Now, it's time for you to get out of here." I grab his arm—probably a bit more roughly than necessary, but what-fucking-ever—and lead him out.

7

Rick

"How could you?" She turns on me.

We're in the conference room adjoining the office at the Alexandra Palace Rink, which is the home ground for the team.

Last evening at the 7A Club's gym, after the run in with the journalist, the security for the club caught up with us. They apologized for the slip up, and I told them off before handing the journalist over to them; but not before I watched her soothe the pap's ego. *Yes, he was in the wrong, but he was still a member of the press,* she said. She wanted to ensure I hadn't made an enemy of him. He could tarnish my reputation in the future, after all. That was her reasoning, all conveyed to me with an eloquent glare. Like I give a fuck.

My sense of right and wrong, honed by my time in the marines, told me the pap made a mistake. Worse, he took a picture of us—of her—without her permission. He infringed on a private moment, on *her* privacy. Ergo, he needed to be punished. At least, that was my opinion.

Only, Ms. PR-Soothe-Things-Over hadn't agreed. She proceeded to smile at him, and he positively preened under her attention. At which point, I wanted to kick him out of the gym—or, at the very least, kick him somewhere else—but she must have sensed my intention, for she turned on me with a livid glower which only served to turn me on. I excused myself and escaped to the dressing room of the gym, where I'd wanked out one.

By the time I'd showered, dressed and returned, she'd dealt with the journalist. I offered to drop her back home, but she laughed outright at that.

Short of picking her up and throwing her into my car—which I was tempted to do, but which would have only pissed her off even more. Hmmm, maybe I should have—I convinced her to allow me to order her a pick-up. She stomped off as soon as her car arrived, without saying a word to me.

I contemplated texting her an apology but decided against it. It's not as if I'm actually sorry. If we're going to work together, she has to get used to who I am. I'm not changing myself for anyone—least of all, a strawberry blonde with a waist so slim I could span it with my palm.

Meeting again this morning, she still hasn't calmed down.

"You're lucky the journalist backed down, once I told him we were compensating him not only for the loss of his equipment, but also for the inconvenience," she fumes.

"I should have smashed his face for trespassing and for daring to click a photo without permission," I say mildly.

She huffs, "Is that your answer to everything? Just break things?"

If I let you, you'd break my heart, but I'm never going to let that happen. I stiffen. *A-n-d where did that thought come from, hmm?* Affairs of the heart and I don't go together. I prefer to live my life uncomplicated by love and any of the messy accompanying emotions.

"You're not even paying attention to what I'm saying." She tosses her head. The morning light slants in through the window and bounces off the copper nestled between the light strands of blonde hair. There she is. The temper I often see flashing in her eyes matches those hidden strawberry colors. She's not the calm, collected blonde she tries to portray. She's closer to the warmer, honeyed tones that she does her best to conceal.

"Rick, I'm talking to you." Golden sparks flare in her eyes. It's a startling combination with the strawberry-blonde of her hair. It's what caught my attention first and made me wonder if the carpet matches the drapes. I'd be lying if I said I don't wank off in the shower to images of her naked and on her knees with her mouth open and ready to receive my cum. My dick lengthens, and thank fuck, I'm wearing my jeans this morning. If I were wearing my sweatpants, nothing would have stopped the fabric at the crotch from tenting. As it is, I widen the gap between my legs to accommodate the action taking place there, then slide down a little in my seat, for good measure.

"Can you say something, instead of looking like you'd rather be anywhere else?" she snaps.

Clearly, my acting skills have gotten an upgrade if I managed to convince her I have no interest in being around her. The only thing that interests me is the twitch in her gorgeous backside encased in that snug little skirt she's wearing. It's black—again—but the way it clings to her butt as she paces about... Not to mention, the shapely turn of her ankles in those stockings with her feet balanced on another of those sexy-as-fuck, six-inch heels designed to give me a heart attack with thoughts of her naked and panting, long legs wrapped around my waist. She straightens and folds her arms under her breasts, which, unfortunately—or fortunately—means her tits are pushed out and straining against the prim jacket she has buttoned up over that frothy something she has on underneath.

"My face is up here, asshole," she growls.

"Eh?" I blink, then have the grace to redden. I manage to tear my glance away from her breasts and train it on Priest, who's been watching our back and forth with a smirk. "What?" I scowl at him.

"We're lucky I identified the remaining players we need for the team from earlier playoffs. The team is ready to start training together. It means, you two have very little time to sort through your differences," he offers in a mild tone.

She tosses her hair over her shoulder. "I have no differences with hIm."

"I have no differences with her," I say at the same time.

I arch an eyebrow in her direction. "You're the one raging around the room like a bull."

"Did you call me a bull?" she snaps.

"I could have said the feminine version of it"—I shuffle my feet—"but it would not have been very complimentary."

Color flushes her cheeks. "Did you refer to me as a cow?"

"I didn't; you did."

"You alluded to it."

I set my jaw. "I did no such thing."

She firms her lips. "Sure you did."

"If you recall what I said, it was something to the effect that you were snorting and pacing about like a—"

"—Don't say it," she warns.

"—you know what," I murmur.

"See—" She turns to Edward. "He called me a cow again."

"I did not."

"You implied it."

"All I was trying to say is you were rolling your eyes like a—"

"Enough!" Priest slaps his open palm into the table. There's no force behind the move but it's enough to bounce the pad of paper and pen in front of him.

She firms her lips.

I scowl. Jesus, did I come close to losing my temper? Me, the man who's calm enough under pressure to have earned the call sign Stone on the field? The man who guided his team through more than fifty missions without losing a single man, until that last time. And even then, I brought them all back home, even though some of them were in body bags. "*Who Dares Wins*," is the motto of the Special Forces I was recruited into after I became a Royal Marine. I swore to look challenges in the face and always stay faithful. To my country, to my fellow marines, to my team. It's the spirit that guided me through the missions. The same promise I intend to lead with as Captain of the hockey team. I allowed my emotions get the better of me in accepting the role. But now that I have, nothing is going to stop me from winning the League. Certainly not the distraction posed by the sprite of a woman who's glowering at me from across the table.

"I'm sorry." I turn to Priest. "It's my fault. I shouldn't have engaged in that childish exchange."

"Now you're calling me a child?" she begins, and I hold up my hand.

"I meant, I shouldn't have argued with you because I was in the wrong."

She blinks. "You were?"

I nod. "I lost my temper with the journalist. No matter that he's a scum of the earth, I shouldn't have threatened him or broken his camera—"

"—you think?" she says in a scornful tone.

"I don't regret it, though."

She stares at me, then a reluctant smile tugs at her lips. "You're one obstinate asshole, aren't you?"

I tip my chin. "It's what's brought me this far in life."

She gives me a strange look, then turns to Priest. "There was no damage done… this time, but—" Her phone vibrates. As do mine and Priest's, at the same time.

Priest is the first to reach for his. He glances at the screen, then holds the device up. "Maybe it's too early to conclude that?"

8

Giorgina

"He called me 'the girlfriend.'" I make air quotes with my fingers. "Like I'm arm candy. Or a dumb bimbo. Why is it that the girlfriend of an athlete of any kind has to be classified as someone without an opinion of her own? Also, I'm not his girlfriend. I'm not even his friend." I begin to pace the floor of the living room of Mira's flat. "And this, after the journalist signed a Non-Disclosure Agreement and had his phone and camera confiscated. How he managed to sneak out a picture, I have no idea."

Mira continues to scroll on her phone. "It's a great picture."

I scoff, "Stupid optics. I stumbled and fell against him."

"He's holding onto your arm. He's shirtless. And you have your cheek pressed into his bare chest and—"

"I know how that picture looks and none of it is true."

"I know you're upset with the journalist, but he's done us women-folk a solid. Look at those abs on that man. And the contours of those biceps, whoa. They're the size of a small tree-trunk. Not to mention the veins of his forearms, OMG. Bet he could carry you with one arm and—"

"Gimme that." I march over and snatch the phone out of her hands and click out of the gossip website she's on.

"Aww, party-pooper." Her lips turn down.

"Go admire someone else."

"He's the captain of the hottest hockey team in the country. Soon, every woman out there is goiIg to be salivating over him," she points out.

I curl my fingers around her phone with such force they hurt.

"Umm, are you going to do a Rick and destroy my phone?"

"What? No." I force myself to relax my grip on her device and hand it over. "Just don't ogle him in front of me, okay?"

"Hmm." She places the phone face down on the sofa next to her. "You jealous?"

I scoff. "Not likely."

"You sure?"

I roll my eyes. "Of course, doofus. It's just—" I pop a shoulder. "I don't want to be reminded of that photo, which is all over the internet. The worst thing is, Priest showed us the pic, and I threw a fit; and that douchebag looked all smug at having been proven right."

"Hmm." She places the tips of her fingers together.

"Okay enough, hmm-ing. If you have something to say, come out and say it."

She pretends to zip up her lips and throw away the key.

I scowl. "That's not helping at all."

She widens her gaze.

"Spit it out already. You look like you're about to burst."

"The two of you look mighty cozy together."

I scowl. "I already told you, it's not like that."

"Okay."

"That's it? Okay?"

"Sure. You can convince yourself it means nothing. I'll go along with what you're saying. For now."

"Okay, enough. Let's not talk about this. I have a more pressing issue. I'm going to have to move."

"You're moving?'

"I've been staying in a hotel paid for by the team, but Priest thinks it's best all the team stays together in a shared accommodation."

She blinks slowly. "You're moving into a house with a bunch of hockey players?"

"I know, right?"

"All the players under one roof?" She tilts her head. "Isn't that a recipe for disaster? Won't they get on each other nerves spending so much time together?"

"It's not unheard of." I purse my lips. "They're a new team playing together for the first time. Other teams have had the benefit of playing together for years, while the London Ice Kings have only recently been formed. It's important for them to bond together off-ice to strengthen their teamwork on the ice. And if there are any differences, it's best for them to come out off the ice so they bond better on the ice. So, in a way, Priest is accelerating the situation, by putting them under one roof. Any differences will emerge very quickly and have to be ironed out before they get to the finals."

"You think they're good enough to make it to the finals?" Her expression is curious.

I choose my words with care. "I'm not a big fan of Rick, but from what I've heard on the circuit, while he's been off the professional playing field, he's still seen as a canny appointment for the post of captain."

"So you *do* think they'll make it to the finals?" she asks with a smile.

"They'd better. My career depends on it." I begin to rake my fingers through my hair before remembering that will destroy the bun I've put it up into. It's important I appear neat and well-groomed. Only, it hurts my head when I use hair pins. It's why I use hair ties instead. My hair looks tidy enough and it doesn't hurt as much. Appearance is everything and the last thing I need is to look as frazzled as I feel inside. My stomach seems to have caught a permanent state of butterflies since I met that horrible man. All the more reason to pretend I have everything together.

Her features take on a considering look. "I understand the players living under the same roof to foster team spirit, but you're the PR manager—"

"And I'm from out of the country, so it's cheaper to provide me with lodgings in the same house as the players. Even the physical therapist is staying in the house. It's helpful to have them on hand to supervise the gym workouts, as well as work on after-practice and after-game injuries." I tap my fingers on my bag. "The coaches have been put in a house separate from the one the team shares, so they can talk strategy."

"All that makes sense, but why do you have to be under the same roof as the players?" A wrinkle furrows her forehead.

"I have a very limited time to get to know the players well enough to be able to pitch them and build their profiles in the media. And Knight, the owner of the team, owns the building the players are going to be housed in, so I suppose it makes it economical. As long as I have my own room, I guess it's going to be okay." I raise a shoulder.

"So, you're going to be the sole woman in the house?" she cries.

"It would seem so, yes." A trickle of awareness tickles my senses.

"Do you trust yourself to live under the same roof as Rick?" she asks with a teasing glint in her eyes.

"What? Of course. I don't even like the man."

"You don't have to like him to jump him." Her smile widens.

"No, no, no. I plan to stay far away from him. I only agreed to this plan because I want to be seen as a team player." I scowl.

"It's going to demonstrate you're a team player, all right." She snickers.

"What do you mean?"

"You poor thing, I pity you." She shakes her head.

"You do?"

She rises to her feet and walks over to me. "You're going to be living in a house with sweaty, hunky, muscled, chiseled, well-hung hockey players, lady."

"Ugh." I shudder. "Imagine being surrounded by sweaty players with stinky feet. Not to mention, hairy chests. And don't get me started on smelly socks and all that belching and farting." I grimace.

She stares at me. "You can't be serious. You're going to be surrounded by eye-candy, and if you were to sample some of the wares—"

"No! Absolutely not." I straighten my spine. "I'm a professional. This is my career we're talking about. I will not have any kind of personal relationships with the players."

She frowns. "Is that in your contract, not to fraternize with them?"

"Well… No—" I shuffle my feet. "But it's an unspoken rule. The fastest way to lose perspective is to sleep with your client."

"The players are not your clients."

"The team is, so by default, they all are."

"Including the captain?" She bites the inside of her cheek.

"Especially the captain." I tip up my chin. "I'm going to be working closely with him, having daily briefings with him, actually."

"Too bad. It's clear from this…" She pulls up that hated photo on her phone and holds it up again. "There's something between the two of you."

"You can tell that from a picture?"

"Of course. Your features are soft, your gaze dreamy. And he looks all possessive, and angry, and snarly, and so macho." Her expression grows dreamy.

"Okay, stop. Maybe there was a moment there, but it was nothing."

"Hmm."

"No, don't hmm me. Please help me out. I don't like the man, and I'm going to have to work with him."

She peers into my features. "This is stressing you out?"

"What do you think I've been trying to tell you all this time?"

"But you're a professional. You're the most focused person I know. You won't do anything to screw it up."

"I wish I shared your confidence." I half laugh.

"You could also go a little easy on yourself, you know. If you did sleep with him—"

"No. Absolutely not."

She rolls her eyes. "From the perspective of a woman who, more likely than not, will end up in an arranged marriage, if I were in your shoes, I'd do it."

"Arranged marriage?" I stare. "Is that still a thing?"

"In my family, it is."

I shake my head. "If I were forced into such an arrangement, it would be the end of the world, as far as I'm concerned."

"But if you did sleep with him"—she waggles her fingers—"it wouldn't be."

Oh, my god, this is what the end of the world looks like. I'm running late for my first meeting. Also, I've been told I don't have a room in the house. "But I've already checked out of the hotel, and I was assured I'd have a room, on the top floor and away from the men."

The woman in charge of admin who met me at the entrance to the house wrings her hands. "I'm sorry for the mix up. But there's only one master room on the top floor, which is allocated to the captain of the team."

"And which I'm willing to share with her." That detestable voice reaches me over my shoulder. *Don't look. Don't look at him. Don't lose your temper, either. You're a strong accomplished career woman. You've worked hard to build a persona and get to where you are. You didn't even let your bastard ex hold you back—so you might have run from the city where he lives but that was self-preservation. This is a new start with the kind of job anyone in your field would kill for. You've got this. You can do this. You can get through today without losing your temper at that asshat.* I glance over my shoulder with a sweet smile. "No, thank you."

He ignores me as he walks over to us. "The room's the biggest in the house; there's enough space for the both of us," he addresses his words to the other woman.

"Oh, that's so nice of you," she says with a grateful smile. "I have no idea how this mix-up happened. And the other rooms are taken by the players." She turns to me. "This is a great solution, until we can work something else out."

"No, it's not." A migraine begins to thrum behind my eyes. I rub at my temple. "I can't share the room with him."

"Yes, you can," Rick says in that calm voice that sends my blood pressure shooting.

My pulse rate spikes. Tension churns my stomach. This can't be happening. Nope, no way. "Can you understand how uncomfortable this could be for me?" I turn on the woman. "Imagine if you were in my place. How would you feel?"

She looks from me to the hulking figure next to me, then back at me. "I'd thank my lucky stars."

The douche next to me shoots her a warm smile. What the—? I've never seen him smile before. Honestly. And he's turning the full effect of his curved lips on this woman who turned my life upside down.

"Thank you, Rick. You're a life saver." She flutters her false eyelashes at him. "If you need anything—"

"We're good," I snap.

She looks between us again, then nods. "I'll try my best to clear things up and allocate you another room."

I open my mouth to tell her off, but she scampers out of there.

In the ensuing silence, I refuse to look at him. I *will not throw a tantrum. Will not stamp my foot. Will not allow my frustration to show. I will be the best version of myself.* I secure my handbag under my arm, then reach for my suitcase. "Where's the elevator in this place?"

9

Rick

"There isn't one."

"What?" She slowly straightens. Her eyes flicker with those golden sparks which only happens when she's close to losing control. Something I'd love to see happen. Woman is wound tighter than a goalie at a shootout. It can't be good for her to keep all that tension locked in. Says the man who's used to never showing his feelings, either. The two of us have more in common than she realizes.

"No elevator. This is a private townhouse. Also, we're on the fourth floor."

"The fourth floor?" She pales.

"Yep, and we're running late." I brush past her, heading for the steps, and she cries, "Wait, aren't you going to help me carry my bag?"

I allow myself a small smile, which I brush off before turning to her. "Do you want me to help you carry your bag?"

"I already said so, didn't I?"

I fold my arms across my chest and look at her steadily.

She shuffles her feet, glances around, then her features light up. "Finn," she calls out to the man walking into the house. "Can you help me?"

Motherfucker! The wankface prowls over and takes in the scene. "You moving in, Gio?" He shoots her a smile, and my stomach clenches.

"That's Mac to you," I say through gritted teeth.

"Mac?" She whips her face in my direction. "What do you mean, Mac?"

"That's your call sign."

"Call sign? Hockey players don't have call signs," she protests.

"On my team, you do. Call it a carry-over of best practices from my military days."

"Call signs?" Finn looks at me oddly.

"Yep." I dare him to contradict me.

He slowly curls his lips. "And I suppose you're the one who decides who gets called what."

"You bet, I'm the captain."

"But why Mac?" she cries.

"Why don't you figure it out?"

She shoots me a look which would take down a lesser man. Luckily, it doesn't affect me at all. If you don't count the half-chub I'm already sporting in my pants.

"And what am I called—" Finn begins, then holds up a hand. "You know what, don't tell me. I don't want to know yet." He reaches for her suitcase, but I'm there first.

"I've got this."

"You do?" She narrows her gaze on me.

I ignore her and jerk my chin toward the living room. "On your way, shit stain."

Finn laughs. "Anytime you need help, my room is on the third floor."

"Get lost," I snap.

"It's the last door on the right, Mac." He shoots her another smile, then ambles off. Bastard knows how to get on my nerves.

I heft her suitcase which is more of a wardrobe on wheels—and gesture to her to go first. She begins to climb, and I instantly know that was a mistake. Between the tight skirt—black, of course—that she's wearing and her usual six-inch-heels, her butt sways in the most enticing of fashions. My half-chub extends, making it fucking uncomfortable to walk, let alone climb. I grit my teeth, grip the handle on her bag tighter, and begin the ascent. We pass the landing of the first floor, then the second. My biceps strain and my triceps begin to burn "What do you have in this, stones?" I grunt.

"Books, actually."

We reach the fourth floor, and I follow her to the door at the far end of the landing. She enters, then looks around the master-room which is big enough to look like a studio apartment. In the living space, a massive TV occupies one wall. Opposite it, there's a sofa with matching armchairs. In between, large French doors open out onto a balcony overlooking the garden below, and beyond that, a view of the city.

"Follow me." I lead her past the sofa and armchairs, which demarcate the living room from the sleeping area, then past the entrance to the bathroom before I pause in front of an expansive wall of mirrors. I slide one open and place her suitcase inside the walk-in closet. When I step out, she's standing in the middle of the space taking in the enormous bed pushed up against the wall. It's a California King; wide enough for at least three of the hockey team.

"If we each keep to our side of the bed, we'll be good."

"What?" She looks at me with horror. "I thought you'd take the couch in the living room."

"Have you seen my size?" I gesture to myself.

She drops her gaze to my chest and flicks her tongue over her lips. She continues to scan me from hip to legs, then back to my crotch. After a few seconds pass, I clear my throat.

"My face is up here."

She blushes a deep red. It's a wonder her cheeks haven't caught fire, that's how hard she blushes. "I'll take the couch." She spins around and stomps to the door. "Also, we're late for the team meeting."

"Now that we've gone over our game plan for the practice sessions, I'm going to ask Gio—I mean Mac—to take us through the publicity strategy." Edward steps back.

Gio glides up to take her position at the top of the conference table. The chairs have been arranged in a classroom seating style and all twenty-three members of the team, along with the physical therapist and the coaches, are in attendance today. Edward had insisted, and I understand why. It's good to get all team members on the same page and get them to buy into the strategy. The game strategy. Why they need to know about the PR strategy, I don't understand.

One of the men whistles from the back while another mops his forehead. A third tugs on the T-shirt he's wearing. All of the men have their gazes trained on her. And I understand why. With her tight skirt and the jacket that clings to her curves, not to mention the sheer stockings she has on with the line running up the back and disappearing into the skirt, and those six-inch heels that make her legs seem impossibly long, she's a wet dream. I know because I've yet to get a good night's sleep since I met her. And now, all these bastards will be imagining her without clothes on. Anger tightens my guts.

I begin to rise to my feet, but Finn grabs my shoulder. "The fuck you doing, mate?" he hisses.

I glare around the room, then at her. She juts out a hip and plants her hand on it. Around me, more than one face wears a dazed look. Gio has that effect on people. As their PR manager, I know I can't restrict the interactions of her with the team, but damn if I'm going to allow them to call her by her name. It's why I decided to give us all nicknames. That way, I can insist no one says her name. That way, her name need not pass through anyone else's lips. Is that taking things too far? Maybe. But if this is one way to buy me some peace of mind, so be it.

Then Gio glances about the room and thrusts out her chest. "I have three simple rules for you boys to follow—"

"Hey, Mac, do you need an assistant?" one of the men calls out.

Unperturbed, Gio flashes him a smile. "Do you need someone to take your place on the ice?" The man shuts up. A laugh runs around the room.

"As I was saying, I have three simple rules for you—" Her fingers fly on her device, and the screen behind her lights up.

"Rule number one: keep it in your pants. Rule number two: keep it in your pants. Rule number three: keep it in your—"

She cups her palm behind her ear, and everyone chants, "Pants."

"Well done, gentleman. You do that, and I can promise you the best damn PR for this team. I'm sure I don't need to remind you we're starting as underdogs for the League. And all of you are media savvy, so I'm sure you'll agree that it's as important to win the game played off the ice as it is to lead in the one on the ice."

"You can lead me anywhere, baby," one of the guys calls out from the back row. I jerk my head in his direction, and Manning 'Odds' Leblanc, one of the defenseman and an original member of the team, winks at me. I glare at him, and his grin widens. Motherfucker. I squeeze my fingers into fists.

"Don't let them get to you, bro." Finn nudges me. "They see your weakness, and they'll be on it like sharks."

"I don't need to take lessons in how to be a team captain from you, Hand," I growl.

"Hand?" He frowns. "The fuck does that mean?"

"Figure it out, *bro*."

"Something you want to share with us, Captain?" she calls out.

Both Finn and I look up to find she's staring at us with a raised eyebrow.

Someone clicks his tongue from behind. "You've been caught: you think she'll want to punish you?"

"She can punish me anytime," someone else replies.

More laughter fills the space.

I resist the urge to turn back and tell off the turdwarts. I'd hear no end of it if I did. Hate to admit it, but Finn is right. If I show these men they're getting under my skin, it'll only encourage them. No, I'll have my punishment on the ice, not to mention, during practice. I *am*, the captain.

Ahead, Gio stiffens. She marches down the aisle past the row where Finn and I are sitting, all the way to the end.

She stares down at the man with the scar around his neck, who replied to the earlier comment: "Jagger Hemsworth, jersey #21, loud when sober, intolerable when drunk. And not a patch on Thor, I might add. I hereby christen you, Shrek."

"What the—?" Jagger's face falls. "Shrek? The fuck does that mean?"

"Oh, didn't I tell you?" I jump in. "I'm assigning callsigns for all you bastards, and I do believe Mac here has the right idea with Shrek."

"Now that you mention it—" The guy next to him looks Jagger up and down. "I see the resemblance."

The only man on the team taller and broader than me slumps in his seat. "I don't suppose I have a say in this matter?"

10

Gio

"I wish my nickname didn't make me sound like a burger." I scowl down at Mira's face on my phone.

She's at the gym but picked up my call. "You have any idea why he decided on Mac?" She sounds a little out of breath. She's on the treadmill, not going too fast, so she can speak to me.

"Because I look like a Big Mac?" I glance down at my waist. I knew I shouldn't have eaten that cheese-toasties for lunch. But damn, if the Brits haven't mastered the art of a toasted sandwich. And the cheddar here tastes heavenly. As for the pickles they slid in between the loaves? They are to die for. I wasn't able to stop myself from devouring it on my lunch break. Then, I decided to take a walk through the park near the rink—before I go back to my desk. I sink down on the park bench and scowl at Mira. "So, I do look like a Big Mac?"

"Jesus, Gio, you're the most svelte, most stylishly dressed woman I know."

I blush a little. "My insecurities are showing, eh?"

Her features soften. "I'm always trying to go on a diet, too. And I guess being surrounded by all those fit men doesn't help, either."

"I've always been like this, though. I'm not sure where it comes from," I lie.

I know exactly where my obsession with my weight comes from, but some-how, I'm not sure I want to share it. Not even with the woman who's fast becoming my best friend.

"Have you thought of going to therapy about it?"

I shake my head. "I don't need therapy. I'll be fine."

"Hmm." She purses her lips.

"No, not another hmm. Your hmms are scary, Mira."

She laughs. "Sorry, it's a habit I can't seem to get rid of. Seriously though, Gio, you are fabulous. I wish I had a figure like you. I wish I could dress like you. Not a hair out of place, perfect make-up..." She looks at me with some-thing like admiration. "You look like you stepped out of the pages of Vanity Fair."

"Is it too much? I still dress like I'm in L.A.? London, I've realized, is a little more low-key, I think." I glance around and take in the people strolling in the park. On the bench next to me is a man in a suit, eating his sandwich and reading his newspaper. On the grass is a woman who's taken off her jacket and her ballet pumps. She's reading a paperback, and her handbag is next to her. Definitely someone who's come out on her lunch break. And she's not exactly dressed up—more smart casual than glamour smart—which is my go-to look. I glance down at my Gucci outfit, my Balenciaga bag and my Louboutins. "Yeah, it's too much."

"You're you, Gio. It's what makes you, you. How you dress, how you walk, how you talk—"

"I might have overdone it this morning." I wince.

"Rick didn't seem to think so, from what you said."

My eyes follow a woman who's walking a dog. A little girl jumps around next to her. She stops to pat the dog, runs up the incline, then back down.

"He confused me this morning," I admit.

"You mean, because he backed up the nickname you gave the defenseman?"

"That *was* surprising." I stare at the little girl bouncing along after the dog. The mother pulls out a phone and types away on it while following at a distance. "I thought he'd bite my head off, but he backed me up."

"So that's good, right? He's trying to make an effort to get along with you." She takes a sip from the bottle of water, then places it back in the receptacle next to the phone on the treadmill.

"Or maybe, he's trying to lull me into a sense of calm, then lower the boom on me."

She laughs. "You don't like this guy, do you?"

"I have no feelings toward him either way."

She guffaws.

I scowl at her. "Now what?"

"You sound a lot like our dear friend Penny, right before she fell head-over-heels for Knight."

"Knight had feelings for her. From the get go, it was obvious the two of them had eyes only for each other. Unlike Rick—"

"Unlike Rick, who's trying his best not to show it?"

I narrow my gaze on her. "You must be mistaken. We hate each other. In fact, we've never been able to stand each other, even when I was the PR manager for Declan and Rick was his bodyguard."

"You know what they say about the boy in the playground who pulls at your braids? He's the one who likes you the most."

"This is not a playground. This"—I wave at the scene around me—"is real life. And I don't wear braids or wear my hair down for a reason."

"Okay." She reaches for her bottle of water and takes a sip.

"Okay? That's it." I look at her with suspicion. "You're not going to try to convince me otherwise?"

"Nah, you know best what it's like when the two of you are together."

"We're not together."

"I mean, when you're interacting. I'm sure it really is dislike on both your parts. Besides, you only have to deal with him at work, right? And you'll have a lot to do with settling into your new room and all that."

"About that..." I wriggle around, trying to find a more comfortable seat on the park bench. "There's been a small hitch."

"A hitch?" She frowns.

"When I checked in, there was no room for me. Some admin mix-up. So, I'm having to share the suite with Rick."

"Wait. Hold on." She slaps at the settings and comes to a complete stand-still. "You're sharing a room with the man you hate?"

"It would seem that way, yes."

"You're sharing a room with the hot captain of the most exciting hockey team in the country?"

"It's a master-suite," I clarify.

"How many bedrooms does it have?"

"One," I mutter under my breath.

"Did you say one?" Her eyes widen.

"He's going to sleep on the couch."

"Have you seen the size of that man? He's got to be at least six feet three inches."

"Six six, actually." I redden. Why do I know his exact height? Oh yeah, because it's my job, that's why.

Her lips twitch, then she schools her features into an expression of disbelief. "And he's going to sleep on the couch?"

"It pulls out into a bed." I bite the inside of my cheek. I have no idea if it does or not. I should feel bad about lying to my friend, but—I'm not sure how to explain that the prospect of being in such close proximity to that rat's ass of a man fills me with both trepidation and a strange excitement. Don't get me wrong, I'm pissed at the entire situation. In fact, I'm sure Rick is having a laugh at my expense, and I definitely do not want to have anything to do with him. Ideally, I don't want to work with him, but given the circumstances, I can either keep complaining or I can suck it up and make the best of it. And no one knows how to make the most of a bad situation the way I do.

"So he's going to be on the couch, and you're going to be in his bed?"

"Technically, it's now my bed," I fib.

She stares at me.

"It's only because all of the other rooms in that house are taken, and only until they figure out a solution."

"And when will that be?"

I scowl. "I didn't get a timeline, which I would have pushed for, except Mr. Grumpface and the admin manager seemed to gang up against me, and that was not a great experience. Also, she only had eyes for him. I doubt she registered that I wasn't happy with having to share a room with him."

"Were you jealous they seemed to be in agreement against you?"

"What? Of course not." I flip my hair over my shoulder.

"Hmm." She makes that irritating noise again.

I throw up my hand. "Fine, okay, maybe I was a teeny-tiny bit. She looked at him like he was a god who'd come to her rescue, and he seemed only too pleased about it."

"Definitely jealous—" She holds up her hand as I try to cut in. "But I'm not one to judge. I don't have time for anyone except my book boyfriends, and here, you get yourself into a forced-proximity, one-bed situation with a gorgeous hunk of a man who—"

"Watch what you say next," I warn.

"—whose dishiness I haven't noticed at all. Not at all," she inserts smoothly.

"Good answer. Also, it's not a one-bed situation. He did say he'd take the couch."

She scoffs. "We all know how that one goes. You're going to have a nightmare, and he's going to slip into bed and calm you, and then you'll wake up with him wrapped around you, and—"

"Stop, right there. I don't get nightmares… Although, keep up the scenarios you're painting and I might. I don't want anything to do with his alphaholeness, at all."

"Ooh, you called him an alphahole."

"Because he is, and that was not a compliment."

"Alphahole?" A voice drawls. I glance to the side to find said alphahole prowling toward me.

"Is that him?" Mira asks excitedly.

"Uh, no, it's a homeless person. I took his bench and now I need to leave—"

"But—" Mira begins.

"Okay, gotta go." I disconnect before she can say anything else.

Mr. Growly-ass slides onto the bench next to me. The man eating his sandwich must have left some time ago.

I begin to rise, when he curls his lip. "You running scared?"

11

Gio

"Of course not." My butt hits the bench with a thump, but I don't look at him. I'm not giving him the satisfaction of thinking he's driven me away. Doesn't mean I have to listen to what he has to say.

He must sense my conflicting emotions, for he raises his hands.

"I'm sorry if we got off on the wrong foot—"

"You have a funny way of showing it." I tip up my chin.

He raises a shoulder. "I'm good at keeping my emotions to myself."

"Is that due to your military stint or because you're British?"

His lips twitch, before he schools his features into that expressionless, yet gorgeous, granite-like-façade he calls his face.

"Is that a personal question?" he rumbles

"Of course not." I swerve my head in his direction. Bastard has a smug look on his face. He's having way too much fun at my expense. I curl my fingers around my handbag. "You know what? I'm leaving." I begin to rise to my feet and he touches my arm.

Shockwaves course under my skin. My belly tightens. My heart collides with my ribcage. My pulse rate shoots up, and fuck-fuck-fuck, what the hell is this response to his mere touch?

He must feel it, too, for he freezes. His green eyes flash for a second. He stares at me with something like shock, then pulls back his hand.

I instantly jump to my feet. "I do need to get back."

"So, you don't want to hear about the proposition I have for you?"

"Proposition?" I blink.

"Something that will help us both make the most of a bad situation?"

I scowl at him. "Why are you being so conciliatory?"

"Because, contrary to your preconceived notions about me, I'm not all unreasonable."

"Preconceived notions?" I snort, and against my better judgement, sit down on the bench again. It's more prudent if I leave. Nothing he has to tell me can be that important.

Also, I must have been imagining the response of my body to his touch. Those kinds of things only happen in the movies or in my smutty novels. I didn't feel every imprint of his finger on my skin as if he'd branded me forever. I tuck my elbows into my sides and square my shoulders. If I knew what was good for me I'd leave but, I'm not going to run away. I'm not.

"My notions are based on how disagreeable you've been so far." I jut out my chin. "How obnoxious you've been, not to mention, bad-tempered, ill-humored, crabby, irritable, grumpy, peevish—"

"Do you carry around a dictionary in your head?"

I snort. "Just love words, is all."

"Hence the books?" He tilts his head. "What's your fave?"

I glance away then back at him. "War and Peace."

"War and Peace, huh?" He looks at me with something like respect in his eyes. "Isn't that Tolstoy's longest work?"

It's my turn to look at him with surprise. "Not many men would know that."

"I'm not many men; my grandmother loves to read."

"She does?" I know I'm engaging in conversation with the enemy, but getting an insight into him, however brief, is more fascinating than I expected.

"Only—" He glances around then crooks his finger in my direction. I lean in; so does he. He looks into my eyes. "She loves to read smut."

"Your grandma reads smut?" I know I'm gaping, and who am I to judge? I love my smutty books, and Rick's grandmother has a right to read them, too, right?

"She loves spicy romance novels. In fact, she started a book club so she and her friends could exchange notes on their favorite spicy scenes."

"Oh?" I blink slowly.

"It's wonderful she's a reader; makes it easy to buy her gifts. For Mother's Day this year, guess what I got her?"

"What?" I murmur. I'm not sure I want to know. Except, *I do* want to know. "What did you get her?"

"A Kindle."

"A Kindle?" I know I'm parroting what he's saying, but I'm finding this entire conversation so otherworldly. This big, rough, grumphole has a grandma who reads spicy books and he bought her a Kindle. Have I been kidnapped by aliens and now I'm living in an alternative world? As long as they're aliens with two penises, I don't mind. Also, ugh, what's this fascination with DP? Where the hell did it come from?

"Her old Kindle was on the verge of dying, so I bought her a top-of-the-line, Kindle paperwhite, the kind you can read—"

"In the sun and which is also waterproof, I know. I have one, too."

"You do?"

"I prefer paperbacks because I can annotate them, though. I often end up carrying my fave ones around so I can read them over and over again. Comfort reads, you know?"

He looks at me with a strange expression on his face.

"What?" I snap.

"You find *War and Peace* a comfort read?"

Oh, that? I blush a little. "I have many comfort reads." I evade the question.

"If you don't want to tell me, that's okay." He raises his hands.

"Reading tastes are personal, you know? It's the one time I can escape my daily worries and not worry about being judged. When I'm between the pages of a book, I can be anyone I want." *And, I can have as many orgasms as I want, with the help of smutty words and my trusted Dan.* It's one of my favorite parts of the day—when I can relax in a bathtub and read with a glass of wine and my toys. More than once, my Kindle has fallen into the bath water, which is why I got a waterproof one. Not that I'm going to share all of these details with him.

"It's not often I find someone who not only loves to read, but who also knows what they like to read, ya know?"

I nod. No way am I ever admitting to you the kinds of books I prefer to read. Not that I have a hankering for a hot man in a mask chasing after me, only to catch me and fuck me until I can't see straight. No, no way, am I telling this grumphole what my secret fantasy is. I pull up my phone and exclaim. "Omigod, look at the time, don't you need to be back for practice?"

He rises to his feet. "Are you going to watch?"

"Gio, right?"

I glance sideways at the lanky man who's come up to stand next to me. Like everyone else on the team he's tall, over six-feet for sure but unlike the players he's lean and lanky, like he went through a growth spurt and never put on weight.

"And you are?"

"Nathan Pitt." He holds out her arm.

"The physical therapist?" I place my hand in his much bigger one. He squeezes gently, his touch careful.

"*C'est moi.*" He dips his head.

"French?"

"Canadian." He nods toward the game in progress on the rink. "Spectacular, isn't it?"

I turn back to watch the men zip around the ice. They're on skates but, whoa, they might as well have wings on their feet. Two of them—Jagger and Enzo, collide. Enzo falls on his back and lays stunned for a few seconds. I gasp, pressing my palm into the plexiglass.

Next to me, Nathan tenses. The next second, though, Enzo is up and off on the ice. He manages to grab the puck and swing it into the goal. His team cheers. And all of that took seconds. Literally, seconds. "Jesus." I shake my head. "I always forget how spectacular it is to watch a game in real life."

Probably because I stayed away from ice hockey games after what my ex-boyfriend did to me. I also stopped myself from following the game online. I through it would hurt to watch the players again on the ice, but strangely, it hadn't upset me too much. Maybe I'm getting over my heartbreak. Or perhaps, it has to do with being fascinated by a certain athlete and his mastery over the puck?

Rick is breathtaking. Clad in jersey, pants, gloves and helmet, he's spectacular. No, more than that, he's breathtaking. There's something about the way his jersey stretches over his shoulder pads and chest protector, and how his elbow pads and protective gloves, padded shorts, shin pads and neck guard, he resembles a beast. Only Jagger, aka Shrek, is taller than him. And then, there's the way he owns the ice, and how he charges. The way he manages to snatch up the puck and swing it toward the goal is poetry in motion. He's more fluid than my asshole ex ever was.

"It's not for nothing, it's known as one of the fastest games in the world," Nathan murmurs.

The coach calls time, and the players glide off the ice. Rick skates up to Enzo, and the two engage in a conversation. Rick does most of the talking, Enzo nods. He seems to be making sure Enzo is okay. Then Rick slaps him on the back and Enzo steps off.

"I'm going to make sure he's okay." Nathan grabs his equipment bag and races off in his direction. The other players head for the locker room, but Rick stays behind to talk with the coach.

Despite the helmet, I sensed the concern on his face as he spoke to Enzo. The man took a solid hit, I and was sure he'd been knocked out. But then, he recovered so quickly, I couldn't believe it. My respect for what the players put themselves through just increased a hundred times. And as much as I hate to admit it, Rick was right. Watching them in action has given me ideas for the kinds of content I need for my calendar for the social media and PR to amplify the team's reputation. I head toward the exit of the rink when Rick falls in beside me. He's taken off his helmet and his dark hair is plastered to his forehead.

"What do you think?"

"Of what?"

"Of having dinner tonight with me?"

12

Rick

"She turned you down?" Finn slaps me on the back so hard my arm shakes. Beer splashes over the side of my mug. Finn decided we needed to get the team together for a piss-up to celebrate our first practice as a team, and thanks to JJ's standing invitation, we ended up at the 7A Club.

The sessions today were brutal. My shoulder hurts from the abuse it took, essentially opening up an old war wound—one I'll never allow to slow me down. Not if I find a way to overcome it first. My calves burn, and every part of me feels the workout I put my body through today. It's clear I need to work much harder at getting in shape. It's also clear age is not on my side.

When Finn suggested heading out, I groaned. But the younger members— which means, the rest of the team—cheered. As the captain, I need to pick my battles, and this—the entire team coming together for the first time to practice and wanting to head out to blow off some steam—is not one of those times. So, after getting my shoulder wrapped up by the team doctor, I took a long hot shower, making sure to keep the dressing dry. Then, I pulled on the extra pair of street-clothes I kept in my locker in the locker room.

No, I wasn't too cowardly to go up to my room. Cowardice had nothing to do with the fact I didn't want to see her before I headed out. Not after she'd turned me down. *Why did I ask her in the first place?* A question that still confuses me. It's not like I want to date her. It's not like I want anything to do with her. Although, she is my roomie, so running into her is unavoidable. It's another reason I agreed to head out. Best to stay out of her way until she's asleep.

Not even the fact that we have to report for training at five a.m. tomorrow had me turning down Finn's suggestion. So here we are. Me and my best friend, who's grinning at me like the joke's on me. Which it is, of course.

"No need to sound so happy." I heft the mug of draft, the only one I'm allowing myself this evening, considering someone has to be sober to ensure none of us got into trouble. Also, I don't mind being that person, since I'm not going to test my body's recuperative powers to that extent... Yet.

"Never seen you look this crushed man," Finn drawls.

"This"—I stab a finger in the direction of my features—"is not the face of a man who's crushed in any way. This is a man who's questioning why the hell he did it in the first place. And then, why he told you about it."

"From the looks of it, I think you owe me." Another voice sounds from my other side. Manning 'Odds' LeBlanc, extends his arm, and Finn groans before slapping a note in his palm.

I sit back on my stool. "You guys had a bet." I glance between them.

"My nickname's Odds, remember?" He smirks.

"What are the bets I'm gonna make you run five extra miles tomorrow?"

"Aww, Stone—"

"Ten then."

He hangs his head. "You're no fun, mate. I call this an abuse of power."

"I call this the best way to train a team." I allow my lips to twitch. "Better make the most of tonight. After this, we're not gonna see the inside of a bar for a long time."

"Jesus, you're killing me here, man." He reaches for my mug of beer and drains it. Before I can protest, he touches his forefinger to his forehead, then spins around and heads over to join two of our teammates who're talking to some women.

"Jeez, don't you think that was unnecessarily harsh? This is *not* the military, man."

"The basics are the same." I raise a shoulder. "Time for the kids to man up. Playing a game on ice is no less lethal than facing down your opponent on the war-front. You need to focus, you need to be present and grounded. You need to be there completely—"

"And they will be."

"Not if they're running around getting pissed and—"

"—flirting with your girl."

"What?"

Finn nods in the direction that Manning headed off in. I follow his gaze to find him and his buddies—I recognize Caspian, Jax and Jagger crowded around the luscious figure of a woman with waves of blonde hair tumbling down her back. She's wearing a dress that ends mid-thigh, in a red that stands out amongst their jeans and dark jackets. She's teamed it with over-the-knees boots with six-inch heels that add height to her figure. But in comparison to the men hulking over her, she seems delicate and vibrant and a flame that I can't help but be drawn to. I raise my mug of beer, realize it's empty and slam it back on the counter. Then I slide off the barstool.

"You realize he's going to win another bet?" Finn cautions.

"And I'm going to make him give me another hundred push-ups if he does that."

Finn barks out a laugh. "Easy, old man, you're losing your sense of humor.

"Never had one to begin with. It's why I'm called Stone, remember?" I begin to walk toward the men when she rises up on tip toe.

She kisses Manning on his cheek, pats Caspian on his shoulder, and nods at Jax and Jagger before making her way through the crowd and toward the hallway that leads in the direction of the ladies' room. As I pass the team, they grin at me.

"Better be careful, Stone, she might be too much for you to handle," Caspian scoffs.

"You'd better be careful, *Prick*, or the practice sessions might get *too* much for you to handle." I head after her.

"Wait, did he say, Prick? Why the fuck did he say, Prick? It'd better not be my fucking call-sign. Hey Stone, how is it you get to pick your call-sign but the rest of us don't?" Caspian calls out after me.

"Because I'm the captain." I raise my finger over my shoulder.

"I need to lodge a protest. " His irate voice follows me.

"Noted and dismissed," I drawl, then continue on in the direction she disappeared.

That's what he gets for coming onto my girl— *Whoa, hold on, not my girl. She's just my roomie. I'm looking out for my roommate. That's allowed, right?*

I head down the hallway, and down the corridor toward the restrooms. I spot her at the far end. Her back is to me and she's talking to a man who looks somewhat familiar. As I draw closer, she tries to brush past him, but he places his hand on her hip.

Something inside me snaps: my heart rate accelerates. My feet don't seem to hit the floor as I hurry toward them. She pushes against his chest, and his smile widens. *Mother. Fucker.* I draw abreast, then grab him by his neck and throw him into the wall.

"Get away from her," I growl.

13

Gio

One moment, I'm trying to get away from my ex—what is he doing in London, anyway? And why is he at the 7A Club? The next, Rick has thrown him against the wall. He has his fingers wrapped around his neck as he glares at the other man. "You dare touch her, asshole?"

Dennis' eyes bug out. He's a little shorter than Rick, but he makes up for it with his bulk, which as I know, is not all muscle. The man's lazy enough to carry more than the requisite body fat, and yet, it hasn't interfered with his role as a defenseman. He has the size to block an opponent's shot and the strength to take the puck away and start play in the opposite direction.

Rick, on the other hand, is 100% pure muscle. His strength is the kind that allows him to take risks on the ice, allows him to block shots and take the attack when he gains possession of the puck. Also he's angry. Very angry. The kind of

anger that gives him the edge. Tension thrums off of him, his entire body vibrating with the kind of rage that signals things are going to go south... And fast. He must cut off the airflow because Dennis claws at Rick's forearm. His features slowly turn from red to purple. Rick lifts his other fist, and the skin across his knuckles stretches white. He pulls it back, and I know without a doubt, if he punches Dennis in the face, it's going to escalate into something that could result in Rick being disqualified from playing. And that's only going to hurt him.

So, I jump forward and grab his upper arm. "Stop."

His biceps flex under my fingers, and holy hell, it feels like I'm clinging to a bolt of lightning, attempting to defuse its power. He stays poised, nostrils flared; the tips of his ears have turned white, a clear sign he's so angry, he's close to losing control. His chest heaves, the sinews of his throat stand out in prominence under his skin, but he stops. He doesn't lower his arm, but he pauses with his fist mere centimeters from making contact with Dennis' nose.

"Rick, let him go." I imbue my voice with a calmness I don't feel.

The pulse at the base of his neck jumps. It's the only sign he's heard me. Every other part of his body is a crackling ball of tension, seconds from detonating in a roar of thunder.

"Rick, please," I implore.

He blinks and begins to lower his hand. He loosens his hold on Dennis, and the bastard coughs. His gaze darts from Rick to me, then back to Rick. He never was very smart. "Pussy-whipped, huh? You do realize she was mine first and—"

With a growl, Rick releases him, only to curl the fingers of his hand into a fist, on the arm I'm not hanging onto, and slams it into Dennis' face.

"You beat up the captain of a rival team?" Edward glares at Mr. Cannot-Keep-His-Temper-In-Check across the floor of the office adjoining the 7A bar.

Turns out, Dennis also decided to leave L.A. and move to London. He was traded to a British team, the Islington Sentinels—the London Ice King's closest rivals— as their captain. I moved to London to make a fresh start; the last thing I wanted was to see my cheating ex here. And since he's the captain of the closest competitor to the Ice Kings, chances are, I'm going to run into to him again. It feels like a bad dream.

Nathan was at the bar and attended to Dennis right away. Not that it stopped him from glaring at Rick and promising to press charges, despite the fact he's the one in the wrong. He's the one who touched me without permission; Rick was only defending me. But when has logic ever stopped Dennis from acting in an impulsive fashion? It's one of the reasons I left him.

"Thankfully, you didn't break his nose," Edward snaps from his position behind the desk.

"Too bad I didn't," Rick growls.

He's seated in one of the chairs facing the desk. I'm on the chair next to him, attempting to bind his lacerated fingers. I tighten the bandage, and he winces. I pay no heed and tug on the dressing. He flinches again but doesn't protest.

I scowl up at him. "You're aware this is a PR nightmare. Hopefully, no one caught it on camera and—" My phone vibrates, as do Rick's and Edward's. I release Rick's hand, pull out my phone and scroll the notifications that have popped up on my social media feeds. "Shit."

"Fuck!" Edward stares at his phone.

Only Rick seems unperturbed. He leans back in his chair and places his ankle over the knee of his other leg.

"You're all over social media." I wave my phone in his direction.

He glances at it and raises a shoulder. "Whoever shot it got a good angle."

"Is that all you have to say for yourself?" I glower at him.

He shakes his head. "Actually, I have more to say."

"Oh?" I tip up my chin.

"I should have thrown the motherfucker on the floor and stomped all over his hands for daring to put them on you."

I blink. A shudder of something like warmth suffuses my skin. My pussy quivers. *No, no, no, I did not find this entire neanderthal act of him wanting to beat up a man for touching me arousing. I did not.* I yank on the bandage so hard his shoulder muscles bunch and yet, he doesn't protest. Stubborn asshole.

"Are you hearing yourself? This is not some street brawl. And even that would have made news, by the way, since you were involved. This involves you and one of the top athletes in the country."

"So?"

"So? This is going to wreck your career, asshole," I snap.

"He needed to be taught a lesson." His gaze narrows on me. "Why are you so concerned, anyway? I thought you don't like me. Thought you'd be happy at my career taking a dip."

I jump to my feet. "My personal feelings don't come into it. You're my client. I work for the team. I'm worried about the reputation of each of you. If one of you takes a hit in the media, we all do, remember?"

He blinks at that.

"You didn't think of that, did you?" I scowl.

"It was there at the back of my mind, but when he insulted you—?" He shakes his head. "Nope, all I wanted to do was make sure the motherfucker couldn't speak for a very long time."

"What Dennis did was wrong." Edward rakes his fingers through his hair. "If I were in your position, I'd beat him up, too, but fuck, if this doesn't put us in a bind. The eyes of the media and the fans are on this team. We're the underdog. And with the negative publicity with the journalist, then with this incident with Dennis, it's making it too easy for people to write us off. It makes us look like amateurs, like we're not focused on the game."

"You're the manager for a reason, aren't you?" Rick lowers his chin to his chest. "I'm aware it's not going to be easy to fix this in the media, but no way was I going to let that asshole walk away after insulting her."

Edward looks at him in frustration. "You're called Stone for a reason. You're the one who keeps your cool under pressure. You're the one who thinks on your feet and doesn't make risky decisions. You're the one who's supposed to set an example for the rest of the team."

"And he did—" The door to the office is pushed fully open and Finn strides in. He's followed by Manning and Enzo, while Jagger crowds the doorway.

Realizing he failed to close the door completely, Edward snaps, "Shut the door, or do you want the rest of the club to listen to whatever bullshit you assholes are gonna spew?"

Jagger steps inside and pulls the door closed behind him.

The space had already felt crowded, thanks to Rick's hulking presence. But now, filled with six men over six feet tall, with huge shoulders and bigger egos, it feels stifling. I resist the urge to edge toward the wall and brace myself against it for support. If I'm going to work with these guys, it's important they respect me. Which means, now more than ever, I'm going to stand my ground.

"It *is* bullshit, Priest, and you know it." Finn folds his arms across his chest.

Edward leans back in his chair and taps his fingers together.

"Anger, fear, aggression. The dark side are they, but sometimes one has to give in to temptation to find oneself," Enzo murmurs.

Behind him, Jagger groans. "Care to translate that for us, Yoda?"

He refers to Enzo as his nickname, so bestowed due to his penchant of speaking like the character from Star Wars.

"I heard what that asshole said to her." Enzo looks between me and Rick. "Rick did the right thing. If he hadn't, I'd have lost respect for him."

I stiffen. "You heard what my ex said?"

"He's your ex?" Rick asks in a hard voice.

I shuffle my feet.

"Gio, answer me." He infuses his voice with a command that slices through to my core. A tone that insists I obey. A pitch that hooks into a primal part of me deep inside and insists I answer.

Before I can stop myself, I find myself nodding. I'm not looking at him, but I sense him stiffen. Damn, why does it feel like I've done something wrong? I didn't engage with that bastard. He's the one who grabbed me, and Rick's the one who reacted when I didn't need him to fight my battle. Also, there is no connection between Dennis and me anymore, so why do I still feel like I owe Rick an explanation? I keep my gaze averted and scowl at Enzo. "Thanks for feeding his ego," I snap.

Enzo's features soften. "I understand why you feel responsible, but you don't need to be. Rick did the right thing and almost all of us agree."

"Almost?" I frown.

"The Prick?" Rick drawls.

"The Prick," Finn agrees.

"The Prick?" I look between them.

"That's Caspian's call sign, one he's not happy about," Enzo adds.

"Never known a name to be more apt." Manning smirks.

"He'll come around," Rick declares.

I turn on him. "And if he doesn't?"

"He will, end of story." He cuts his palm through the air in a sign that says he won't brook any argument. I glower at him, and he meets my gaze with a raised eyebrow, as if daring me to defy him. Which I so badly want to do, but I'm not stupid enough to do it in front of everyone. I haven't known him too long, but common sense dictates it's best to pick up on this when we're alone. So I contend myself with glowering back at him. And that, for some reason, makes his lips twitch. *Bastard.*

"And what about Dennis?" Edward cuts in.

"What about him?" Rick wrenches his gaze away from me and some of the tension drains out of my muscles. Being in such close proximity to him is like imbibing a testosterone overload, one that's making my belly quiver and my breasts tighten in anticipation. I shuffle my feet, then squeeze my thighs together, in the hope of relieving some of that tension in my core. Only he senses it, for his nostrils flare. He doesn't look at me, though, thank god. *It must be my imagination that he's as tuned into me as I am toward him, right?*

Edward's phone rings. He looks down at his screen and his gaze widens. He answers the phone. "Priest." He listens to whoever is on the other side, then his brows knit. He rubs the back of his neck, looks at Rick, then nods again. He sets down the phone and his features tighten.

"What?" I clear my throat. "What is it?"

14

Rick

"No, absolutely not. You are not doing this." She paces back and forth across the floor of the living room. We're back at the house, and the rest of the team are sprawled around in the space.

Finn lounges in the chair opposite me. Enzo and Manning take up most of the couch, while Jagger leans a hip against the wall. The TV on the wall has been turned off—for the first time since we've occupied the house—a measure of how serious the topic of discussion is.

Caspian stands with his feet wide apart, a sneer on his face. The rest of the guys take up the chairs that've been dragged in from the rest of the house. All twenty of them are here. Guess there's some use for the group chat Finn has instituted. Not that I'm part of it. But Finn had shared the message on my behalf and the guys responded at once. Now their gazes are trained on the woman who stands in the middle of the room and scowls at me. Her golden eyes crackle with fire. Her blonde hair is piled up in its usual bun. She hasn't changed out of her work clothes or her heels, while the rest of us are in our jeans and sweatshirts.

"This is not going to help things." She turns on Finn. "Why don't you make him see sense?"

"Actually," — Finn edges forward in his seat — "I'm not sure he has a choice."

"Actually, he does." She slaps her palms on her hips. "He can turn down Dennis' challenge to a fight."

"And lose face? If news of this gets out, he'll become the laughingstock of the internet."

Caspian's statement is followed by silence. The rest of the team look at him. The expressions on their features range from anger to frustration to derision.

And I'm the one who did that. I'm the one who put us all in this quandary. When I lunged for that wanker, Dennis, I didn't think of my team at all. For the first time in my career, I put myself first. Not my teammates. And while it surprises me, I don't regret it. Not one bit. There's no way I could have allowed him to walk away after he insulted her like that. No, I did the right thing. I wish the rest of the team didn't have to be impacted by it.

"Shut the fuck up, Prick," Finn growls.

"Fuck you, too, Hand," Caspian shoots back. "What kind of a call name is Hand, anyway? If it's supposed to indicate the size of the organ between your legs, we both know mine is larger, longer, broader and—"

"—no match for mine." Finn smirks.

"Oh?" Caspian looks him up and down. "If you want to compare—" He reaches for his waistband, as does Finn.

"Fucking hell." I rise to my feet. "Can't we get anything done without the two of you reverting to primates?"

"It was him." Both point to the other.

I crack my neck, then jerk my chin in their direction. "Shut the fuck up, you two."

They shut up. Or at least, Finn does.

Caspian glances at me with a measuring look. "You have to do it. You don't have a choice."

"He doesn't have to do anything," Gio retorts.

He turns on her. "Are you worried about him because he's the captain, or because the two of you are fucking each other?"

"Don't talk to me like that." She marches up to him and stabs a finger in his chest. "I'm the PR manager of this team. I might not play on the ice, but as image conscious as you are, you know that it's in my hands how I paint you in the media."

He blinks, then seems to get a hold of himself. "You don't scare me," he scoffs.

"Oh?" She draws herself up to her full height, then taps the toe of her right stiletto. "All I have to do is put out a few whispers about the size of your package. Perhaps, even leak some limp dick pics and ensure the trail leads back to you, and then we'll see."

His jaw drops, then he laughs, the sound uncertain. "You wouldn't."

"Wouldn't I?" She rubs her nails on the collar of her Chanel jacket. "I know enough people in the right places in the media world to make this a reality."

He surveys her features, then nods slowly. "You made your point; I'll back off. For now. But there's nothing stopping me from leaking to the media that the two of you are sharing a room, either."

She stills, then tips up her chin. "Try me, buster. The same people who'd attribute a dick pic to you, would hold back news about me."

"Also, there's a reason we're sharing a room." I prowl over to stand between them. "You going to tell them, babe?" I soften my gaze as I meet hers.

"Eh?" She scowls. "Tell them what? And why are you ca—"

"You see, there's a reason we're sharing a room, and it's not only because there's no extra room for Gio here."

She angles her head.

"It isn't?" Finn taps his fingertips on his thigh.

"It isn't?" Caspian asks slowly.

The unsettled expression on his features is almost as satisfying as the shock on her face when I drawl, "It isn't. Because what Gio and I failed to tell the rest of you, is that we're engaged."

"Engaged? You told them we're engaged?" She leans against the door to the room and folds her arms across her chest. Her voice is deceptively mild, and that's the first sign there's a side of her I haven't seen before. "You told them that you and I"—she points between us—"are involved in a relationship."

I hold her gaze, and underneath the golden sparks in her eyes, I spot silver flashes. Not something I've seen before—a sign that she's pissed, I'm sure of it. The fine hair on the nape of my neck rises. My subconscious, honed by my many tours, warns me this is a situation not to be taken lightly. All my senses home in on her. "Umm, can we talk about this?"

I slowly raise my hands, so as not to incite her further, and her eyes flash. The pulse at the base of her neck kicks up. If we were in a superhero movie, there would be flashes of lightning sparking off of her skin.

"You want to talk?" she asks, again in that tone of voice that almost has cheerful lilt to it. One that makes me very, very wary. If I don't answer her, it's going to make things worse. If I do—? I'm not sure it's going to make things better. The only thing I'm grateful for? She waited until we got behind closed doors before she decided to lower the boom.

I nod slowly. "I do want to talk, yes."

"So talk." She taps her foot, clad in those six-inch heels with the red soles. Not sure which designer created it, but fuck, if it doesn't add height to her legs and push out her butt, as well as enhance the thrust of her tits. Which is chauvinistic, I'm aware, but I'm a red-blooded male, and I can only resist looking at her assets to a point. Besides, it's Gio—not any woman. The kind of woman I've dreamed of meet for years.

"You have to admit, it was an inspired way to nip the gossip at the source."

"Inspired?" She pushes a finger into her cheek and pretends to think. "Let me see... What do I think?" She directs her gaze back on me. "I agree."

"You do?" I stare at her, trying to peer through that expression of serenity on her face and failing.

"It was inspired. And so is this." She bends, slips off her stiletto, then lobs it at me.

15

Gio

"Motherfucking, twat-busting, rat's ass of a manhole," I fume.

He steps aside and my Louboutin crashes to the floor.

"That's a very expensive pump, you douche-hat." I hop around on my bare foot, then slide off the other stiletto and pitch it at him. He catches it. Of course, he does, asshole athlete that he is. Then he brings it up to his face and licks up the inside of the sole.

I gape at him. "Did you just —"

"Lick your shoe?" He lowers the heel to his side, then picks up the other one. Without taking his gaze off of me, he brings it to his face and inhales it.

"Umm…" I hesitate. "I'm not sure that smells very good."

His lips curl. "Everything about you smells like you, and that's all that matters."

A ripple of heat licks up my spine. If I look down at my chest, I know my nipples will be outlined through my blouse and my jacket. The lust that slices through me is not a surprise. It's been there, bubbling and rising inside me, increasing in size every day, slowly, slowly.

He's a master of seduction, that's for sure, with his words—when he speaks —and his actions, and his every move intended to make an impression on me, until I can't help but be aware of him when we're in the same room. And when we're not, I'm searching for his ugly mug—okay, his devilishly handsome mug—and the sight of his broad shoulders, that wide chest, the tapered waist, those powerful thighs, which could hold up my weight without a second thought. Only, I'm not going to let myself be taken in by his gorgeousness, his beauty, the sheer masculinity of his presence that has already imprinted itself on me.

"Everything about *you* makes me want to turn my back on you and walk away," I shoot back.

"Oh?" He prowls over until he's standing so close the heat from his body surrounds me like a welcome embrace.

That fresh snow and cut grass scent of his envelops me. I draw it in, and my head spins. My blood begins to pump harder; a pulse throbs at my wrists, my ankles, behind my eyes, all of it coalescing into a molten beat that thuds between my legs.

"You want to leave?" he asks in a silky-smooth voice that does weird things to my belly. Gah, why is everything about this man designed to turn me on? He's one big sex-machine, and Tom Jones has nothing on him.

"Do you, Goldilocks?"

I huff out a choked breath. "And which one of the three bears are you?"

"How about all three combined into one?" He bends and drags his nose up the side of my cheek. "I certainly have the appetite to rival it."

He draws in a breath, followed by a growl of approval.

The sound grates over my nerve-endings, and my pussy clenches. Moisture trickles out from between my legs, and I squeeze my thighs together to clamp down on that growing emptiness between them.

"I do want to leave," I burst out.

He freezes at once, his azure eyes flashing. He takes a step back, then another. He nods in the direction of the bedroom. "Run along before I change my mind."

Something like disappointment squeezes my chest. Damn, I didn't want him to kiss me, did I? I don't even like him. I'm attracted to him, but I have nothing in common with him. I have a career to focus on, and he needs to get his team to the finals of the League and win it. We have our jobs cut out for us, and a liaison of any kind would only make things more difficult. Not to mention, after my bastard of an ex, I've sworn off men in general, and hockey players in particular.

"Not before you tell me why you said we're engaged? And it's not only about managing the gossip, is it?"

The lust in his eyes recedes enough for a shrewd look to come into them. A cunning expression settles on his features. That's when I realize I've misjudged this man. I underestimated him. I mistook him for being laid-back. Now, I realize it was all a front. Is this how he lulls his enemies into a sense of complacency, only to finish them off? Just like he's killing me with the desire that laces his expression.

"You're right, there's more to it," he drawls.

"So tell me"—I look between his eyes—"why did you tell them that?"

"You want revenge on your ex—"

"And you concluded that how?" I snap.

"I saw the look on your face. He hurt you, and you want to hurt him back."

"And you figured that out in a few minutes?"

He peers into my eyes. "I'd wager you're still in love with him."

Fire lights up my face. I squeeze my eyes shut. I should deny it. But the fact is, I am not a person who takes relationships lightly. When I was with Dennis, it was because I was ready to commit. Because he ticked all the boxes and seemed like the man I'd like to spend the rest of my life with... on paper, at least. And look how that turned out.

"I didn't mean to upset you," he murmurs in a soft voice.

I manage to compose myself and open my eyes. "You may be right. I was in love with him. At least, I thought I was. And I'm not the kind who gets over feelings quickly, you know? So yeah, maybe a part of me is *still* in love with him, much to my chagrin."

Something flickers in his eyes. Surprise? No, he's the one who said it. Disappointment? Nah, why should he be disappointed?

"I know. What does it say about me that I might still be in love with him after he cheated on me? But I'm realizing I'm not the kind who can turn my feelings on and off, you know?" I hunch my shoulders. "He hurt me; he broke my heart, so I don't want to get back together with him. I need time to mourn the loss of my dream. I had everything planned out—my career, my life, my future—and then it all went to pieces." My nose tickles, and the backs of my eyes burn. I refuse to cry over that asshole. He doesn't deserve my tears.

"He doesn't deserve you. He should be whipped for what he did to you."

The violence in his voice sends a jolt of shock through me.

In all the time I was with Dennis, not once, did he ever use that tone of voice with me. I never sensed that kind of passion in him. I was the arm candy girlfriend. The one he loved to take to official events, to be seen in the media with, to share pics with me on social media. The ideal girlfriend, couple goals... That's what we were.

Rick, though? In all the interactions I've had with him, it's clear he doesn't give a damn about his social standing or his image in the media. And that anger on my behalf in his tone? It…it sends a pulse of longing shooting through my veins. I take in the set of his jaw, the nerve that tics at his temple, the steely flint in his eyes. He's not just angry, he's enraged. On my behalf.

For some reason, that thickens the ball of emotion in my throat. I manage to swallow around it and tip up my chin. "You're right, he doesn't deserve me. I can do better than him. I know that. And I can't believe I'm still thinking of him. I need to get over him and move on, I know that. I haven't managed to do it… yet."

He scans my features and slowly nods. "He's a goddamn fool to not have held onto you."

Warmth pools in my chest.

"He doesn't know what he's lost. If you were mine, I'd treat you like a queen. I'd make sure nothing ever hurts you. That you're always taken care of, that all of your needs are met. That you're"—he lowers his voice—"satisfied in every way."

My heart descends to the space between my legs. A dull throb flares to life in my core.

"When I saw you with him, it was clear you were pissed off. I couldn't hear the argument you two had, but your body language screamed you didn't want to be anywhere near him. He wasn't man enough to respect your wishes."

I swallow. "And you'd respect my wishes?"

One side of his lips twist. "For now."

The promise in those words shoots a pulse of longing through my soul. Jesus, how can make me feel these emotions at such a deep level? Then he steps back, and I draw in a breath. He spins around and, still holding my Louboutins, walks over to stand by the window. "Also, I need a fiancée to take home to my Grams."

"Eh?" Of all the things he could have said, that was not what I expected.

"My grandmother refuses to have a heart operation that would save her life, unless I show her I'm serious about settling down. Hence…" He raises a shoulder and continues to look out the window.

"So you're going to lie to her?"

"If it means convincing her to get the surgery, then yes." He uses his free hand to rub the back of his neck. "When you meet Grams, you'll understand. She's as feisty as you."

"I'm not feisty."

"And stubborn," he goes on, completely ignoring my reaction. "You can't make that woman do anything she doesn't want to do. She's been morose since her diagnosis. It's why, on my last trip home, I left Tiny with her."

"That mutt has a way of lightening up things around him. But wouldn't he be too much for her to take care of?"

"She has a companion who spends the day with her and helps her around the house. Part of her duties include walking Tiny every day and making sure he gets his exercise. And before you worry, she was thrilled to have Tiny there. She knows how to handle him, and there's no additional demand on Grams' energy. And Tiny is wonderful with her. He's a gentle soul, and he livens up things and makes her laugh."

"It's true; the only time I've seen you crack a smile is at his antics."

He turns to look at me over his shoulder. "I smile," he says with a frown on his face.

"Ha, ha, did you crack a joke?" I chuckle.

His lips twitch, drawing attention to that puffy lower lip, and that thin upper lip that promises there's a streak of meanness running through him. A spark of anticipation fires up my nerve-endings. I can't ignore the clenching in my belly, either. Gah, why can't I go a few seconds without reacting to his lethal good looks?

"Also, why ask me to do this? Why not someone you know?"

"Like who?"

"An ex-girlfriend, maybe?"

His frown deepens, then he turns and leans back against the windowsill, my Louboutins dangling from his fingertips. It should look incongruous, but the delicate stilettos only serve to heighten his masculinity in comparison. "I don't have an ex."

I mentally fist-pump. Outwardly, I narrow my gaze on him. "You never dated? Or had a girlfriend?"

"Never had time. I had lots of sex, of course."

"Of course," I huff.

His eyes gleam. "Lots and lots of sex, in all positions, and once with triplets, all of whom I satisfied—"

I swallow.

"—and at the same time."

Heat flushes my cheeks. "I don't need the details."

"Isn't that why you're asking me questions, so you can find out more about me?"

"Don't flatter yourself."

"You should be flattered I asked you to pose as my fiancé," he drawls.

My eyeballs almost pop out of my head. "I hope you have the equipment to back up your massive ego," I burst out.

"Wouldn't you like to find out?" He drawls.

I survey his features for some sign that he's joking, but nope. Those features are unruffled. No sign of emotions or some crack in his façade. Except for his narrowed gaze, I may as well be talking to a stone.

"So, what do you say?" He bends his knees and peers into my eyes. You pose as my fiancée on a trip home. In return, I help you show that asshole that you've moved on from him for good."

16

Rick

Her frown deepens. "Can I think it over?"

"There's nothing to think over. It's a neat solution to all of our problems. Also, the team thinks we're engaged."

"And whose fault is that?" She glowers at me.

Mine, and I'm not apologetic about it. Though, no one was more surprised than me when I said it. It seems my sub conscience was several steps ahead of me, as usual. Once I heard myself speak, I was convinced it was the right way forward.

"Of course, considering they haven't seen us kiss or hold hands, we'll have to convince them about our intentions toward each other."

I tilt my head and allow the lust to, once more, diffuse my features. The air between us heats at once. I can see she senses the chemistry, for her lips part.

Her breathing grows choppy, then she glances away. "No thank you," she says in a prim voice. "If we did this and"—she raises a finger—"I'm only saying *if*, then there'll be no sex."

"No sex with others." I nod. "You didn't have to say that. Once I commit, I'm all in."

"No, no, no." She shoves her fingers through her hair, and a strand breaks free from that complicated hairdo she loves to wear. "I mean, no sex with each other."

"Okay." The moment the word is out, I curse myself. That wasn't convincing at all. The suspicion in her eyes confirms my suspicion.

"So, you're fine with sleeping on the couch?"

Hell, no. I wince. "That sofa wasn't made for sleeping, in case you hadn't noticed."

She purses her lips. "It's not the most comfortable piece of furniture in the room," she admits.

That's an understatement. The couch is not one of those pieces of furniture that encourages you to sink into it. It's straight-backed and feels out of place in comparison to the cushioned armchairs, which seem to have come from a different set.

She begins to speak but I hold up my hand. "I promise, I won't share the bed if that reassures you about my intentions."

"So you won't sleep on the couch or on the bed?" She frowns.

"Don't you trust me?"

"Is that a trick question?" Her eyes flash. "For the record, I don't trust your intentions, but considering you haven't left me with much of a choice..." Her shoulders slump. All at once, she looks defeated and tired. I notice the dark circles under her eyes, the hollows under her cheekbones.

"Have you not been sleeping well?" I walk toward her. "And when was the last time you ate?"

"Okay, hold on. We need some boundaries. You don't need to put on the act of a caring fiancé when we're on our own." She gulps as I come to a stop in front of her.

I look down at her from my immense height. She's so much shorter than me. And slimmer. Even soaking wet, I'd be able to carry her with ease. Which I would have if I were her fiancé, which I'm not, as she's reminded me. Instead I nod, then

"—also"—she swallows—"you can hand over my Louboutins."

"Eh?"

"My pumps. Can I have my pumps, please?"

I shake my head. "So you can heave them at me again? I don't think so." I walk past her and head toward the part of the room that doubles up as the sleeping area.

"Where are you going?" she calls after me.

I veer toward the closet, slide it open, then walk over to the row of shelves opposite my clothes and place them on the bottom shelf. When I turn, it's to find her staring at her stilettos with a strange look on her face. "What is it?"

She swallows, then shakes her head. "It's nothing."

I frown. The hurt in her eyes, the downward curve of her lips, the dejection that's written into every dip of her features, twists my heart. I walk to her, notch a finger under her chin so she has no choice but to look up at me, and ask, "What is it?"

"Told you, it's nothing." She tries to pull away, but I place a hand on her shoulder.

"You can tell me, Goldie."

"*Now*, it's Goldie?" She scoffs. "Why not call me Mac?"

"That's for them. Goldie is the name only I can use."

"And why would you want to do that?"

"Because you're my fiancée, remember?"

"Fake fiancée."

"Still my fiancée."

"But fake."

"Still my—"

She throws up her hands. "I can't win any argument with you, can I?"

I allow my lips to quirk and shrug. "You're so cute when you're angry, you know that?"

She scowls. "I'll show you how cute I can be."

She bends her knee and raises it, but I step aside. The next moment, I've grabbed her arm and twisted her around so her back is to my chest. I wrap my arms about her. "There, much better."

"Let me go," she snarls.

"Only if you tell me what's wrong."

She continues to struggle for a few seconds. When she realizes I'm not letting her go, she sags against me. I hold her close, and inch by inch, her muscles relax. We stay there, unmoving, and I tuck her head under my chin. There's a comfort in this, despite the fact that her butt is nestled against my crotch, and the blood is draining to my groin, and I can feel every soft dip and curve of her tight little body against mine. Despite the fact that I have a raging hard on, there's still an ease in holding her like this. A contentment, a sense that all is right with the world. A feeling of peace I've never felt before. A sensation of having found my place, finally.

It's only when a growl rumbles up my chest that I realize how much I've allowed myself to draw comfort from this closeness. She must realize it, too, for she stiffens. I should release her now. I should walk away and stop probing about why she seemed so sad, but I can't. I'd do the same for any other team-mate, minus holding any of them so intimately in my arms, of course. I resist the urge to speak, and instead, simply hold her. It's the right decision, for she melts even further into me.

"I always thought I wasn't worth much. I didn't think I'd ever find anyone who could understand me. And then I thought I had." She swallows.

"You mean Dennis Dickface?"

She snorts out a laugh. "Yeah. I know you saw us arguing, but during the time we were together, we never did. We seemed to make space for each other, and he seemed like the perfect boyfriend—"

"Until he wasn't?"

She nods.

"What happened?"

A shudder grips her, and I tighten my hold around her. It's not in me to offer comfort so openly. Hell, if anyone had told me I'd be holding a woman for anything other than the act of safe sex... Always safe, never without a condom, and only for as long as needed to get myself off. I always ensured they orgasmed, too, before I left their bed and never saw them again. Anyway, if anyone had told me I'd be doing this, I'd have called them a liar. Yet, here I am, comforting her and insisting she tell me what's bothering her. Last I checked, I had my balls intact, though, so there's that. It must be this enforced proximity, thanks to us being roomies, which is making me want to make her feel better.

"You don't have to tell me—" I begin when she bursts out, "I walked in on him with another woman in our bed."

17

Gio

Oh my god, did I blurt that out? Fire streaks my cheeks. I try to pull away again, but of course, he doesn't let me go. "You got what you wanted; can you release me please?" I manage to croak out the words through a throat that feels like I've been screaming.

"You don't have to be embarrassed about what happened. It was on that asshole that he didn't realize the value of what he had."

"And you do?" I shake my head. "Ignore what I said. My emotions are all over the place. This is why I don't like to talk about what happened. I wish you hadn't forced me to share it, now I feel like a complete idiot."

"He's the wanking toss-arse who didn't deserve you in the first place."

I choke out a laugh. "You're creative with your insults."

"As are you."

"One of my redeeming features," I murmur.

"I can think of a few more."

"Oh?" I still. "Like what?"

"You looking for compliments?" he asks in a light voice.

"Of course not." I wriggle in his hold, then freeze when my butt brushes up against the very thick, hard column in his pants. "Umm—is that—?" I swallow. "Did I just—"

"Rub up against the evidence of how aroused I am? Yes, you did."

I twitch my backside and, once more, connect with that very sizable bulge.

This time he groans. "What are you trying to do, Goldie?" His voice is slightly breathless, and that makes me feel good. He should hurt for how he makes me want to slap his ridiculously handsome face, then jump him, before throwing myself down and demanding he fuck me every time I see him. It's only right he feels some of the—whatever it is that's been growing between us since we met. I squirm in his hold, and this time, the hockey stick in his pants stabs into the valley between my butt-cheeks.

I freeze. "Oh."

"Indeed," he says in a droll voice. One that's bereft of any emotion. Which tells me how much he's feeling. Which is a lot. Funny how I can already read between the lines of his grunts and one-word replies.

"I think you should let me go," I manage to say around the ball of sensation in my throat.

"I think I should throw you over my shoulder, march you over to the bed, toss you down, and tear up your pussy until you stop sassing me."

"Excuse me?" I squeak.

"You heard me."

Oh god, oh god, oh god. If he does it, I'm not going to protest. Nope. I'm going to lay back and take everything he gives me. I'm going to climb him like he's a California coconut palm and suck face with him. I'm also going to squeeze other parts of him. And let him squeeze me, too. Aargh, the fire in my cheeks intensifies until it feels like an inferno.

"Only, I'm not going to follow through with my thoughts, sadly."

Before I can open my mouth to ask him why not and disgrace myself further, he releases me. I stumble forward, then turn and stare at him. "D-d-d-did you just say what I think you did?"

"Which part are you talking about?"

"Uh, all of it."

"And if I did?"

"I'd say you've got a hope in hell for that happening." I spin around and prance out of the door, then stumble over the carpet in the bedroom because goddamn, but I'm better at walking with heels. And that's a fact.

I manage to hold onto the remaining shreds of my dignity as I head past the bed and into the closet. I snatch up my nightdress. It's a silk kimono, and damn, if I'm going to wear anything else. If he has a problem with it, he can jump out the window.

I hear his footsteps behind me and race into the bathroom and slam the door shut, because I'm a coward. Because if I look at that gorgeous body of his, I won't be able to keep my hands off him.

I drop my clothes onto the small table in the corner of the bathroom, then step into the shower. I switch on the water and step under it. The steam envelops me, sinking into my blood. My already sensitized skin prickles in reaction. I press my forehead into the tiles and close my eyes, then slide my fingers down between my legs. It's okay. He can't hear me—not over the sound of the shower. I know he's hurting, but so am I.

I can still feel the strength of his body around me, the hard edges of his pecs as they dug into my back, and the blunt heaviness of the equipment he carries between his massive thighs. My pussy clenches, and my nipples tighten into points of acute hardness. I trace the outline of my throbbing clit and a moan wells up my throat. I'm so damn close. I stick my fingers into my squelching pussy and begin to fuck myself. In-out-in again and again, but it's not enough. I thrust a third finger and a fourth, stretching myself around the girth, already knowing it's nowhere near the thickness I crave. I bring my other hand to my breast and pinch my nipple.

Instantly, my pussy squeezes down. My breath catches, my skin tingles and I part my legs further, trying to give myself better access, when the hair on the back of my neck rises. I freeze, then turn and glance over my shoulder to find he's watching me through the glass wall of the shower cubicle. My gaze catches with his, holds. Those cerulean eyes of his turn almost indigo. I gulp.

The steam rises between us, adding to the dream-like feel of the moment. I cling to the strength in his piercing gaze and begin to move my fingers in and out of my channel. His nostrils flare, and I know he knows what I'm doing. He also knows he caught me as I was masturbating to thoughts of him. And there's a certain safety in being behind the wall of the shower cubicle and surrounded by the water that rains over me. It gives me the courage needed to increase the pace of my movements. I work my fingers in, and my entire body shudders. I bring my other hand down to pinch my swollen clit and cry out. I continue to work myself and rub on the swollen bud. The tension behind my pussy walls grows and builds and becomes bigger until it thuds through my veins, my arms and legs and just like that, it explodes. My back curves, I arch up to tiptoe, unable to look away as I gasp, "Rick." The orgasm pushes me over the edge.

My eyelids flutter down as I slump against the wall and slowly, slowly drift back to earth. When I manage to crack open my eyelids, the doorway is empty.

18

Rick

That was the hottest thing I have ever seen. Goldie shattering with my name on her lips. I saw her body tremble as she fell apart. I felt her fall apart, despite the distance and the incessant drumming of the water from the shower. I took a step forward, intent on marching over to her and pushing her up against the wall, replacing her fingers with my cock. A-n-d the only thing that stopped me was the fact that she made it clear there's to be no sex between us.

I'm no gentleman—make no mistake—but she deserves to be treated like a lady. Until she gives me her consent, that is. Until she gives me her yes to take from her without her assent. Until then, I'll respect her wishes. I can't take her —not after she revealed that particular secret, which I'm sure she hasn't told too many others. She's vulnerable, and I cannot take advantage of that. Much as I want to feel her cunt strangle my cock as I fuck her, this isn't the time.

So, I marched out of there and out of the room. I could not allow myself to stay there a second longer. I could not let myself imagine how it would feel to sink down on my knees and thrust my mouth between her thighs, to eat her out and make her orgasm again. To kiss her with pussy breath, then turn her into the wall and fuck her from behind. To wrap her up in my arms and feel her shudder and pant and yell my name over and over again.

When I proposed the charade of her being my fake fiancée, I did it, confident it would be just that—a pretense. I didn't think I'd be tempted to act on the attraction between us and cross the line to fuck her.

When I took on the role of captain, it's because I saw as it my path to redemption. I ran from the Royal Marines, then tried my hand at private security. But nothing has come close to the satisfaction I felt when I played for the NHL. I never thought I'd get the chance to strap on the skates and hit the ice again. And when Knight offered it to me, I almost convinced myself I wasn't ready. But when he mentioned she was going to take on the role of the PR manager and would work closely with the captain, something inside me clicked into place. Even though I suspected the bastard was trying to manipulate me. I knew this was my chance to get close to her. Also, I didn't want anyone else spending so much in such close proximity to her, so I made a decision.

No one else would have the opportunity to brainstorm with her, or plan with her—or share a room with her. No one but me. My subconscious was, once again, way ahead of the curve and waited for the rest of me to catch up. Of course, it provides me the perfect opportunity to show my grandmother I'm serious about getting married and embracing domesticity. Everything has come together... but for this all-consuming chemistry between us throwing a wrench into my plans.

I have to resist it, else it could distract me from my goals. Knight relies on me to lead the team to victory. It might not be the same as leading a team on the war-front, but the feeling sure comes close. This is my second chance to prove to myself, I still have what it takes to play professional hockey. I can do it. I simply have to stay clear-headed and keep my head in the game.

I psyche myself up enough so that by the time I reach the kitchen on the first floor, I almost feel like myself again.

Anyway, I do owe her a meal. She confided in me. In return, I can ensure she's fed. Not that I know how to cook, but a man has to start somewhere. I head for the refrigerator, then pull it open and stare at the contents. Beer, more beer, wine, bread and eggs, ham and cheese, hmm!

"What are you looking for, asshole?" Finn drawls from over my shoulder.

"It's late; we have an early start tomorrow. Shouldn't you be in bed, dick-face?"

"If you're looking to make dinner for her—"

I scowl. "And if I was?"

"I'd say, since your culinary talents are not the best, you should stick to making her an omelet."

I grab the eggs, butter, cheese, ham and straighten, then turn to find him hovering at my elbow.

"You going to supervise?" I scoff.

"When were you going to tell me you two are pretending to be engaged?"

My fingers slip. I almost drop the egg, then manage to hold onto it at the last moment. "What makes you think it's a pretense?"

"The fact that you didn't tell me about it earlier? Oh, also, let me see... We worked together on our last project when we were assigned as bodyguards to Solene, and I didn't see any evidence of the two of you being together."

I slide a skillet onto the range and light the flame under it. "Just because you didn't see it doesn't mean we didn't get together then." I crack the eggs and beat them up. Then begin to dice the ham.

"Considering we were together almost day and night on the job and not once did I see you as much as get on the phone to Gio—"

"That's Mac to you."

He blinks. "—to Mac, it's safe to say the two of you have decided to take part in this pretense for a reason."

I heat the butter in the frying pan and when it's foaming, I pour the egg mixture onto the skillet and cook it until it begins to set. Then I add the cheese and three-quarters of the ham in the center of the omelet.

"And if I were to take a guess, I'd say you decided to help her get revenge on her dick of an-ex."

The cheese begins to melt, and I increase the heat to high and cook the omelet further. Meanwhile, I pop two slices of bread in the toaster.

"You could have told me," he continues in a hurt voice.

"There's nothing to tell because it's all true." Goldie's voice sounds behind me.

I stiffen, but continue to watch the omelet, checking the bottom to make sure it browns. Once I'm satisfied, I fold it, then slide it onto a plate. I sprinkle the remaining ham. Only then, do I turn to find Finn contemplating her.

Goldie looks unperturbed. Her face is flushed from the shower, and her hair is tied up in a pony tail. Her face is bare of make-up, and she looks fresh-faced and gorgeous. Also, she's wearing a silken kimono that comes to above her knees and leaves her legs bare. I narrow my gaze on her; she tilts up her chin.

Finn looks between us. "You mean to say you're engaged to this douchebag? You, who couldn't stand the sight of him?" Finn widens his stance. "If I remember correctly, the two of you could barely see eye-to-eye every time we had a discussion about Solene's security detail."

She waves a regal hand in the air. "That was foreplay."

I cough.

Finn seems taken aback.

"Ever hear the old enemies-to-lovers adage? That's us. We were enemies—"

"—but now we're lovers," I pitch in helpfully.

Finn barks out a laugh. "You expect me to believe that?"

She arches a shoulder. "Honestly, it's none of your business, and I don't care what you believe. But because Rick's your best friend, I understand you feel a little left out. Maybe this will convince you."

She glides across the floor in her red ballet flats. When she reaches me, she rises up on tip-toes, wraps her palm around the back of my neck, and urges me to lower my head to hers.

19

Gio

I press my lips to his, and I must take him by surprise, for he allows me to brush my mouth over his. His breath smells of mint, and the heat of his body is scorching hot, but the kiss itself is soft. Unremarkable, even.

A part of me is happy that the chemistry I imagined between us, clearly, doesn't translate to anything. But the emptiness in my stomach, and the hollow feeling in my chest say otherwise. And I was so sure there was something between us, that it would be explosive when we finally kissed.

I begin to pull away when he flattens his big palm over my hip. He holds me in place, tilts his head, and his mouth firms. He licks my lower lip, and I gasp. Instantly, he slides his tongue over mine, and I melt into him. He pulls me close, deepens the kiss, and drinks from me. He sucks on my tongue, and my head spins. My knees wobble. I grab at his shoulders to hold on as he kisses me and kisses me. My nipples tighten, my breasts hurt, my pussy clenches, a thousand little flares fan to life under my skin… And then I'm free. I sway, and he holds me until I regain my footing. I stare into those arctic blue eyes, now dotted with silver sparks. As they fade away, his usual noncommittal mask falls into place.

Behind us, Finn clears his throat, and I jump back. I spin around, pop my hip out, and plant my palm on it. "See?" I clear my throat. "The engagement is not fake."

"Well, it's clear the two of you can't keep your hands off each other, but if you want to convince the media, you need to get a ring."

"The media?" The blood drains from my face.

"Don't tell me the two of you didn't think about the media attention this is going to generate when it gets out that the captain of the London Ice Kings is engaged... And to the PR manager of the team?"

I stiffen. To be honest, I hadn't thought this through. And I'm in charge of publicity for the team. It should have been the first thing I thought of when he announced to the team we're engaged. But I was so taken aback, all thoughts of PR slipped out of my head. The only images I held were those Rick's hot body and the things I wanted him to do to mine. There was this nagging sensation that I was missing something when I agreed to pose as his fake fiancée, but I allowed my lust for him to blind me. I mean, sure, it'll help me show my asshole ex I've moved on, but it's also going to fuel a paparazzi frenzy. It's a miracle the word hasn't leaked to the press already. It's only a matter of time before someone outside the team gets wind of it.

"I should have realized this." I wring my fingers together. "I should have thought this through. I should have—"

"It's okay; we'll handle it." Rick places his palm on the small of my back. The gesture is comforting—more than it should be. It also feels like the heat from his touch is branding me. Despite the turmoil in my mind, those tiny flares fan into flames. I manage to push aside the lust that licks at the corners of my senses.

"This is my job. I should have foreseen this. I should have had a plan. I—"

"You do have a plan."

I frown, then glance at him over my shoulder. "I do?"

"Sure, we're going tomorrow to pick out a ring for you, remember?"

"Oh, r-right...." I stammer.

He nods. "Also, you decided to give the scoop to one of your most trusted journalist friends. And I've arranged for us to have a meeting with her, over lunch."

"Uhhh..." I gape at him.

"In fact"—he pulls out his phone and taps on the screen— "I've messaged James Hamilton to book out his restaurant so we can speak to the reporter without anyone bothering us."

"James Hamilton?" I frown. "You're talking about the leading Michelin-starred chef on the continent?"

·He nods.

"And he's going to book out his restaurant and swallow the losses for you?" I fix him with a disbelieving look.

His phone vibrates. He looks at the screen, then holds it out to me.

JH: Done. Anything for you, buddy.

O-k-a-y. "Why would he do that for you?"

"He owes me," Rick says simply.

I narrow my gaze. I shouldn't be interested in his past. I don't care to know why James Hamilton would owe him. Anyway, I have bigger issues here to worry about. Namely, the fact he said we're going to pick out a ring and that I'm supposedly engaged to him. Also, did we plan all this and now I don't remember it? Nah, that's not possible. I'm too careful, too much of an organizer to have decided all of this and forgotten about it. No, the only explanation is that he's come up with this on the fly.

The toaster pops, and I snap out of my reverie. Before I can open my mouth to ask another question, he bends and presses a kiss to my forehead. "We'll talk about this later," he says in a firm voice.

I'm so shocked by the tenderness in his kiss that all I can do is gape. It's the only reason I don't protest or pull away. Yep, that's why I stay silent. It doesn't explain why I lean into the warmth of his body.

"You guys going to keep kissing or are you going to eat?" Finn says from behind us.

I stiffen. Rick pulls back and searches my features, then nods as if satisfied by what he sees. "I made you an omelet."

"I can't walk into a jewelry store and pick out a ring." I pace the floor in front of the bed in our room.

Gah, I called it our room. It *is* our room, but calling it our room makes this arrangement all too formal. It was only yesterday I ran into my ex, and today I'm pretending to be engaged again. And now, the entire world is going to find out I am engaged. How did this happen? Everything is moving too fast, and that's a first for me. I'm used to being in control. I'm used to planning my day down to the last minute, and now, it's as if everything I've worked for is slipping through my fingers.

"I can't go through with this."

He looks at me from where he's sprawled on the bed. He takes up so much space, the massive mattress seems to shrink in size, so it might as well be a single.

"Can't go through with what?"

"This… stupid fake engagement you've gotten both of us into."

"I thought you said it was a great way to solve both of our problems." He flings his arm behind his back. His biceps bulge. He's wearing a white T-shirt, which has seen better days. It stretches across his shoulders, outlining his pecs, as well as his nipples. Since when do I find a man's nipples erotic? The T-Shirt rides up, and a strip of tanned skin shows over his waistband. My mouth waters, and my thighs clench. Jesus, this walking sex god is my roomie.

As if that weren't enough, he's a brave man who faced real enemies on the front line. He won the Victoria's Cross, the highest military honor in this country, and he can make a mean omelet. Also, he cares enough about his grandmother to want me to pose as his fiancée. Jesus, could he be more perfect? Also, did I mention he kisses with his entire body? Like he's completely present—heart and mind and body and tongue and lips and mouth and sculpted chest and powerful thighs. The man almost made me orgasm with the meeting of our mouths. How would it feel to have that tongue on other parts of me? A blush sweeps my face.

He looks at me with interest. "Care to share what you were thinking?"

"I was thinking it was you who said it was the answer to our problems, not me."

"And it's late. I need to be up at five a.m. for practice."

"That's all you're going to say?" I plant my palms on my hips. "This is my future at stake."

"And mine."

"You've already proven yourself with your military career. In fact, I still don't understand why you needed to accept this role as captain. It's not going to be easy to lead this team," I warn.

"I'm aware." He rises to his feet and keeps rising so I have to tilt my head right back to meet his gaze. "And I had to do this."

"But why?"

"It's almost one a.m. Let's talk about this tomorrow after practice, okay?"

He closes the distance between us, and his scent, his nearness, his presence —all of it instantly overwhelms me. It's not fair he can distract me so easily.

"Good night, Goldie." He presses a chaste kiss to my forehead, then walks toward the closet. He emerges with a pillow and a duvet, which he throws down on the floor next to the bed.

He lays down, throws his arm over his eyes, and just like that, his body is still. I'm standing there, while Mr. Jerkosauraus falls asleep.

I glance toward the living area. I could take the couch to put a little more distance between us, but even though I'd be able to stretch out lengthwise on it, the bed is so much more inviting. I march over to the bed, and throw myself under the covers, then switch off the lamp. I turn my back on him and close my eyes. All the ups and downs of the day must take their toll, for I fall asleep at once.

Something infiltrates my layers of sleep, some sound, a cry, maybe? I hear it again and my eyes snap open. I sit up in bed, turn on the lamp, and turn to find Rick thrashing around.

He digs his fingers into his hair and tugs. His eyes are shut, but his features are scrunched up. Sweat beads his forehead, and as I watch he cries out, "Stop, don't do it." The sound of his voice is filled with so much helplessness, my heart stutters. Before I can stop myself, I've slid off the bed and knelt next to him. His chest rises and falls; the tendons of his throat stand out in relief. He shakes his head again, then flinches—and to see this big man flinch, this confident, dominant male who's the most self-possessed man I've ever met, so vulnerable and in pain, makes my insides twist.

A surge of protectiveness fills my blood. I need to console him. To somehow make him feel better. His chest rises and falls. Sweat beads his forehead, and when a shudder grips him, I can't stop myself. I lean in and touch his shoulder. "Rick, wake up, you're dreaming, you—" The next moment, I'm flat on my back and he's on top of me with his fingers around my neck.

20

Rick

"Rick, stop! It's me, Gio. Rick, please—" Her voice cuts through the noise in my head. I stare into her wide golden-brown eyes—eyes currently filled with fear and alarm, both emotions I put there. I take in her pale features, her fingers wrapped around my wrist; the wrist attached to my fingers which are wrapped around her throat. I release my hold and push away, landing on my back next to her, adrenaline pumping, sweat dripping down my chest. "Fuck, fuck, fuck." I draw in a breath and my lungs burn. I throw my arm over my eyes, trying to regain my composure. "Fucking fuck." I almost killed her. I— There's a touch on my arm, and I wince.

"Don't," I force the words out through my throat that is so raw, it feels like I've swallowed acid.

I sense rather than see her retreat. Feel the nervousness coming off of her. I lower my arm and take in her concerned features. "Are you okay?"

She nods, her movements jerky. "You were having a nightmare."

I lurch up to my feet then head to the bathroom and turn on the tap. I dunk my head under and allow the water to flow over my hair and face. I stay there with my eyes closed for a few seconds. When I feel a little more in control, I raise my head. The water drips onto my T-shirt and when I look into the mirror, I meet her eyes. Her features are pinched, but at least, her face has more color. I reach behind me, pull off my T-shirt, then hold it under the tap until I drench it.

When I turn to face her, she flinches and that cuts a swathe of pain through my chest. "I won't hurt you."

"Oh, I know that." She waves a hand in the air. "I'm more worried about who hurt *you*."

I firm my lips. "It's nothing."

"It's not nothing. I saw you cower in your sleep. I heard you cry out. I sensed your fear. For the first time since I've known you, I saw the emotions you hide under that grumpy facade you always have on and that" — she holds up a finger — "is not nothing."

I can't stop the slight quirk of my lips. "You're so goddamn sexy when you get pissed off."

She scowls. "Don't try to distract me."

"Is it working?'

"Do you think it's working?"

"I think you should let me take care of you." I nod toward her neck.

"Oh." She touches her fingers to her throat. "You marked me?"

Satisfaction flushes my chest. "I won't pretend I regret seeing the imprint of my fingers on your skin, but I'd much prefer it to be in the throes of passion, and not as an offshoot of when I might have hurt you. Unless —" I close the distance to her, and her pupils dilate.

"Unless?" She swallows.

"Unless you *asked* me to hurt you." I press my wet T-shirt to her throat with a light touch.

Her breath catches.

"Unless you want me to give you a hand-necklace..." I curl my fingers lightly around the nape of her neck and she shivers. "But that'll be when you ask me for it."

"I can buy my own jewelry, thank you very much," she scoffs.

"Not this one, you can't." I lower my wet T-shirt and survey the skin about her throat. "It'll fade soon enough." *Unlike my feelings for her.* A-n-d, that's my cue to back off. "Come on, I have some ointment that'll help it heal faster."

I walk away from her, tossing my T-shirt onto the counter on the way out. By the time I've snatched up the tube of salve from my kit, she's seated on the bed. I sink down next to her and push her hair over her shoulder. She swallows, her breath uneven. She's trying not to stare, but her gaze keeps wandering to my chest. She must notice the tattoo over my heart, but she doesn't ask about it. Instead, her gaze slides down my abs.

I know I'm in good shape. An offshoot of my daily exercise regime from my NHL days, not to mention, my time with the Royal Marines. It's something I kept up during the time I worked in professional security. Once I realized I was going to take on the role of Captain, I upped the intensity. I've lost a little weight since I left the NHL, but I'll make up for that with the new dietary regimen I've adopted. All of which means, I'm in better shape now than when I was playing for the NHL the first time. I smear some of the liniment on her skin, and a shiver runs up her body.

"You cold?"

"A little." I take in the swell of her breasts bared by the neckline of her kimono. I'd be lying if I said I hadn't noticed her state of undress, but seeing the imprints of my fingers on her had pushed everything else out of my head. That burn of possessiveness in my guts, the intensity of needing to own her, to stake my claim over her—all of it had taken me by surprise. I don't want to acknowledge these new feelings and yet—they feel so right.

I raise my gaze to hers to find her features are flushed, her lips parted. The air between us thrums with awareness, the honeysuckle scent of her seems to sink into the depths of my soul. I lean in, and so does she. She glances down at my mouth and swallows. And I know then, if I kiss her, there's no looking back.

If I touch her, I won't be able to stop. I'll throw her down on the bed and fuck her until neither of us can think straight, and that—would be a mistake. I need to keep this relationship between us professional. That's what we are, teammates. And partners in a role-play that'll benefit the both of us. Besides, I gave her my word I wouldn't sleep with her—and my word is something I value too much to go back on. I rise to my feet and walk past her and into the closet. I pull on a fresh T-shirt, then walk back to her and hand her my jersey. "Put it on."

"Why should I?"

"You're cold; this will keep you warm."

She accepts it without argument and slips it on. It dwarfs her, not that it covers her shapeliness. Her tits are so firm, her nipples thrust out against the fabric. I gesture to her, and when she holds out her arm, I roll up the sleeve for her, then on the other, before I sink down on my haunches. I take her much smaller palms in mine. "I'm sorry I hurt you. If anything had happened to you, I would have never forgiven myself."

She swallows. The air between us thickens. My pulse begins to race. I want to lean in and kiss her, shape her features with my fingers and memorize them. My fingers itch, and if I look into her eyes any longer, I won't be able to stop myself.

"Let's get some rest."

I pretend not to notice the disappointment on her face and throw myself back onto my temporary bed. Fucking hell. Tearing myself away from her when I wanted to kiss her then bury myself inside her is the hardest thing I've done in my life. Harder than watching friends killed in action. Harder than walking away from the NHL. Harder than swallowing my pride and joining the security agency and taking on assignments as a bodyguard. Harder than this goddamn floor I'm trying to sleep on. "Trying" being the operative word here.

I roll over on my side, keeping my back to her, fold my arm across my chest, close my eyes and count backward from ten, but every part of me is focused on the woman who's lying on the bed not two feet away from me. The light clicks off. I can hear her soft breaths, feel her presence; every cell in my body is tuned into her and—

"You can share the bed with me," she says in a small voice.

Not if I want to keep my promise to you, I can't.

When I don't reply, she huffs out a breath. "I know you can hear me, so why don't you get into bed? It's big enough for both of us, and if we each keep to our sides, it should be fine."

"I used to pride myself on my self-control, but with you, I'm not so sure," I growl.

There's silence for a moment before she says, "What if I want you to lose your self-control?"

21

Gio

I did not say that. I can't believe I said that. Shit. I said that. Out loud.

"You're tired." He pauses. "Get some rest."

I freeze. *Did he turn me down?* He turned me down. Heat flushes my cheeks. I tell him I want him to fuck me... And what does he do? He goes to sleep.

"I can hear you thinking," he says in the darkness.

I hunch my shoulders.

"I want you so much now, I'm tempted to go wank off before I go to sleep, but I won't."

"You won't?" I squeak.

"I prefer to let the anticipation build, so when we finally fuck—and we *will* fuck—I'm going to make you come so hard, you'll forget your name and that of your arsehole ex, and only remember what it feels like to fall apart around my cock."

Ohmigod! My entire body seems to detonate. Those tiny flames in my body multiply until it feels like there are a million of them building upon each other and setting fire to my blood, my muscles, my flesh. They're seared by the potency of the lust that laces his words. I curl my fingers into fists and draw in a deep breath, which only intensifies his scent and turns the flesh between my legs into a melting puddle of moisture. I squeeze my thighs together, and that's when he interrupts my thoughts.

"Not able to sleep?"

I shake my head. I'm afraid to answer him. He already turned me down once.

"Need help?" He sounds closer now. Is he sitting up?

I mumble in the affirmative.

"I did say I wasn't going to fuck you, but that doesn't mean I can't make you come, does it?" His tone indicates he's asking himself the question, and that he doesn't expect me to answer but I let out a soft moan anyway. The next second, he's on his feet and standing at the foot of the bed. I can see him well enough from the light coming through the French doors.

"Take off your shorts."

"What?" I gape at him.

"Take. Off. Your. Shorts. Goldie." He lowers his voice, the tone barely above a harsh whisper, but the intent in his words is unmistakable. Heat spools off of his body and presses down on my chest.

I gasp. Something inside me melts, leaving me free to obey. I shove down my shorts until they pool around my ankles. He bends, slides them off, then brings them to his nose and sniffs. My belly quivers, and my thighs tremble. Why is that so filthy, and so erotic? He tosses my shorts aside, then grabs my ankles and tugs. I squeak. He positions my feet on the edge of the bed, then places his big paws on my knees.

"Open for me"

My face heats. My pussy trembles. I slide my legs further apart, and he stares down at my exposed cunt. "Good girl."

I almost fall apart. My heart descends to the space between my legs. The beats are heavy, and so intense, I can feel it at my temples, behind my eyeballs, in the swollen nub of my clit.

"Show me your tits."

I reach for my shirt and pull it up; cool air hits my exposed flesh.

"Good, now hold your pussy lips apart."

"What?" I clear my throat.

"Not gonna repeat myself." He glares at me and sweat breaks out over my brow. My fingers tremble, but I manage to pinch the engorged lips and pry them apart.

"Whatever happens, don't let go." He sinks down on his knees, then swipes his tongue up my slit.

I cry out. My eyes roll back in my head. He licks me again, and my channel squeezes down. My breasts swell. My nipples are so tight they feel like they could cut through glass. My arms tremble. I try to squeeze my thighs together, but he loops his arms under my knees and pushes them, so I have no choice but to stay exposed. Then he curls his tongue around my clit. Those thousand little fires he ignited earlier come to life and multiply, until every inch of my skin is tingling with pleasure. He bites down on the nub, and I yell. He begins to eat me out in earnest. I want to let go of my hold on myself, but I can't. Not when he told me to stay in this position. Sweat pools in my armpits. I arch my back, trying to pull away, but I'm pinned down in his hold. "Rick, please, Rick. Rick. Rick."

He releases his hold on me, only to fit his thumb between my butt-cheeks. He plays with the rosette there, plunges his tongue inside me and uses his other hand to rub on my clit. With a sudden fury, my climax crashes over me.

I open my mouth to cry out, but the orgasm is so intense the sound is unable to escape. I writhe, shudder, and submit to the orgasm. He continues to lick me through the aftershocks, and when I slump, he wraps his fingers around my wrists, crawls up and over me, twists my arms over my head and presses his lips to mine. I open my mouth, and he kisses me thoroughly. The taste of my cum on his tongue sets off another chain of tingling in my blood. He lays down on the bed and pulls me into his arms. I press my cheek into his chest and close my eyes.

When I wake up, I'm alone. I sit up and reach for my phone on the bed-stand. It's nine a.m. The daily team meeting is at nine-thirty a.m. *Oh my god! I'm late.*

I jump out of bed—there's no time to shower—change, and rush out of the house. By the time I reach the offices above the rink, I'm already ten minutes late. Damn, I've never been late for a meeting in my life. Never. I burst into the conference room and come to a stop. The two men seated on opposite sides of the table turn to look at me.

I gape. "What are you doing here?"

22

Rick

"Gio, I'm so glad to see you." Douchecanoe—a.k.a. her ex— a.k.a. the captain of the team of our sworn rivals—rises to his feet. Before he can walk in her direction, I jump up and plant myself between them.

"Baby, did you manage to get some rest?" I cup her cheek. "When I left, you were sleeping so soundly, I didn't want to wake you up. Also, how are you feeling today?"

Her gaze widens.

I search her features and infuse concern into my expression. "I saw you limping, honeybun. Is that an after-effect of our strenuous night?"

She glowers up at me.

"Not that I'm complaining. In fact, if it were up to me, I'd fill all your holes and—"

"What are you doing?" She slaps at my chest.

I feel her touch all the way to the crown of my cock. Goddamn, this woman. A touch from her, and I'm ready to rut into her like the beast I turn into when I'm around her. I wrap my arm about her shoulder and draw her up to her toes, then press my lips to hers. She melts into me, and I deepen the kiss. I thrust my tongue between hers, suck from her, ensure she's plastered to me as I share her breath and drink from her, until her knees buckle. Only then, do I release her mouth, and peer into her flushed face.

"Much better." I grin.

She meets my gaze with eyes that are clouded with lust. And damn, if I don't want to throw her down in front of her bloody-ex and take her right here.

The wankenstein clears his throat from somewhere behind me.

She blinks, then seems to remember where she is. "Have you lost your mind?" she snaps.

"I have from the moment I saw you," I agree.

Her flush deepens, her pupils dilate, then she glances away. "Rick, please —" She swallows. I peruse her features, and the blush deepens.

"You smell like me, baby, and fuck, if that doesn't make me happy." I bend and press a kiss to her forehead, then turn, and with my arm about her shoulders, face Dennis.

"What are you doing here?" she asks.

He looks between us, a pinched look on his features. He takes in my arm about her and his eyes flash. He also has a bandage over his nose which pleases me no end. If I could, I'd smash my fist into his face until his features are re-arranged, but I'm going to have to save that for a time when neither of us are playing. I don't want to risk the careers of my team members by getting embroiled in another controversy. A part of me wants to say fuck it to everything and simply punch him until he doesn't dare to set eyes on her again.

"I came here to apologize, Gio," he begins.

"That's Mac to you," I snap.

"Mac?" He blinks.

"Her call sign. Ergo, that's what you call her from now on, understand?"

His frown deepens. "What's happening Gio? I wanted to see you and apologize and—"

"You've apologized. Now get gone. Also don't call her Gio."

"Now look here." He thrusts out his chest. "I'm talking to my girlfriend—"

"Your ex-girlfriend, who is now my fiancée."

"—and who are you to—" He does a double take as if my words have only registered. "Did you say your—"

"Fiancée, whom I'm very much in love with so, if you'll excuse us…" I nod in the direction of the door.

The bastard's jaw hangs open. "You're engaged?" He frowns at her.

"I am," Goldie murmurs.

"Talk to me, not to her," I say at the same time.

She shoots me another glance, a plea in hers asking for me to stay quiet. A plea I ignore. No way am I going to stay silent while he stakes his claim on her. Not when I'm right here.

"We're engaged. Didn't you hear me say that already?" I snap at him.

The color fades from his features. He looks from her to me, then back to her. "Gio, I can explain what happened."

"What happened is that you cheated on me and now you're standing here telling me you're sorry."

"I am." He swallows. "It was a mistake. I shouldn't have slipped up like that. But I was lonely, and you were so busy. And I needed you that day, Gio, but you weren't there. I told you not to go on that trip, but you were focused on building your career and I… I needed to be with someone."

"So, you decided to cheat on me with my colleague?" A shiver runs down her spine. Her shoulders shake, and I wrap my arm about her and pull her closer.

He looks away before addressing her again. "I miss you, Gio. It's been terrible without you. As soon as I saw your face that day, I knew I'd made a mistake. Forgive me, Gio, please. What can I do to make it up to you?"

She swallows then says slowly, "Actually, there is something."

"There is?" he brightens up.

"There is?" I turn on her.

She keeps her gaze firmly on Dickface. "Call off the fight with Rick."

"Don't—" Before I can complete the sentence, Dennis nods.

"Done. Now, will you forgive me?"

She makes a strangled noise at the back of her throat, and I can't take it anymore.

I thrust out my chin and stab a finger at him. "Okay, that's enough. You need to go, right fucking now."

His jaw tightens, anger blazes in his eyes, then he nods. "I'm going, for now, but this is far from over."

"You shouldn't have provoked him." She scowls.

"And you shouldn't have asked him to call off the fight."

I narrow my gaze on the road ahead. After the run in with that shitstain, Dennis, she refused to meet my gaze. Edward joined us shortly after, and we quickly ran through the most important points of our meeting. She responded to his questions with short answers. I stuck to monosyllables. Edward gave both of us curious looks but didn't pushed it further. I told him we'd broken the news of our engagement to arsehat, Dennis. At that, she paled and muttered that it was going to be all over the internet before the day was out. The result?

I pushed up our lunch, and she called up the journalist she'd promised the exclusive to and told her we needed to meet in the next hour. Now, we're on our way to meet her.

"Dennis is a slimy bastard. If that fight had gone ahead, he'd have seriously injured you," she says in a low voice.

"I'd have injured him first."

"And he'd have sued you after...or found another way to get back at you, and things would have escalated into a mess that would have ended your career."

"Not if I killed him first and disposed of the body."

She gasps. "How can you joke about this?" She surveys my features.

When I don't reply, she tenses. "You *were* kidding, right?"

I raise a shoulder. "Yea, sure. Let's go with that."

She shakes her head. "I forget you have a military background. Killing people is not new for you."

I tighten my grip on the wheel. "I was doing my duty to protect my country, and I'll never apologize for it."

She glances out the window. After a few moments, she says softly, "I'm sorry, I shouldn't have said that. What you did for your country was honorable, and I made it sound sordid."

I grunt in response, and neither of us speaks for several minutes.

"He's going to get his revenge on the ice," she remarks.

I scoff, "We'll see."

"I'm not saying you're not a good player. It's just... he has a track record."

"So do I."

"Rick, you haven't played professionally in years."

"Are you saying I can't hold my own against him?"

"I'm saying he's younger than you, he has more stamina than you—"

"You weren't complaining about my stamina when you were falling apart around my tongue."

23

Gio

I draw in a sharp breath. Fire embraces my cheeks. "I can't believe you'd throw that at me," I say in a low voice.

His fingers tighten around the steering wheel, then his shoulders bunch. "I'm not sorry I made you come, but I am sorry I threw it at you like it didn't mean anything." He glances in my direction before looking back at the road. "You have to understand, I couldn't have stood by and allowed that man to talk to you like that."

"I still think you shouldn't have been so impolite." I tip up my chin. "He's the captain of the rival team. He can make things very difficult for you and the team."

He makes a growling noise at the back of his throat, and my nerve endings spark. He doesn't even have to speak. All he has to do is make his grumpy, growly, beast-like noises and, apparently, I turn to putty.

When he doesn't say anything, I search his features. "I'm serious. You shouldn't have pushed him like that. You shouldn't have told him to—"

"Fuck off? I should have punched his throat, then followed it up with a few to his face, then kicked his legs out from under him, before jumping on his chest and—" He shakes his head. "Fucking hell, you should have seen your face when he was speaking to you. You should have seen how hurt you were, how you were drawing into yourself, and Goldie...any man who makes you feel like that deserves a lot worse."

"There you go, threatening to kill him again."

"If necessary."

I narrow my gaze. "Don't do anything stupid, you hear me?"

"Who, me?" He points at himself. "I'm the epitome of playing by the rules."

I make a rude noise, and one side of his mouth twitches.

"For someone who's so straitlaced, you always surprise me when you do something so irreverent."

I toss my head. "I only seem to do that with you."

He draws in a breath. "If anyone hurts you, in any form—emotionally, mentally or physically—I won't hesitate to take them out."

My heart stutters. My belly flip-flops. I should be upset. I should be alarmed by how this man can deliver that ultimatum in such a matter-of-fact tone. I should not be aroused by that hint of menace in his words, how his jaw is set, how his cheekbones cut through the air. How the nerve pops at his temple, hinting at the violence that rolls under his skin. I thought Rick was grumpy—and he is. But, underneath that facade of hating the world, he's so much more intense. He might pretend not to care about anything much, but he sees everything, takes in everything, doesn't miss a nuance.

He has to be that way, given his past. It's probably ingrained into him to spot everything that happens around him. It's what would have saved his life in the past. This...intensity about him is also the most arousing thing for me. He won't do anything by half measures. He won't say one thing and do another. He wouldn't cheat on me with another; that's the kind of person he is.

It took me a while to realize that. Maybe subconsciously I did, which is why I agreed to move into his room and then went along with his plan of pretending to be engaged. I wouldn't have done that if I had any concerns about his character or about the kind of man he is at heart.

Sure, he's not an easy man to understand, but that's also part of his appeal. The guarded face he puts on against the world makes me want to find out what he's hiding. That fury that flashes in his eyes when he forgets to hide his emotions. That look of hurt that accompanies it sometimes, which is so slight that half the time I'm sure I'm imagining it. That gentleness I sense under that tough exterior of his. The way he planted himself between me and my ex as if he wanted to shield me from his gaze. All of it points to a man who's intense and complex and has a heart so passionate, I can't wait to get to know him better.

"Pull over," I burst out.

"Eh?" He shoots me a sideways glance.

"Pull over, Rick, right now."

He must see something on my face, for he flicks on his indicator and turns onto a side street before guiding the car to a stop on the side. "What are you—?"

The next second, I've unsnapped my seatbelt and straddled him.

"Goldie, you—"

I throw my arms about his neck and press my lips to his. He stays still, his lips unmoving. That is, until I bite his mouth.

A growl rumbles up his chest. He grabs my hips and fits me over the tent at his crotch, and his thickness stabs between my legs. A sharp lash of lust zings up my spine. I push my breasts into his chest and plaster myself to him, as close as his seatbelt will allow. I dig my fingers into the short hair at the base of his neck and tug. A shudder runs up his back.

He keeps one hand on my hip; with the other, he clamps his fingers around the nape of my neck, and it's so primal, so possessive, that the fires under my skin that always seem to dance to his tune are igniting like sizzling fireworks. My belly clenches; my pussy begins to throb. That yawning emptiness gapes between my legs, and I grind down on him. His chest rises and falls, and he hauls me even closer. Our teeth clash. Our tongues tangle. He angles my head, then sucks on my tongue and I feel it all the way to my core.

I moan, and he answers with that deep throated growl that spikes my pulse and sends adrenaline racing through my blood stream. My heart is hammering so hard in my ribcage, all I can hear is the drumbeats emanating from my chest. I grind down on that thick ridge that's grown even bigger in the last few seconds, and his thigh muscles shift under mine. I begin to rub myself up-down-up on that tented portion of his jeans, that's when he tears his mouth from mine.

"Get yourself off." He glares into my eyes, and a shiver of anticipation, of such overwhelming lust, of so much want, spirals over me and threatens to engulf me.

I manage to keep my eyes on his, manage to hold onto his shoulder as I begin to rub that most sensitive part of myself against his thick ridge. My breasts swell, my nipples are so hard I wish he'd bite on them to alleviate the pain. He commands me with his gaze, and I'm enthralled. It's so intimate, so raw, the orgasm bursts out from behind my pelvic bone and up my spine. I curve my back, open my mouth, and cry out as I shatter. That's when a flashbulb goes off outside the window.

24

Rick

The flashbulb highlights the curve of her neck, the sharp edges of her cheekbones, and the helpless lust that sparks her eyes as she climaxes. Then, the shock cuts across her face and she turns to face out the window. So do I. Which is how the photographer snaps the second picture of the both of us — arms about each other, features flushed, anger on mine, surprise on hers.

"Oh my god," she gasps.

"Fucking hell, I'm going to get him." I lift her back onto her seat, then throw open my door and shove my legs out, but the seatbelt holds me back. "Bloody fuck!" I unsnap my belt, jump out, but by then, the paparazzi has turned and scampered across the street. I race after him, up the sidewalk, back to the main road. He runs across, and before I can follow him, the lights change. Traffic pours out in front of me. I curl my fingers into fists and watch as he hightails it up the sidewalk and out of sight.

"Rick, are you okay?" She grabs my arm, but I shake it off.

"I lost him."

"It's best not to get into scraps with these guys."

"He took a photo of us."

"It's okay."

"It's not okay." I turn on her with such menace that she shrinks back. I see a flash of apprehension in her eyes and draw in a sharp breath. *Don't lose your temper. Not now, not when you've been doing so well.* I squeeze the bridge of my nose. "He took a picture of you at your most vulnerable. I'm not going to let him get away with it."

"Leave it be. These things happen. You have to expect it now that you're much more in the public eye."

"He took. *Your.* Picture. As you climaxed. It is not okay. No one can catch you in that unguarded moment but me. That was for my eyes only. For my delectation. For my appreciation. For *me* to snapshot and hold in my mind's eye so it fuels my dreams. It was for *me. Only* me."

She swallows.

"I will not let him publish that picture. This, I swear."

A flash of something like—lust— flares in her eyes, then she swallows. "Let it be, Rick. Don't make it worse, please."

"I promise, I won't."

Some of the worry in her features recedes.

"Doesn't mean I'm not going to hunt him down and teach him a lesson."

She searches my features. "I shouldn't find that so hot. I should be worried about how you seem to have no qualms about doing something that is on the grey side of the law, and yet—"

"And yet?"

"And yet—" she looks away, then back at me, "I find that such a turn on."

"Rick Mitchell," a voice rings out. I swing my head to the side to find the traffic has come to a standstill. A man jumps out of his car and points his phone in our direction.

"Shit—" I turn my back on him and plant my body between her and the traffic. "Let's get out of here."

"You promised me an exclusive, but it's not one anymore." The journalist we're meeting for lunch at James Hamilton's restaurant holds up her phone.

On the screen is a blurry image shot through the glass of a car of a man and a woman caught in the middle of making out. Their features are a little blurry, but there's no mistaking the distinctive curve of her shoulder, nor the jut of my chin, or the anger in my eyes. It's clear it's the two of us.

After we were caught out by the road, I hustled Goldie back to the car and got out of there as fast as I could. We reached the restaurant with enough time for her to freshen up, by which time the story was already out in the media. I knew the journalist would publish the picture, but I didn't think he'd do it so quickly. Goldie warned me. News, nowadays, is instantaneous, but I didn't think interest in my personal life would be this extreme.

"You're the first to know we're engaged," Goldie interjects in a smooth voice.

"Engaged?" The journalist glances down at her left hand. "I don't see a—"

"Now you do." I slide the ring out of my pocket, then take Gio's left hand in mine and slide it onto her ring finger.

"Oh my god," Goldie gasps.

The journalist inhales a sharp breath. "Is it okay if I take a picture?"

Gio nods. "If you're okay with it," she chokes out, looking in my direction.

"I'm okay if you're okay," I murmur.

"And I assume I can record this interview?" the journalist asks.

Gio's staring down at the gold eternity band that wraps around her left ring finger. She manages to nod; so do I. She moves her fingers this way and that, and the light bounces off of the tiny diamonds set amid the swirling design.

"It's"—she clears her throat—"it looks like an antique."

"It belonged to my grandmother, then my mother."

"Oh, Rick." She looks up at me and a single tear squeezes out from the corner of her eye.

I raise my hand and swipe it away with my thumb. "Didn't mean to make you sad."

"I'm not," she declares.

"You're crying."

She sniffs, then inhales deeply. "I'm surprised is all."

"I know we said we'd pick out your ring together, but I wanted to surprise you—" I raise a shoulder.

"You did, in a good way. I wasn't expecting this."

I look between her eyes. "Neither was I."

She swallows, then glances away. "When did you have the time to get it?"

"My grandmother gave it to me when I turned twenty-one. She told me I'd know who the right woman was for it."

She jerks her chin in my direction, her eyes wide with shock.

"I kept it in a safety deposit box in the bank. I took it out the first time I met you in L.A."

"You've been carrying the ring around since L.A.? That was months ago." She swallows.

"What can I say, I have good instincts."

Our gazes hold, and the hair on the nape of my neck rises.

The space between us thickens further with unspoken emotions.

Everything else fades away except for the longing in her eyes. Her cheeks stain, her lips part, and the chemistry that connects us is so potent, a bead of sweat slides down my back. Her golden eyes turn amber, and I know she's aroused. I lean in; so does she. Our breaths mingle, our noses almost bump, our eyelashes brush against each other... The whisper of a camera beginning to click cuts through the hair's breadth of space between us. She begins to pull back, but I plant my fingers around the nape of her neck—a gesture that signals my possession and one which feels so right, too right, but that's something I'll think about later. For now, I hold her in place and search her features. "I'm going to kiss you now."

25

Gio

He swoops down and closes his mouth over mine. I'm aware of the journalist watching us, of her recording this, and I know I should care, but I don't. All that matters is the firm grasp of his on the nape of my neck, which makes me feel cherished and possessed and his, his, his. And the scent of his, which I draw into my lungs, the hard feel of his lips on mine, the gentle swipe of his tongue against mine, and the tenderness of his licks slay me. As he cajoles me to open my mouth and allow him to slip his tongue between my lips and draw from me, he brings his other palm up to cup my cheek, and his touch sinks down to my core.

The dominance of his presence pins me down, holds me in place and yet, his touch is gentle. His assertive touch, combined with the openness with which he shares himself with me, makes my head spin. None of our previous kisses were this...potent. This intense. This searing. This all-consuming. So consuming he seems to have branded himself into every cell in my body. Then he releases me, slowly, with reluctance.

When he draws back, I chase his mouth with mine, and a low chuckle rumbles up his chest. "We have an audience, baby, and you know how much I hate sharing any part of you with anyone else," he whispers in a voice intended only for my ears. Moisture pools between my legs.

I draw in a breath and fight for composure as he increases the distance between us. He still holds my gaze, and only when he's sure I'm steady, does he slowly release his hold on me. Even then, he twines his fingers with mine and places our joined hands on the table, which the journalist steals glances at through the rest of the interview.

"So, how did the two of you meet?"

I freeze. *OMG. OMG.* We never did discuss and decide what story to tell the press. And that's PR lesson one-oh-one. Never meet the press until you have your story down. Something I've always gotten right in the past. It's a testament to how off-kilter I am that I never thought of coordinating my narrative with his.

I open my mouth, but he interjects, "It was love at first sight."

I blink.

"It was?" The journalist looks between us.

"Indeed. I walked into a restaurant and was waiting for my meeting to turn up, and I looked over to the table next to mine to find she was seated alone. Of course, I was entranced right away."

"You were?" The journalist asks with interest.

He was? I begin to frown, then manage to school my features into an expression which doesn't reveal the surprise I'm feeling.

"You bet I was. She was the most beautiful woman I'd ever seen. Not in the conventional way. Gio is too unique to fit the normal conventions of beauty. It was her flashing eyes and her haughty stare at her date when he finally arrived that drew me in. Then, the two of them got into a fight."

The journalist gasps.

My eyebrows begin to knit again, and I smooth them out. *You're a PR professional. You know how to keep a mask on your emotions.* Not as well as him, though. Who'd have thought the stony-faced Rick would turn out to be a consummate liar?

"It was clear she wasn't happy, but when she jumped up and tried to leave, the asshole—pardon my swearing, but he was one—stepped in her way and grabbed her arm. That's when I jumped up from my seat. I walked over, draped my arm around her and said…"

The journalist is practically salivating, waiting for his big reveal.

So am I. He's so convincing. I'm half sure all of this happened, and I forgot about it. Except, if it *had* happened, I *wouldn't* have forgotten about it. My every single encounter with this man is etched into my memory. That's how much of an impression he's made on me. So, he's making all of this up right now. He flicks a glance in my direction and his mouth curls. "I said, 'Take your hand off my wife.'"

"Oh my god." The journalist fans herself.

Heat flushes my skin, and my toes curl. My wife. He said, *my wife*. He doesn't mean those words, but the possessiveness in his tone, the protectiveness that laces his words, that thread of dominance that runs through his tone, not to mention, the craving in his gaze... All of it wraps its net around me like a spider's web around a helpless firefly. The tension builds, and the hair on the back of my neck rises. We stare at each other, and the intent in his eyes is so salacious, so carnal, so filled with promise, a shiver sweeps through me.

"What happened next?" the journalist interrupts.

"Oh, he lowered his hand and walked away."

"And then?"

"Then"—he tears his gaze from mine—"then I asked her to join me for dinner."

"And did you?" She turns to me.

Trying desperately to weave some truth into his lies, I continue the deception. "I didn't want to... But he told me I owed him. He also said if I didn't join him, he'd understand but—"

"You joined him anyway," she says with satisfaction.

"He said he wouldn't keep me for more than a drink," I murmur.

"But you stayed for dinner."

I open my mouth to deny it, but Rick steps in. "After which, we walked by the river, and we couldn't stop talking until the wee hours of the morning."

"Hmm." She taps her fingers. "So, you must know a lot about each other then?"

His forehead creases, then he nods. "Oh, I made it my mission to find out everything about the love of my life."

Her features soften, then she seems to get a hold of herself. "So, you wouldn't mind if I asked the two of you to take a quiz about the other?"

My heart rate accelerates. *No, no, no, I can't do that.* I don't know that much about this guy. This is going to be a car crash. I begin to shake my head, but once again, Mr. Know-it-all jerkhole beats me to it.

"Of course, we'd be happy to oblige you."

"You okay with that?" She turns to me.

"Umm." I bite the inside of my cheek. If I say yes, she'll figure out we're lying. If I say no, she'll know something is wrong. I try to pull my hand away from his, but his grip tightens. I try to signal to him with my eyes that I don't want to do this. He shakes his head, and I know he's right. We don't have a choice. We need to do this. I manage to tip my chin down, then up.

"Awesome." The journalist's features light up. "My first question is for Rick. What is Giorgina's favorite color?"

Ha, no way, does he know that. I try not to smirk, but I'd be lying if I said my lips don't twitch.

His eyebrows draw down, he opens his mouth, shakes his head, then says, "Red."

She turns to me and asks, "Is he right?"

Rick

Goldie seems taken aback, then slowly nods. To be honest, I'm a little surprised I got that right. But I've noticed how she favors red heels, which makes me wonder how it would be to have them digging into my back; and red lipstick, prints of which I've imagined around my cock; and red painted nails, with which I want her to mark my skin.

"And Rick's favorite color?" the journalist asks her.

"That's easy, it's black," Goldie scoffs.

"It is," I affirm.

"Which season is her favorite?" The journalist asks me.

"Autumn," I say without hesitation. When the gold of the leaves matches the sparks in her eyes.

Gio's gaze widens, then she tosses her head. "And his is winter." *A season as cold as his heart* is what she communicates with her eyes.

I chuckle, then release my hold on her hand, only to wrap my arm about her shoulders. I pull her close and kiss her forehead.

The journalist smiles.

Goldie stiffens, then inch by inch, she melts into my side.

"Giorgina's go-to karaoke song?" the journalist asks.

"I will survive by Gloria Gaynor," I reply.

Goldie draws in a sharp breath, and I know I'm right. Again.

The journalist turns her attention to her. I glance down to find her forehead furrowed, then she juts out her chin. "Rick wouldn't sing but if he did, it would be Highway to Hell by AC/DC."

I bark out a laugh. "Apt choice."

"If Giorgina were on a deserted island, what's the one thing she'd take with her?" She tilts her head in my direction, a look of challenge on her features.

That's a tough one. What would she take with her? What would she? What would—"Her phone. She's a PR professional. She has to be connected. Her phone is the one thing I know she can't do without. Case in point—" I glance down to where her phone has been placed screen down next to her.

"Given there is no Wi-Fi on the island, and her phone would be useless, what else would she take?" the journalist persists.

Goldie pulls away from me, and this time, I let her. I glance into the distance, trying to make the connections in my head.

A few seconds pass. Goldie shuffles her feet. The journalist watches me closely. When a few more minutes pass and I haven't come up with a reply, a look of disappointment comes into her eyes. "Well, that was a difficult question, to be fair, and—"

"Her Kindle."

The journalist frowns.

Goldie looks at me in shock.

"Is he right?" The journalist turns to her.

"Oh, I know I am." I place the tips of my fingers together. "I'd have said all her favorite novels, but a Kindle is easier to carry, and this way, she can keep herself entertained until help arrives, which would be me, of course."

"Of course," the journalist laughs. "And what about Rick? What's the one thing he'd take to a deserted island?" she asks Goldie.

"Nothing. Except himself, that is."

I narrow my gaze on her.

So does the journalist. "Care to explain?"

"Rick's very resourceful. He'd use whatever he found on the island to fashion a shelter for himself. He'd manage to catch fish with his bare hands, and keep himself fed. He'd find a way to gather rainwater or, no doubt, find a plant from which he could drink sap to keep hydrated. And he's so sharp, he'd keep himself occupied with his thoughts. And I bet he'd manage to flag down a ship in the distance by making a fire, or attract the attention of a plane flying overhead in no time."

Silence stretches. The journalist looks at us with something like envy in her eyes.

Gio avoids looking at me, though. "So, what do you say? Do you have everything you need?" she asks the other woman.

We drive back to the rink in silence. The journalist was more than happy with our answers. She declared she'd never seen a couple more in love, wished us the best in our life together, then wrapped up her interview. Apparently, we pulled off the impossible. We convinced her we're made for each other. Goldie must have been as stunned as I was; neither of us attempted to start a conversation on the way back.

I park in front of the arena where her office is located. Neither of us moves. She stares ahead, and I stare at her. The silence extends.

"What?" she finally snaps.

"That last thing you said about me. Did you mean it?"

"This ring you gave me. Did you mean it?" She raises her left hand, and I glance at my grandmother's ring on her finger.

"I wouldn't have given it to you if I didn't."

Her breath catches. "Rick, this is a fake engagement."

"And we need to make sure everyone believes it isn't."

"So you gave me a family heirloom?" she bursts out.

"I'm all set to let you feel up the family jewels; a family heirloom doesn't seem like much in comparison."

She looks at me stunned, then a laugh bursts from her lips. "Who'd have thought the surly captain of the Ice Kings has a wicked sense of humor?"

"Who'd have thought the thorny PR manager of the Ice Kings knew me so well?"

She looks away, then back at me. "You answered all the questions about me correctly."

"You seem surprised."

"No more than you."

We stare at each other, and the tension building during the course of the ride threatens to spill over.

"What are we doing, Rick? What's happening between us?" she bursts out.

"What's happening is that we're attracted to each other. And now that we're engaged"—I reach for her hand, encircle her wrist and raise it so the ring on her finger stands out—"I think we should fuck it out."

Her jaw drops. "Typical man. Have a problem? Sex is the answer, of course."

"Not any kind of sex. I'm talking sweaty, heated, erotic, kinky, no-need-for-lubrication, toe-curling, heart pounding, fuck-you-till-you-can't-walk-straight for days—"

"I get the picture," she cuts in. Her voice is shaky, her breathing roughened. Color sweeps up her neck and paints her cheeks, and damn, but she looks hot and bothered. And so fucking adorable. Did I say adorable? I meant, sexy. I mean, *also* adorable. But definitely, sexy.

"So, what do you say?" I lower my chin to my chest.

She tugs her hand from mine and shoves the door open. "I say, go to hell."

26

Giorgina's To Do List

1. Wake up at 5 am, meditate for fifteen minutes. *(OMG, I can't meditate. Every time I close my eyes, I see his face. And feel his skin. And imagine I have my nose buried in between his pecs, and the throb of his cock under my palm — stop, stop, stop.)*
2. Go to the gym at 5 am - half-hour workout. *(WTF? This is the third day in a row I've forgotten to set my alarm. This has never happened before.)*
3. ~~Healthy breakfast = oats? Croissant.~~ Chocolate croissant. I deserve it after putting up with that alphahole!
4. Get to the office by 8 am and get through all emails by 9 am.
5. Avoid thinking about the Dick. Newsflash: His dick really is BIG. (Why am I thinking about his dick?)
6. Healthy lunch – salad, no dressing.
7. ~~Search for new flat ASAP~~. For the time-being, the room at the hockey house will do. It's not because there's a guilty pleasure in sharing the room with the Dickhole. Nope. That's not it.
8. Start that grapefruit diet??????
9. Need to shave legs, and other parts. It's not for him. Nothing to do with him. This is for me.

10. ~~Make time for Steely Dan. Why does the Dickhole's dick seem bigger than the Dan? Why make time for Steely Dan when I can peek at the sleeping dickface and his dick? It's okay to ogle right?~~
11. Read 110 spicy books this year. 51 down, 59 to go => *gah, I can't focus. This has never happened before. Every time I try to read, my fiancé, I mean, my fake fiancé's face, and other parts of him appear in front of my eyes.*
12. Make list for tomorrow.
13. Put this down for the satisfaction of crossing it off the list.

27

Gio

I flounce out of the car and up the steps of the arena. There's no one around, thank god. The team must have left after practice, and my footsteps echo in the empty corridor as I head for the stairs. I take the steps as fast as I can and reach the second floor, then march down the short hallway. I nod toward my assistant and enter my office. It's a quarter of the size of the one I had in L.A. And I don't have a team, only an assistant. But the position pays well, and given how I left my last agency in L.A., I was lucky to get this job. As I must keep reminding myself.

As for this stupid fake engagement thing? It'll blow over. It's only temporary. It's only until we convince his grandmother we're for real. To be honest, the look on Dennis' face when Rick told him we were engaged already makes this move worthwhile. Now, I only need a few more opportunities to rub it in. To make him feel as wretched as I felt when I walked in on him with that skank, Tiffany. Of course, she'd have to be called Tiffany. How typical.

I head for my desk, drop into my chair and open up my laptop. The screen comes to life and the first thing that pops ups is that grainy picture the paparazzi shot of Rick and me making out in his car. The headline declares:

• • •

Can This Ice Kiss Melt Stone?

Ugh! Trust a hack to come up with *that* headline. I click out of the website as Rick prowls into the office.

He shuts the door, locks it, then leans against it with his hands crossed over his chest.

"What do you want?" I scowl.

"You didn't answer my question."

"What question?"

"You know which one."

I lean back in my seat and fold my arms over my chest, mirroring his stance. "I have no idea what you're talking about."

"Sure you do. It's why you flounced off without bothering to reply."

"If I remember correctly, I told you to go to hell," I scoff.

"Only if you follow me there. Come with me, and I promise you, I'll turn it into the kind of heaven you read about only in your books."

I frown. "You have no idea about the kinds of books I read."

"You mean like *The Seven Habits of Men Who Know How to Give Highly Effective Orgasms*?"

My jaw drops. I manage to scoop it off the floor and begin to laugh, but turn it into a cough. "Did you play on *The Seven Habits of Highly Effective People* by Stephen Covey?"

"Or it might have been a play on the spicy novels you love to read and hide."

This time, I jump up and plant my palms on either side of my laptop. "Get out."

"Or what?" He takes a step forward, and another.

I swallow. A frisson of fear runs up my spine. I can't let him touch me. I can't. If I do, I won't be able to stop myself from enjoying it. From giving in to the pleasure it evokes in me. I won't be able to stop myself from begging him to throw me down on this desk and fuck me. And if I do that, I'll lose all respect for myself. He moves toward me; I straighten. He pauses halfway across the floor, then crooks his finger. "Come 'ere."

I toss my head. "You haven't got a hope in hell of me obeying you."

"I have high hopes of cramming my dick into your pussy and making you come all around my shaft—and with your consent."

A thousand butterflies flutter in my belly. Moisture squeezes out between my lower lips. *I do not find his dirty talking a turn on. I do not.* I draw in a breath. My chest rises and falls. But he doesn't glance away from my face. Doesn't break that contact between us, which is like a laser beam that binds me to him every time our eyes meet.

"You want this, baby. You're always so in control, and it must be exhausting. This is a safe space. Here, it's you and me. I'm not the captain of the London Ice Kings. You're not the PR manager. We're not pretending to be engaged. Here, with me, you're simply Goldie, the woman who wants me to do to her as I wish. The woman who wants to feel how it is to let go and feel every inch of my cock inside her. The woman who"—he leans forward on the balls of his feet—"wants to give into her desire and orgasm without constraints."

The butterflies in my belly take wing, a cloud of sensations rising to my chest, ripples of awareness spreading to my extremities.

"I… I don't want that."

"Yes, you do." He widens his stance, and my gaze is drawn to his powerful thighs that stretch the material of his jeans. And then there's the tent between them. *Ohmigod, is he already aroused?* Although, considering the size of his shaft, that might be his resting dick phase.

A giggle boils up my throat and I quell it. It's not like me to make stupid jokes that make me crack up when I'm nervous. I'm normally in control. I like to keep track of exactly how I spend my time. I plan my day so I can fit as much as possible into it and work toward climbing my career ladder… All of which has been shot to hell since I met this man.

"I. Don't. Want. That. I don't want you," I announce.

One side of his lips twists in that half smirk he's taken to wearing whenever he knows I'm saying something I don't mean. He prowls forward, reaches my desk and pats the surface.

I scowl back. If he thinks I'm going to obey him, he can keep dreaming.

"You know, you do," he murmurs.

I shake my head.

He narrows his gaze, then he holds out his hand. "Trust me."

Do I trust him? Do I want to trust him? Do I want to do as he says? I don't dare look inside myself because I know what the answer is going to be, and I don't want to acknowledge that. I don't want to give in to this need inside of me that insists I obey him. I want to tear my gaze away from his so he can't influence me further, but it's as if I'm locked into it with no escape.

The heat builds under my skin. A bead of sweat runs down my neck, and his eyes follow it down to the valley between my breasts. He licks his lips, and it's as if he's touched me with his tongue. A shiver grips me. I lock my fingers together and feel the metal that encases my left ring-finger.

I can't stop myself from tracing the tiny diamonds on it. An infinity ring, something that says forever, and an antique one that belongs in his family. I already love the weight of it on my hand. I already want to wear it all the time. He rakes his gaze down to where I'm toying with it, and I stop.

I don't want him to know how much this gesture of his moved me. He didn't have to get me a ring— certainly not one so symbolic—but he did it. He didn't have to be so in sync with me during the interview with the journalist, but he was. It was as if we'd rehearsed our answers before going in, which we hadn't. We were attuned to each other—so much so, we correctly guessed the right answers for the other. It was as if we knew each other intimately—which we don't—*yet*. Eh? No, no, no I don't intend for that to happen. I don't intend to get to know him better, not beyond what is needed to do my job well. And that's all the interview was about. A job well done.

And maybe, he used the fact that we were so on the same wavelength as an opportunity to further his plan, but in the end, it worked out.

The journalist was satisfied, and the ensuing publicity is going to help the team. It's going to help me grow their reputation and meet my PR goals, even though, this time, I'm the story.

Everything that has happened in the last few days has turned my emotions upside down, and that's a first. I'm not used to feeling so out of sorts. As if events in my life are overtaking me and I can only watch. I glance at his outstretched hand, and my heart begins to pound. My pulse points go into overdrive. My blood begins to pump with such speed, I feel breathless and dizzy and... *Don't do it. Don't give in. Don't give up control to this man.*

"It's your choice. You have the power to say no at any time. You're in the driver's seat here, baby," he says in a soft voice.

Something knotted inside of me dissolves. *Would it be so bad to find out if what he's saying is right?* I glance down at his palm, then back at his face. He must read the struggle going on inside of me.

He jerks his chin. "Give me your hand, Goldie, you won't regret it."

I'm going to regret it. But I'm going to do it anyway. I slide out from behind my desk, then walk around to stand in front of him.

I place my hand in his, and his shoulders relax. Strange. *Was he worried I wouldn't comply with his request? Was there ever a chance that I wouldn't?* "What if I had said no?" I ask.

"Then I'd have let you go." He sets his jaw, then shakes his head. "Not."

I begin to pull away, but he tightens his grip in my hand.

"Stay, Goldie, I promise to make it worth your while."

"Oh?

28

Rick

I could have ordered her to comply. I could have demanded that she walk around and drop to her knees in front of me. I could have infused my voice with enough dominance that she'd have given in much earlier... But I didn't.

I need her to agree of her own accord. I want her to trust me to make decisions for both of us. I need... Her. There, I admit it to myself. I yearn to feel the touch of her skin under my fingers, the give of her curves as I squeeze them, the jab of her nipple as it pushed into my chest, the...fan of her eyelashes as they graze my cheek. I run my finger over the ring on her hers, and she swallows.

"Stay with me," I urge her.

And when she nods, that tightness around my chest eases. I tug on her hand, and she stumbles forward. Instantly, I grab her hips and lift her onto the desk.

She squeaks. "What are you doing?"

"Shh." I place a finger on her lips. Her pupils dilate. The black spills out until there's only a ring of gold surrounding it. She flicks out her tongue and licks my finger. All of the blood drains to my groin. She must realize what she's done, for the pulse at the base of her neck speeds up.

"Rick — " she begins, but I shake my head.

She subsides. I place my thumb on her lower lip and press down. She opens her mouth, and I slide my thumb over her tongue. She sucks on it, and I feel it all the way to the crown of my cock. I step between her legs, forcing her to widen the gap between them. She swallows, and the slurping sensation shoots a ripple of lust down my spine. She releases my thumb with a pop, and I drag it down her chin, her throat, to the hint of cleavage visible at the neckline of her blouse. When I slide it under, she gasps.

"Kiss me," she demands.

I allow myself a chuckle. "You're not in control, baby."

She pouts a little. "I thought you said I was in the driver's seat."

"To the extent that if you don't want this, you can tell me your safe word."

"Safe word?" She blinks.

"Choose one."

"But —"

"Do you or don't you trust me?"

"I wouldn't be here if I didn't," she scoffs.

"Then. Choose. Your. Safe word."

She chews on her lower lip, and goddamn, but my cock seems to be linked to her mouth by an invisible thread. My balls harden, and I widen my stance to accommodate the erection. She senses my movement and glances down. Her cheeks turn bright red. She reaches for my waistband, and I click my tongue.

"Not yet."

She lowers her hand, then looks up at me, a look of petulance on her features. "Then when?"

"When I say so."

"And when will that be?"

"Wouldn't you like to find out?"

"Are you playing games with me, Stone?"

I wrap my fingers around the nape of her neck and peer into her eyes. "That's Rick to you."

She bites down on her lower lip and my stomach muscles tighten.

"Say my name," I demand.

She tightens her mouth, and I increase the pressure around her neck. "Don't defy me," I say in a low, hard voice.

She swallows, then tips up her chin. "Stone."

A flash of lust zips through my blood. I lean in until my breath mingles with hers. "Say. My. Name."

She swallows, her breathing intensifies, then she murmurs, "Rick."

Warmth coils in my chest. My cock extends. I lower my other hand on her hip and slide her forward so she's snug against my tented crotch. She gasps. Her gaze widens further. Her mouth opens in an 'O' that's perfect to wrap around my cock. The thought oscillates another spiral of desire through my veins. My heart threatens to burst out of my rib cage.

"Fuck." I push my forehead into hers. "I haven't touched you properly, and I'm ready to come in my pants like a teenager."

She huffs out a laugh. "Is that a confession?"

"It's an acknowledgement of how much you weaken me," I admit.

"You weaken me, too, and I'm not sure how I feel about it."

I lean back so I can stare into her eyes. The connection that stretches between us snaps into place, knotting my heart to hers. *Thump-thump-thump.* My pulse booms at my temples, behind my eyes, even in my balls. I've never wanted a woman as much as I want her. I slide my hand down the curve of her butt and squeeze.

She shudders, opens, then shuts her mouth. "I think I'm going to melt into a puddle right here," she groans.

"Not yet. Not until I've had my way with you."

I lower the zipper on the back of her skirt, then step back and set her down on her feet. I tug on the skirt, and it pools around her ankles. I unbutton her jacket, push it off her shoulders, then grip the hem of her blouse. She raises her arms and I pull it up and off, then unhook her bra. When she brings her arms to her sides, it slides down her shoulders. I slip it off, then tug both of her hands behind her back. She looks at me in surprise as I wrap her bra around her wrists, then pull on it to secure it. It results in her thrusting out her chest so her breasts stand out in prominence. I weigh them in my palms, and she groans.

"Suck on them, please."

I chuckle. "What did I tell you earlier?"

"That I don't direct the proceedings?"

"Exactly."

"But I want you to pinch my nipples," she whines.

"Like this?" I squeeze one erect nub between my thumb and forefinger, then twist tit. She cries out. I lower my mouth to the other and suck on it.

A keening cry emerges from her lips. She pushes her breast into my mouth, and I nibble on the hard flesh. "Oh god, oh god, oh —"

"Rick." I lick the reddened point of her nipple. "The name is Rick."

"Rick," she gasps out.

Finally, fuck. I straighten and survey her features. "What's your safe word, Goldie?"

She stares at me. I contort her nipple again, and she groans. Her eyelids flicker down, and I slap her nipple. Instantly, her eyes snap open. "Penalty," she chokes out.

"Your safe word is penalty?"

She nods.

I can't stop the chuckle that rumbles out of me. "You're something, you know that? And as a reward..." I reach down and tear off her panties.

She cries out, "Rick, what are you—" but her words are cut off as I stuff her panties in her mouth.

I sink to my knees and push my nose into her pussy.

29

Gio

He draws in a deep breath, and my entire body quivers. That's so primal, so erotic, so dirty, so sexy. My knees begin to buckle, and he squeezes the backs of my thighs to hold me in place. Then he licks up my slit, and my eyes roll back in my head.

"Rick, Rick, Rick." I chant his name. It comes out muffled through my panties, and for some reason, that only sends my desire further into overdrive.

He closes his teeth around my clit and tugs; goosebumps scatter across my skin. I tug on the bindings on my wrist, wishing I were free to grip his hair and tug on it. Wishing I could moan out his name, but the very fact that I can't, that I'm at his mercy, with him on his knees in front of me, and his tongue inside me, and his fingers sliding between my asscheeks to play with my puckered hole, is also an aphrodisiac. He stabs his tongue in and out of me, in and out, then brings one hand around to play with my clit. He rubs on the swollen nub and sensations shoot through my veins.

I feel like someone jammed a syringe of adrenaline and something more potent into my bloodstream. Something that goes straight to my head and pushes me to the edge. So when he curves his tongue inside me and pinches my clit, I explode. The orgasm slams through me, and I'm catapulted over the edge like a puck into the net of the opposing team. I cry out, and a part of me is relieved he gagged me. I hate to think the rest of the admin and accounts team who work next door might have heard me. The climax goes on and on, and I swear, I see lights in front of my eyes. He pulls back and the orgasm dissolves. My bones turn to mush.

I begin to slump, and he rises to his feet and hitches me up and onto the desk. I crack open my eyelids, which I must have closed at some point. My gaze is instantly captured with his blazing blue ones.

He pulls my torn panties from my mouth, slides them into his pocket, then urges me to wrap my legs about his hips. His monster-cock throbs through the crotch of his pants and against my sensitive core.

"I'm not going to fuck you... yet."

Before I can say a word, he propels his hips forward so his rigid shaft stabs into my swollen clit. Shockwaves zip under my skin. I open my mouth to cry out, but he wraps his fingers around my throat and squeezes. The pressure is enough to lock the sounds in my throat while allowing me to breathe. He glares into my eyes, and the lust burning in his sends pulse-waves of need shooting through my veins.

He's not fucking me, but he's showing me how good it'll be. He'll be too much. Too big. Too hard. I'll be stretched around his dick, and oh my god, I can safely say, I've never had anything this humongous attempt to infiltrate my pussy before. Even though he'll make sure I'm aroused and well lubricated, he'll still stretch me around his cock until I'm sure he'll skewer right through me. He'll be so deep inside, I'll be able to feel him in my throat. The thought pulses a bullet of excitement through my blood.

A helpless noise escapes me. His gaze instantly intensifies. He flicks out his tongue to lick his lips, which are swollen from how he went down on me. Moisture glistens around his mouth, and I imagine the taste of my cum is heavy on his palate.

How would it feel to taste myself on him?

As if he senses my thoughts, he loosens his hold on my throat enough so I can speak.

"You didn't kiss me," my voice comes out hoarse. I sound like I'm pleading, but I don't care. And when he leans in, the warmth from his body swirls around me like heat waves rising off a desert floor. The strength of his dominance is a corporeal presence that pins me in place. I gasp.

The blue in his eyes deepens. He brings me closer, then proceeds to kiss my forehead, each eyelid, my nose, each cheek, my chin. His touch is so tender. So sweet. So soft. Such a contrast to his almost uncaring hold on me that tears prick my eyes. I can't feel this...moved. This yearning. This wanting to strip him and me of our clothes and fuse into him. I *can't*.

"Rick... please... you—" Before I can complete my sentence, he fits his mouth to mine.

His lips are firm, his breath on my face soft. He stays there with his nose bumping mine, his eyes holding mine. And somehow, it feels even more intimate than when he had his tongue inside my pussy. Then he licks my lower lip, and a groan tumbles from my mouth. Instantly, he sweeps his tongue over mine, and the sweet taste of my cum interlaces with that darker, deeper, more complex taste that is Rick.

Contradictions. That's what this man is about. The way he holds me by my neck like I'm his possession or his pet is in contrast to how he kisses me like I'm something precious. Something he wants to savor and relish and appreciate. He licks into my mouth, swipes his tongue across my teeth, and more moisture pools between my legs.

My nipples harden until they're pinpoints of pain. He sucks on my tongue, and my entire body seems to catch fire. That's when he kicks his hips forward.

The zipper of his pants rubs up against my sensitive core as the thick column at his crotch nestles against my slit. He's so big, so hard, the heat against my center feels like an inferno waiting to erupt. He's not inside me, and yet, I can imagine how it would feel to have every inch of his hardness in that space deep inside me where no one has ever been.

Sensations ignite my nerve-endings and I cry out. He absorbs the sound and stays in place as my channel contracts and comes up empty.

I push up and into that heavy ridge in his pants. And again. And again. Each time I rub up against him, a spark of lust coils in my belly. My clit throbs. My pussy contracts. My breasts grow heavy, the ache within them spiraling until I am dizzy with need.

I moan into his mouth, beseech him with my eyes, and his grip on my throat tightens. With his other hand, he continues to massage my breast, and the sensations zip down to combine with the tension that builds in my lower belly. *Oh my god, I'm going to come again.*

I wind my arms about his neck and hook my fingers through his hair. I tug, and the column in his pants swells further.

I feel consumed by his presence, violated by the thickness of his shaft, no matter that he's not inside me.

He may as well have breached me, his presence is that potent. I'm surrounded by his scent, his absolute confidence commanding me to give in to him. He releases my lips, then leans back enough to search my eyes.

When I feel him swell against the rim of my entrance, I know he's gathering himself.

That if he'd been inside me, he'd have fucked me so hard I'd likely forget my own name. That even though he isn't in me, he's going to ensure I never forget this experience; a-n-d he doesn't disappoint. He thrusts forward and hits my clit at the right angle. A whine wells up my throat as he stays there. For a second. Another.

He continues to scan my features as if waiting for something. Something. My entire body is covered with a million tiny fires rapidly spreading to transform into an inferno that I know will burn through me. I open my mouth, try to say his name but all that emerges is a guttural cry. It's so primal, I barely recognize it as my own voice. It seems to reach him, though, for he nods. Then he releases my throat, grips my hips and hauls me up against his swollen erection with such force, the entire desk moves. Something crashes to the floor behind me, but we both ignore it.

He bends his head until his mouth is close to my ear. "Ride me, baby."

Before I can react, he's urging me up and down, up and down as he dry humps me. Well, not so dry, because my pussy is a melting puddle of need which must surely dampen the fabric over his crotch. But it doesn't deter him from dragging me over his thickness. That tightness in my belly folds in on itself. My thighs quiver. It's only his hands steadying me on my hips that keep me in place. A dense cloud of heat seems to spool off of his body and slam into my chest. I swallow, my throat so dry it feels like I have been screaming since the beginning of time.

The entire experience is primal and erotic... And different, because he's turning me on, but also making it known he's not going to fill me with his girth. At the same time, I can feel how it would be if he did. It sends my imagination into overdrive and turns me inside out.

A tear squeezes out from the corner of my eyes. He instantly licks it up, and when he straightens, his features soften. He brushes his lips over mine, once, twice, his touch now gentle, and when he pulls me up, his movements are firm but slow, almost languorous. Where he'd been racing to the climax, he's now almost unhurried. His thick cock brushes up against me, and I'm sure I can feel him in that that secret place deep within me.

A groan wells up my throat, and his cerulean eyes glow with an inner light. He holds my gaze, then wraps his thick fingers around my throat again. I'm possessed. And owned. And he's stamped himself into my cells without penetrating me. The trembling starts from deep within, and he feels it, too, for his movements speed up again. He holds my hips and surges forward.

"You will not"—thrust—"come"— thrust—"until I"— thrust—"give you permission."

"Please, Rick. Please," I gasp, as the pressure inside me tightens and builds until it seems to fill my entire body, my every pore. "Please," I cry out. "Please."

His hold around my throat tightens enough to cut off the oxygen.

My lungs burn, and my eyes grow wider. Every part of me waits, waits...Tears fill my eyes, my mouth falls open, I tug on his hair, squeeze down on his hips with my knees, dig my heels into his back, and plead with him, with unspoken words.

Then he hauls me up against him, fits me over the thick ridge in his pants with precision, and moves me up and down his length—slowly, making sure I feel every centimeter of his shaft, making sure I don't miss how big he is, making sure I realize I'd struggle to fit all of him inside me if he were *actually* fucking me. And the thought turns me on even more. It fills me with a yearning which pushes me to the edge.

That's when he growls, "Come. Right now."

30

Rick

I release my hold on her throat, and she throws back her head, sucking in air. Her mouth opens in a soundless cry. When her eyelids begin to flutter down, I snap, "Look at me."

She cracks her eyelids open as her body bucks, and she shatters. She's so fucking beautiful, a beacon that entices me to follow her over the edge. My balls draw up, and I grit my teeth to stop myself from coming. Instead, I hold her gaze and revel in the rapture of her orgasm. See the lust, the need, that absolute ecstasy that overtakes her, and that relief as she slumps against me. I cradle the back of her head and hold her against my chest. With my other hand I rub slow circles over her back. When she stills, I notch my knuckles under her chin and tip up her head. I press a firm kiss to her mouth. Her sweetness, her essence, her scent... All of it is goes straight to my head, and my cock twitches again.

I lick her lower lip, my favorite curve of her body, then whisper, "I'll be right back."

When I step back, she winces.

"Did I hurt you?"

She nods.

"That's good."

"Wha—?" She gapes.

I chuckle. "This way, you won't forget the first time we almost fucked." Then, because I can't stop myself, I kiss her again.

"I don't understand why you couldn't fuck me for real?"

"Just heightening the anticipation, baby."

"I'm beginning to think you're a sadist." She tips up her chin.

"I did let you come," I point out. "But if that's what turns you on, I could ensure you don't the next time and prolong the expectation even more…"

"There's not going to be a next time." She scowls.

My lips twitch.

She sees the confidence on my face, and her scowl deepens. When she opens her mouth, I silence her with mine and she instantly melts into me. I deepen the kiss, find myself leaning into her, and groan. "I'll never get enough of you."

She scoffs, "You're a piece of work, Stone."

I pull back, then slap her pussy lightly.

"Ow," she gasps. "What was that for?"

"My name. Is. Rick. You feel me, Goldie?"

She nods.

I hold her gaze a bit longer. Then, satisfied by her response, I nod. I grab her clothes from the floor. Then I scoop her up in my arms.

"Hey, what are you doing?"

"Gonna get you cleaned up."

I carry her over to the ensuite, then lower her to the counter near the sink. I wet a towel and press it between her legs. She winces.

"I did hurt you." I frown.

"Nothing I can't handle. I'm tougher than I look, Sto—I mean, Rick."

"As far as I'm concerned, you're fragile and need to be taken care of."

She chuckles. "Who, me?"

I toss the towel into the basket near the sink, then help her slide into her bra. I reach around to hook it up, but she protests, "I can do it."

"So can I."

"Had much experiences with women's lingerie?"

I raise a shoulder.

"What's that supposed to mean?"

"That it's common sense how to work the fastenings of a bra. Also—" I grunt as I stretch the band, then stretch it further, and finally manage to clasp the hooks. "Okay, maybe not that simple, but I succeeded."

"You did." She adjusts her tits in the bra-cups. Her movements are practiced. No doubt, she does that every time she wears her bra, but fuck, if it doesn't jiggle her breasts. My still hard balls threaten to blow. I managed to stop myself from coming, even as I encouraged her to climax, but this casual way she handles herself is more intimate, more arousing, more...everything.

A warmth steals over my skin. I help her down from the counter, then pull out a pair of panties from my pocket and sink down on one knee and hold it out for her."

"W-h-a-t? You were carrying an extra pair?"

I curl my lips.

"So you planned to tear off my panties?" She frowns.

"Didn't plan on it. But also knew I wasn't going to stop myself if I wanted to do it. I knew I wasn't going to let you out of my sight without panties. Not when the scent of your cunt would be too freely available for anyone else to smell. And only I get to enjoy the smell of your freshly-fucked pussy.

Her eyes flash. A combination of anger and desire, which turns me on even more.

"I can't decide if I should be angry at your presumptuousness, or moved by your thoughtfulness or—"

"—as long as my words heighten the moisture between your thighs, I'm good."

She rolls her eyes. "I can't even with you. Also, I can dress myself."

"Humor me." I tilt my head, and she finally relents. She steps into her panties, gripping the top of my head for support. When she tugs on my hair, my cock instantly responds—not that it's a surprise. Where she's concerned, I'm in a state of permanent arousal. I slide the panties up her legs, and because I can't stop myself, I press a kiss to her pussy lips—which makes her gasp—before I smooth the fabric over her hips. Then I hold her hips and press another kiss to her belly button.

She moans and grips my hair tighter. "What are you doing?"

"Taking care of what's mine." I glance up to find she's looking at me with a mixture of lust and need, and it's never felt more right to kneel in front of a woman like this.

"I'm not yours," she reminds me.

"You're my fiancée."

"Your fake fiancée."

"Real, as far as the world and my grandmother are concerned." Just then, the phone in my back pocket vibrates.

"Are you going to get that?" she murmurs.

"Only if I continue to inhale your pussy scent while I talk to whoever is on the other side." I pull out my phone, glance at the screen, and stiffen. *Oh hell.*

"Are you okay? Who is it?"

"My grandmother." I sigh before bringing the phone to my ear to answer it, "Hey, Grams."

"There you are, darling boy. You're all over the internet with that beautiful fiancée of yours."

Of course, she noticed. Grams is tech savvy. She might be eighty-two, but she's very connected with world events. She scans the news every day on her tablet, and until a month ago, invested in the stock-market using an online app. She's also physically active. She goes for daily walks and takes part in social activities with her book club. Which is why it came as a surprise when she was diagnosed as having blocked arteries in her heart a month ago.

Dr. Kincaid said it was age-related. He advised her to cut back on stress, which is when she handed over her investment management to a consultant. The doc had been clear: it was best to have surgery and have stents fitted into her heart to prevent the possibility of a heart attack. Grams refused to get the procedure done until I settled down.

"Is she there with you?" she asks.

"Yep, she's here." *Very much here.*

I press my cheek into the soft skin of her belly. She melts into me then squeaks, "You're talking to your grandmother."

She tries to pull away, but I hold her in place. "I was going to tell you about her, Grams, but things got a little out of control, and we had to give an interview this morning—"

"—no matter. When are you bringing her over?"

"Soon." I turn my nose into her belly and bite down on the skin lightly.

She trembles, then grabs the hair at the back of my head and tugs on it. "Stop it," she admonishes in a low voice.

"Is that your fiancée? Her name's Giorgina, right? Can I talk to her?"

I blink, then slowly straighten and hand the phone over to her. "Grams wants to talk to you."

"What?" Goldie's eyes grow so big, they seem to fill her face. "What do you mean, she wants to talk to me?"

I raise a shoulder, then wave the phone under her nose.

"Giorgina, is that you?" My grams' voice can be heard through the receiver.

Goldie glowers at me then takes the phone and holds it to her ear. "Hello, Grams. This is Giorgina."

31

Gio

"I've been waiting for so long to meet you. My prayers have finally been answered," Grams gushes. The emotions pour through the phone, and I freeze. Oh wow, she does believe we are engaged to be married. And she's happy about it. Considering I don't have anyone else in my family I needed to notify about the breaking news of my fake engagement, it's overwhelming to have this kind of reaction from someone who clearly cares for him. I hold his gaze, then glance away. "That's a very sweet thing to say, Grams."

"You two look so cute together. And you only have eyes for each other. I knew when he finally fell it would be for a woman who's strong and confident. Someone who won't put up with his shenanigans."

I chuckle. "You haven't even met me and—"

"And I'm good at reading the nuances, young lady. That kiss between the two of you is somethin' else. And he has eyes only for you in every picture. He's smitten, Giorgina, and with good reason. From what I gathered, you have a firm head on your shoulders. And you're beautiful, too!"

I bite the inside of my cheek. "Thank you, I guess?"

"So, when am I seeing the both of you?"

I glance up at Rick who murmurs, "Tomorrow?"

"Tonight, for dinner," Grams announces.

"Ah, well, I'm at work and—"

"My time is short, Giorgina. Every minute wasted is one I won't get back. I'm going to see the two of you this evening at dinner. You tell that grandson of mine to bring you home by six p.m."

"But Grams—" the phone goes dead.

I lower it, and he takes it from me, sliding it into his pocket.

"I assume you heard that?"

"Loud and clear." He rubs the back of his neck. "You don't have to come. My grandmother can be a handful, but if you're uncomfortable with it—"

"I'll come." I reach for my skirt and slip into it, then pull on my blouse before shrugging into my jacket. "I mean, that's one of the reasons for this entire charade, isn't it?"

He nods slowly. "I don't want you to feel compelled to do something you're not comfortable with."

"The only thing I'm not comfortable about is that your Grams sounds genuinely excited about our engagement, and it doesn't feel right that we're acting out a farce in front of her, you know?"

"But the end result is that she'll agree to the procedure that'll give her a chance to live."

I nod slowly. "Couldn't you have done this for real?"

"Done what for real?"

"Found a woman and gotten engaged to her?"

"What's this then?" He points at the space between us.

"You and I both know our engagement is as fake as the snow in that indoor ski-resort in Dubai."

"Dubai has an indoor ski-resort?" He frowns.

"That's not the point."

"Then what is?"

I throw up my hands. "You know what I'm trying to say here. Your grandmother seems to think we're engaged."

"That was the idea. And our little interview earlier with the journalist clearly did the trick."

"But she sounded so thrilled and so looking forward to seeing us..." I lock my fingers together in front of me. "It doesn't feel right."

He scans my features. "It's bothering you, huh?"

I nod.

"If it's making you uncomfortable and you don't want to go through with this, then—"

"That's not what I'm saying, either."

He rubs at his temple. "I'm not sure what you're trying to tell me here, Goldie. Do you want to meet my grandmother or not?"

I draw in a breath. "Yes, yes I do. She's looking forward to seeing us. I don't want to let her down."

"Okay, good." He seems relieved. "Let's take it one step at a time. Let's get through dinner today and we'll take it from there?"

"Am I over-dressed?" I run my sweat-soaked palms down the fabric of my dress. Thankfully, I packed a range of clothes in my suitcase when I moved from L.A. I might have left in a hurry, but I had enough presence of mind to pack my favorite outfits, which include this pale blue, silk shirt-dress that comes to below my knees. It's made of a flowing crepe de chine fabric with a collar, a wrap detail bodice, and a belt that cinches in at the waist. It's timeless and elegant and something I know makes me look good.

After that call with his grandmother, he left me in my office to get on with my work and promised to be back to pick me up at four-thirty p.m. I told him he didn't need to, but he said we should for the sake of appearances. Of course, Edward is in his office down the corridor from me, as are his assistant and the admin and finance teams, so I suppose he's right.

Also, his grandmother was right. I saw the pictures from the interview, and the one of us kissing is smokin'. And the other pictures all have Rick looking at me like I'm the love of his life. There's even a slight curve to his lips in one, and his eyes have this look of adoration that made my heart go flip-flop. Ugh, he's a better actor than I am; other than the kiss where I'm leaning into him, I look a little uncomfortable, like I'm not sure what to do with myself.

Fact is, as a PR professional, I'm used to managing the profiles of my clients. But now that I'm in the spotlight myself, it's making me realize I don't like having the attention on me. I've also gained a new understanding of how difficult it is for clients to keep their composure when they're faced with prying questions. Still, it's already been worth it. That look of shock on Dennis' face when he'd found out I'd moved on made it worth it. And if this coerces Grams to get her operation, then it's worth all the scrutiny over my life and having to share living quarters with the Grumphole, right?

"Well?" I turn to him. "Am I dressed appropriately for this visit?"

He eases the car to a stop at a traffic-signal, then turns and drags his gaze down my face, my chest, my legs, which I cross over each other. My skirt slides up my thighs. He takes in the skin exposed above my knees, and goose-bumps pop on my skin. I resist the urge to pull down the fabric and cover myself up.

"You haven't answered the question," I remind him.

He brings his gaze up to my face, and his blue eyes flash with desire before he banks it. "You are the most beautiful woman in the world."

Heat flushes my cheeks. This man… He makes me blush like I've never been complimented before. Which I have been, but coming from him? It's different. It's special. It's personal. It feeds something primitive inside of me. Something I can't understand, something that makes me want to please him even more. Something that makes me want to earn his praise and feel contented.

The signal changes, and he faces forward before taking his foot off the brake. His thick fingers grip the wheel with practiced ease. He's changed into slacks and a blue button-down shirt with the sleeves rolled up. As he steers the car, veins stand out on his forearms. The dark hair peppered there, the chiseled muscles that flex as he drives… All of it elicits a familiar prickling between my legs. I squeeze my thighs together to assuage the emptiness that yawns there. The emptiness which is now stamped by the shape of his cock.

He must sense it for he growls, "Spread your legs."

32

Rick

"What?" she says in a breathless voice.

"Don't make me repeat myself," I say in a hard voice.

I'm sure she's going to refuse, then she slowly slides her legs apart. I keep my attention on the road—doesn't mean I'm not tuned in to her. Enough to have noticed she was turned on. Enough to have smelled her arousal and sensed her squeeze her thighs together. Enough to wrap my fingers more firmly around the wheel and ensure I don't look at her. If I do, I'll lose control, and I can't have that, not when my pillow princess is riding in the car with me.

"Pull up your dress," I order.

Her breathing grows rougher, then I hear the whisper of the fabric over her skin as she draws it up. That sweet scent of her arousal intensifies, and my mouth waters. The blood drains to my groin and my balls grow so hard, I have to spread my own legs to accommodate my erection. Jesus H Christ, all I have to do is smell her and I'm so turned on I want to pull over, yank her to me, fit her over my erection and thrust up and into her, over and over again, until she orgasms. The air in the car thickens. That unseen chord that has bound us since we met tightens.

"Now slide your fingers inside your panties."

"What?" she squeaks.

"You heard me, Goldie."

She draws in a breath, then I sense her following my instructions. I know when she's brought her fingers to her core, for she moans.

"Touch your clit for me, baby."

"Rick, no, please. I'm so sensitive there. I can't do this. I can't."

"Yes you can."

I know she's blushing something fierce, for the heat in the enclosed space dials up a few notches. A bead of sweat slides down my temple, and my vision narrows. My fingers tingle, and I'm this close to saying to hell with the trip, turning right back so I can take her back to the room and fuck her until she's screaming my name. But I promised Grams I'd bring her for a visit, and until I met her, Grams was the most important woman in my life. So, I can't disappoint her. "Don't disappoint me, Goldie. Feel how swollen that little nub of yours is. Feel how moist your channel is as it prepares itself for my cock."

"Rick, oh my god," she gasps, then cries out, and I know she's fondling her clit.

"That's it baby, like that. Circle that little bud for me."

She shudders, then arches her back as she follows my orders.

"Now slide two fingers inside yourself."

The slurp of her wet skin giving as she fucks herself with her fingers fills the air.

"Did I give you permission to get yourself off?" I growl.

"What the—" she begins to protest.

I cut her off. "If you swear, I'll have to punish you for it, and I'll take great pleasure in it, too."

She makes a sound halfway between a snarl and a groan.

A chuckle rumbles up my chest, but I manage to swallow it back. She's so fucking adorable when she gets all antsy and so filled with lust that she can barely think straight. And I'm the one who got her there. Not that asshat of her-ex. Her soon to be no-longer-ever-in-her-thoughts ex, if I have my way. I'm going to show her how much pleasure I can give her. How much in touch with her moods, her emotions, her every little need I am. I'm going to take such good care of her, she won't want anything to do with him.

"Now, stuff a third finger inside yourself."

"Another one?" she cries.

"In comparison to my cock, three of your slim fingers is less than half the size."

"One fourth, but whatever," she mumbles under her breath, but I hear her.

"What did you say?"

"That there's a reason your ego's as big as an arena."

I allow my lips to curl. "Did you compliment me there?"

"I suppose I did," she scoffs.

I frown. "And how many have you seen?"

"Is this the conversation you want to be having while I have my fingers inside myself?"

I shoot her a sideways glance, then look back at the road. "Just for that, cram a fourth finger inside yourself."

"What?" She gasps, "If I had long manicured fingernails—"

"You don't. Do it, Goldie. Now."

A whimper spills from her lips. Then she throws back her head, "Oh god—"

"Oh, Rick," I correct her.

"Oh, Rick. I'm so close. So, so, close."

"You may now start fucking yourself."

The slap of wet flesh against flesh fills the air. The sweet scent of her cum is so intense, it goes straight to my head. I force myself to stay focused, then flip the indicator and take the turn off that leads to Grams' place.

"Faster," I snap.

The intensity with which she's fingering herself increases. She gasps, groans, and wriggles her hips as she obeys me. Her entire body shudders. Her movements get more frantic. I know she's there. I know she's about to come.

"Stop."

"Eh?"

"Pull your fingers out, right now."

She does so, then inhales. The tension vibrates off of her body as I guide the car to a stop. I turn, circle her wrist with my fingers, and bring hers to my mouth. I lick the cum off her fingertips, and the honeyed taste adds fuel to my arousal. I hold her gaze, curl my tongue around her fingertips, and her pupils dilate further.

"Why didn't you let me come?" she cries.

"Do you think you deserve to come, Goldie mine?"

She blinks rapidly.

"Do you?"

She slowly shakes her head.

"Good girl."

Her chest rises and falls; a whine escapes her lips. "I am so aroused, I might self-combust."

"Excellent." I reach for one of the wet wipes on the dash and rub it over her fingers. Then I bring them to my nose and sniff. I wipe them again, sniff, then nod.

"What are you doing?" She clears her throat.

"Making sure no one else can smell the evidence of your arousal."

Her already flushed features turn a bright red. "Do you have to be so uncouth?" She coughs.

"Do you have to be so coy?"

"You don't have to spell out every little detail of our... Whatever it is we're doing." She waves at the space between us.

"You mean my bringing you to the edge without even touching you?"

She glowers at me. "You don't have to look so pleased, and you better let me come next time, you hear me?"

In a flash, I've unsnapped my seatbelt, leaned toward her and wrapped my fingers round the nape of her neck. "What did you say?" I ask in a voice infused with dominance.

She draws in a sharp breath, and a flicker of excitement threads through her gaze. "I said, you'd better let me come, you—" She gasps, but I swallow the sound as I close my mouth over hers. Her lips, her scent, the beating of the pulse at the base of her neck, the bite of her fingertips as she digs them into my shoulders and holds on... All of it sinks into my blood, empties my mind of all thought, and cranks up the lust in my bloodstream, until all I can feel is this overpowering need to own her, possess her, to have her in every way possible, to make her mine. *Mine. Mine.*

I tilt my head, deepen the kiss, and with a sigh, she melts into me. She kisses me back with a hunger that has my lust flaring, deepening, extending to every part of my body, my cells, my very soul. I tear my lips from hers, pull back enough that she has to withdraw her hands, and stare at her, chest heaving, breath coming in pants. *What insanity is this that I only have to touch her to feel like every part of me is being taken over with this overpowering need to claim her? What witchcraft is this that she holds so much power over me? Why does she affect me so? Why her? Why now? Why, when I've been happy with my life so far? When I've rededicated myself to the game I love. When I ...*

She reaches up to touch my face, and I grab her hand. "Don't. If you touch me again, I won't be able to stop."

"So don't."

"I also think you were right."

"About what?"

"We need to set some boundaries."

"I don't understand." She blinks.

"I mean"—I release my hold on her neck and sit back—"I think we should keep up the pretense of being a couple only in front of others and not when we're alone."

"What do you—"

There's a rap on my window. I turn to find Grams peering in through the glass. "You two coming in any time soon?"

33

Gio

We need to set boundaries. Boundaries. So that's it? One minute, we're kissing; the next, the man's withdrawn his affections and his touch and sucked all the warmth back into himself.

A shiver ran down my back. I knew what he meant. The bleak expression on his face made it clear he was having second thoughts about us plunging headlong into a relationship, which seemed as real as the act we put on in front of the journalist earlier... Which hadn't been an act at all, either. In fact, since we commenced this farce, nothing is as it seems.

He said I was his fake fiancé, yet he gave me a ring that belonged to his grandmother. He said it was a pretend relationship, yet the way he kissed me was so intense, I was sure he was catching feelings for me. There are no half measures with Rick. Everything he does, he puts his entire self behind it. Both on the ice and off, especially when he held my gaze and never looked away as he made me come.

And now, he's talking about boundaries? After breaking every possible rule, spoken and unspoken, between us.

I glare at the rat's ass of a man who's bent over his grandmother. Rosemary is nothing like I imagined she would be. She's not the stereotypical little grandma who loves to knit and wears old-fashioned clothing. Rick's grandma is sprightly, with silver hair cut in a fashionable blunt cut that set off her features. Her eyes are bright and only a little less faded blue than Rick's. She's also wearing a Chanel suit, complete with a string of pearls and a pair of *Manolo Blahniks*. Yep, the woman is sporting a pair of black pumps that are both stylish and comfortable. She hadn't seemed surprised at all to have found us kissing in the car parked outside her house. If anything, I have a sneaking suspicion I went up in her estimation for being found making out with her grandson.

She embraced me, then hooked her arm with mine and walked me inside her home. We'd barely stepped in when the pony... I mean, Tiny, came dancing over to us. He stayed quiet and waited for Rosemary to pat him, then looked at me with his big melting grey-brown eyes—so different from the cold-fire eyes that are Rick's—until I gave in and rubbed his big head. He pushed his big body into my hand and turned to present his hind quarters.

When I looked around in confusion, Rosemary chuckled. "Clever boy, he wants you to scratch his back; he can't reach there." So, I did.

He woofed his happiness and let me pet him. Until Rick walked into the house, that is. Then, forgetting all about me, he barked out a greeting and threw himself at Rick.

To Rick's credit, he took the brunt of what was, surely, a hundred and fifty plus pounds of Great Dane planting his paws on his chest. Rick scratched Tiny behind his ears, massaged him under his jowls, and patted him with sweeping strokes that sent the mutt into an ecstasy of happy woofs. He flopped onto his back and Rick tickled his tummy. When Rick hit the sweet spot, his leg shook, prompting a laugh from everyone. That prompted Tiny to straighten and lick Rick's face until Grams called him to heel.

Rick excused himself to go wash up, with Tiny on his heels. I was sure Grams would use that alone time to quiz me about my relationship with Rick, but she didn't. Instead, she led me to the sunroom and invited me to take a seat. She introduced me to her companion, a young woman called India who hugged me and said she'd already heard so much about me, before setting off to lay the table for dinner. When Rick returned, he'd walked over and embraced Grams properly.

Now, India walks in to announce dinner is ready. Grams rises to her feet; so do Rick and I. Grams walks over to me, hooks her arm through mine again and pronounces, "Walk with me."

India leads Tiny into the kitchen, and I let Grams lead me in the direction of what I assume is the dining space. We walk through a hallway decorated with pictures. My steps slow as I take in the family snapshots. A man whose height and build is very similar to Rick's, and a woman who's brilliant blue eyes and features resemble Rick's. There are pictures of a baby Rick with his eyes closed, with his mother holding him and his father with his arm around the both of them. Rick, as a toddler with a mischievous grin on his face, those mesmerizing blue eyes, and curly dark hair on the beach with his mom holding his hand. The trio at a barbecue. Rick, when he must have been five, wearing a Santa hat and surrounded by Christmas gifts and wrapping paper. What looks like a ten-year-old Rick, with a face smeared with ice-cream. A teenaged Rick, almost as tall as a younger Grams with hair that hasn't yet gone grey, wearing another Chanel suit with the same string of pearls she's wearing now. An older teenaged Rick with a girl his age, both of them grinning in front of Grams' house.

"That was his first girlfriend."

"She wasn't." Rick comes up behind us.

"You dated her for six months," Grams points out.

"I hung out with her." He raises a shoulder.

"You took her to prom."

"Only because I had to go with someone. If it hadn't been her, it would've been someone else."

I frown at him over my shoulder. "That's not very nice."

"It's true. I never did have feelings for anyone, until you."

Grams' gaze bounces between us. She's following our conversation with great interest. It's the only reason I don't respond to his comment. Instead, I walk forward and peer at another picture. This one is of a younger Rick, in his late teens or early twenties, dressed in full hockey gear. He's on the ice, leaning on his hockey stick and grinning widely at the camera. He has his helmet tucked under one arm, and his hair is longer, curlier and falls over his forehead. He looks more carefree, more unguarded. His eyes are not shadowed, his gaze more open. "You look different in this picture," I murmur.

"I was different. That was before."

I shoot him another glance. "Before what?"

"Before I joined the Marines."

I want to ask him why he left the NHL, why he moved back to England, what made him decided to play hockey again. I don't even know where he and his family lived in the US. There's so much I don't know about this man. And now, perhaps, I never will, considering he's decided to re-impose the dividing lines between us.

I turn to Grams. "I'm hungry; what's for dinner?"

34

Rick

"So how did you two meet?" Grams looks between us. "I read the interview but would prefer to hear it from you in person."

I exchange glances with Goldie. The look in her eyes says she'd rather I take this one. I nod and turn to Grams, but before I can reply, India walks in and serves Gio and me. Then she returns with another plate of food and places it in front of Grams.

"Grilled mackerel with mustard sauce on a cous-cous salad, enjoy," India announces.

"Mackerel?" Grams makes a face.

"It's good for you, Grams. You know the doctor advised you to be careful with your diet."

Grams' frown deepens. She opens her mouth, no doubt, to protest, but Gio interjects. "Yum, this looks so good." She turns to India. "I love mackerel."

"Me too," I lean back in my chair.

India flashes us both a smile.

All three of us turn to Grams who huffs, "Fine, okay, I'll eat it."

India voices a silent thank you to Gio and leaves.

Grams stays silent for a few seconds, then nods in Gio's direction. "You have a good one here, my boy. I hope you hold on to her," she says without looking at me.

"Not telling me anything I don't know," I murmur.

Grams is on a special diet to manage her heart condition. While the food looks, smells, and is no doubt, tasty to eat, she hates the constraints imposed upon her. But Gio's timely intervention helped put Grams at ease.

All of us dig into our food—which I can attest is tasty.

After a few mouthfuls, Grams raises an eyebrow in my direction. "You were telling me how you two met?"

I clear my throat. "It was as we told the journalist. I rescued her from her date."

Grams places down her fork, "Your words, as I recall reading were, 'Take your hands off my wife'?" She makes air quotes with her fingers.

I resist the urge to look at Goldie and nod. "Umm, yes."

"*My wife*, hmm?" She leans back in her seat, then taps the table. "My. Wife."

"You have a question, Grams?" I ask lightly.

"Indeed, I do." She purses her lips. "Why are the two of you hiding things from me?"

I stiffen. "What do you mean?"

"You didn't tell the entire story to the journalist. There's stuff you're holding back. Things which I think I deserve to know, since I'm not the public. I'm your grandmother, your only surviving blood relative, too."

Grams can be good at guilt-tripping me. It's how she almost always gets me to do what she wants. Not that I hold it against her. I love her too much. I should have also known better than to try to get her to believe in my fake engagement.

"Let me explain. There's a reason I decided to do it this way, and—"

"And nothing." Her features form into firm lines. "You never told the journalist that you love each other."

Goldie frowns.

I stiffen. "Umm, Grams? We're engaged; it stands to reason we're in love."

"Why didn't you tell the journalist that? If you were trying to convince someone of your feelings for each other, wouldn't that be the first thing you mention?" She looks between us. "If it weren't for how the two of you looked at each other before you started smooching, I'd have been sure you were pretending to be engaged so you could convince me to have my surgery."

My heart slams into my ribcage. My guts churn. It's bad enough I feel guilty about suggesting this charade, and now I have to lie to her all over again. But if it means she'll agree to the operation, it'll be worth it. I square my shoulders and school my features into an expression which I hope makes it clear I'm sincere.

"Well, I'm telling my fiancée now, in front of you," I turn to Goldie. Her eyes widen. A hint of panic creeps into them, but before she can say or do anything which could give away this pretense, I lean over and place my hand on hers. "I love you, Goldie. I loved you before I knew what it was I felt for you. I love you in a way I've never loved anyone before or ever will after. You're it for me. You're my sun, my moon, my stars, my everything. You're the woman I've been waiting for. As soon as I saw you, I knew you were the one. I'd pick you out in a crowd. I'd pick you out among the billion stars in the universe. I'd pick you over and over again. Only you."

Goldie swallows. Her chest rises and falls. Her pupils are dilated, her color high. She looks like what she's meant to be, a woman in love.

Grams looks between us and sighs. "That was so romantic. I brought you up right, boy."

Goldie draws in a breath, something flashes in her eyes. Desire? Need? Longing? Then she turns her palm and twines her fingers through mine. "I love you too Rick. I don't know why. I often question myself why it is I have these feelings toward you... Why it's you who should elicit this need in me... Why you draw me in... Why, when I'm not with you, I keep thinking of you... Why I miss you even when I'm with you, and then I realize, it's because the emotions I've felt since I met you are so different from anything I've ever felt before."

"They are?" I ask in a cautious tone.

"Mmm-hmm," she nods. "It's because I love you. I love you, Rick, and you better believe it, for I've never said that to anyone else before."

"Not even to your twatarse of an ex?"

"Rick!" Grams admonishes me.

"Not even him." Goldie's lips twitch.

I lower my gaze to her lush mouth and don't look away. Her smile fades. Her throat moves as she swallows. And when I tug on her hand, she comes closer without complaint. I fit my mouth to hers, keeping my gaze open as I stare into her eyes...as I take in the sincerity, the intensity, the lust that clouds her eyes when I deepen the kiss. I share her breath, draw in of her essence, suck on her tongue, and when the blood drains to my groin, I pull away before I remember Grams is an eager spectator.

Grams claps her hands. "Now, that's a kiss!"

Goldie blinks. The expression on her face is dazed. Good. This dinner isn't going how I planned. That declaration of love was spontaneous, but damn, if it didn't sound convincing. And her words, even more so. If I were a spectator, I'd have been persuaded we're in love. Which was the entire point of this exercise.

So why is my pulse racing? Why is sweat dampening my brow?

This doesn't mean anything. They were empty words. I was acting my part, and so was she. That's all this is.

"You guys, it pleases me so much to see the two of you so in love," Grams exclaims.

I don't look away; neither does Goldie. Our gazes seem to be engaged in a dance of their own, one I don't want to interpret. And as long as it helps Grams buy our story, it doesn't matter.

"Not sure why you doubted us, Grams," I murmur.

Gram blows out a breath. "You'd think that it would be the logical conclusion when two people get engaged—that they're in love. But who knows? Your mother's generation was bad enough, but you guys? You'll go straight to anal before you even speak the L-word."

Goldie's face mirrors my shock, then, "Grams!" She whips her head in my grandmother's direction.

"Grams!" I'm not only gaping at my nana, but I swear, there's also a blush stealing up my neck. It's not every day you hear your eighty-two-year-old Grams mention the A-word.

Grams scoffs, "What, you don't think I know about a—"

"—Okay, enough. I know you're with it, Grams, and know your way around the internet and social media—"

"I don't have fifty thousand followers on my platform for nothing," Grams reminds me.

"Fifty-thousand?" Goldie exclaims in awe. She tries to pull her hand from mine, but I tighten my hold.

"Apparently, people like to hear me read from my favorite smutty romance novels. They find it endearing." Grams rolls her eyes.

"You read from your spicy romance novels on your social media platform?" Goldie murmurs. Again, she tries to tug her hand away, but I bring her fingers to my mouth and kiss them.

Grams sighs, "You two are adorable."

Goldie's face flushes. She darts me a sideways glance, then looks back at Grams, who has an expression of satisfaction on her face.

"My followers love it," she says with a wide smile.

"In fact, they demand I read from my dark romance novels, which are my favorite, by the way. And my latest book is a hockey romance novel, which—"

"Please, don't tell me that our love story is what inspired you to read hockey romance," I interject.

"It's true. Your interview and how you met is what inspired me to pick up a hockey romance, and I was hooked." She snaps her fingers.

Goldie looks at her with awe. "You're quite something."

"You're only as old as you think you are. And you're only young once." She looks between us again. "Know what I mean?" She addresses her question to me.

"Um, not really?" I admit.

"Your declarations of love and the way you two kissed have convinced me we need to set a date."

"A date?" Goldie exclaims.

Grams nods. "Surely, you two must have discussed a wedding date?"

"A wedding date…" I pale, then reach for my glass of water and drain it.

"Isn't that the logical next step, or am I missing something?" Grams frowns.

"It is the logical next step, but to be honest, we hadn't discussed it yet."

"Not at all," Goldie adds.

"You don't know when you're getting married?" Grams' lips turn down.

"First, you need to take care of your surgery," I say gently.

Her shoulders hunch, and for a second, my usually confident Grams looks uncertain. Then, she seems to get ahold of herself and fixes me with a shrewd look. "So, if I get the surgery, the two of you will get married?"

"You told me if I found a woman and settled down, you'd schedule the surgery," I remind her.

"I should be the one nagging you," she says with a small smile.

"We can nag each other; it's allowed." I reach over with my free arm and take her hand in mine. Her fingers are slim, the skin paper thin. I'm struck anew with how fragile she seems. She's always had this larger-than-life image in my mind. As a child who spent summers with her in London, I was very influenced by Grams' resilience and zest for life. When my grandfather died, she was only fifty, but she didn't let that get to her. She grieved, then moved on, even managing to have a couple of relationships—not to replace her husband, but so she could make the most of the present. That's always been her philosophy—stay engaged and always make the most of the moment. For her to show apprehension tells me how much she's been trying to put up a brave front.

"You're not alone Grams, you know? You have me." I squeeze her fingers.

"And me." Goldie says softly. "I can only imagine how scary it must be to think of going through something like this on your own. But we're here for you Grams."

Grams' eyes shine with unshed tears.

She reaches for the glass of gin and tonic that's been placed next to her plate and takes a long drink from it. When she places it on the table, she seems steadier. "Thanks, dear." She holds out her free hand to Goldie, who doesn't hesitate to take it. Goldie squeezes my hand while holding onto Grams'.

"I'll talk to Dr. Kincaid and arrange a date for the operation."

"Why don't you let me—" I begin, but she scoffs.

"I may be old, but I'm not dead yet. I can arrange for my own procedure."

"But you'll let us know when, so we can be there for you?" Goldie asks.

A cunning look comes into Grams' eyes. "If you let me know what the date is for your wedding."

35

Gio

"We're not in love or getting married. And we're certainly not setting a date. How did we even get here?" I spin around on my sock-clad feet and glare at the alphahole sprawled out on the bed. We're back in our room in the shared house.

After that pronouncement, Grams didn't seem bothered when neither of us were able to assure her we'd set a date soon. Rick, however, managed to extract a promise from her that she'd tell us when she was going in for the surgery so we could be there with her.

After that, Grams seemed to tire. She didn't push further about us setting a date for our wedding. We got through the rest of the meal, with Rick updating her about the London Ice Kings and the upcoming exhibition matches against the Islington Sentinels — Dennis' team.

We exchanged glances when he mentioned the team name, but neither of us brought up Dennis. Not during dinner and not on the trip home, during which we were both silent. The meal was delicious, and despite my strictly regimented diet, I wasn't able to resist the sticky toffee pudding — a dessert I never had before. But it looked and smelled delicious, and before I knew it, I'd inhaled a couple of mouthfuls. Then, Grams coaxed me into eating some more, and before I knew it, I'd wiped my plate clean. And instantly, I felt guilty.

I began to feel sick and stayed quiet on the way home, then managed to rush into the ensuite and turn on the shower so the sound of the water drowned out the noise of my retching. It's one of the reasons I was so reluctant to move into the same room as Rick. So far, I've been good with what I've consumed, so I haven't felt the need to stick my finger down my throat. But I gave into temptation today. Blame it on Grams talking about our getting married. I felt nervous, but also, something inside me loved the idea of being married to this man. *No, no, no I'm not going there.* Apparently, faking it until you make it is real. Faking it with this guy has made me feel like I'm in a relationship with him, which is why he mentioned drawing up boundaries on the way to Grams, of course.

Also, I don't want to catch feelings on a rebound. I trusted one man, and look how that turned out. It's not that I have feelings left for Dennis—contrary to what I hinted to Rick. I did so, perhaps, out of self-preservation? Because I didn't want him to think I was open to catching feelings for him either. As for Dennis, he doesn't merit a second thought. But I invested so many years in that relationship, and the betrayal has left me feeling raw and exposed. Not that Rick is anywhere as unreliable as Dennis.

I haven't known Rick for long, but seeing how caring he was with his Grams, how he played with Tiny at her place, and how he inquired after India and made sure she had everything she needed to support her role as Grams' companion... All of it made me realize, he's not in the same league as Dennis. Rick is a much better man in every way. Too bad neither of us is ready for a real relationship yet.

After I empty the contents of my stomach, I jump into the shower, then pull on my stretchy pajamas and my comfiest socks. I pad out of the bathroom to find him sprawled on the make-shift bed on the floor. I take in his bare-chested torso and the pair of grey sweatpants he's wearing.

Argh! Of course, he had to wear grey sweats. Which mold to his powerful thighs and tent at his crotch. *Look away. Look away.* I try. I swear, I do. But I simply can't stop my eyes from tracing the outline of that monster cock, which I know his sweats are hiding. In fact, if I look closely enough, I can make out the crown of—

"I'm commando," he declares.

"What?" Fire engulfs my features. I manage to keep a straight face, despite my cheeks that are scarlet with embarrassment. I tip up my chin, walk past him and lower myself onto the bed.

"I don't wear briefs to bed."

"TMI. TMI," I sing out.

"Didn't seem like you had any problems with the information gathering when you were getting an eyeful of my pocket python."

"Pocket python?" I choke out the words. "Did you say—"

"Pocket python, or you could call it my moisture-seeking-missile, my hand grenade, my Garfield, my—"

"Stop." I sit up in bed and stab a finger at him. "You're saying all this to shock me."

"Am I succeeding?"

"You're succeeding in upping the cringe factor, yes."

"Why did you tell Grams we're in love?"

"Why did you tell our teammates we're engaged?"

He throws his arm behind his neck, and his biceps bulge. That wide chest of his might as well be carved from marble, as faultless as it is. If I were a poet, I could write an ode to it. But I'm a marketing and PR professional, so I reach for my phone and snap a picture.

He frowns.

"Why'd you do that?"

"It's a great picture for your social media feed." I look up from perusing his sex-on-a-stick, faultless, click—*jeez, the man looks delicious, and I'm not sure I want to share this picture for everyone to see.* "You look like a growlier Henry Cavill, if he had a bad attitude and a resting dick face."

"A what face?" He glances down at his crotch. Typical man.

I circle my face. "Your face. I'm talking about your face. In fact, I'd say you have CRDF."

"Eh?"

"Chronic Resting Dick Face. When you always come across as disgruntled, angry and annoyed. Like you're going to bite someone's head off."

He leans back into his pillow. "Just because I don't go parading around like some grinning idiot, doesn't relegate me to the abjectly miserable."

"You don't look miserable, just peevish, crabby and short-tempered."

He raises a shoulder, and that makes his muscles move like tectonic plates under the earth. Oh god, did I compare him to an earthquake? He certainly rocked my world when he made me come in my office.

My nipples pucker, and my lower belly clenches. I keep my legs still, making sure I don't squeeze my thighs together. Okay, maybe a little bit. Just a little wriggle, but he catches it.

"Right now, you look hungry."

On cue, my stomach growls.

He looks at me with interest. "Are you hungry already?"

"No, no, that's my stomach digesting my dinner."

Skepticism flickers in his eyes. "You sure? We can head down to the kitchen, and I can make you a sandwich."

"You don't have to pretend to care for me," I say primly.

He frowns. "I do care for you. As a friend."

"So, if any of the other guys on the team were hungry, you'd make him a sandwich?"

"Nah." He turns over on his side and faces me. His sweats dip a little at his waist, baring more of that V-shaped Adonis belt of his, and that happy trail that disappears under the waistband and--

"My dick-face is up here," he drawls.

That blush sweeps over my features with a vengeance. "I was admiring the goods, is all," I say honestly.

He rakes his gaze down my chest, the space between my legs, my thighs, and by the time he meets my eyes, that blush is, once again, an out-of-control forest fire. "So was I," he replies in a low, hard voice.

The air between us thickens with unspoken words; the heat in the room seems to increase ten-fold. A ripple of heat eddies down my spine. All of my senses seem to pop, and I'm very aware of how he's looking at me like he wants to eat me up.

Then, he squeezes his eyelids shut and shakes his head. "Shit, this isn't working, is it?"

"If you mean setting up boundaries between us, yeah, probably not. Especially not when you're—" I jerk my chin at his naked torso.

He glances down as if surprised, then reaches over, grabs a T-shirt and pulls it on. "Better?"

"Umm." I take in the way the soft, much-washed fabric clings to his shoulders, outlines his pecs and nipples, and traces the narrowness of his waist. I blow out a breath and close my eyes. "I'm too aware of you, and it's all your fault. The way you dry-humped me earlier has made me hungry for more of the same." I open my eyes, then yelp, for he's standing over me, arms over his chest. I didn't sense him move. For someone so big and bulky, he moves so lightly, he may as well be wearing skates, even outside the rink.

There's hunger in his eyes, and also, frustration. "We only need to make this work until Grams gets through her surgery."

I nod slowly, "at least I stopped the fight with Denni—" His glare intensifies, I correct myself, "I mean my ex."

His features soften. "Were you worried about me?"

"Of course I was." I slap at his shoulder. "I'm wearing your ring. It means...something." *Oh god, did I say that? How could I have let that slip? It means nothing that I'm wearing his ring. Nothing. This is an arrangement, that's all it is. So, why do I feel sick inside at the thought of him putting his life and his career in jeopardy?*

A slow burn starts somewhere behind his eyes, until that cold fire crackles in his irises. It feels like the dark blue air bubbles you see trapped under a sheet of ice. Bubbles which ebb and flow and burst, lending intensity to his expression, the one that has always pinned me down and rendered me helpless to his influence.

"Forget it; it's your life. Do whatever you want to do with it." I lower my hand and begin to turn away, then gasp when he clamps his fingers around my neck and pulls me into him.

36

Rick

She stumbles into me. Her sweet honeysuckle scent teases my senses and goes straight to my head. Her gaze widens; she looks up at me and her pupils dilate. "Wh-what are you doing?" she whispers.

"The ring means something to you, hmm?"

She swallows, then holds up her hand and looks at the circle of diamonds. "I don't want it to. It's an empty gesture, so the rest of the world can believe our farce, but from the moment you slipped it on my finger"—she laughs, a low confused sound—"it felt like we were connected."

"I felt it, too."

She jerks up her chin. "You did?" She swallows.

"Do you still have feelings for that douchebag, Dennis?"

She hesitates. And it's as if she's plunged a sword into my chest. Anger sparks at my nerve-endings; my chest tightens. She must see something on my face for she shakes her head. "You're misunderstand. I told you I was in love with him when we were in a relationship. And at least according to how I felt then, I thought I was in love. I know now it probably wasn't. But I'm still upset from walking in on him with another woman, someone who was my friend, no less."

"She was your friend?" I frown. *Why the hell didn't I know about this?*

"*Was.* She worked at the same agency as me. She worked on different accounts, and we competed to get promoted in the company...for awards...to win the biggest accounts. I thought we were friends, but I guess she didn't. Which became painfully clear when she decided my personal life wasn't off limits, ya know?" Hurt clings to her expression. The sides of her lips draw down. "When I think about it now, I realize it wasn't so much that I was sad to lose Dennis. It was the betrayal that hurt—the idea that two people I trusted, two people I considered allies, would do something behind my back that they knew would hurt me... She was a colleague. I thought of her as a friend, but she viewed me as an adversary." She sighs. "I don't know, I suppose it was my fault. I was so focused on building my career, I didn't have enough time for Dennis and—"

"Stop. Don't blame yourself for what happened. No matter what went down, I know you gave it your best shot. She's a bitch and never deserved to have a friend like you. And it's Dennis's fault that he didn't understand you and support you. If you'd been mine, I'd have never allowed you to get hurt. I'd have done everything in my power to make you happy. I'd have supported your career, and been there for you emotionally, mentally"—I bend my knees and peer into her eyes—"physically."

She swallows. "When you say these words with such conviction, I'm almost sure you mean it."

"I never say anything I don't mean."

"And the way you always know what to say to calm me down, it's just..." She shakes her head. "It's so right."

I massage the muscles at the base of her neck which have wound up as we've been talking. I dig my fingers into the tendons and work out the knots.

She sighs and melts into me. "Thanks." She pushes her forehead into my chest, then wraps her arms about my waist. "That feels so good."

I bring up my other hand and continue to knead her back, her shoulders, then the dip at the base of her neck. "Oh my god," she groans, and the blood drains to my groin.

She makes a humming sound at the back of her throat, and my cock instantly lengthens. My balls tense, and my pulse rate speeds up. She moves in closer, and when her pelvis cradles the tent at my crotch, she freezes. "Umm... You're."

"Ignore it," I say through gritted teeth.

She looks up at me, and her eyes are languorous. Her features are flushed. "I want to help, but I have my period."

"So?"

She blinks. "There's… a lot of blood down there."

"I'm not one to shy away from a rainbow kiss, baby."

Her features turn as red as the blood she referred to. "You mean you'd—"

"Kiss your pussy while you're on your period? Absolutely—"

"—not." She begins to back away, but I tighten my hold on her. "Where do you think you're going?"

"Oh, um, I don't think it's sanitary, you putting your mouth down there when I'm…you know—" She winces a little.

I frown. "What's wrong?"

"Cramps, that's all. I get them when I have my period. Also, my breasts get tender." I glance down at the jut of her chest. "And my legs hurt sometimes, and I feel all bloated and yucky, so—"

"So you're not in the mood to fuck."

She winces again.

"It *is* fucking, isn't it?" I watch her reaction closely.

"Only fucking," she says in a remote voice, and it pisses me off. And I don't know why. It *is* fucking. That's all there can be between us. So, why do I want to kiss that sad look off her face, and smooth out the furrows in her forehead, and hold her close and soothe and tell her…what exactly? That we're no longer playing make-believe? That I'm developing feelings for her?

Which is why I told her I was setting boundaries, in the first place. I'm running scared. I can face down a puck traveling at 170 miles per hour, but at the first sign she's getting to me, I'm ready to run?

No, I'm not a coward. I have other things I need to focus on. I can't let this go any further, but I also can't turn my back on her. Not when we convinced Grams to go in for her surgery. Once she's completed it, then perhaps, I can break off this engagement and focus on proving myself in hockey.

Hockey is the one thing I've always wanted in life, the one thing I haven't been able to have. I had to settle for an alternate career, and it always rankled me that I couldn't pursue my dream of leading my team into the finals of the Cup. And while the League isn't the Cup, it's as important in this part of the world. It'll give me a chance to redeem myself in my own eyes. Give me a chance to be noticed among my peers around the world. This is the chance I've been waiting for. The only chance I'll get. I only have a few more years left of playing professionally on the ice.

I cannot afford the distraction that comes with getting involved with a woman. I *almost* fucked her… but it cannot go further than that. I release her, then step back. "Lay down."

37

Gio

"Excuse me?" I frown up at him. "Didn't you hear what I said? I'm not in the mood to fuck."

"There won't be any fucking involved."

"Then why do you want me to—"

"I thought you said you trust me?"

I lock my fingers together and begin to play with the ring on my left hand, then realize what I'm doing and stop. I cannot get used to this piece of jewelry. I'll have to return it to him, at some point. Soon, by the looks of it. His grandmother will have the procedure, and Dennis will give up any hope he harbors of getting together with me. The thought doesn't upset me as much as I thought it would. Perhaps, I'm getting over what he did to me? No doubt, all this interaction with Rick is helping me move on, as well.

"Do you, Goldie?" He tilts his head. "Do you trust me?"

I'm attracted to him, a lot. I'm not sure, yet, if I like him. But trusting him? Yeah, my instinct says he's not like Dennis. He's not using me as arm candy. He's not going to take advantage of me—not unless I ask him to—and he's not going to do anything I don't want. I do trust him. More than I ever did

Dennis. More than I do my own mother, with whom I've never had a great relationship.

I've always trusted myself, always held myself up to high standards. I've always relied on myself to get things done, to overcome challenges. And I should think of him as one, too, only, I know there's more to it than that. This connection I've felt to him since the first time I saw him signals to me I can trust him.

When I nod, he releases a breath. His shoulders relax. He nods toward the bed. "Lay down, Goldie."

I lower myself back onto the bed and, instantly, feel even more at a disadvantage. I open my mouth to tell him this is a mistake, but he beats me to it.

He jerks his chin. "I'll be back."

To my surprise, he spins around and heads out of the room. My stomach spasms again, I grimace. I should get up and get myself a painkiller. In fact, a hot water bottle would be great, too. Except, I don't have one. In my hurry to leave L.A., I left so much of my stuff behind, and I haven't had the time to buy a new one. Also, more of that massage which started this entire episode with Rick.

I try to breathe through the next eddy of pain. Damn, why do periods have to be so painful? I curl into a ball trying to lessen the pain, not that it helps. I squeeze my eyes and breathe through the next wave. I must have drifted off, for the next thing I know, I hear his voice saying, "Take this."

I open my eyes and peek up to find he's holding out his hand with what looks like painkillers and a glass of water. Huh? I sit up, take it from him, then down two tablets with water. He places the glass on the nightstand, along with a mug of steaming liquid and a tiny bottle of essential oil.

"What's all this?"

"Yoda's big on essential oils and herbal teas, so—" He shrugs.

"So, you went over and asked him for some of it? What did you tell him?"

"That you have your period."

"You told him I have my period?" I cry.

"Of course not." His lips quirk. "He wasn't in his room, so I helped myself to his stash."

I open my mouth to protest, but he shakes his head. "He won't miss it. Now, drink your tea."

"Why are you being so nice to me?"

"I'd do the same thing if one of my teammates was suffering from an injury."

"Hmm."

"You don't believe me?"

No, I don't. "It doesn't matter." I reach for the cup of tea and blow on it. The scent of lavender fills my senses, and already, I can feel my body relax further. I take a couple of sips, then place the mug back on the side table.

"Lay back now and pull up your kimono."

"Why?"

"Only so I can massage this into your stomach."

"You don't need to do that."

He glares at me. "Lay. Back. Goldie." He infuses enough authority into his voice, goosebumps pepper my skin. A heavy pulse flares to life between my legs. I comply, and his gaze flickers with an emotion I can only classify as satisfaction.

"Good girl," he says in that low, hard voice, and my scalp tingles. My toes curl. A flush of pleasure tugs at my lower belly and overrides the discomfort there. My entire body feels heavy. My limbs sink into the mattress. I manage to grip the edge of my kimono and pull it up to below my breasts. I'm baring my panties, but he's already seen me without them so it shouldn't matter that he's seeing me in such a state of undress. Besides, I'm in too much pain and that massage sounds heavenly.

He pours some of the lavender oil into his palm and rubs his hands together. A floral and woodsy scent fills the room. He swipes his palm gently across my lower belly, and the hairs on my forearms stand on end. His palm is big and warm and engulfs my stomach. I glance down to where the contrast of his dark skin with my much paler skin sends a primal thrill zipping up my spine. My thighs clench. I manage to not squeeze my legs together, manage to hold myself still as he rubs circles over my stomach. He must sense the tension radiating off of me for he murmurs, "Relax, I've got you."

That's what I'm afraid of.

"Close your eyes and focus on the movement of my hands on your body."

The flush of pleasure between my legs turns into a heavy pulse. This time, I can't stop myself from squeezing them together. A sharp inhale from him tells me he's noticed my reaction. However, he doesn't stop those circular motions over my middle. The comfort of his touch seeps into my blood and vibrates out to my extremities. My muscles relax, one by one. I close my eyes. It's as if it's a signal, for he increases the circumference of his movements, and each sweep brings him closer and closer to my breasts. He slips his fingers under the side of my waist then back up, and again, and when he brushes the curve of my breasts, a delicious sensation vibrates out from his touch. A sigh ripples up my chest.

"Better?" He clears his throat.

Without opening my eyes, I nod. On the next sweep, he slides his fingers under the kimono and cups my breasts. That melting sensation deepens and encompasses my chest. My nipples tighten, but not in a painful manner. He continues to caress my body and every part of me seems to be melting. My brain cells dissolve, and my arms and legs feel heavy. Even my eyelids seem to be weighed down. I'm a puddle on need reflecting back his image. I'm sinking, sinking into this oblivious space where I can no longer feel pain.

This...is better than any painkiller, better than trying to drown my pain with alcohol, which I'm afraid I tried to do in the past, when the cramps became too much for me to bear. It's not healthy, but I'd often reach a point where I was unable to cope with my agony. Normally, it'd be me suffering alone in the house while Dennis was off at some event or another. His need to be seen by the right people and add to his image meant he was out of the house most nights, including those when I had my period. I never mentioned to him how much having my periods caused me distress. It's not as if he was interested in my comfort, anyway. Unlike Rick.

His firm yet gentle touch fills my pores, my cells, even permeates my extremities. I fall back further into myself, that thick quagmire of sleep drawing me in. I'm so loosened up that when he touches the kimono bunched around my chest, and asks, "Can I take this off?", I jerk my chin.

He turns me on my side. I worry about the oil staining the sheet, and I try to say that aloud, but my words are slurred. Still, he understands me for he murmurs, "Don't worry about it." Then he unties the kimono and slides it down my shoulder. He tugs it off, before coaxing me onto my back and pulling the silken fabric down my other arm.

I sigh. That feels good. My body unwinds further, and when he circles my nipples, a whimper of satisfaction spills from my lips.

38

Rick

My cock is hard, my balls are hard, and my thighs are... hard. All of the muscles in my body are—you guessed it—fucking hard. This is torture. Touching her, massaging her body, kneading her muscles so the pain leaks out of her tissues. And I know I'm succeeding in easing the pain from her body; she's more relaxed than I've ever seen her.

Her breathing is deep. Her chest rises and falls and her tits... Her gorgeous tits gleam as a result of the oil I'm stroking into them. Her nipples are pink and juicy, and my mouth waters to take a taste, but I will not. This, right now, is about her comfort, her relaxation, relieving her soreness. I whisper my thumbs across her nipples, and the pulse at the base of her throat speeds up. She parts her lips, and the scent of her arousal intensifies.

My fingers tremble, and my heart rate speeds up. I slide my hands under her breasts and weigh them. This time, she moans, and the sound is so fucking erotic. It's a call to the primitive side of me to bury myself inside her. To mate her. To claim her. To make her mine. She is mine. There's no doubt in my mind, and I'll do everything in my power to keep her happy. And that means, not making love to her now. That means, finding a way to squeeze out the last dregs of discomfort from her flesh so she can drift into sleep.

I bend and blow my breath over her nipple; she whines. I trace my fingers around her nipples again, then down the center of her stomach. Her ribcage stands out under her skin. I pause.

She's so thin. Isn't she eating properly? Whenever I make food for her, she finishes everything on her plate. She even finished the dessert at dinner with Grams. So why does she feel so fragile? And it's not because her build is tiny. Maybe her metabolism is such that she burns off everything? Maybe. But maybe, I should keep an eye on her. I trace the space between each rib, and she shudders.

"Rick," she murmurs. Her voice is sleepy, and lust drips from each syllable. My dick instantly hardens further. I manage to swat away my desire and drag my mind back from the need-filled space it's ventured into. This is about her, remember? About her. Only about her. I trail my fingers toward the waistband of her panties, then under it.

"Take 'em off," she slurs.

I want to. You have no idea how much I want to. But if I do, I won't be able to hold myself back, and I don't want that, Not for tonight. Instead, I dip my head and press my lips to her lower belly. She moans again, and my pulse rate goes through the roof.

Shit, when I started to massage her, I didn't mean for it to go down this route. And I'm not going to fuck her. But she's turned on, and if I can make her come, it's bound to relax her even more and draw out any remaining pain from her body. Only challenge: I'm going to have to do it without touching her pussy. I know if I do I'll lose the last vestiges of my self-control. I slide my hands up to cup her breasts, then drag the scruff of my chin around the outside of her waistband. This time, a full body shudder grips her. I nibble little kisses to her lower belly, then pass my nose into the apex of her thighs.

"Rick, please." She thrusts up her pelvis. No matter, she's still wearing her panties. It doesn't stop the heady scent of her arousal from saturating the air. The sound of her panting reaches me and drains any remaining blood to my groin. I drag my nose up her fabric covered pussy lips, then caress her nipples again. She arches her back, pushing her lower body up, chasing her release. I continue to very gently brush my fingertips back and forth over her nipples, and again, then drag my whisker-covered chin over her fabric covered core.

"Oh Rick," she whimpers. Her hips quiver, and her thighs clench. She gasps, and I know she's close.

I release her breasts, only to bring my hands down and under her butt. I squeeze the rounded flesh, and a low cry emerges from her lips. I rise up and over her, and still massaging her rounded arse, I place my lips over hers. I share her breath, fill my lungs with her fragrance, then blow lightly up her cheek.

"Come for me, Goldie," I whisper, and with a silent tremor, the orgasm rolls over her. She opens her mouth in a soundless cry, and I place my lips over hers. Not kissing her, simply absorbing her wordless pleasure. As her body twitches with the aftershocks, I allow myself to press a kiss to her forehead, then I roll over and position her again on her side. "Sleep, baby."

Her breathing deepens. Her eyelids are shut, and with a final twitch, she stills. I slide the kimono out from under her, and she doesn't stir. Then, draw the sheet over both of us and spoon her. Despite the hardness between my legs and that agonizing need to empty my balls, I wrap my arm about her, place my hand over her lower belly where she was hurting and drift off to sleep.

When I open my eyes next, I'm alone. I touch her pillow and find it's cold. How did she wake up and get out of bed without rousing me? I'm a light sleeper, at the best of times. And since the accident that took my parents from me, I've yet to manage a good night's sleep. Apparently, the cure for my insomnia is being curled around the body of my fiancée. I mean, my fake fiancée.

I sit up, glance around the empty room, and a knot of apprehension squeezes my belly. Or is that a result of my morning wood? I roll out of bed, stand, then groan when the throbbing heaviness between my thighs makes itself known. Fucking dick, doesn't know when it needs to keep down and out of the way. If there's time, I'll go to the bathroom and jerk off before heading downstairs.

I snatch up my phone, then groan when I realize it's dead. In my hurry to spoon her and hold her last night, not to mention the temptation that was her body, I forgot to charge my phone. Fucking fuck. Judging by the early morning light slanting through the windows, I've overslept. And I'm the team captain. I cannot afford to be late for practice. No time to change, I grab my kit, pull on a sweatshirt, step into my sneakers and run down the stairs.

The scent of coffee beckons me from the kitchen. That and the sound of her voice, interspersed with male laughter. What the fuck? Who the hell is in there with her and at this time of the morning? I speed up until I'm almost running, and when I burst into the kitchen, come to a stop. She's standing with her hand on Finn's arm. And he's looking deeply into her eyes.

I move forward. "Get away from her."

39

Gio

I take a step back, but Finn, damn him, catches my arm. There's a smirk on his face and a mischievous glint in his eyes. I scowl at him, but his grin only widens. Heavy steps approach us, but before Rick can reach us, Finn has pulled me in. At the same time, Caspian — Mr. Prick himself — steps up behind me. He's not touching me. Neither is Finn — but for his fingers around my wrist — but I'm sure from where Rick stands, and considering how pissed off he sounds, it seems like I'm sandwiched between the two men. A prospect I might have welcomed before I met my very own wet dream of a man.

"Let her go." Rick reaches us and glares at where Finn is holding me.

"Or what?" Finn says in a jovial voice.

"Or I'm going to sink my fist in your face." He turns that burning blue gaze onto Caspian. "And that goes for you, too, asshole."

"You'd raise a hand against your teammate?" Caspian scoffs.

"For her, I'd have gone against my own family. She comes first. Better get that into your thick skulls."

Finn and Caspian exchange glances, then Caspian holds out a hand. "You owe me."

Finn groans, then steps back, before pulling out a bill and stuffing it in

Caspian's outstretched palm. Instantly, Rick pulls me into him and tucks me under his arm.

Of course, I melt into his side. Tingles course up and down my body. That was...

"Arright—" Caspian holds up his other fist, and Finn bumps it. Caspian turns to Rick with a shit-eating grin on his face. "Keep this up, Rickster, and I'll be singing all the way to the bank."

"Fuck the both of you. And why are you still here? Aren't you late for practice?"

"So are you," Finn points out.

"Couldn't miss the chance to get under your skin, and I have to say, it was disappointingly easy." Caspian laughs.

"I'm going to hand you your arses in practice." Rick's voice is mild, but under my cheek, his heart is pumping so hard, he might as well be having a cardiac event.

I manage to lean my head back a little—because the man's holding me so tightly, I can just about draw a breath. "You okay?"

"Why wouldn't I be?" he asks without looking at me. "Out!" He glares at the two other men, then nods toward the door.

"We asked the bus to wait for us. You could thank us for that, by the way," Caspian murmurs.

"Also, we may have stretched the truth a bit. We have just enough time to get to the rink in time if you make it out in the next five minutes," Finn drawls.

"Get the fuck out you guys, or—"

"Bye Gio," Caspian calls out.

"That's fucking Mac to you," Rick growls.

"Bye G—" Finn says in a sing-song voice.

Without releasing me, Rick reaches over, grabs a wooden ladle and lobs it at him. It misses Finn, who ducked, and is already at the door. His laughter reaches us as he heads toward the front door.

"Jesus, you're in a violent mood," I scold him. "You could have hurt, Finn."

"Nah, I'm a crack shot." He looks into my eyes and it's like I'm being struck by the intensity of his eyes for the first time. Those cerulean blues of his hold a world of pain and secrets, and am I ever going to get to know him enough to find out what's playing out in his mind?

He holds my gaze for a few seconds more, then his own softens. He tucks a strand of errant hair behind my ear. "I wouldn't have hit him unless I wanted to, which I did, but I wasn't going to. Also, arshole's too fast. He has to be, to be the goalie. His reflexes are still as sharp as when he played in the NHL. The bastard hasn't lost any of his agility —"

"Unlike you?" I search his features.

He looks rested, but his cheekbones are more prominent than when I first met him.

"Oh, I'm fast, but Finn's always been the slippery one on ice. He's fast, flexible, and has very quick reaction times, not to mention, his hand-eye coordination is incomparable. If anything, he's faster than when he played at the NHL."

"But the two of you never played together, am I right?'

"He joined the NHL after I left."

"Why *did* you leave?"

He blows out a breath. "Let's park that discussion for now, shall we?"

"But you'll tell me?" I persist.

"I will, I promise," his voice grows lower in tone, all rumbly and growly, and my pussy instantly dampens.

"How are you feeling this morning?" he asks in that same edged-with-sex voice.

"Amazing."

"No cramps?" He looks between my eyes.

I shake my head.

"And the blood flow. Are you —"

"Jesus, Rick, can we stop talking about my period?"

He frowns. "Why? It's nothing to be ashamed of."

"It's not, but it's also not something I want to talk about with my fiancê first thing in the morning the night after we — ah —" I clamp my lips together.

"After we? You mean, after I, don't you?" The left side of his mouth twitches. Bastard's having a good ol' laugh at my expense.

"Fine, fine. After you massaged away my cramps, then made me come and forget all about the invasion of the red tide."

He blinks. "Invasion of the red tide?"

"Or you can call it Shark Week."

His lips twitch. "That one, I like."

"Of course, you would. " I roll my eyes.

He cups my cheek. "I'm glad you're feeling better, Goldie, and you should know, a little period blood wouldn't have stopped me, except you were in pain and I didn't want to add to your discomfort.

The tenderness in his eyes throws me. Sure, he showed me last night how in tune with my needs he is. In a way, no one ever has been before. Not my ex, and not my family. Yeah, I avoid thinking about my family, unless I absolutely have to. But after meeting Grams, I feel the lack of parental figures in my life even more.

That's what happens when you never knew your dad and you have a junkie mom who loves to take out her frustrations on you by beating you up.

That's what happens when you grow up in a trailer park and keep walking in on your mom turning tricks to score. That's what happens when your mother's boyfriends start eyeing you up when you hit puberty. Good thing I managed to leave home before any of them touched me. It's a tired story; one you must have heard before. But when you're in it, it scars you forever, and I'm living proof of it.

I'll save you the time of psychoanalyzing me. It's the reason why I started starving myself, which was easy because there was never anything to eat at home. But even later, once I started earning and could provide for myself, I felt guilty about eating. As a result, I now have an unhealthy relationship with food. It's why I make long to-do lists, so I can take control of my life. If I get through my list, everything will be okay. If I cross things off, I've achieved something. Not that my to-do lists ever get shorter.

I don't need a shrink to tell me that every time I cross something off the list I get a burst of happy hormones in my system, which make me feel good. Like how you feel when you post on social media, and someone likes your update.

Which is why I also know I should see a shrink about my habit of not wanting to keep food down after I've eaten. I thought I had it under control, too, until Dennis' betrayal unraveled things and I felt myself slipping back. Yeah, it shows me how delicate this balance is. Something doesn't go according to plan, and I slip back into old habits. Not that it's a habit. It was a condition, I know, I know. But I had it under control... Until I didn't.

It's why I can't afford to get involved with anyone else. It's why I'm pretending I don't have feelings for Rick. It's the only thing that will keep Rick from getting involved with me for real. Though, after last night, I'm not sure anymore. Maybe he is catching feelings for me? Maybe I've begun to invest emotionally in him, too. Gosh, this entire situation is another slippery slope, and I can't afford to slip up. "Rick, don't."

40

Gio

I step back, and he lowers his hand to his side.

"Don't what?" he murmurs.

"Don't go all soft on me now."

His brow knits. "If you mean taking care of you last night—"

"That's exactly what I mean." I run my hands down my skirt. Yeah, I managed to shower and change into my work clothes before I came down. It wasn't easy to ignore the man-chest of the alphahole sprawled on the bed, but I managed to keep my gaze averted as I dressed.

Okay, I lie, I snuck quick peeks. He threw off the sheet while I was in the shower, and while he was still fully dressed, his T-shirt clung to every ridge and valley of his sculpted abs, not to mention the tent at his crotch. An erection from last night compounded by morning wood. As far as I know, he didn't come. I'm pretty sure he didn't leave the bed to go off to the bathroom and jerk off. At least the one time I woke up, he was wrapped around me, and I could feel the thickness of his length between my asscheeks. I fell back to sleep before I could do anything about it, either. That's how relaxed I was after his ministrations. And he didn't have to do that last night. He didn't have to be so sweet.

"I can't reconcile this side of you with the grumpyass you normally are."

He searches my features, then nods. "I can understand why it must seem so confusing. This is a charade, and here I am, doing things a real-life fiancé would do for you."

I tilt my head. "I can't understand how you are so reasonable sometimes."

"I'm *always* reasonable," he murmurs.

"You're joking, right?"

His lips kick up on one side, so he has that one-sided smile on his face that's so freakin' sexy. My heart stutters a little.

"Maybe I am... a little," he agrees. "But I'm not unnecessarily unreasonable."

I stare at him.

"I don't go out of my way to be cheery, but I also don't make things difficult for other people."

"And what do you call asking me to move into your room, knowing full-well there was only one bed, and then asking me to pose as your fiancée, *and* making it impossible for me to refuse?"

"I call that a transaction." He raises a shoulder.

"It didn't make my life easier, necessarily."

"It helped you get back at your wankhole of an ex."

"It did." I look away, then back at him. "I guess I'm confused because you said you wanted to re-instate boundaries and then you were—"

"Massaging away your pain?" His forehead furrows. "It's a little confusing to me, too. I hadn't meant it to turn into a seduction routine or make you come — Okay, maybe I did want to make you come, but only because I knew it would relax you further. But I'm all for the boundaries."

I rub at my temple. "This entire discussion is giving me a headache. Also..." I lower my hand and scowl up at him. "You told me you'll tell me about your family."

"If you tell me about yours?"

I fold my arms about my waist. "I don't talk about my family with anyone."

"Neither do I."

I jerk my head in his direction. "You introduced me to your Grams."

"But you don't know about my past."

I have a sense of it from the pictures I saw on the walls of his grandmother's house, but I also noticed they stopped when he was a teenager. After that, there are no pictures of them together as a family, and I have to admit, I'm curious.

"The only reason I want to know about your past is so I can do a better job as the PR manager of the team." I tip up my chin.

He widens his stance. "And the only reason I want to know about your past is so when I'm interviewed about you by the media, I know enough to keep this charade alive."

"O-kay." I nod slowly.

"Okay." He holds out his hand. "Shall we do it over dinner tonight?"

"So, he's taking you out to dinner?" Mira squeals over the phone.

I increase the distance between the phone and my face. "Jeez, pipe down, will ya?"

"He's taking you out to dinner; that's a big deal."

"He's taken me out to dinner before," I remind her.

"That was to his grandmother's place which, if you ask me, is already a big deal."

"And one of the main reasons we embarked on this farce of an engagement." My emotions have been on such a roller-coaster, I had to confide in her about the reality of the situation and make her swear to secrecy. Which is unusual. I'm not used to confiding in others. I'm used to relying only on myself. But being in a different country and in a new job has made me more vulnerable than usual. That's the only reason I confided in Mira—I only know her through Solene, but she's been so warm and friendly, and I get the impression she's not judgmental, so I couldn't help but share the true situation with her.

"You don't sound happy about it," she murmurs.

"I'm not." I train my gaze down at the men gliding along the ice. I'm standing in one of the VIP boxes that overlooks the rink and gives me a bird's-eye view of the practice session. I've positioned myself sufficiently to the side so if any of the players look up, they won't spot me at once. From my vantage point, I can make out the #13 jersey, and even if he didn't have a number on the back, I'd know it was him from his size and the breadth of his shoulders. All kitted out in his protective equipment, the man looks like a beast, and damn, but I'm even more attracted to him now.

As I watch, Rick bends low with a controlled motion, then lifts the puck off the ice and over the defender's skates. Caspian picks up the puck and throws it at the goal. Finn, the goalie, drops down on his knees in a butterfly stance but is unable to stop it. Yeah, I'm learning about ice hockey and my vocabulary is improving. I can even tell you that was a saucer pass Rick used with the puck. The men break into cheers; Rick and Caspian high-five each other. Apparently, their enmity is forgotten on the ice. And that's how good professionals are. And Rick is a professional, no matter that he's going to face that ass Dennis in a real-life brawl.

If the press gets wind of it, it's going to be ugly. It's a PR professional's nightmare, to be honest. Especially if they find out that the woman at the center of the brawl is me.

Below me, the whistle blows, and the players slow to a stop. Rick and Finn bump glove-covered fists, then pat each other on their backs before they follow the others off the ice.

"Gio, you there?" Mira's voice reaches me.

I shake out of my reverie and give her my full attention. "Sorry, was watching the practice match."

"Ooh, so did the two of you drive there together, like a real engaged couple?"

"No, we didn't, because we're not a real engaged couple."

"Hmm," she scowls.

I roll my eyes. "Okay, enough with your hmms. What are you thinking? Out with it, woman."

"Just that the chemistry between the two of you in the pictures I've seen online seems real. If you hadn't told me it was all pretend, I wouldn't have guessed it."

"So you thought I moved to London, fell in love with the captain of the hockey team, and got engaged to him in the space of weeks?"

"When you know, you know."

"Oh boy, you're such a romantic."

"And you could do with being more of one." She half smiles.

"I read enough spicy books to know romance only belongs between the page flips of a Kindle and not in real life."

"Oh my god, that's so cynical."

"That's me."

"And yet, you read romance novels?"

"That's *why* I read romance novels," I correct her. "There's something reassuring about reading about all that groveling and all those declarations of love and grand gestures, not to mention the spicy scenes which—" I pause.

"Which?" She tilts her head.

"Doesn't matter."

"No, go on. You can't leave me hanging like that. What were you going to say?"

I flush. "Nothing."

She surveys my features, then that smile on her face broadens. "You were going to say that you thought the spicy scenes only belonged in the smutty romance novels you read, but now that you've slept with that sex on-a-hockey-stick, you realize it's not the case anymore."

My flush rises to my scalp. "We may have slept together, but we haven't had sex."

She blinks slowly. "So, you two did sleep together?"

"Only we didn't sleep 'sleep' together." I make air-quotes with my fingers.

"Well, maybe you need to sleep 'sleep' together." She mirrors my air-quotes. "Maybe you should give him a chance. He might live up your book boyfriends on all other fronts."

"You haven't been listening to me. There is nothing between us. Nothing except—"

"Intense, panty-melting, chemistry which will likely lead to hot, sweaty sex?" She smirks.

I shake my head, then sober. "I'm not convinced it's just sex, either."

"Eh?" She blinks.

"He took care of me last night."

"What do you mean?"

I bite the inside of my cheek. "I had bad cramps from my period, and he massaged lavender oil into my stomach and—"

"He massaged lavender oil into your stomach because you were on your period?" she cries out.

"—and then he spooned me all night." I'm not going to tell her he made me come without touching my clit which—oh my god, Dennis hadn't even managed to do with his penis.

Yeah, it's a penis. I can't call it a dick. It would be a disgrace to dicks everywhere to call that pale, less-than-average-sized, utility tool my ex sported in his pants a dick. The one I saw when he'd fucked my "friend" in our bed. That's when I realized I wasn't missing anything. Ricks' cock, though... It's a cock's cock. A master-of-all-he-surveys cock. A cock that would give an anaconda a run for its money. I squeeze my eyes shut.

What is wrong with me? It's like my mind has a mind of its own—ha-ha—traveling down paths of thought I don't want it to. This has got to stop.

"That's not all, is it?" Mira chuckles. " I'm not going to force you to tell me if you don't want to. The very fact that he spooned you, woman? That's like hot and sweet and seriously sexy."

What is it about a man curving his body to fit the contours of your own that makes it more erotic than having his dick, and his fingers, and tongue inside you, all at the same time?

"Spooning releases 'cuddle hormones.' It's why it's so awesome. Of course, I have to admit, I love savage sex and make-up sex, as well as spooning after sex," she says with a huge grin.

He's already delivered on the third—without the sex—and I'm sure he'd be good at the first and the second, as well. Not that we're going to have a lover's quarrel, because we're not lovers. Which makes us *almost*-sex buddies. More like puck buddies, and—my phone buzzes with an incoming call.

I groan, "I have to take this. I'm sorry, Mira."

"I'm seeing you at Abby's house tomorrow for a girl's night, right?"

"Okay." I nod, though I'm not going for the girl's night. That's not my scene.

"If I don't see you, I'm coming to your place to drag you there," she warns.

"Fine, okay. I gotta go." I disconnect and answer the other call.

"Hello, Dennis."

41

Rick

I prowl into the empty VIP box and find her holding her phone up to her ear. She's looking into the distance, a wrinkle between her eyebrows. Her lips are turned down, her shoulders hunched forward. Whatever the conversation is about, it's not making her happy.

"I understand, but—" she begins, but must get cut off because I can hear the person on the other end say something. The words are not comprehensible, but the depth of the voice makes it clear it's a man.

"I know we had a plan, but Dennis—" She squeezes her eyes shut and listens to him.

Anger twists my guts. I'm thankful I didn't stop to shower but only stripped off my protective gear, pulled on my sweatshirt and changed into my trainers before getting here. I knew there was a reason I had to hurry here after I saw her peeking through the glass panes. Oh, she thought she'd hidden herself, but all it took was a curve of her shoulder, and I knew who it was.

"You're right. We were together for almost a year, but you have to understand—"

I reach her, grab the phone from her and bark, "Keep away from her. She's my fiancée, and if I catch you trying to reach her again, I'll kill you when we fight." I disconnect the call and slide the phone into my pocket.

"That's my phone."

"And you're not going to get it back if you keep talking to your ex."

"The entire point of this fake relationship is so that I piss him off."

"Exactly. It's not about you getting all warm and cozy with that doucheface."

"What's it to you, anyway?" She throws up her hands, and the light bounces off of the diamonds on her ring. "Our relationship is fake. We established that earlier today. You have no rights over me. No rights."

"What did you say?" I glare at her, and the color pales from her cheeks.

She swallows, then tips her head back. "Your D-Dom voice doesn't faze me."

"Oh?" I take a step forward, and she sidles back. I close the distance between us and crowd her until her back touches the glass wall. She stiffens.

"What are you doing?" she asks in a breathless voice.

"I'm going to punish you for your sass."

Her gaze widens, and her pupils dilate. The pulse at the base of her neck kicks up. "P-p-punish me? Why would you punish me?"

"Because you spoke with your ex. And I don't share, Goldie. You're my fiancée—"

"F-fake fiancée," she stutters.

"—and I intend to show you what that means."

I bend my knees and peer into her eyes. "Of course, you could make a run for it."

"What?"

"Run, Goldie, and if you manage to make it out of this room, I'll back off."

"You're crazy. We agreed we'd have boundaries in place."

"I changed my mind."

She stares at me like I'm crazy, which admittedly, I am—crazy with jealousy since I overheard her talking to her ex. That churning feeling in my stomach spreads to my chest. My heart pounds into my ribcage. Adrenaline laces my blood. It's as if I'm back on the ice, in pursuit of the puck... Only, in this case, there's so much more at stake.

"You shouldn't have threatened him; he might use that against you."

"Fuck him," I snap.

"You need to care more about your future."

"I care about you."

"What?"

"Fuck!" I squeeze my eyes shut, then shake my head to clear it. Not that it helps. When I look at her, she's staring at me with a myriad of emotions in her eyes, the most obvious one of which is confusion. *Fuck, fuck, fuck, I didn't mean for that to come out. Hell, I hadn't even admitted it to myself yet, and here I am, saying it aloud. It's only after I heard myself speak… I realized I mean it, too. And I don't want this. This was not part of the plan.* "You'd better run, baby. If not, I'm going to take it as a sign that you're giving in without a fight."

She scowls. "Giving into what without a fight?"

"Fuck or flight, baby."

"Excuse me, did you snow clone fight or flight?"

His smirks before he decides to ignore me. "You have until I count to five."

"I can't believe you're doing this, you—"

"Five…" I reach for her.

She squeaks, "That's cheating."

When it comes to you, I'll do anything to make you mine.

She ducks and slips past me, only because I let her, of course. I wait. Wait until she's halfway across the floor, and only because it's going to make the chase so much more satisfying. Then, I set off. She hears me coming and increases her speed. Her high-heeled pumps thump onto the floor. She reaches the door and slides one foot out. That's when I reach her and clap my fingers around her neck, turning her to face me. Her chest rises and falls; her eyes shine. She opens her mouth, and I'm sure she's going to scream. Instead, she slaps me. The sound echoes around the empty room. Her gaze widens until her eyes seem to fill her face.

I click my tongue. "You shouldn't have done that, Goldie." I release her long enough to bend and throw her over my shoulder.

This time, she yells, "What are you doing?"

I carry her over to the glass wall—pocketing a paper napkin from the bar counter on the way— and lower her to her feet.

She sidles back until her back is flush against the sheet of glass. Her cheeks are flushed, her eyes flashing those golden sparks that cut me to my knees. She's so goddamn gorgeous, so alive. She tries to stay in control, but she's a fiery, sassy, ball of light that illuminates the dark corners of my life. I kick her legs apart, and she raises her hand and slaps me again. My cock extends, and my balls are instantly hard. All that suppressed need from last night roars forward. I lean in until the edge of my thigh rubs into her core. She gasps, her breathing grows rougher, then she raises her hand again.

Before she can slap me a third time, I've grabbed her wrist and flipped her around, so her chest is pressed up against the glass. Her cheek is smashed into the pane, her chest flattened against it, I twist her arm behind her back and step into her. She gasps, and I know it's because she can feel the evidence of my arousal between her arse-cheeks.

She looks at me from the corner of her eyes. "Let me go." Her voice is breathless, her features flushed... With anger? With excitement? Both, likely.

"Not until you pay for what you did."

"What did I do?"

"You made me admit my true feelings for you."

Gio

"Also, you slapped me." He continues as if he hasn't dropped the biggest truth bomb on me. He cares for me? He truly cares for me? And he said it aloud, just like that? And what am I supposed to say? I care for you, too? I do, but I'm not sure if I want to. I'm not ready to be in a relationship yet, am I? And this was supposed to be a farce, a fake relationship. The thing is, I'm not ready to tell him about the myriad of thoughts buzzing around in my head, so like the coward I am, I ignore what he said earlier.

"You deserved it," I manage to gasp out.

"And *you* deserve this." He takes a step back, kicks my legs out further, and before I can protest, he brings his palm down on my butt. The sound is loud in the empty space. The shock slices through me, and for a second, my head is clear. For a second, every pore in my body is open and my senses are focused. All other sounds recede; all other thoughts dissolve. Everything around me fades away. Everything except the feel of his big hand massaging my throbbing backside. Through the fabric of my skirt, he rubs the pulsating ache into my skin. It sinks straight to my core where it sits, heavy, thick, swelling my clit, setting off tiny vibrations of lust in my core.

Then, he spanks my other ass cheek, and I cry out. Everything comes back into focus as he slaps me, alternating cheeks. One, two, three, four, five... He stops. The sound fades away, I can hear his harsh breathing, feel his chest rise and fall, sense the heat that ricochets off his body like he's a living furnace. The force of his personality is a heavy, dominant presence that presses down on me and pins me to the glass wall.

"Rick," I wheeze, "Please."

He bends in close enough for his hot breath to sear my cheek. I flinch, and at the same time, my pussy clenches down on nothing. Damn, but I'd do anything to feel his cock between my legs…and his fingers squeezing my breast…and his lips whispering down my cheek before he bites down on the curve of my shoulder and— He licks up the corner of my mouth, and I moan and shudder and press the fingers of my free hand into the glass for support.

"Tell me what you want, Goldie," he murmurs in a low, hard voice that sets off a fresh burst of trembling down my spine.

You, I need you. Your tender words and your harsh touch, your ability to maneuver my body into any position you like, your masculine scent, your hard lips, the gentle rustle of your eyelashes over my skin, the confident touch that turns me into a melting icicle of desire, your capacity to understand exactly what I want, when even I don't know what it is I'm looking for. I open my mouth to say that, but all that comes out is a whimper. And he seems to understand what I want, for he pulls up my skirt, then tears off my panties. I cry out, then draw in a sharp breath when he cups my core.

"Who does this pussy belong to?" he snaps.

Oh, my god, did I hear that right? And why do I find that so hot?

"Tell me, Goldie, who does this clit belong to?" He circles the swollen nub, and my eyes roll back in my head. I lean my head back against his chest and shuffle my legs further apart. Cool air sighs up my thighs. It brushes up against where he brushes the slit between my legs. A shudder grips me.

"Want me to fuck you with my fingers?"

I nod.

"Then answer the question. Who does this melting slit, these pussy lips, that hot, tight cunt-hole of yours, who does it belong to, Goldie? Tell me, right now."

"You," I gasp, "it belongs to you."

"Good girl. How's the blood flow?"

"What?" I groan.

"Your period, Goldie, are you still on your period?"

"I am, but the flow is much lighter today."

"And the pain?"

"Almost non-existent."

"In which case, we can dispense with this." He pulls a paper napkin from his pocket, and in one move, slides out the tampon, wraps it up in the tissue, and tosses it aside.

"What are you—" I gasp because he's replaced it with two of his fingers in my channel.

My period may be almost over, but my channel is over-sensitized. A trembling vibrates out from where he begins to weave his fingers in and out of me, in and out.

He drags his whiskered chin up my cheek, then stuffs a third finger inside my melting channel.

"Oh my god," I cry out as he stretches me, and curves his thick digits hitting that spot deep inside. A trembling starts deep inside, and as if on cue, a man drives a Zamboni out onto the rink. The vehicle makes its way across the ice, smoothing it out while ripples of sensation undulate out from where he's finger fucking me. He twists his fingers inside me, and I throw back my head, and moan, "ohgod, ohgod, ohgod."

"You mean 'oh Rick,' don't you?" I hear the smirk in his voice and try to dredge up a semblance of anger, but I'm too focused on how he's shoved his fingers down the front of my blouse and is squeezing my nipple, how he's grinding the heel of his hand into my clit, how he's stroking my inner walls with the blunt tip of his fingers, how his big body feels like a wall against which I'm rubbing myself. How the climax begins to swell up my insides, up my spine, and I close my eyes and brace for it... That's when he pulls his fingers from me and steps back.

The orgasm trembles for a second, then begins to recede. What the—? Below me, the Zamboni driver continues his progress, leaving a smooth sheet of ice behind. Which is the opposite of how I feel. Waves of pleasure lap at my subconscious, hinting at the release I've yet to experience. My knees wobble, and he grips my shoulder and steadies me. I scowl at him over my shoulder. "Why did you stop?"

"Why do you think I stopped?"

"Can't you answer a question without posing one back?"

He pretends to think then shakes his head. "What do you think?" I can hear the smirk in his voice, and it's like a little bomb going off in my brain. I spin around, raise my hand, but when he glares at it, I pause, then curl my fingers into a fist and lower it to my side.

"What are you getting at? Why didn't you let me come?" I whine.

He tucks a strand of hair behind my ear, then bends his knees and peers into my eyes. "Because you're a brat, and you need to learn you don't direct the proceedings when we fuck. And by the way,"—his lips firm—"you will not come until I give you permission."

42

Rick

"Check." I glance down at my cards. This has to be the worst hand I've ever been dealt.

Only consolation? The scent of her arousal is imbedded in my nostrils. After I commanded her not to come, I pulled out the pair of panties in my pocket—I wasn't joking when I said I've taken to carrying them around—and ensured she stepped into them. Then, I straightened her clothes, walked her out of the arena, and dropped her home before I joined the guys for our weekly poker session.

We're in the den in the basement of Sinclair's townhouse in Primrose Hill. Next to me, Edward raises the bet and slides a few chips across the table. No one reacts. Talk about playing poker with a tough audience. With Sinclair, JJ, Michael, Knight, and Edward, it's safe to say I may have met my match when it comes to not letting any emotions show on my face. And *I'm* called Stone.

A chuckle wells up, and I tamp down on it. In front of these guys, I might as well be called "too emotional." These guys are as tough as they come. 'Course each of them has been through their journeys, professional and personal, and they've come out of it stronger and with the women of their dreams next to them.

Except Edward. I don't know the exact story, but I heard he walked away from his calling as a priest and then lost his woman to his best friend. He's been traveling around the world ever since, returning to London when Knight asked him to take on the role of General Manager of the London Ice Kings. You'd have thought he'd struggle to adjust to this position, but it turns out the challenges he's faced in his life, combined with his ability to listen, which he honed when he was a priest, means he's perfect in this role. He even has a flair for navigating the politics of trading players, as evidenced by the stellar line-up he's put together.

Not that it helps me here at the poker table. When he suggested I join him and the others at the newly instituted weekly poker night at Sinclair's place, I agreed—only so I could put some space between me and Gio.

After almost making her come, then refusing to let her come and enjoying the shock followed by rage on her face, I took advantage of her temporary surprise to straighten her clothes, then haul her to my car. On the way home, she turned her face away and focused on the passing scenery, which suited me fine.

It gave me time to work through my actions and reactions toward her. I certainly hadn't meant to blurt out that I'm coming to care for her. She noticed it, but she didn't ask me anything further about it, thank fuck. It's something that was in the height of passion and doesn't mean anything—except it does. And I can't get that damn confession out of my mind. Catching feelings for her? That was never part of the plan.

This was only meant to convince Grams to agree to her operation, which she has, so there's no reason for us to be together. Except, Grams texted me twice today asking me when we're getting married so she can ensure she's recovered from her operation in time to attend. Something I didn't tell Gio, and no doubt, what messed with my composure enough for me to trip up and allow those words through my lips. And then, I couldn't wait to dump her at the doorstep to the house and get the fuck out of there. Coward that I am.

"Your turn," Hunter murmurs from next to me.

I glance down at my cards, then slap them down. "I fold."

"And I thought you were a fighter." JJ smirks.

"Fuck off," I say without heat.

"Something bothering you?" he asks with interest.

"Nope, nah, not being pulled into this discussion with you."

"Pulled into what?" Hunter frowns.

"You've been too busy governing the country to keep track of how these three here"—I nod toward JJ, Sinclair and Michael—"have been conducting interventions which have resulted in many of our mutual friends biting the dust."

Hunter moves the cigar to the other side of his mouth. "It'd be remiss of me not to admit that they had a hand in my coming to my senses and marrying the woman of my dreams, too. It's what makes everything worth it."

I narrow my gaze. "Makes what worth it?"

"Everything. Winning the vote, becoming the Prime Minister, working twelve hours a day, as long as I can return home and see Zara and Enzo every evening." His features soften, and his eyes shine with what I can only assume is love. For a few seconds, he's not the leader of the country whose every decision will impact the future of generations to come. He's a man in love—head over heels in love—and someone who cares deeply about his family.

"Huh?" I blink.

"And what about you?" Sinclair drawls.

"Me?" I lean back in my chair. "What about me?"

"A-n-d there it is. The very fact that you'd think we were talking about you is a sign of guilt." JJ guffaws.

"Guilt? The fuck you talking about, old man?"

JJ smiles wider. "Don't deflect. I'm comfortable with my age, unlike you."

"Now you're going too far." I cross my arms across my chest, knowing my posture is belligerent, but what-fucking-ever.

"I'm not the one who signed up to captain a team of whippersnappers decades younger than me."

"And I'd think you'd respect me for it," I snap.

"Not that I don't, but—"

"But?"

"But"—he raises a shoulder—"I don't have a point to prove."

"And I do?" I frown.

"Do you?" JJ lowers his chin to his chest. "What ghosts from your past are you running away from, hmm?"

"Maybe they're not ghosts. Maybe they're here and alive, and I'm exactly where I'm supposed to be."

JJ meets my gaze, then nods slowly. "Your engagement is going as you intended?"

"Of course it is." I look between him and the rest of the men, all of whom are looking at me with skepticism.

"What? If any of you wankers have something to say—"

"What they mean is that this entire pretending to be engaged situation you have going on isn't fooling anyone," Edward offers.

I shoot him a sideways glance. "Think they can speak for themselves. Anyway, it's not pretend."

JJ snorts.

Sinclair smirks.

Michael looks at me with an are-you-fucking-with-me look in his eyes.

Hunter has a half-smile on his face. He looks like he's about to say something, then shakes his head. "You might as well spit it out."

He removes his cigar from between his lips and gestures toward me. "We understand how it is," he says gently.

"You do?"

"Of course, we do, you arsewipe. This is how their respective relationships with their wives began. Not mine, of course." JJ reaches for a fresh cigar and lights up.

"No, you stole your son's girlfriend."

"Ex-girlfriend."

"Who is your son's age."

"True love knows no boundaries," he says in a serene voice. "Also, I didn't steal her. One look at each other, and we knew."

I blink. When I came here, I didn't expect a candid conversation. Hell, I wasn't expecting to talk at all. A poker night with the lads is meant to be strong silences, the shuffle of cards, the clack of poker chips sliding across the table, the hiss of a cigar being lit, the gulp of beer being swigged... All of which is there, in addition to the grilling these guys are subjecting me to. I've faced cross-examinations by war-veterans, and grappled with hockey players faster than me, but being at the receiving end of the knowing looks from these five guys has me straightening my spine in defense.

"Just like I'm sure you and your fiancée knew," Sinclair offers.

"Which is, of course, why the two of you announced your engagement so quickly," Michael drawls through a puff of cigar smoke.

"Of course." I run my finger under the collar of my sweatshirt. "Is it hot in here?" I glance around the space.

"The air-conditioning is on, so the answer would be a no," Edward murmurs.

"You nervous ol' chap?" Hunter asks in an interested tone.

I laugh, and the sound does come out *nervous*. I reach for a cigar, then stop myself. Nope, not going there. Truth is, I am struggling to keep up with the younger players. And after a day of heavy practice, the number of aches and pains that riddle my body has made me reconsider Edward's offer of using one of the massage therapists the team employs to limber up. So far, I've resisted it.

In all my years of playing professionally and then with the military, I've always bounced back from the hardest of schedules with a spring in my step. But since I've started the drills with the team, I wake up feeling every ache and pain. My body is not bouncing back the way it used to. And I'm never going to admit it aloud.

Just like I'm never going to confess that the relationship with Goldie is a sham. Nope. Nah. We're going to break up soon enough. They'll know when it's over. No need to pre-empt the upcoming severance of the connection between us. My heart thuds in my ribcage, and my pulse rate falters. Splitting up...

I'll be splitting up with her soon. And then she can go back to her loser of an ex, for all I care. No, not her ex, she can do better than that wanker. *Like you? Not me. Someone else.* Someone who didn't start the relationship with a lie. Goddamn it, why did I have to start our alliance with a lie? Only good thing is, she doesn't know about it yet. And she never will. It would only hurt her, and while I can't stop the impending cutting of ties, I can spare her the ignominy of finding out the real reason I asked her to pose as my fiancée. Yes, yes. Of course, it was to help persuade Grams to agree to the procedure, but there was more than that.

My phone buzzes. I pull it out of my pocket, and stare at the photograph attached to the message. *The fuck —?* I jump up so quickly, my chair overturns.

JJ's eyebrows shoot up. "Emergency?"

43

Rick

"What's the emergency?" Caspian side-eyes me from the couch in the living room where he's sprawled out, fingers on the controller; on the massive TV screen in front of him, a zombie is blown to bits.

"Gotcha!" Jagger crows next to him.

"Fuck!" Caspian jerks his head forward. The split-second of inattention caused him to lose the game.

I charge past the morons, and up the short hallway toward the kitchen. If they're still there… I'm going to kill that mofo. I burst into the kitchen and come to a stop. She's standing in front of the island. Her back is toward me and she's wearing her blonde hair in that messy bun on top of her head. Tendrils of hair cling to her neck from where they've escaped. She's wearing yoga pants that cling to her thighs, and which I know must cup her butt, the shape of which I can't see… Because she's wearing a jersey. The number on the jersey is eight, and the name above it is Kilmer. *She's wearing Finn's fucking jersey.* She stirs something on the pot in front of her, then turns and holds up the spatula to the man standing next to her. "Taste it," she offers.

Finn, that motherfucking twatface, bends and licks the broad end. "Yum."

He straightens, then uses his finger to scoop up some of the mixture from the spoon and offer it to her. "Taste it."

Anger pulses through my veins. My vision tunnels. My feet don't seem to touch the ground as I close the distance to them. Before she can lick the concoction from his finger, I've stepped between them. "Get the fuck away from her," I snap.

Finn's gaze widens, then a big smile splits his face. "You got my message, hmm?"

"What message?" Gio tries to peek out from around me, but I slap my arms on my hips so she's blocked from his sight.

Finn messaged me a photograph of her wearing his jersey, knowing full-well it would piss me off. "The fuck you playing at, Hand?" I growl.

"Moi? I'm not playing at anything."

"Get out of my way, you neanderthal." Gio punches me in the side, and my cock twitches. This woman… If she only knew her anger turns me on more, she probably wouldn't be very happy.

"You know what I mean." I lean forward on the balls of my feet.

"I have no idea." Finn brings this finger to his mouth and sucks on it.

"Hey, we were trying to cook, and you're in the way," Gio huffs from behind me.

"Good," I say without looking back. Going by the waves of anger emanating from her, I know she's working herself up into a good ol' temper tantrum.

"You're pissing me off," she snaps.

"And *you're* pissing me off." I stab a finger into Finn's chest.

"Hey, I'm talking to you," she yells.

"I'll talk to you later!" With a final glare at Finn, who smirks back at me, I pivot on my feet.

"What's wrong with you? I'm trying to cook dinner and you barge in and upset everything."

"Oh, I'm upset all right, and you have no idea how much."

She throws up her hands, including the one holding the spatula and some of the sauce splatters across my face.

"Oops." Her eyes round before she covers a smirk.

Without taking my gaze off of her, I lean into her, then rub my sauce-stained cheek against hers.

"Oh," she gasps.

"Indeed." I straighten and take in her cheek, now stained with the mixture.

"You're crazy." She swallows. The pulse at the base of her neck speeds up.

"And you're wearing his jersey."

"Eh?" She looks down at her chest, then up at me. "I spilled water on my T-shirt and didn't want to go all the way up to the room to change it. Finn loaned me his sweatshirt, and—"

I reach behind me and pull mine off. "Take it off."

"Oh please, you're pissed off because I wore his jersey—"

"I'm not pissed off."

"No?" She blinks.

"I'm freakin' enraged, fuming, seething, on the verge of killing him right now. Take your pick."

Finn whistles from behind me. "This is where I leave you two." He reaches over and turns off the burner on the stove—"Good thing the sauce is done"—then turns and stalks off.

"Shut the kitchen door and stay on guard," I call after him.

He glances over his shoulder, and whatever he sees on my face makes him realize how serious I am, for he nods. The door to the kitchen snicks shut behind him.

"What are you doing?" She looks from me to the door, then back at me.

"You don't ask the questions," I snap.

"Oh?" She scowls.

"Oh, yes, is the right answer here."

She firms her lips. "You're acting weird."

"And you haven't taken off his jersey."

She places the spatula on the island top, then folds her arms across her chest.

"Take. It. Off." I lower my voice to a hush. The color drains from her face. She swallows, then reaches down, grips the hem and pulls off the jersey. I snatch it from her, throw it over my shoulder, then pull my sweatshirt over her head. She threads her arms through the sleeves and smooths the fabric down her thighs. She's swallowed up in it, and I roll the sleeves up to her wrists.

She looks down at herself, then up at me. "This is bullshit."

"What's bullshit is you dared wear someone else's jersey."

"It was temporary," she protests.

"Like our engagement?"

She pales further. "It is temporary, whatever this is between us, isn't it?"

Of course it is. But right now, the way I'm feeling, I don't care. "Right now, we're engaged. We're both playing a role which the media has bought into. A role which has convinced your ex you're out of his reach, which is making him want you even more. A role which my grandmother believes is real. Which my teammates are convinced is authentic. A role which, if it gets out that this is fake will result in a media shitstorm, not to mention, break my Grams' heart and show your ex the extent you'd go to take revenge for what he did." I frown. "Or perhaps, that's your plan. You want him to know our relationship is fake, so the next time he asks you for forgiveness, you can go back to him."

She shakes her head. "You're the one who came up with this cockamamie idea!."

"And? Are you telling me you don't want to go back to him?"

"Of course not."

I frown. "Wait. You don't?"

"I admit, I was confused, at first. Coming out of a relationship and meeting you and having all these strong feelings for you, it made my head spin. So, I told you I wasn't sure about how I felt toward Denn—

"Don't speak his fucking name in front of me."

She swallows. "I mean... him. I wasn't sure how I felt about him, but now I know."

"You do?"

She looks away, then back at me. "I realize now, he was nowhere as caring as you. I know he didn't respect people the way you do. I know he didn't feel as passionately about things as you do."

"You must have me mistaken for someone else. I'm not a passionate person."

She laughs, then stares at me. "You pretend not to be a passionate person, but you are."

"Oh?"

"If you weren't, you wouldn't have marched into this kitchen and gotten all hot under the collar because I was wearing someone else's jersey."

Heat flushes my neck. "That's different."

"Oh, and how about the time you saw me speaking with Denn— I mean, my ex, and you marched up to us and punched him. And that time the pap took a photo of—"

"Alright. I admit those are all times I lost my temper. A rarity."

"Except when it comes to me."

I blink.

"You seem to suffer from bouts of extreme emotion when it has anything to do with me."

"Because I know it turns you on when I do."

She opens and shuts her mouth. "Wow, so you're blaming your inability to keep your composure on me?"

"Obviously."

She scowls. "And you're saying all this to rile me up?"

"I'm saying all this to let you know I haven't forgotten what you did, and that you need to take your punishment."

"P-punishment?"

44

Gio

My voice trembles, and my pussy quivers. All of my nerve-endings seem to spark. I glance toward the door, then back at him.

"Oh no, you don't—" He clicks his tongue. "There's no escape for you this time."

And the thought of that turns me on. Anything this man does turns me on, no surprise, but when he goes all hard and mean and threatens to make me pay for my mistakes, it makes me so horny, and I can't understand why. Or maybe I do. Maybe he calls to that part of me that always wants to be in control. Maybe I've always been attracted to that dominance in a man. But he's the first man I've met who's strong enough to allow me to feel secure enough to know he's safe. Enough to drop the pretense I'm always in control and allow him to take over. Enough to reveal that hungry, needy part of me that wants him to take me in hand and make choices on my behalf.

Maybe he touches that part of me I don't want to rein in, the part of me I've been forced to restrain because if I showed who I really was, I'd be punished. If I asked for what I really wanted, I'd be turned down. If I shared the real me, I'd be ridiculed and...

Yeeesh, I don't need a therapist to tell me why I'm attracted to him. I've tried to control my life so far, and things haven't worked out how I've wanted. He makes me feel secure enough to give up control... For the very first time. To trust in him to do with me as he wants, to challenge him enough so when he punishes me, I know he cares. A tear squeezes out from the corner of my eye.

His gaze widens, then he leans in, scoops up the tear with his thumb, and sucks on it.

"Why did you do that?" I whisper.

"Damned if I know." He cups my cheek. "You make me act in ways that surprise me."

"Me too."

"I'm not going to not punish you."

"I'm counting on you not, not to."

He surveys my features, then nods. "Turn around and hold onto the edge of the island."

"Only if you promise to make me come."

It's been two days since he told me I couldn't come without his permission. The last two nights, he's come to bed after I've fallen asleep, and woken and left for practice before I was up. If it weren't for the mussed-up sheets on his side of the bed, I wouldn't have known he'd come to bed, at all. I'm not ashamed to say, I buried my face in his pillow, drew in his scent, and tried to get myself off. But each time I try to rub out one, the alphahole's command stops me.

Judging by the expression of satisfaction on his face, he knows it too. "I take it, you're frustrated?"

I firm my lips.

"Want me to do something about it?"

What do you think?

"Do you, Goldie?"

He holds my gaze, and those blue eyes of his pin me in place. Lying is pointless because he's going to be able to tell I am right away. But I'm not going to give him the satisfaction of saying it aloud, so I content myself with a nod.

"Good." He makes a twirling motion with his finger.

I swallow, then turn around and grab the edge of the counter. I sense him moving to stand behind me. The heat from his body wraps around me, then he grips the curve of my hips and pulls me back so my butt juts out. In this position, I feel vulnerable and open, and I know I need it. I want him to do this. I do...but in the right way.

"My mother used to spank me with a wooden spoon," I burst out.

He pauses, then heads to one of the drawers of the far side. I hear him rifling around. He walks back to me and shows me the two large spoons he's acquired. "Which one?"

I take in their size, then nod toward the one with a larger base.

"Is this similar in size to the one she used to spank you with?

I nod.

He looks between my eyes, "I'm going to replace the memories that brought you so much anguish with new ones that bring you pleasure."

He sets the other one aside, then takes up position behind me. "Hold on."

Heat flushes my skin. My knees knock together. I dig my sneakers into the floor, lock my fingers onto the edge of the counter and hold…and hold and hold and… The whack of the spoon against my backside sends a line of fire zipping up my spine. I yelp, and almost fall forward, but he steadies me with his hand on my hip. I gasp, then draw in a breath.

"You okay, Goldie?" There's concern in his voice, and the pressure behind my eyeballs builds.

I will not cry…will not. I swallow down the ball of emotion in my throat, then tip up my chin. "I'm good." My voice comes out strong, and that gives me even more confidence.

"You sure?"

I scowl at him over my shoulder. "Don't go soft on me, Stone. I want you to spank me… I want you to—"

He brings the spoon down on my other ass-cheek, and I gasp. Then turn and push out my hips. His grip on my waist tightens then, whack-whack-whack, the spoon connects with my backside again and again. Each time, it seems to sear into my butt. The vibrations begin at the base of my spine and build and grow and become thicker and stronger and coil in my core, and still, he doesn't stop. The next time the spoon connects with my backside, I groan. My pussy trembles, the waves of tension swirl in on themselves until they tighten and fold into themselves, and knot and tense up. And then, he brings down the spoon across both of my butt-cheeks.

The pain arrows to my center, and it's like a key that opens the ball of sensations twisted tightly there. Just like that, the knot unravels. The orgasm pours over me, and my back curves. I push my cheek into the counter and cry out as I come. The aftershocks rip through me.

I'm aware of him placing the spoon aside and massaging my backside through the seat of my yoga pants. The pain sinks into my skin, into my blood, and coils around my swollen clit. Then he straightens me and lifts me into his arms.

"Wha 're ya doin'...?" The words come out slurred. A heavy weight seems to drag down my eyelids.

"I'm taking you to our room."

Our room. I love the sound of that. I try to tell him that, but the words come out garbled. I turn my face into his broad chest and draw in a lung full of Rick. Then close my eyes and allow myself to lift off. I dimly hear another voice — Finn, maybe — ask a question followed by the rumble of Rick's voice as he answers, then darkness embraces me.

When I wake up, I'm in my bed with the covers pulled over me. My hair must have come out of its bun, and I shove it out of my eyes, then turn on my side and find Rick asleep on top of the covers. His hand is flung out toward me. There's enough space between us that we're not touching each other. He's wearing the same pair of jeans I saw him in when he burst into the kitchen with the same threadbare T-shirt he wore under the sweatshirt; it clings to the ridges of his pecs. The dog tags he wears have fallen out.

I reach forward and touch them. When he doesn't stir, I drag my fingers over the bulge of his pec toward where his nipple is outlined against the cloth. I look up at his face — his eyes are still closed — then circle the nub.

That dull pulse between my legs kicks up in intensity. The slight soreness of my backside only accentuates the emptiness in my center. I whisper my fingers up his chest, between the strong cords of his muscles to that prominent chin, and when I take in his face, I'm not surprised to see his eyelids are open. He's staring at me, and those eyes glow with the silver sparks that never fail to entrance me.

I cup his cheek, and when he doesn't stop me, I push off my covers. I realize I'm not wearing my yoga pants or his sweatshirt a few seconds before I throw my leg over his waist and straddle him. When I bend over him, my hair curtains his face. I lean in closer, until my mouth is positioned on top of his. My nose bumps his, and our breaths mingle. My nipples tighten, and the moisture between my thighs tells me I want him. I need him. I can't do without him. I lower my chest into his, and my breasts flatten.

His gaze narrows, and his eyes flash.

That's when I fit my core over the tent at his crotch and whisper, "Fuck me, Rick."

45

Rick

"No."

"What?" She gapes. "What did you say?"

"You don't call the shots." I slide my hands down to cup her arse-cheeks. I squeeze, and she gasps.

"Rick, please."

I push her down on my thickening erection, and her pupils dilate. Color flushes her cheeks. She pants, brings her lips down on mine. I allow her to kiss me, allow her to deepen the kiss until her breathing quickens, until the pulse thumps at my temples, behind my eyes, even in my eyeballs, then I flip her over so she's on her back and I'm between her legs.

She locks her ankles around my hips and throws her arms about my neck. "Please, please, Rick," she whines.

I can't stop the chuckle that bubbles up my throat. Can't stop myself from pressing down into the cradle of her core, can't stop myself from digging the column in my crotch between her pussy lips.

"Oh my god, stop teasing me," she whines.

"I'm not. Not more than I'm teasing myself," I confess.

"Why can't you fuck me?"

"Because if I do, the way I feel about you, I might get attached, and I can't afford that."

She seems taken aback. "You don't want to get attached to me?"

It might be too late, I already am, but I don't tell her that. Instead, I shake my head. "This isn't what I had in mind when I asked you to pose as my fiancée. I hadn't anticipated Grams wanting to attend our wedding." Which, in retrospect, is the height of stupidity. Why wouldn't she?

"Wedding?" She pales. "We can't get married. I don't want to get married to you."

A hot sensation stabs at my chest. I push it aside. "Neither do I," I assure her. "It's why I don't want to fuck you, either. We need to keep our distance." I take in her flushed features, her parted lips. "We… I need to stop wanting to get inside of you."

She nods, then tightens her hold about my waist. "I agree." She pushes her breasts up and into my chest, and a growl of satisfaction ripples up my chest.

"On the other hand," I reason, "we could take this night to fuck this attraction out of our system."

"Just this night." She licks her lips, and my cock extends further.

"Just this night."

"Just this—" She tips up her chin.

I lower my head and close my mouth over hers. I thrust my tongue in between her lips, and drink from her. The fact that she's under me, in my bed, at my mercy—open and willing—is an aphrodisiac that fills my veins. The blood drains to my groin. I tear my mouth from hers and straighten so she has to lower her arms to her sides. Then I reach behind me and pull off my T-shirt.

She draws in a sharp breath, drags her gaze down my torso, then reaches up to trace the tattoo over my heart. Her fingertips flutter over the script carved into my skin.

"Diana," she reads aloud. Her forehead furrows. Does she recognize the name? I didn't see anything to indicate she did the first time she noticed the tattoo. I watch her features closely but there's only puzzlement in her eyes. "Who's Diana?"

"My sister."

"You have a sister?"

"Had."

"Oh." She frowns.

I scrutinize her face, but all I see is sympathy and curiosity.

"I didn't realize," she murmurs.

Of course the name doesn't mean anything to her. Why would it?

I look away. "Grams removed all pictures of her after her death. She doesn't like to talk about her. She loved Diana more than her own daughter, my mother."

"What happened?" Her frown deepens.

I turn and lock my gaze with Gio's. "She committed suicide."

"I'm so sorry." Gio slides her hands up to cup my face. "I truly am."

So am I, for what I'm going to have to do to you. But not tonight. Tonight, I'm going to forget what brought me here. How I've been playing you all along. How I'm going to hate myself for seeing through what I planned. How I have no choice if I want revenge for what happened. How... I've fallen for you without meaning to. How I'm damned, but I have to go through with this. I have to.

I turn my face into her palm and kiss the soft skin. Then sit back on my haunches. I hold out my hand, and when she places hers in mine, I tug. She straightens, and I release her hands, then reach for the camisole she's wearing and tug it off. The creamy globes of her breasts tempt me to bury my head between them, but if I do, I won't stop. And I want to see her naked. Want her to see me naked. This time, I want us to be skin-on-skin, nothing in between. I reach for her panties, and when she raises her hips, I slide them down her thighs. She bends her knees, and I pull them off, then bring them to my face. I sniff, and she makes a noise at the back of her throat. "You're filthy."

"You have no idea." I stuff the panties in the pocket of my jeans, then shove them down and aside. My cock springs free, and her gaze is instantly captured by it.

She stares at it, then swallows. "You're so big."

I curl my lips, "I'm about to get bigger."

She scowls but doesn't take her gaze off my dick.

I reach over her and toward the nightstand for a condom when she touches my shoulder.

"I'm on birth control."

"And I'm clean."

"I've never—" She presses her lips together.

"Never—?"

She glances away, then back at me. "Never been with anyone who hasn't worn a condom before."

"And you won't be with anyone else except me after this."

She jerks her chin in my direction, opens her mouth to ask a question a-n-d... I'm tired of trying to justify my actions, when all I do is trip up around her. I fit my lips to hers, position my cock at her opening, and in one smooth move, I thrust inside her.

She jerks, and a cry rolls up her throat, I swallow down the sound and freeze. My cock pulses inside her. So tight. So hot. All the muscles in my body lock. I release her mouth, and stare into her pain filled gaze.

"I'm going to fuck you now."

46

Gio

I'm not a virgin. I've never been with a man before, but I *have* used vibrators to get myself off. So, there's no reason it should have hurt as much as it did when he penetrated me. But this is Rick. And his cock is bigger than my XXL-sized dildo. He's too much, too huge, too everything inside me. I'm stretched around him, pinned down and unable to move. It's a pleasure-pain that focuses my entire attention on that part of my body where we're joined and sends a line of sensations zipping up my spine.

Then there are his filthy words? They are so over-the-top. I've read the heroes of my smutty novels talk dirty to their women, but coming from Rick, it's more erotic, more primal, more raw. More real. Duh, of course, it's more real. But It's more than that. It's more him.

I hold his gaze, and the intent in his eyes is laced with lust and need, but there's something more. Something I don't dare identify. Something so intense, it brings tears to my eyes. I try to pull away, but he curls his fingers around the nape of my neck and stops me.

"Don't be ashamed of how you feel." His voice is soft, and so tender and there he is, the man under that ice-cold exterior, the man I'm falling for. The first man I've been with because I know, he's the one.

And no way, am I going to explain that to him because who reaches the age of twenty-nine without being with a man? All of my experience comes from my smutty novels and my creative usage of my Steely-Dan. This is my secret, one I've never shared with any of my girlfriends. Because really, someone as confident as me, someone who loves power-dressing and is confident enough to make it in a cut-throat profession like PR... who'd guess I'd never had sex with a man? The thought crossed my mind when I met Dennis, but I was secretly happy when he didn't want to sleep with me until we got married.

On some level, I was relieved to find him cheating. It meant I didn't have to sleep with him because, the truth is, I hadn't been attracted to him that way. But he ticked so many boxes, assumed the problem was me. I simply wasn't interested in sex with a man. So, I opted to pour all of my energies into building my career instead.

Of course, I'd hoped to one day meet a man who'd sweep me off my feet. Who'd know what I wanted when he met me. Who'd be the kind of man who would be my partner in every part of my life. Who'd fulfill me in bed and emotionally satisfy me. A man who'd make me feel secure. A man like Rick. A man with whom I don't have a future.

"Don't be ashamed of *what* you feel." He tilts his hips, a subtle movement, but one which sends the blood roaring in my veins.

"Rick," I gasp.

"You're so tight, Goldie. So wet." His gaze intensifies. "If I were to die now, I'd have no regrets, because I'm inside you."

My heart stutters. A warmth fills my chest. No one has ever said those words to me. No-one else can match his passion, his ardor how he makes me feel. There's no-one else except him for me. "Me too," I whisper.

His eyes flash, the blue a glowing azure which makes my breath catch. "Fuck, baby, you're making it difficult for me to control myself."

He grits his teeth, and a bead of sweat slides down his temple. His biceps bulge as he balances on his arms. His cock stretches me, and it feels so good and so full and just a tad painful as he throbs against my sensitive inner walls. Then, I flex them, and a growl rumbles up his chest. The sound is so primitive, so raw, my nerve-endings detonate. My brain cells melt, and all thoughts empty from my head. I lock my ankles around him, tilt my hips up, and he slips in further.

His gaze narrows, a nerve pops at his temple. "Don't try to top from the bottom," he growls in that familiar hard voice, and I'm instantly wet... I mean, wetter. My slit quivers around him, and he must feel it, for he unhooks my ankles from around his waist, only to prop them over his shoulders, so I'm almost bent in half. Then he unclasps my arms from about his neck and twists them over my head. He curls my fingers around the border of the headboard. "Hold on."

Before I can say another word, he pulls back until he's balanced at the edge of my slit, then thrusts forward. He buries himself inside me in one smooth move, and I swear, I can feel him in my throat. I open my mouth, but no words emerge. He holds my gaze, stays where he is, allowing me to feel every ridge, every groove, every pulse of his cock inside me. I've never been more owned, more possessed, more everything. He slides his hand up the back of my thigh and squeezes. Then, holding me like that, he drills into me again with such force, the entire bed moves.

Something crashes in a corner of the room, but he doesn't stop. He plunges into me again, and when I cry out, he's already there. He kisses me again, absorbing the sound, and buries himself inside me at an angle where he brushes up against the most secret part of me. The orgasm swells to a crescendo, and I'm swept up in it. His gaze still holds mine as he releases my mouth long enough to whisper, "Come," and I shatter.

He fucks me through the waves of my climax, the blue in his eyes turning almost completely silver, until finally, with a low groan, he follows me over the edge. He presses his forehead into mine as we both pant and come down from the high. His cock pulses inside me, and it's the single most intimate experience of my life.

I'm changed from here on. I'm no longer only my own. I've given him a part of me—and I don't mean the fact he's my first. It's more than that. I've allowed him into a part of my life no one else has been welcome before. I've allowed him a peek into the mess that is my heart and my soul and my mind, and I'm not sure if he's even aware. When he begins to pull away, I shake my head and cling to him. He kisses me again, and I almost burst out crying and... *Nope, nope, nope, I'm not going to be that cliché of a woman who cries after the first time she's had sex..*

I swallow down the emotions that block my throat, focus on his lips on mine, his tongue sliding over mine, the feel of his cock between my thighs, focus on how good it feels to have his weight on mine.

When he pulls away again, I let him slide my legs down. He glances down and I follow his gaze to the blood on his cock. I flinch. "In case you're wondering, I'm not a virgin."

"Did I hurt you?" His features harden. "Did I, Goldie? Is that why you're bleeding?"

I nod. "You *are* enormous. Thicker than I'd anticipated."

His eyes gleam. "Was I too rough?" He bends his knees and peers into my eyes. "Not that I regret it, but, if I caused you pain—"

I place my hand on his lips. "You were perfect. You were everything I imagined and more."

He searches my features but doesn't seem convinced, "I caused you to bleed." His jaw tics. "If I made you suffer in anyway, I'll never forgive myself."

"You did make me suffer by making me wait so long before you fucked me."

"And the anticipation built, and every part of your body was primed for release, so when you finally came, it blew your mind," he says with that arrogance that is so very Rick. So very annoying. But also arousing. My lower belly contracts; moisture coils between my legs.

He must sense my reactions for his eyes gleam, "Admit it, it was worth the wait."

I set my lips.

"Go on say it."

I tip up my chin. "It was worth the wait that you were my first."

He looks up at my face, and his eyes widen. "What do you mean, I'm your first?"

I look away. "You're the first man I've been with."

"But you're a—?" He shakes his head. "It's not possible." He peers into my features. "Is it?"

"I'm not a virgin, but you *are* the first man I've been with."

"But how—?" He clears his throat. "I don't understand."

"Because…who reaches the age of twenty-nine without being with a man, right?" I begin to pull away, but he leans his weight on me.

"Hey, no hiding from me. You can tell me anything, Goldie." The tenderness in his voice is my undoing. Tears prick the backs of my eyes, and I blink them away. The understanding in his features squeezes my chest. The empathy in every angle of his body unlocks something deep inside of me.

"My mother was an addict. I spent my teenage years defending myself from her boyfriends. Ran away at sixteen, moved to L.A, lied about my age and joined the mailroom of a PR company and worked my way up. By eighteen, I was the assistant to the PR manager of a very famous Hollywood actor."

Something flickers in his eyes. Something like anger? But it's gone so quickly, I'm sure I imagined it.

"And you didn't sleep with anyone during that time?"

"Not that I didn't want to. But I was nowhere as confident or as put-together as the woman you see today. I had to work on that, on my appearance, on using the money I spent to finesse my appearance. I didn't approach men and shut down anyone who showed any interest. Anyway, I didn't miss it. I was too busy building my career. Besides, I had my toys—"

"Toys?" He frowns.

"Sex toys."

"Which you won't be needing anymore."

"Not to mention my smutty book-boyfriends—"

"Who you're not allowed to think of again," he growls.

I arch an eyebrow. "Is that an order?"

"It's a statement of intent. The only man in your life from now on is me. The only toy you'll be needing is this one." He reaches for my hand and places it on his still erect cock. And this, after the man just came a few minutes ago.

"You're insatiable."

"Only for you, baby."

"And a sweet talker."

"Only when it comes to you." His eyes gleam, then he stiffens. "What about your douche ex—"

"Didn't want to sleep with me until we were married. We were together for a year, and I thought it was romantic he wanted to wait until our wedding night. I realized later he was getting it on the side." I squeeze my eyes shut. "This is so mortifying. I don't want to talk about it."

"Hey, don't be embarrassed." He cups my cheek. "I'm your first. Do you have any idea how that makes me feel?"

This time, it's me who shakes my head.

"It makes me want to…" He swallows, seems to get a grip on himself, then thrusts out his chest. "It makes me wish I'd never been with anyone else before you. It makes me realize the others don't count because nothing felt as perfect as when I was inside you. It makes me"—he leans in until our eyelashes inter-twine—"want to fuck you over and over again, until I've marked every part of you as my own. Until I've branded you with my cum and rubbed it into your skin, so you never get rid of the scent, so if any man ever comes close to you again, they'll know you're taken."

His words send a visceral thrill up my spine. "And you say you're not passionate?"

He blinks, then a slow smile curves his lips. "You bring out a part of me I didn't know existed. I've saved the best parts of me only for you, Goldie." He kisses me again, then rolls off the bed and walks toward the ensuite.

A-n-d I can't take my gaze off that tight butt of his, or his powerful thighs or the way he moves like he's still on ice, or the scars that mark his back. I hear the water run then he comes out with a damp towel that he presses between my legs. I wince, then sigh as the remnant of pain dissolves. He tosses the cloth aside, then slips under the covers and pulls them up over the both of us. Then, he turns me over and spoons me, and oh my god, this is even better than the fucking. Okay, almost as good as the fucking. I push back so my butt nestles against his groin. I wriggle a little more, trying to find that groove where I'm surrounded by him completely...

That is, until he growls, "What are you doing?"

"Making myself comfortable."

"Any more comfortable, and I'm going to have to take you from behind in this position."

"Oh." I freeze.

"Oh, indeed," I hear the humor in his voice.

His thigh muscles flex and I'm aware of the hard length nestled between my butt cheeks. "Oh," I gasp again.

He blows out a breath. I feel his chest swell, then still. "Go to sleep."

I close my eyes, sure I'm not going to be able to do so, then surprise myself when I surrender to the darkness. When I open my eyes, I know I'm alone. On the pillow beside me is my phone. I pick it up and swipe the screen to find a message: "Gone for practice. See you after work. Dress warmly. I'm taking you out."

My phone buzzes with an incoming call. I accept it as a voice call.

"I can't see you, why can't I see you? Are you naked, Gio?" Mira's voice filters through.

"I'm—"

"You're naked and freshly fucked, admit it."

"Okay, fine, are you happy now?"

Her screech almost takes my ear off, and I hold the phone at a distance. "I knew it. Does this mean you two are together?"

47

Rick

"So, the two of you are together?" Finn asks.

I pull on my T-shirt, then my sweatshirt and sit down on the bench to pull on my socks.

"Is that why you're taking her out on a date?"

"It's not a—" I stop. Actually, it is a date, so can't deny that, but still how did he—

"How did I know it was a date?" He chuckles.

I finish tying up my shoelaces, then straighten and scowl up at him. "How did you?"

"You were so nervous during practice, your performance was all over the place."

"It wasn't all over the place."

"It was not only all over the place, it was under the ice. If it had been any deeper, I'd have had to look for you and found, not the captain of the ice hockey team who's already tipped to lose the league, but one who's head and heart are not in the game because they're somewhere else." Edward glares down at me.

Finn winces. "To be fair, it wasn't that bad."

"It sucked arse," Edward snaps.

Finn hunches his shoulders, then jerks his chin. "Catch you later, Stone." He sidles off. Coward. I glower after him.

The rest of the dressing room empties out in a hurry, until it's only the very angry General Manager of the team and me.

"What the fuck is wrong with you?" he bites out through gritted teeth. At least, he waited until we were alone before he chewed me out. That's something, I suppose. Not that it matters. I knew how badly off-form I've been lately. Which is why it doesn't surprise me when he sinks down next to me and runs his fingers through his hair. "I can see by the look on your face you already know what I'm going to say."

"So don't—" I begin, but he holds up his hand.

"You're not like the rest of them. You're older, more mature—"

"You mean, past my prime?"

He frowns. "You know as well as I do that, while it might take more time for you to recover from a game, what you have in experience both on and off the ice makes you invaluable as a captain."

Yes, I'm aware. No, I don't need someone else to tell me that. No, I'm not insecure… Not normally. Not until a siren swept into my life and blindsided me. I blow out a breath.

His frown deepens. "You're not a man known for his lack of confidence. In fact, it's your larger than average ego that's helped you come this far. And it's an asset when you're leading a team on the ice."

And it's the one thing I have in pucks… Still have in pucks… Just not when it comes to this relationship thing that I seem to have stumbled upon. I don't say a word aloud, except good ol' Priest intuits what's on my mind. He lowers his hands and drops down onto the seat next to me. He leans forward and lowers his arms between his knees, mirroring my posture. For a few seconds, we stay that way, then he rolls his shoulders. "Life isn't linear. It snakes around corners of heartache, pain, and suffering. It requires endurance and perseverance and every other trait you can think about and more. Oh, and a good dollop of humor, too."

"Like hockey?"

"Like hockey." He turns to me. "Fear causes hesitation, and hesitation will cause your worst fears to come true."

I frown. "Did you quote *Point Break*?"

"You're showing your age." He flashes me a smile.

"Was that a trick question?"

"There are no right answers."

"Better Swazye than Cruise."

"Says the man who's named after Maverick."

"Shh." I look around the dressing room. "I'd never live it down if that came out."

Priest brightens. He cups his hands around his mouth and pretends to yell, "If you want to know what Rick's full name is, it's Maverick Mitchell, and—"

I lunge toward him, and both of us hit the floor with a thud and roll over. We end up with me straddling him, my arms around his throat. I press down, and he holds up his hands, signaling he's giving up. I release him and he coughs.

"Not that I don't want to fight you, but I'm the GM and you're the captain, and I don't condone the fighting. Not to mention,"—he twists his body, and I go flying through the air. I hit the floor with a thud, on my back, and lay stunned—"I don't fight fair." He springs to his feet and holds out his arm.

I look at it, then up at his face. "Arsewipe."

"Wankface," he replies obligingly.

"Knobhead." I grab his hand.

He hauls me to my feet. "Shag-Bag"

I tilt my head, *since we're trading eighteenth century insults, apparently.* "Lob-cock." I smirk.

He laughs. "Okay, you win this round."

But I'm going to lose this attempt at playing the farce that is my supposed engagement.

"You'll figure it out." His features soften.

"Go annoy someone else on the team, man. Your mind reading skills are weird as fuck."

He winces a little. "I need to tone it down, eh?" He rubs the back of his neck. "Guess you can take the priest out of a man, but you can't take the man from the priest—" He frowns, and I burst out laughing.

"Oh, were you that kind of priest, then?" I tease. I resist the urge to ask him how he feels about altar boys because... Well, it's not really something to joke about, is it?

He reddens. "Absolutely, not." He pauses as if he wants to say more, then shakes his head. "But you know what I mean, right?"

"Yeah." I nod slowly. "You okay, man? How're you coping not following your calling?"

"How are you coping now that you *are* following your calling?"

I shuffle my feet. "The jury's out on it. I thought this opportunity is what I was waiting for, ya know? I thought once I was back on the ice, everything in life would fall back into place. Turns out, it's only complicating things further."

"Hence the saying, be careful what you wish for. Sometimes, when you do get it, you don't know what to do with it."

Like having her in my life? I wasn't prepared for my life to be shaken the way it has been. Not that I actively wanted to find my woman, but if I had, it would be very much a woman like Gio I'd want next to me.

She was so good with Grams, too—those two fell for each other at once. And that only makes things more complicated. When I tell Grams we're separating? I wince. It's going to get ugly. Of course, first Grams needs to get her procedure done. Only a few more weeks, and once she's recovered, I can slowly clue her in on the reality.

My phone buzzes, and when I see the name on the screen, I draw in a breath. "It's my grandmother. I need to get this."

48

Gio

"She won't have the procedure until we get married?" The blood drains from my features.

"She confirmed." Rick's features resemble that of the stone his call sign is. His jaw tics, and his cheekbones stand out even more in contrast. There are hollows under his eyes. Clearly, he's been training hard—and he hasn't been getting that much sleep, considering we'd both been busy until the early hours of this morning.

"Do you think she knows?" I frown.

He rolls his neck. "Knows what?"

"That the two of us are faking it?"

He stills. "Only, we aren't faking it, are we?"

I wince. "I don't want to talk about it." Mainly because I can't see an end to this resolution. Not until we can walk away from each other, and I can move out of the room I'm sharing with him. Which means, leaving my job—which I can't afford to do. Not until I find another, and it's not going to be easy to find another, considering my track record is far from stellar at the moment.

He raises a shoulder. "Whether you want to or not, fact is, we need to figure this out because it seems there's no getting away from it." He grabs the glass of water the waiter poured him and chugs it down like it's alcohol.

We're sitting in another restaurant run by James Hamilton. This one perches atop one of the tallest buildings in the city with a spectacular view of the Tower Bridge, otherwise known as London Bridge to the rest of the world. The place is so exclusive, we had to go through security before we were ushered up.

I spotted an Academy Award-winning actress, a politician who was recently in the news, and a pop singer with her entourage, to name a few. The tables are separated enough to provide complete privacy, the staff were discreet, and we have a corner table looking down on the Thames with the sun setting over the horizon in the distance. It's romantic.

Except for the paparazzi who were waiting for us as we entered. Which, I confess, is my fault. I leaked the news of our arrival to the press. I may be the fiancée of the captain of the hockey team, but I'm first and foremost, a PR person. I had to make the most of the opportunity. Rick played his role, too. He pulled me into his side and kissed my forehead. The resulting picture will seal our reputation as one of the most popular couples across the internet. My work is going well. So why doesn't it feel all that rewarding?

"I don't want to marry you," I burst out.

He doesn't seem surprised by my outburst. "Neither do I."

My stomach twists. What was I expecting? A declaration that he's ready and willing to do what his grandmother wants without hesitation? Which isn't fair, considering I'm the one who said I wasn't on board with the idea.

"If she doesn't have the operation, she'll die."

He firms his shoulders. "Of course, she's not your grandmother. You don't have to agree to the marriage."

"And if I do agree to get married—?" I swallow.

"At least, she'll have a chance. The odds are not in her favor; she's already delayed too long. But this gives her a chance."

"Shit." I reach for my glass of wine and knock it back. I, too, need to be up early tomorrow for work, but damn, if this occasion doesn't call for alcohol. A waiter materializes by my side and tops me up, then fades away. I curl my fingers around the stem of my wine glass. I'm so distracted that when Rick touches my outstretched hand, which I've placed on the table between us, I startle. Some of the wine splashes onto my blouse. "Oh, no." I grab my napkin and dab at it, then jump up to my feet. So does Rick.

"Stay." I glance away. "I… I'll be right back." I rush toward the hallway and into the restroom at the far end. I'm glad for the reprieve, because he's right. If I want to help save his grandmother's life, we have to get married. *Shit, shit, shit.*

I grab one of the towels from the counter, wet it under the tap, and dab at the blotch of red on my blouse. I had to drink red wine today, and of course, I'm wearing white. I rub at it and the blouse sticks to my bra through which the outline of my nipple can be seen. Ugh. I ball the towel in my hand and am about to throw it when the door behind me opens. I look up and gasp, "What are you doing here?"

Dennis saunters in. "I was looking for you."

"How did you know where to find me?"

He holds up his phone and comes to a halt behind me. On the screen, I see the picture of me and Rick that the journalist snapped an hour ago. Plenty of time to post it and for other media outlets to pick it up.

"What do you want?" I toss the napkin into the basket and straighten.

His gaze drops to my chest, and color flushes his skin. "You've lost weight since I last saw you."

"So?"

"It suits you."

I grip the edge of the counter. "You need to leave."

"Not before I find out why you're doing this." He shoves his hand in his pocket. "I've apologized to you so many times for what happened. She didn't mean anything."

"Does she know that?"

"Yes, I told her. Tiffany and I are no longer together."

"Good for you." I flip open the tap and hold my hands under the water so I have something to do.

"I love you, Gio."

"I don't."

"You said you did."

"I don't anymore. Infidelity can do that, you know."

"But we had it all planned out. Me, the successful athlete. You, the well-known PR guru. A wedding, consummation on our first night together—"

"*You* had it planned out."

"I wanted to do everything right. I wanted to have you for the first time after we were man and wife."

"But the rules didn't apply to you."

"That's what I mean, she didn't mean anything. You did. It's why I didn't touch you. Plus,"—he raises a shoulder— "you didn't seem very interested in sex anyway."

"Wow." I slap the tap shut, wipe my hands again on another towel and fling it into the basket. "You have some nerve coming to talk to me, especially when I'm engaged to someone else." I hold up my left hand, and the light blinks off the ring.

His features darken. "You mean your sham engagement?"

"Nothing sham about it. I have a fiancé who loves me. Unlike you. You must be either completely crazy, or stupid, or both, to think I'd ever forgive you for what you did to me."

His gaze narrows, and his eyes gleam. "Is it because I didn't fuck you? Is that why you're trying to make me look like a fool?"

"This isn't about you. Well, it is, because you slept with my friend—or at least, someone I thought was a friend. I suppose, I should thank you for exposing her for what she is. As for you? You did me a favor by sleeping with her. You saved me from getting married to you and"—I gasp as he grabs me by my hair and tugs. Pins scatter, and a strand of hair breaks free. He tugs again, and pain sizzles down my neck. I arch my back to try to get some slack, but he only tightens his hold on me. I paw at his wrist, but he doesn't budge.

Anger pours off of him. My eyes water, and when I meet his gaze in the mirror, I swallow. He has a look on his face that makes my stomach twist. My skin crawls. "Did he fuck you already? Is that why you're marrying him? First taste of sex and you think that's the best you can get?"

"I don't *think*. I *know* it's the best I can get," I spit out.

He bares his teeth, then pushes down with such force, I have to grab at the sink to stop myself from falling over. Another zip of pain, this time more intense, shivers down my neck. My back protests, and my shoulders hurt. The fine hairs on the back of my neck rise. *Shit, shit, shit, I shouldn't have aggravated him, but I'm so tired of playing safe. So tired of feeling torn. And I hate him. This much I know. And I don't want anything to do with him.*

"I'm going to show you what it means to be fucked by a real man."

He palms my butt, and I cry out, "Stop!"

His smile widens before he reaches down and grips the hem of my skirt.

"Rick, help me!" I scream.

That's when the door crashes open.

49

Rick

He has his hands on her. *He. Has. His. Hands. On. What's. Mine.* My feet don't seem to touch the floor as I close the distance to where he's standing behind her. He has his fingers in her hair. Adrenaline laces my blood. My vision tunnels. I strike at his forearm, and he cries out. He releases his hold on her and staggers back. And I step between them. I sense her shudder, feel the terror coming off her in waves, and the last hold on my control dissolves.

With a roar, I smash my fist into the side of his head. He stumbles back, and I'm sure he's going to keel over, but to my surprise, he shoots out his fist. I block, land another punch in his stomach. He wheezes, and I continue to punch him. One-two-three. I'm aware of her clutching at my shoulder, but I shake her off, and continue to bury my fist in his side, his chest—he cries out —his throat. He makes a choking sound.

The next second, arms grip me and pull me away, and someone does the same to him. I manage to get in another punch, this time, to his nose. Blood blooms and drips down his chin.

"Stop this." Edward steps between us. "Stop it, right fucking now."

"Get the fuck out of my way, Priest." I raise my fist, but Edward grips my wrist and squeezes.

"Get a hold of yourself."

"He touched her," I growl. "He fucking touched what belongs to me."

"Hey…" She steps around from behind me. "I-I-I'm not a possession."

"You're mine. And I don't share."

"I'm n-n-n… not yours." She sets her jaw.

"Oh?" I lower my hand, then grab her hand with Gram's ring on her finger. I raise it, so she has no choice but to look down at it, then at me.

"This says otherwise," I snap.

"Th-that… is not"—she glances at Edward, who's looking between us with narrowed eyes—"what it seems," she whispers.

"Knew it." Her bastard ex crows—or tries to, for his voice comes out muffled, thanks to the towel he's holding against his nose.

"You're right," I snap.

"I-I am?" She blinks.

Edward lowers his chin.

Sensing the tension in my muscles, and no doubt, noticing how my shoulders bunch, they tighten their holds on me.

Even her douche of an ex falls silent. The security guys from the restaurant who'd shouldered their way in on Edward's heels hold him back.

I take advantage of the silence to slide my jacket off and place it around her shoulders. "It's not what it seems because things have changed."

She frowns and opens her mouth, but I bend and scoop her up in my arms, bridal style. "We're getting married."

"What?" Edward gapes.

"What?" she cries.

"What the fuck?" Arsemonger—yep, this is the right name for him— Dennis takes a step forward. "You can't do this; you fucking can't."

She wriggles in my arms, but I tighten them about her and flash a grin in her ex's direction. "We are."

He makes a strangled sound, then leans forward on the balls of his feet. "You can have her. She's a fucking bitch who—" His eyes roll back in his face because Edward releases me and moves so fast, he almost blurs. His fist connects with fuckhead's face, and the arsemonger would be on the floor were it not for the security team holding him up.

That's when a flashbulb goes off from the doorway.

"Are you okay?" I glance down at where she's huddled in my arms. We're in an office in the restaurant, not far from where the photographer snapped our photo. He managed to evade the security posted around and in the restaurant and get to us. These paps will do anything for a scoop. And captains of the two hottest hockey teams in the country, who are also bitter rivals, fighting each other over a woman, is bound to fetch him thousands when he hawks the pictures to the tabloids.

I left Edward to deal with Dennis and the journalist and carried Gio out of the restroom. Turns out, he was here in the same restaurant for a meeting and spotted first, Dennis, then me. He saw me leave the table in a hurry and decided to follow me out. He also alerted the security team.

The restaurant staff directed me to this space, and not a second too late. If I'd stayed, I was liable to kill her bastard of an ex with my bare hands, and I promise, that's not a euphemism. Gio was right, I killed men when I was on the front line, and sure, that's because it was my duty to do so, but it lowered the barrier in my mind to taking a life. And his, I gladly would—he touched her, threatened her, and made her tremble so much that when I hauled her up in my arms and walked out, she didn't try to push me away. And that bothered me. It's not like Gio to be this passive. I'd rather she be her usual, sassy self, and the fact that she isn't is testament to how disturbed she is. "Gio?" I cup her cheek.

She shudders, then seems to come out of wherever she'd gone to in her head.

"I'm fine," she says in a listless voice.

"You're not fine." I reach for the pitcher of water the staff left us, fill a glass, and offer it to her. She takes it without comment, takes a sip, then begins to put it aside.

"Drink some more."

She obediently raises the bottle to her lips and takes a few sips, and that only makes me more anxious. I take the glass from her, set it aside, then bring her closer. "Tell me what you're thinking."

"Nothing."

"It's something."

She swallows. "How could I have misjudged him like that? I thought I was in love with him. I thought he loved me. I was so wrong."

"It's his fault. He's the one who couldn't be loyal to you."

"He didn't want to sleep with me. He wanted to wait until we were married, and I thought that was a sweet, loving gesture. Little did I know it was because he was fetishizing it and wanted to sleep with other women, and—"

"Stop." I place my palm over her mouth. "I will not let you do this to yourself."

Her gaze widens; she looks at me over the top of my hand.

"You're a gorgeous, beautiful, smart, ambitious woman who's going to be my wife, and I will not let you beat yourself up over some man who had no idea how lucky he was for you to even be in his proximity."

Tears gleam in her eyes.

I shake my head. "No, don't. He doesn't deserve you to cry for him."

When a drop squeezes out of the corner of her eye, I bend and lick it up. I move my palm down to her throat and curl my fingers around the slim column. When I press down, her breath catches. Her pulse rate speeds up. I whisper tiny kisses down her cheek until I reach her mouth. I hover my lips over hers and stare into her golden eyes. There's a plea in them, a silent ask. One I know I want to give her... Just not yet. "You've been through an emotional encounter; you need to recuperate."

"I need"—she clears her throat—"you to fuck me right now."

"Not when you're vulnerable."

"Now, when I'm vulnerable. So I can feel you inside me, and on me, and all around me. So I can use you to wipe out the feel of his hands on me, the sliminess of his touch, the heat from his body that made me sick to my stomach. I need it now, so I can imprint you in all of my senses. So I can purge every last memory of him from my mind, my body, every part of me that only you have the right to."

My heart smashes into my ribcage, and my blood pulses at my temples. I lean back into the chair, taking her with me, and when I lift her by her waist, she throws her leg over my lap and straddles me. "Please, Rick. Please." She peers between my eyes. "I'm begging you to fuck me."

"I cannot... will not fuck you," I murmur.

Her features crumple.

"But I will make love to you."

50

Gio

Make love to me? Did he say make love to me? I'm almost not surprised because, somewhere along the way, I became sure he'd developed feelings for me like I'd done for him. Only right now, I don't want the tender side of Rick. I want the part of him that is Stone—immovable, mean, smashing everything that comes in his path to smithereens. Throwing me down on all fours and mounting me from behind without mercy. I want the Stone who was my first, who smacked my butt and made me come, who took his pleasure from me and denied me my orgasm until he was ready. I want that Stone—the one who filled my body with his and pushed all the thoughts from my mind. Especially the thought of how I'd trusted someone who'd not only cheated on me but also would have raped me if Rick hadn't been there at the right time. Oh my god, my horrible ex could have marred me in a way I might not have recovered from.

"Look at me," Rick snaps.

I blink, then focus my gaze on his, and his aquamarine blue eyes capture mine. The silver sparks in them and I'm drawn in.

"You will not think of him again. You will not think of what happened. You'll focus on my touch." He slides his big palms down to cup my butt.

"You'll bring your attention to how your core fits around my length." He lowers me down to the ridge between his legs, and an electric current runs up my spine. And when he thrusts up and into me, I can feel his length stab into my core through the barriers of clothing we're wearing.

"I need to feel you inside me," I gasp. Sweat pools under my armpits, and my skin feels too tight. My scalp tingles, and I dig my fingers into his shoulders, wanting to feel every part of him against me.

He holds my eyes for a second longer, then nods as if coming to a decision. He maneuvers me up, so I'm balanced on my knees on either side of his lap. Then he pulls up my skirt and tears off my panties.

"Oh." All thoughts disappear from my mind. He's done this before, but it never stops turning me on. I can feel my cum trickle down between my legs.

"Open," he growls.

When I part my lips, he stuffs my panties between them. Then he lowers his zipper. I glance down to find his cock jutting up, the head swollen and purple, with pre-cum drooling from the slit. My mouth waters, I reach down, needing to touch him, and he clicks his tongue. I glance up to find a fiercely intent look on his features. Then, he positions me over his dick, and pushes me down, so I'm impaled.

Thick, hard, and so right. I'm spread around his girth, stretched around his monster cock, that leaves no room for anything but the feel of his shaft throbbing inside me. I grip his thick wrists, and feel his skin give under my fingernails. And it's primal, and satisfying, and so carnal. It's what I need right now. I squeeze down with my inner muscles, and a growl rips from him. I lower my chin, peer into his eyes, and the fierceness in them makes me flinch. He raises me, holding me up like I weigh nothing, until I'm once again balanced over the crown of his cock, then he pushes me down, breaching me in one smooth move. I cry out, the sound muffled against my panties, throw my head back and pant, letting the pain from his intrusion seep into the pleasure that sparks in my cells.

He holds me there, giving me a chance to adjust to his size, then begins to raise and lower me, again and again. Each time, his length seems to grow bigger, broader, more immense. The tell-tale trembling starts at my knees, and then I'm lifted off of him and placed on the table. He urges me to wrap my legs about his waist and positions his cock at my entrance. Then he pushes forward and sinks into me. The orgasm continues like there was never a break. And when I whimper and throw my arms about his neck, he yanks out my gag, pockets it, and closes his mouth over mine.

With one hand on the nape of my neck and the other on my hip holding me in place, he pulls out, then ploughs into me, absorbing the cry that wells up my throat. He leans in, and the world shifts.

I'm on my back, looking up into his eyes, clinging to his shoulders, with my legs wrapped around him. Without pausing, he drills into me with such force, the table creaks. Something crashes to the floor. The sound of flesh meeting flesh fills the space, the scent of our combined arousal sinks into my blood, and the dominance of his personality pins me down.

My chest feels like it's being cleaved open, and everything I feel for him pours out of me. "I love you," I choke into his mouth. I'm not sure if he heard it. I'm not sure if I said it aloud or in my mind. Either way, he must glean the sentiment, for he tears his mouth from mine, and lunges forward, hitting a spot deep inside me that sets off a tsunami of sensations that travel up my spine and burst behind my eyes.

"Come," he snaps, and I shatter. With a low cry, he follows me over the edge. When I open my eyes next, I'm in his lap, gathered close into his chest, and my clothes have been straightened. His jacket is draped over me again, forming a cocoon.

The door opens and Edward walks in, followed by Knight. They don't seem to notice anything amiss. Edward leans a hip against the table. Knight glowers between the two of them before turning to Edward. "And I thought you were the mature one," he bites out.

"He deserved it," Edward replies.

"He touched her. I'm going to kill him," Rick says in a flat voice that's so devoid of sentiment, it's clear he's serious. I glance up at the hard ridge of his jaw, feel like I should protest, but...

"Shut up." Knight stabs a finger in his direction. "I'm not saying what you did is wrong. If I were in your place, I'd have done the same thing, but there are ways of dealing with the situation without your being directly involved."

I blink, then the ramifications of what he's saying sinks in. I stiffen. "Are you saying what I think you are?"

"All he's saying is that Rick is too important for us. He's the captain; we need him." Edward rubs the back of his neck. "We can't jeopardize the chance for him to lead the Ice Kings against the Sentinels."

"And I don't fucking care if it means I'm getting benched. I am going to make him pay for what he did. He is going to regret every bit of pain he caused her," Rick bites out.

I swing my head in his direction. O-k-a-y, I wasn't expecting that kind of vehemence. I knew he was pissed, and I confess, I'm shaken by what almost happened, but... I swallow down the ball of emotion that blocks my throat. He deserves everything that Rick's threatening, and it'd please me no end to see Rick get his hands on him, but I can't let Rick risk his career, I can't. He's worked too hard for it. He has too much riding on it. Not least of it is the fact he needs to prove himself in his own eyes. More than anything, it will wreck his confidence if he doesn't face off against the other team and win this game.

I reach up and cup his cheek. "I'm okay."

He looks into my eyes and his shoulders relax. "Doesn't change what he did to you. What he almost did to you..."

"And you can have your revenge where it benefits everyone, on the ice."

51

Rick

"You're not going to hold back," Finn says with finality as we wait for the gates to open and let us on the ice. The Sentinels finished their warm-up session first, followed by us. They've been introduced and are on the ice while we're queued up in the tunnel waiting to enter. The chanting of the crowd grows deafening. We're not the home team, and the support is with them, but it's not going to deter me from gunning for that douchecanoe Dennis on the ice.

"At least pretend like you're not going to kill him," Finn murmurs.

When I don't reply he slaps me on the shoulder. "You hear me, Stone? Don't go crazy."

"I know what I have to do." I crack my neck, grip my hockey stick, and bend forward. The gate opens, I glide out and am introduced, followed by the rest of the team. The national anthem is played. Then I glide forward to the center of the court; so does Dennis. We are both captains and play center— a-n-d today's not his lucky day. I'm going to make him pay at every turn. We glare at each other through our helmets. I lean in; so does he. Our gazes clash. Around us, the noise ebbs and flows as our teams take their stance. Then Solene—in her role as the hottest pop star since Taylor Swift— releases the puck. Instantly, the noise rises to a crescendo.

She's escorted off the ice and the game is on. Fuckface reaches for the puck. I leap forward, smack his chest with my shoulder, putting enough force into the move that he stumbles back. I twist, follow it up with a hip check, and yep, fuckface overbalances and hits the ice. I raise my stick, intent on pinning his throat to the floor, but Jagger sweeps in from the side, nudging me along with him. The fuck?

He glares at me through his helmet, then jerks his head toward where Caspian has the puck and is moving toward the Sentinel's goalie. He tosses it to Maddox who shoots it past the goalie.

Cheers erupt. Some of the burning in my chest subsides.

I glide back to the center to face off with Douchecanoe. The referee drops the puck, and before it even hits the ice, I'm on him. This time, I body check Douchecanoe with such force, he loses his stick. Jagger glides by, sending it flying, then Maddox, then Enzo, until it hits the board.

I rejoin my team, this time, snatching the puck from Caleb and shooting the goal. Douchecanoe has to head to the bench to get a new stick, and when we face-off the third time, he's prepared. Finally. I need more of a challenge.

This time, he bodychecks my hip. I hit his shoulder, we jostle, then I lean my full weight into his torso, and he loses his footing and overbalances on the ice. Once more, he loses his stick, and it's swept away in the melee. I bare my teeth at him, not missing the rage in his features, before racing off to support my team. Enzo shoots the goal, and the whistle blows for the end of the period.

I glance around, until I spot her and glide over to the plexiglass above the boards. I place my hand on the glass, and the crowd around us yells its support. Gio flushes, looking like she's about to run away. I tip up my chin and drag my gaze down to the jersey she's wearing, which has my number. When I look at her face again, her flush deepens. Even across the distance, I sense the shiver that grips her. She walks forward and places her palm on the glass over mine. The crowd rises to their feet in the stands behind her, camera flashes going off. I bring my glove-covered palm to my chest. Gio's chin trembles. I shake my head, and she manages to smile, then I turn and glide off the ice.

When I meet fuckface at the next face-off, it's clear, he's better prepared. We bodycheck each other, neither of us giving way, while the puck is swept away. I grapple with him for a second, then another. He breaks free, hooks his stick around my leg and tugs. I stumble back. The referee blows his whistle, indicating a minor penalty. Fuckface grins, then glides off the ice.

He's replaced by another player, and the game continues. Finn's unable to save the next two goals, and by the time the whistle blows for the end of the second period, we're two goals each. In the dressing room, the mood is tense. I rehydrate, stretch, then turn to my team. "I'm not sorry I'm gunning for Captain Fuckface, and I promise, I will not let the team lose."

Caspian frowns at me. "You should have never become captain. Your play so far shows where your priorities lie."

"My priorities lie with my fiancée," I growl.

"And that's what you get for having someone with experience lead us." He snickers. "Now, if I were the captain, I'd put the game before anything else."

"Which is why you have a ways to go before you become captain," Edward interrupts. He walks over, dressed in his usual dark suit, and plants his hands on his hips. "What you do off-ice affects how you perform in there." He stabs his thumb in the direction of the rink.

"Exactly what I'm saying," Caspian begins, but Edward cuts him off.

"And when you're obsessed with the game to the exclusion of everything else, your performance is lopsided. It makes you—"

"Focused?" Caspian sneers

"Blinkered," Edward says in a firm voice. "You're too focused on the end result, to the extent that you'd sacrifice anything to get to your goal."

"Duh?" Caspian looks at Edward with a frown on his face.

"You need a balance, some perspective, the ability to look at the big picture which is what Rick"—he jerks his chin in my direction—"brings to his role."

Caspian's features harden. "And that's why you overlooked that he's engaged to our PR manager? A fact that—"

"Is unorthodox but which has generated positive publicity for the Ice Kings and put us in the running as a possible contender for the League, which your shoddy performance in today's game might unravel." Edward lowers his chin. "You have a burning desire to excel, Prick. That's your competitive edge, but it's going to be your undoing when you take it to the extreme."

"That fucking call sign." Caspian glowers at me.

I shrug. I call it as I see it, and that motherfucker is a prick whose ego is bigger than mine, and *that's* saying something.

"Combined with Rick's insights and expertise and the skill of the remaining team members, we have a chance of making it through to the finals—assuming the lot of you pull your heads out of your arses and focus on the prize."

The second period goes better. We score two goals, the Sentinels score none. I take the opportunity to body check the fuckface, but in a way that doesn't get me banned—not that I give a fuck about it, but I owe it to my teammates to keep my head in the game, and more importantly, keep the team in the game. I'm also flagging. I wouldn't ever admit it aloud, but the truth is, I feel it as I limp off the ice. I make sure to meet her gaze, but don't going up to the plexiglass this time, but only because I need to do this much for my teammates.

And fuck, if that doesn't twist my heart. Because when it comes down to it, I'd choose her over the game any day, and it wasn't meant to happen this way. But when I saw his hands on her and noticed the anguish on her face, something in me changed. I knew then, she's more important than the game, and that revelation took me by surprise.

I'm still dealing with it, still unsure what to make of it. I gave into that feeling when I skated over to her earlier, and much as I want to do that now, my guilt over the feelings I developed for her, along with Edward's words ringing in my ears, ensured I continued off the ice after a final glance.

The intermission goes quickly, especially because I focus on stretching out the aches and pains, and chugging down a sports drink. Finn and Caspian spend the time in a game of who can do more push-ups, and while I'm tempted to join them, I'm not stupid enough to do so. Even a few years ago, I'd have been leading them in the race, but now, I know when to conserve my energy and when to compete. And while I'm confident I can outdo the two upstarts, it's more important I go out and finish this game on a high.

We head back to the ice. I face-off with Arsemonger, the puck drops, and he moves first. He raises his stick and hits me on my shoulder. Pain rips up my arm, but I shake it off. Everything in me wants to lower my head and butt him, but if I did that, I'd face a match penalty which would cripple my team. That wouldn't help any of us, and definitely not Gio, who'd have a PR disaster on her hands. I content myself with tripping the douche and slashing at his shoulder when he falls as I glide off.

I catch the puck from Caspian, throw it to Jagger, who shoots it home. The home audience boos; our supporters in the audience cheer. I glide back to the center where Arsemonger is back on his feet. Neither of us were charged with a penalty, an oversight which the audience is not happy about. It also means the next time I indulge in unsportsmanlike behavior, I'm going to be sent off the ice.

The puck drops, and we lunge at each other. He tries to hook me. I step aside and hit him with the shaft of the stick. The whistle blows, and the referee indicates we're both to be sent off the ice for two minutes. I glare at the douche then glide to the bench while Joshua, aka Ghost, takes over. However, the incident seems to have broken the focus of the team, for the Sentinels score. Their home crowd cheers, but ultimately, we win 3 - 2.

As we glide off the ice, Arsemonger skates past, but not before he digs his elbow into my side. "I don't know what you're hiding, but whatever it is, I plan to dig it out."

I turn, grip his shoulder and pull him close, so to anyone watching, it'll look like we were having a conversation. I tighten my hold on him, and his features redden. He tries to yank free, but I squeeze down. His features slowly purple, he opens his mouth to speak, but nothing comes out. I bare my teeth. "By the time I'm done with you, you won't have the strength to move. If you dare come near her—if you dare even look at her again—if you dare so much as be within a hundred feet of her, I'll fucking—"

"Rick!"

52

Gio

I yell through the plexiglass, sure he won't hear me over the noise, but he stiffens. He heard me. He must hear me, or at least, he must sense me. "Rick, stop, please."

Tension is embedded in every hard plane of his body, but he releases Dennis, pivots and glides off the rink without looking at me.

I hurry up the aisle between the rows of people beginning to stream out. When I reach the top of the seats, I turn toward the room where the post-match media-debrief is going to be held. Making sure all of the arrangements are in place, I withdraw to the side. The reporters file in, and in a few minutes, the seats are taken. Then Edward walks in, followed by Rick, the Sentinel's General Manager, and Dennis. All four take their seats on the podium, and the journalists start firing questions.

"Is it true that Rick's fiancée was your girlfriend, Dennis?" One of the journalists asks Dennis the question, but Rick cuts in with, "She's not his; she's mine."

Oh my god, does that man have no self-preservation? How could he say something so caveman, and with a straight face, a-n-d — I take in the faces of the journalists, all of whom have serious looks on their faces. They're taking him seriously. Don't they see how ridiculous it is that he claims me as his in front of all of them, as if he owns me, and all of them take it as the gospel truth?

"Were the two of you exchanging words? Anything to do with her?" Another journalist asks.

I flatten myself against the wall of the conference room. Good thing I chose the furthermost corner from the platform. I look down, making sure not to meet anyone's gaze.

"Isn't this press-conference about the game?" Edward asks in a pointed fashion. "I prefer it if we leave the player's personal life out of the questions."

"You can ask about my personal life any time. I'd be only too happy to answer," Dennis says with an oily smile on his face. How could I have thought of him as charming? I'll take Rick's rare smiles over Dennis' any day. Rick's smiles are so genuine, they hit me in the guts and twist my insides, and always have my ovaries all excited.

"In which case, I'd love to know why the two of you had an altercation on the ice," a journalist pipes up.

"Altercation?" Rick rubs at his chin. "That wasn't an altercation." There's laughter from the audience, then Rick rises to his feet and growls, "This is an altercation." He turns, hauls Dennis to his feet, and before the man can react, he's buried his fist in his face.

"Couldn't you control yourself?" I dig my fingers into my hair and tug. Strands of my hair rain down around my face and I push them back. I've never known a time when I've been this distraught. Not even when I'd walked in on my ex and my friend. But watching this man bury his career is agonizing. And arousing. The fact he doesn't care one whit for his public image and that he proclaimed me as his in front of the world and on national media is the hottest thing anyone has done for me. Also, the scariest thing. This is irrevocable proof that this guy is nothing like my ex—which I knew, but which he confirmed today. And all the more reason he needs to keep playing. He's the best player on the scene, and the best captain this team could have, and I can't let him fuck it up for me.

"You gave me your word," Edward warns from across the table. The usually unruffled GM looks this close to flipping his temper.

"I stuck to it."

"So what was that out there?" He stabs his thumb in the direction of the conference room. We're in the office adjoining it, where Edward and Finn managed to drag Rick away after he'd punched Dennis in his nose—the one which Rick already broke previously.

Dennis howled like a banshee, and the flashbulbs went off like fireworks. My phone has been pinging with updates ever since. I have no doubt the pictures of the two of them will be all over the internet again, and by default, me too. One of the reporters spotted me and moved toward me, but I evaded and ran out of the room, then got on the phone to my contacts in the media to try to put damage control measures in place, but there was not much I could do. It was a disagreement captured live on camera, and the press was going to have a field day with it.

"What do you have to say for yourself?" Edward bites out.

"I stuck to my promise of not fighting on the ice. I didn't say anything about off the rink."

"Motherfucker." Edward throws up his hands. "Do you have any idea how difficult it was to convince the chairpersons of the League not to penalize you?"

"Those ass-twerps? I'm sure they're enjoying the extra attention I'm bringing to the league. The enmity between me and that douceface, is no doubt driving many square inches of media attention. It's benefitting them, putting bums on seats for the next game, and shining the spotlight on the game in the country."

Edward sets his jaw. "It shows you as being unsportsmanlike, a man who'd take the rules in his own hands, a man—"

"Who's driving heightened levels of sponsorship money into the sport," Rick drawls.

Edward's jaw tics, the veins on his throat stand out, and OMG, that only draws attention to his smoldering good looks. I'd have to be blind not to notice how appealing he is when he's all worked up...and when he's not. Except, he doesn't do anything for me. He doesn't have the same effect on my body as Rick.

I flick my gaze in the direction of my fiancé to find he's glowering at me. I frown back at him. An assessing glint sparks in his eyes, one that promises me retribution for—he couldn't have realized I found Edward attractive for about a second, right?

Edward draws in a sharp breath. "I saved your arse this time, but it may not happen again. Don't push your luck, Maverick. One of these days, you're going to be caught up in the turbulence of your own making, and we all know how that ended for Goose."

Maverick? I blink in Rick's direction and find him sitting stiffly, his shoulder muscles bunched under his team sweatshirt.

Edward spins around and walks out, the door slamming shut behind him. I keep my gaze on Rick, who has a distant look on his face. A vein pops at his temple. The muscles of his jaw are so wound up, it's a wonder he hasn't cracked a molar by now. His gaze is distant. Those blue eyes of his resemble a frozen tundra. As I watch, that promise of retribution in them deepens into an expression that tells me he's not going to hold back. He rises to his feet, and I take a step back. He kicks his chair out of the way, his movements deliberate. I gulp, resisting the urge to glance at the door behind me. He prowls toward me, and I stumble back. My back hits the wall, and I gasp. When he steps into my space, I tilt my face back, and further back, so as not to break the connection. I will not be the first to look away. I won't.

I need to distract this guy before he touches me. If he does, I won't be able to resist him. So, I say the first thing that comes into my head. "Who's Maverick?"

53

Rick

"Who the fuck do you think he is?" I bend my knees and peer into her eyes.

She flinches. "I-I don't know."

"Why are you stuttering?" I lower my voice to a hush, and she shivers.

"I-I'm not."

"Lying, Goldie?" I lean into her space, so my chest is pressed into hers, and she shudders. The pulse at the base of her neck kicks up, and damn, but I can't stop myself. I lower my head and close my mouth around the skin where her blood pounds in her veins. She whimpers, and the blood drains to my groin. I nibble my way around the base of her throat, then release her, only to curl my fingers around her neck. I squeeze, and her gaze widens. Her chest rises and falls. The scent of her arousal bleeds into the air, and my balls tighten. "My hand-necklace looks so fucking good on you." With my free hand, I grasp her butt and lift. She gasps, then locks her ankles around my waist and clings to my shoulders. She raises her chin, but I evade her lips. "I'll kiss you when I'm good and ready," I growl.

She pouts. "Why can't I initiate a kiss?"

"Because you're a brat who needs to learn how to earn what she wants."

"But—" she begins to whine, and I narrow my gaze on her.

"Keep that up, and I won't be doing anything else, either."

"Like I want you to—" She groans, for I've pushed my crotch into its happy place, also known as, in the cradle between her legs. My dick instantly lengthens, and I know she can feel it stab into her center, for color flushes her cheeks. She begins to grind down on my cock, and her breathing grows choppy. Her eyes are dilated, her lips parted, and all I want is to remove the barriers of our clothing and push into her…

Like that douchecanoe wanted to do. If I hadn't arrived there in time— The blood pounds through my veins. My guts churn. Asshole deserves to die. If only I didn't have to wait until the team makes it to the finals of the league before I have my revenge.

And meanwhile, you're going to string her along? And allow your feelings for her to deepen. Allow her to fall in love with you, too? How much of a sadist can you possibly be? How can you do this to her?

She looks into my face, and a furrow appears between her eyebrows. "What's wrong?"

I draw in a sharp breath. *Since when have I unable to keep my feelings to myself? Since when have I begun showing what I felt inside on my face? Since when has she read me so well?*

"Rick?" She cups my cheek in a gesture that's so familiar, so heartfelt, so everything. A line of sensations runs from where she's touching me to my chest. My heart falters. My scalp tingles. The words I want to speak die in my throat. I spread my fingers so they cover the sweet column of her neck, and all I can think is, *she's mine. Mine. Mine. Mine.*

"Rick? Baby?" A flash of panic ignites in her eyes. "Rick, talk to me."

I open my mouth to tell her the real reason I asked her to share a room with me the day she arrived at the house, when my phone buzzes in the back pocket of my jeans. I ignore it, lower my chin until my mouth is over hers, and draw in her sweet breath. The phone stops, then starts again.

"Aren't you going to get that?" She asks in a breathless voice.

I blink.

"Rick, it might be your grandmother."

Fuck, she's right. How could I have forgotten Grams' condition? I pin her to the wall with my hips, pull out my phone and answer. The voice on the other side echoes through my head. When I lower the phone, she takes in the look on my face, and her expression changes to one of sympathy.

"She's going to be okay." Goldie places her hand on my shoulder, but I shrug it off. If anything happens to Grams, I'll never forgive myself. She's my only surviving relation. I should have checked in on her more.

I called her to tell her I was getting married, and she was elated. She promised to set the date for the procedure with the surgeon. I didn't follow up after that. I was too caught up with preparing for the game, and my mind was too full of Goldie and my changing feelings for her. I was selfish again. I didn't make time for Grams, just like I wasn't there for Diana when she needed me most. If I hadn't been busy pursuing my career as an NHL player, I'd have been able to be there for my sister.

After our parents' deaths, Diana was everything to me. Grams brought us both up, but she was never able to control Diana. She only listened to me. When I got the opportunity to play for the NHL, I didn't want to go, but Grams convinced me. She told me my parents would have wanted it. That if I didn't follow my passion, I'd regret it.

I didn't want to listen to her, until Diana found out. She was seventeen then but mature enough to insist I follow my dream. I promised I'd always be there for her, no matter how busy I was. But, NHL commitments meant there was no way I could fly back to see her as often as I wanted. In fact, I only managed to get away for Christmas each year.

Whenever I made it back home, things were strained between Diana and my grandmother, but I didn't realize how bad things were. Not until Grams called to tell me Diana had moved to L.A. to launch her career as a director. Even then, I wasn't alarmed. Diana had always been stubborn; she'd always known her mind, and had been mature for her years.

Even though she and Grams didn't often see eye-to-eye, they loved each other. I kept in touch with Diana by phone, calling her every week, and she kept me updated on her progress. Things were tough. She was pitching her script and waitressing to pay her bills, but she never lost faith in her talent. Neither did I. I was convinced she'd make it as a director. She was talented and beautiful. Then the calls stopped. I wasn't able to get hold of her. I hadn't been particularly alarmed. I hadn't time to be alarmed, I had entered a particularly challenging phase of my career, and all my mind-space was taken up with making it in the NHL. Then the call came.

"Rick?" Goldie's voice cuts through my thoughts. "Dr. Kincaid's here."

I glance up to find a man in scrubs walking toward me. His features are tired, but his gaze is bright, and that gives me hope. I rise to my feet; so does Goldie. She takes my hand, and this time, I let her. He stops in front of us, then his face curves in a smile. "I'm Dr. Weston Kincaid. Your grandmother is doing well."

I blow out a breath. "How long will the recovery be?"

He turns serious. "I won't lie. She's at an age where it will take her time to recover from the effects of the operation, but she's a strong woman and a fighter. I'd told her to not delay the operation. Her heart was weakening every day, but the woman was stubborn. If she'd agreed to the operation earlier, it wouldn't have come to this." He shakes his head.

Guilt twists my guts. My stomach churns, and bile boils up my throat. I'm responsible for Grams condition. I should have set a date for the wedding and insisted that Goldie go through with it. That way, Grams would have gone through with the procedure before she collapsed. I curl my fingers into a fist at my side. I tighten my hand around Goldie's, and sensing the tension emanating from me, she stiffens.

Neither of us says anything.

Dr. Kincaid looks at the engagement ring on her finger, then back up at me. His feature soften. "She's a tough one. I'm confident she'll be back on her feet soon."

A shudder of relief grips me. My knees buckle, I sway, and Goldie wraps her arm about my waist to steady me. For a second, I lean my weight on her. I realize again, she's not fragile as she seems. For the first time in my life, I've depended on someone else. *But why does it have to be her?* I put distance between us, so she has to lower her hand. I sense the hurt on her face, but I don't look at her.

"Can we see her?"

"She's still in recovery and will likely be sleeping off the after-effects of the anesthesia. I suggest you go home and do the same. You can come tomorrow morning, by which time, she should be awake."

When I hesitate, Dr. Kincaid turns to Goldie. "Take your man home. Both of you seem ready to drop." He nods in my direction. "You're no good to her if you run yourself into the ground."

He turns to leave, then stops. "She was asking for Tiny when she was brought in. Who's he?"

54

Gio

"We're getting married," Rick announces.

He spent the entire journey from the hospital brooding. I wanted to console him, but after the way he pulled away from me earlier, I wasn't sure if I should. He had a car with a driver waiting for us outside. I assumed he'd ordered one earlier. But when we slid into the backseat, he greeted the chauffeur. He didn't introduce the other man, who frowned at him, then introduced himself as Charles.

He's Grams' driver and has been the Mitchell family's driver for more than thirty years. It's another piece of information I added to the 'Rick's space' area in my heart. Somehow, he's never volunteered information about his family. He only took me to see Grams because that was part of our deal.

Fact is, I might know Rick in the carnal sense, but emotionally, it's another matter altogether. The man has never been open to sharing information about himself. He's never bothered to ask me about myself, either. If it hadn't been for that journalist's interview where she tested us about our knowledge of each other, I wouldn't have realized how much he knows about me. Things he's learned by observing, and no doubt, asking the friends we have in common.

Still, I'd have preferred he ask me face-to-face, like going on an old-fashioned date. But when you're roomies and the chemistry between the two of you is always a third presence... It's difficult to keep your mind on anything else except jumping him, and licking him up, and coaxing him to sink that big, fat cock of his inside you. Heat flushes my skin. Why am I thinking of sex, when his grandmother is in the hospital?

I'm a horrible, horrible person. I reined in my thoughts and ended up falling asleep in the car. When I opened my eyes, it was to find he was carrying me into' the house. I protested, but he ignored me and that had pissed me off. But I was too tired, so I decided to close my eyes, snuggle into his chest, and enjoy the ride up the stairs.

Then, he prowled into the room, lowered me to the bed, and loomed over me until I opened my eyes. That's when he made his intention known, and all sleep vanished.

I spring up in bed. "What?"

"It shouldn't come as a surprise to you. I already told you this was inevitable."

"But Grams already had her operation," I protest.

"And if we had gotten married earlier, she wouldn't have waited until she'd collapsed to be rushed into surgery. She almost died." His jaw hardens. A nerve twitches at his temple, a sure sign that he's pissed.

I recognize this man's little tells. I know that he likes to fuck rough, that he enjoys primal play, even as his touch is so tender it brings tear to my eyes. That he'd do anything for his family and for his team, that he has feelings for me, even though he hasn't outright confessed to it, but a woman's instinct knows when a man is affected by her. He hasn't said 'I love you,' but he's told me he cares for me, and more importantly, he's shown me how much he wants me. And Rick 'Stone' Mitchell, captain of the hottest ice hockey team on the continent, is drawn to me, and not just physically, even though he's loathe to admit it.

"I'm sorry Grams didn't have her operation earlier, but she's fine now."

"And if she finds out we're not getting married, all the progress she's made will be reversed."

I rub at my forehead. Every part of me hurts after spending the night on the unforgiving hospital chairs, even though Rick and I had been ushered to a comfortable waiting room on what seemed to be a private floor of the hospital, the kind I didn't think existed in the country. And while the coffee from the machine was terrible, the corridors were carpeted. There were a few other waiting rooms on the floor, and a reception with someone at the desk all night, and there were nurses coming in to keep us updated, something I didn't think would normally happen. The entire process gave off the feeling that there was a lot of money cushioning the process. And his grandmother's home was beautiful, with that gorgeous private garden behind it... but it wasn't ostentatious... But add the car and uniformed driver who had picked us up, and the dots join in my head. "You're rich," I exclaim.

He stares at me, a question in his eyes.

"I mean, you're rich. The kind of rich where you don't have to make your bed every day or cook your own food or lift a finger to do anything. It's why you have a chauffeur who's worked for your family for decades."

He tilts his head. "Your point being?"

"Don't you want me to sign a prenup?"

"So you are going to marry me?" Something flashes in his eyes, but he banks it.

"If we don't, Grams is not going to be happy. It'll upset her and put more strain on her heart, so you've said."

"Is that a yes?"

I bring up my knees and hug them to my chest. "It's not like I have a choice."

"Marrying me is the ultimate way to piss off your douche-ex."

"I suppose."

"Don't you want to get revenge for what he did to you?"

"Oh, I do." But somewhere along the way, this had become less about Dennis and more about me and Rick.

"So what's the problem?"

"It's just"—fatigue knocks at the back of my eyes—"every time I think I know you, something happens, and I'm sure I don't."

He seems about to say something, then shakes his head. He tosses his jacket aside, reaches behind him to pull off his T-shirt, then shoves his jeans down. OMG that expanse of his ripped chest, with the tattoo over his heart, the concave stomach, those powerful thighs—my mouth waters. My nipples tighten, and I squeeze my thighs together to control that gnawing in my core. He rakes his gaze over me, and I'm sure he knows the effect his striptease had on me, then he mutters, "Scoot over."

"Wha—"

He slides onto the bed, so I have no choice but to follow his direction. He pulls the covers over both of us, then adjusts me so I'm on my side and his arm is under my neck. He adjusts his body to mine so he's spooning me, and oh my god, heaven is the feel of his hard thighs against mine, the wall of his chest pressed into my back, my head tucked under his chin, with his heavy arm pinning me to him, and that thick length of his cock nestled into the curve of my butt.

"Rick," I begin, but he tightens his hold on me. "Sleep, we'll talk later."

"You're too hot," I protest.

When he doesn't answer, I sigh. "I mean, your body is like a furnace, I'm sweating, I need to take off my clothes."

"Not stopping you," his voice is slurred, like he's half asleep already.

I manage to shuck off my slacks, then my jacket and my blouse, as well as my bra. Clad in my panties, I burrow back into his chest. He pulls me close.

"Rick, I haven't brushed my teeth, and neither have you," I protest.

He makes a noise at the back of his throat which I interpret as 'fuck that.'

I sigh again, "Rick, I do need to brush my teeth."

No answer.

"Rick,"—I dig my elbow in his side, but his granite-like body absorbs it— "did you hear me? *I have to* brush my teeth."

This time, he's the one who sighs. "We'll brush each other's teeth tomorrow morning with our tongues." he mumbles under his breath.

What the--! That's gross, so why does warmth bloom between my legs? Why are my nipples peaked? I ignore the reaction of my body, try to turn and tell him off, but his hold around me tightens, holding me immobile. His breathing deepens, his body twitches, and I know he's asleep.

It's annoying how easily men seem to switch off that thinking part of their brains and get their body to obey. Except for that thickness that continues to stab me between my ass cheeks, that is. Not that it's stopped him from falling asleep. I close my eyes and drift off.

When I awaken, we're both in the same position. Only, that thickness that's poking my behind seems to have gotten bigger, harder and more insistent. I turn and stare into the face of my fiancé, my husband to-be, my lover, the man to whom I gave my virginity. The man who I know better than my own family. And yet, in so many ways, he's still a mystery. *What are you hiding from me, Stone?*

I slide my palm down and squeeze the column outlined against the crotch of his boxers. A muscle jumps in his chest. I massage him from base to crown, and again. His erection grows even bigger. Even through his boxers, I can sense the throbbing of the blood, the intensity of heat which sears my palm.

My mouth waters. Sweat pools under my arms, and my breathing grows ragged. A trembling runs up my spine, and whoa! I might come from how aroused I am with feeling how rigid and solid and unyielding he feels. I raise my gaze and gasp.

55

Rick

Her golden eyes are pools of sunlight. Her cheeks are flushed, her hair mussed from sleep. She watches me watching her as she reaches into my boxers and begins moving her hand up and down. Then, in a move which mirrors the throbbing of that tell-tale pulse at the base of her throat, speeds up as she pumps my cock. I can't stop the growl that rumbles up my chest. Her lips part, her pupils dilate, then she squeezes even harder.

The breath hisses out between my lips. I shoot my hand out and grip her throat. Her eyes grow so big, they seem to fill her face, but she doesn't stop. I loosen my hold on her throat, only to drag my palm down her chest. I pinch her nipple through her bra, and she shudders. I tweak it, applying enough force that she groans. The sound goes straight to my head. I slide my palm down her stomach and inside her panties. When I cup her pussy it's my turn to growl, "So, fucking wet, do you want me to take your cunt, my little whore? You're a slut for my cum, aren't you? You want me to bury my cock inside you and fuck all thoughts out of your head. You want me to stuff my fingers into the hole between your arse-cheeks and tease your most forbidden places while I thrust my tongue inside your—"

"Stop"—she gasps—"please don't—"

"Stop?" I cram three of my digits inside her sopping wet channel.

"Don't stop," she cries out.

I weave my fingers in and out of her, in and out. Each time I shove my fingers inside, her entire body jerks. It mirrors the way she's clamping down on my dick with her fingers, the way I shudder when she swipes her fingers up to the crown.

"Fuck." I rub my thumb into her swollen clit, and her eyes roll back in her head. She arches her back, and a shiver spirals up her body. "I'm coming," she gasps.

"Don't you dare come, Goldie." I pull my fingers out of her, and when she opens her mouth to protest, I thrust them between her lips. She sucks on them greedily, and I feel the pressure at the base of my spine. She licks her tongue up my fingertips, and my balls tighten. I'm going to come in my pants any moment, like I'm a teenager. I tug my fingers out, then wrench hers from around my cock.

"But I wanna make you come, too," she whines.

"Oh you will, just not like this." I reach down and tear off her panties.

She cries out, "You're an animal."

"And you love it."

Color suffuses her features. "You have such an insufferable ego. If it weren't for the fact that—"

"I have the balls to go with it?"

She firms her lips.

"That's what you were going to say, hmm?" I lower her hand to my balls and cup them with her fingers.

She swallows, and when she cups them, I can't stop the grunt that wells up my throat.

"Enough of this playing around." I pull her hand off my balls, then sit up. I lift her up and position her so she's lying on her side.

I curve her body, then position myself so her sweet pussy is in front of my mouth and my cock is lined up with her face. Once I'm sure we're in the sideways 69 position, I push down my boxers.

"Oh, my." The awe in her voice drains all remaining blood to my groin.

I push my head into the flesh between her legs and inhale deeply.

"Did you sniff me?" she cries.

"And now, I'm going to lick you and suck on your clit. Then, I'm going to gather your cum and uses it to lubricate you before I fuck your arse."

"No." She tries to shuffle away, but I squeeze her hip and hold her in place. Then I lick her from slit to blackhole.

She moans, "Oh my god."

"You mean, 'oh, Rick,' don't you? Also, my cock isn't gonna suck itself, so chop-chop."

I stab my tongue inside her channel, and she pants. I rub on the swollen nub between her pussy lips, and her entire body jerks.

"Oh god, oh god, oh god," she whimpers.

I slap her pussy, and she cries out. "You bastard."

"The only name I want from your lips is mine, and don't you forget it."

"You're a jerk."

"And if you don't jerk me off right fucking now, I'll—" My breath catches, for she's closed her mouth around my dick. She digs her fingernails into my thighs hard enough to leave marks, and fuck, if that doesn't turn me on more. I circle her clit with my tongue, while she begins to lick me from crown to balls again and again. Then she clamps her lips around my dick and swallows.

A line of fire zips up my spine. My head spins. I groan into her pussy, draw in more of that heady essence of hers, and a primal need fills me—to fuck her, to take her, to make her mine, to... stamp her pussy with the indelible impression of my cock, to imprint the heat of my breath on her skin, the feel of my fingers on her tits, to carve my thoughts into her mind, etch my name into her soul, to fuse our skins so we become one, even if it's only for an instant, and ensure she'll never forget me. *She'll never forgive you, either.* My heart squeezes. *And isn't that what you wanted?*

She bobs her head, and I glance down in time to see my dick disappear inside her mouth. It's the most erotic thing I've ever seen. Then she deep throats me, and all thoughts disappear from my mind. I grab her hips, bring her even closer, and begin to eat her out with renewed vigor. She gasps around my dick, and my balls draw up. I will not come, not until I've taken her to the edge. I attack her pussy like it's the puck I'm after on the ice.

I stab my tongue inside her melting channel, then flick her clit. Her body jolts, and when she bites down on my shaft, the shockwaves spark a chain reaction that ignites all of my brain cells.

Sweat beads my shoulders, and I rub on her clit, then curl my tongue inside her, and the shudders that grip her body multiply. Moisture bathes my mouth and drips down my chin. I release my hold on her, reach across, and grab her hair. I tug on it, and when she looks at me, I growl, "I'm going to fuck your mouth."

56

Gio

That's all the warning I get. He holds my hips to pin me in place, then pistons his hips forward. His dick plunges down my throat. I gag, and tears squeeze out from the corners of my eyes. He pulls back, I gasp for air, and drool dribbles down my chin. It mirrors the glistening moisture on his unshaven one. I have no doubt that's my cum, and it turns me on more. That, and the fact he's using me as a receptacle to give him pleasure.

My sole focus in life is boiled down to how I relax my jaw and stop fighting the singular reality that I am meant to satisfy him. I am his to use as he pleases, to fulfill his urges, to gratify his need for control, to serve his urge to dominate, to slake his hunger, his urge to take revenge. He's so single-minded, so driven to cause me pain that's on the verge of pleasure when he fucks me. It's as if he can't stop himself from taking me into the pleasure zone, but would rather use sex to cause me pain. As if he's punishing me. But for what? It's not like he wants revenge…does he? I've done nothing to make him feel this way…have I?

He must sense my thoughts, for his movements grow more frantic. I dig my fingernails into the backs of his thighs and hold on; and when his cock thickens down my throat, I know he's close, so close. That's when he releases me and pulls out.

In the same move, he flips me over so I'm on my back and face-to-face with him.

Without breaking the connection, he plants himself between my thighs. Then, he reaches down, scoops the moisture from around my slit and smears it around my back-hole. I flinch, but don't look away.

"Do you want me to stop?" He peers between my eyes. "Say the word and I will, I promise."

He's giving me a choice, and that makes it worse. And *that* confuses me further. He reads the confusion on my face and lowers his, until I can make out the individual silver sparks in that icy expanse of his eyes. "You'll always have a choice with me; the power is in your hands."

"I thought you were the one in charge of our relationship."

"I lost control the moment I saw you talking to yourself the first time."

I flush. "You saw me talking to myself?" It's a bad habit. A way to self-soothe I've never gotten over, but which I hope I've managed to hide from the world—Not from him, though.

"The first time I saw you walking to your car in L.A. You were on your own and didn't think anyone was watching."

"But you were?"

He nods. "I haven't been able to get you out of my mind. You've burrowed under my skin, and there's no way I can get rid of you." His eyebrows draw down.

"You don't seem happy about it."

"Not like I have a choice."

"But you're giving me one now?"

"Always." He lowers his voice to a hush, "Only you have the power to wreck me."

There's something in his eyes, something I can't quite unpack. A mixture of anger, helplessness, and lust...and love? Is he in love with— I gasp, for something big and blunt edges the forbidden hole between my butt-cheeks.

"You know why I'll never fuck you from behind, not even when I'm taking your arse?"

I shake my head.

"Because I want to see you when I shag you. I want you to see my eyes as I bury myself inside you. I want you to be aware of who's bringing you to climax. Every second that your body responds to mine, I want you to be conscious of who's wringing pleasure from you."

Oh my god. Just when I think he can't outdo himself, he comes up with words which will be seared into my memory forever. A thousand bees hum under my skin. Sweat beads my lips. I open my mouth to tell him I want him to fuck me any which way he wants. That he can have me anytime, anywhere, in any position. That he doesn't need to ask me for permission. That I'd prefer for him to not ask. That I want him to surprise me, shock me, break me... And put me back together in a form that carries his name etched into every fabric of my being. But nothing comes out. My brain cells have frozen. The words have turned to shards of ice in my throat.

He searches my features and frowns. "Yes or no, Goldie?"

When I stay silent, his jaw tics. A shutter comes down over his eyes. His features turn into that mask that doesn't allow me to read his thoughts, but I know now, this is how he puts up walls. This is how he hides that caring, sensitive man inside who feels too much. It's why he puts up the barriers—so he doesn't get hurt. It's why we're the same in so many ways, and yet, we're also the opposite of each other. It's why I'm so drawn to him. It's why I know I can trust him. It's why I'm going to give up my remaining virgin hole to…him. Only him.

"Yes," I murmur. "Yes," I tip up my chin and say in a stronger voice.

His shoulders relax. "Thank fuck." He lowers his lips to mine and kisses me. I taste myself and him, and it's a combination that melts any remaining doubts I had. I'm his. Irrevocably. No one has made me feel so safe as him. I hook my legs around his waist, push up, and his cock breaches my forbidden hole. Pain shivers up my spine. I groan into his mouth, and he stares deeply into my eyes as he stays. Stays. Allows me to adjust to his size. Which I don't think I ever will. "It hurts," I manage to choke out.

One slide of his lips twists. "Good."

"What?" My gaze widens. "What did you say?"

"Relax, I was joking."

"You don't joke." I frown.

He straightens his lips. "I don't. I thought I wanted to see you in pain. Now, I'm not so sure."

"You're confusing me," I whisper.

"I'm confusing myself," he says through gritted teeth. "You feel so fucking tight, so hot, so fucking everything. It's better than anything I've experienced in my life."

A bead of sweat slides down his temple. Before I can stop myself, I lift my head and lick it off. His blue eyes flash, a thousand little sparks joining the silver ones already there, and oh god, it's like I'm peering into his soul.

Remember, I said he feels too much? I had it wrong. It so much more than that. He perceives every single emotion deeply, much more deeply than me. And he's been hurt... *By me?*

I swallow. That's not possible. Since we met, I've been helpless in front of his dominance, his charisma, the force of his personality. Since we met, he's been in charge of whatever it is that sparks between us, that connects us and pulls us together even more strongly when we try to stay apart. He's known it; I've known it. Only, I've never known how to harness it, but I thought he had figured it out. Now, I realize, he's as buffeted by the potency of the chemistry that sparks between us.

"Rick, I lo—"

"Don't." He swoops down and closes his mouth over mine. His kiss drugs me, the warmth of his body cocoons me, relaxing my muscles enough that when he thrusts forward, my muscles let him sink in an inch, and another. I groan into his mouth, and he swallows the sound, then pulls out until he's balanced on the rim of my entrance. When he kicks his hips forward, he impales me to the hilt. I cry out, more from the shock of how thick and heavy he feels, how strange the sensation is, how—as he begins to move inside me— how he slides his hand between us and rubs on my clit, how he tweaks my nipple, and my entire body catches fire.

He doesn't stop kissing me, either. I'm burning up. My brain-cells have long since dissolved into a puddle of want, every cell in my body alive and needing that last push to get me over the edge. I push my breasts up into his chest, dig my fingernails into his shoulders, my heels into his back and meet his next thrust. He hits that intimate spot deep inside. The climax sweeps through me, and when he releases my mouth long enough to growl, "Come," I instantly shatter. He fucks me through my orgasm, and with a low roar, bathes my insides with cum. And when his body weight grows heavier, I feel subsumed by him, buried under him... Exactly how I want it. I close my eyes and instantly fall asleep. When I open my eyes, he's fully dressed on the chair next to the bed. "We need to talk."

57

Gio

"No." I shake my head. "Don't do this." I don't realize I've uttered them aloud until I hear them reach across the space between us, an involuntary response to what I'm seeing in his eyes. Something I sensed was coming, given the intensity with which he took me. It felt like it was the last time we'd be that intimate. I attributed it to the intensity of the emotions I've been feeling, but seeing the bleakness in his eyes? I know, now, I didn't imagine it. My heart pistons against my ribcage, and my pulse-points go into overdrive. This sense of foreboding. *Where is it coming from? I haven't done anything wrong, have I?*

"You always mean what you say," I whisper.

He nods.

"So, I'm not sure I want to hear your words."

He turns his palms face-up and stares at them. "I think you need to."

"No, I don't." I sit up in bed and pull the covers up under my chin.

"If you don't, you'll hate me."

"Will I hate you less if you don't tell me?"

He winces, then shakes his head. "It's best you hear it from me now."

"I don't want to."

"You have to."

"No, Rick. No. I don't. I just found you; I don't want to lose you."

"You'll never lose me." He swallows. But the fact he looks so uncertain for the first time since I've met him, the fact that this big, grumphole of a man looks like his world is collapsing around him, sends a jolt of panic through my insides.

I throw off the covers, and when I rise to my feet, he sweeps his gaze down to my breasts, then to the flesh between my legs. His chest rises and falls, and when I look at his crotch, I spot the tent in the grey sweatpants he's wearing. *What is it with him and grey sweatpants?* No one should look this hot wearing a pair of faded sweats and an even more faded black T-shirt that clings to every angle of his musculature.

"You're trying to distract me," he growls.

"No, I'm not." I spread my legs, then slide my hand between them. "Now, I am."

A noise rumbles up his throat—something between a chuckle and an admonishment, and it's so freakin' hot. A feeling of power surges through me. I raise my other palm to my breast and play with my nipple.

Spots of color paint his cheeks. He curls his fingers into fists at his sides, and the fact that he's stopping himself from doing whatever he has in mind sets off alarm bells in my head, and my need to distract him multiplies. "Don't you want to touch me, baby?" I croon.

His nostrils flare. His throat bobs. His gaze is fixed on my pussy—my very wet, throbbing, pussy. I take a step forward, and new aches and pains make themselves known. I wince, and he jerks his chin up.

"You sore?" he asks with interest.

I firm my lips. *Of course, I'm sore. You put that monster cock of yours in a hole that's roughly one-millionth of its size, or at least, it felt like that,* is what I want to say, but I don't. It'll only serve to increase the ego of this man, and he can do without that.

"You're sore," he concludes with a satisfied quirk of his lips. That half smirk of his draws a fluttered response from between my legs. I move toward him, and when I reach him, he leans back to put distance between us. "I know what you're doing," he says in a low voice.

"Oh?"

"You're trying to distract me."

"Is it working?"

"You don't need to try to get my attention; you always have it."

I swallow.

"You walk into a room, and I know where you are. You're in the stands, and I know exactly where to find you. You could be in the other side of the world, and I swear, I could sense you. There's this invisible connection between us that's so real, it feels like a third person."

Tears prick the backs of my eyes. It's so close to the thoughts I've had about this pull that binds us that I swear he's read my mind. "Rick..." I'm not sure what to say. And again, he deciphers my unsaid words, for he pulls me into his lap. I straddle him, then wrap my arms about his shoulders and push my nose into the base of his neck where his scent is the strongest. I breathe in pure Rick, and a calmness descends. "Whatever you were going to say, it doesn't matter."

"It does." He pinches my chin, so I have to tilt up and meet his gaze. "I asked you to share my room because—"

"Rick, we're gonna be late. You said you'd ride with us today. Coach is ready," Finn's voice reaches us through the closed door.

He groans. "I did promise them I'd be riding with them from now on."

"That's good for team spirit," I agree.

"Maybe it's a mistake. You're more important. Maybe I should tell them I'm taking the car today with you and—"

I silence him by pressing my lips to his. He instantly thrusts his tongue into my mouth and takes control. He sucks on my tongue and draws from me, enveloping me in his big arms, and I'm hot and aroused, and moisture slides out from between my legs. The man has some kind of radar where I'm concerned, for he reaches between us and hooks two fingers inside. I mewl into his mouth, and that turns him on, for the column under my butt grows thicker. "You're fucking soaking, and I'm not leaving you needy."

"What are you—" I draw in a sharp breath when he urges me up long enough to pull down his sweats. Then, he positions me over his already erect cock, thrusts up his hips and breaches me. I cry out, then hold onto him as he begins to pound up and into me, over and over and over again. Each time he enters me, he hits my G-spot. *How is that freakin' possible?* The man's a sex god, and his dick has a homing device when it comes to that invisible, innermost, most sensitive part of me. He holds me steady with one hand on my hip. The other, he wraps around the nape of my neck. His fingers are so thick and so long, they meet in the front of my throat. And when he punches up and into me again, I feel completely possessed. Owned.

He's my dominant and I'm the submissive who'll give him anything he wants. I've already given him my heart and my trust, and now he takes the only thing left, my will. I'm crumbling to dust, and every particle says his name. *Rick. Rick. Rick.*

He pistons up and into me. "Come," he snaps, and I cry out as I shatter. With a grunt, he pounds into me and empties himself inside me. For a few seconds, we stay there, eyes locked, breaths blended, my fingers digging into his shoulders, his palm heavy on the nape of my neck, his cock pulsing inside me. Then, he picks me up and sets me on the floor. His gaze turns bleak, and he looks away. "I need to go."

58

Rick

"Whatever it is you need, you've got to sort it out," Edward glares at me from across the floor of the locker room. He's alluding to how I sucked at practice. And it's not only because I'm worried about Grams. Hockey has always been my escape. But now, getting on the ice reminds me of how much I miss her when she's not in the stands.

Gio messaged me to say she was going to the hospital to visit Grams, then sent me a picture of the two of them. Grams seemed pale in the picture, but there was a smile on her face. Gio sent a second text that said what followed was dictated by Grams: "I'm doing great, and Gio is here, so I don't need you. I prefer her to you anyway. *wink emoji* Focus on the game."

O-k-a-y... Clearly, Grams is doing well. I'd fully intended to head there after practice, only Edward cornered me. I wanted to brush him off and leave, but while I'm stubborn, I'm not stupid. Also, although Gio comes first, it won't help either of us if I commit professional suicide—again. Not when she's the PR manager of the team and her professional reputation is tied to mine. This time, I won't have a chance to resurrect myself.

"The Japanese have a word for it." He leans forward in his seat. "Hara-kiri."

"I'm not trying to destroy myself," I lie.

He scoffs. "Have you heard yourself? You wouldn't be able to convince yourself with that tone, let alone me."

"You're right." I pinch the bridge of my nose.

"The fuck is wrong with you?" he snaps.

"Yeah, when are you going your head out of your arse and tell her?" JJ prowls up.

"Oh, fuck." I open my eyes, then close them again. "When I open them again, will you be gone?"

"Not likely," JJ booms out a laugh.

"Where are the other two musketeers?" I slouch in my seat, not looking forward to this conversation.

"Someone call me?" Sinclair ambles over and stands next to JJ.

"And I was hoping to avoid this conversation." Michael glowers, then stops on the other side of JJ.

"Time to get this party started." Knight slips onto the bench next to me.

Edward lowers himself onto my other side.

I glance between them, then fold my arms across my chest. "Guess I should have called you all Robin and his merry men, the way you lot seem to multiply," I say in a bitter tone.

"There were four," Knight reminds me.

"Four?" I frown.

"Athos, Porthos, Aramis, and d'Artagnan," Knight adds.

"Not following," I growl.

"There are four main characters at the heart of the story." JJ rocks forward on his heels. His eyes gleam. Asshole's enjoying himself. In fact, I'd say he lives for these little run-ins where he gets to share his love of the classics. His lips curve. "The title refers to the three whom d'Artagnan befriends, even though—

"Yes, I know. Your point being?"

"You haven't figured out your shit yet," he replies.

"That's what I've been trying to tell him," Edward agrees.

"I thought you guys already staged your intervention," my voice comes out sullen. I wince. I sound like a surly teenager, which is what I feel like when I'm confronted with these guys. Not Edward. I feel more of a kinship with him, considering the man has ghosts to deal with. Though you wouldn't know it, given the polished appearance he's taken on since becoming GM. Gone are his jeans and leather jacket. He's more likely to be seen in the tailored suit like the one he's wearing today. As are the four other men? Each on their own is a force to be reckoned with, but together, they pack enough assertiveness to not be ignored.

"I do not need you guys all up in my business."

JJ scoffs, "If you'd come to your senses, we'd have left you alone, but since you haven't—"

"We didn't have a choice," Sinclair adds.

"You need to figure things out before this gets out of hand." Michael glowers at me.

I glance at my watch. "I need to get to the hospital to check in on my Grams."

"We've done so already," Knight murmurs.

I stare at him.

"Gio's there with her; so is Penny. Your Grams is conscious and in good spirits," Edward interjects.

"All the more reason to see her and make sure for myself," I snap.

"Which you will, once we've had this little tête-à-tête," Sinclair drawls.

"I don't want to talk to you guys." I rise to my feet, but Knight grips my shoulder.

"Sit down, man." His voice is serious, the expression on his features even more so. I sink back down slowly, then ball my fingers into fists.

The men exchange looks, some kind of silent communication passes between them, then Sinclair folds his arms across his chest. "Why haven't you come out and told her the real reason you wanted her to marry you?"

I arch an eyebrow in his direction. "I asked her to marry me because I love her."

"No denying that. No man would look at a woman the way you look at her if you didn't love her." JJ's voice softens.

Seems nothing stays hidden from my friends, assholes that they are. But they are *insightful* assholes. Smart enough to glean that not all is as it seems with me.

"But it's not only that, is it?" Sinclair butts in.

"I don't know what you're talking about."

"Sure you do. And you don't need to tell us what it is," Knight adds.

"But you need to tell her, before you marry her." Michael glares at me.

"You think I haven't tried?" I squeeze the bridge of my nose, then pause. "Also, how did you guys find out?" I lower my hand and glance between them again.

"You think anything stays hidden from us?" Sinclair drawls.

"We take care of our own." Michael shrugs.

"What does that mean?" I scowl.

"That between us, we have the resources to ferret out skeletons in everyone's closet and"—I begin to protest, but JJ holds up his hand—"we're not apologizing. Since you weren't getting a move on, and it was beginning to affect your performance—" he raises a shoulder.

I turn on Edward. "You're behind this intervention?"

"I had to do something. The future of the team is at stake."

"It's my future at stake." I thrust out my chest.

"And I care about you, but I'm also the GM of the team. I need to do what's best for everyone."

I glower at him, then deflate. "Can't say I blame you. If I were in your shoes, I'd do the same thing." The team comes first. I'm the captain. I know that more than anyone else. And I need to tell her, I do. So, what's stopping me? I jump up to my feet, then shoulder my way through the men and begin to pace. "Why is this so hard? Why does it feel like I'm going to lose everything?"

"Because you might?" Sinclair offers in a droll voice.

"Easy for you guys to say this. You all have your women and are all smug and content and—"

"—and each of us went through our own difficulties to find our soulmates," Sinclair adds.

"Soulmates?" I scoff.

"You don't believe in soulmates?" Knight lowers his chin to his chest.

"Soulmates are for men who have souls." *And I'm not sure I have one, especially after what I'm going to do to her.*

"After I returned from being held hostage at war, I was sure I could never feel again. I shut down, refused to allow anyone and anything to touch me. Until her." Knight shifts his weight from foot to foot. "I was disillusioned. I had abandoned all pretense of being human in any way. I was focused on amassing power. I thought that was the only way forward."

"And love cured you?" I scoff.

Knight's lips quirk. "Love gives you a reason to cure yourself. The rest you have to want hard enough to do the work."

"You guys are not making any sense." I run my fingers through my hair. "If it hurts this much, if it turns my guts-inside out, if it makes me weak at my knees and tightens the band around my chest and pushes down on my shoulders until I can't breathe, then—"

"You're on the right path," JJ murmurs.

"You need to keep going." Knight nods.

"Don't stop," Sinclair growls.

Michael jerks his chin in my direction adding his encouragement. He's one scary motherfucker. And *he* believes in love? Correction, not only does he believe in love, but he's married to the woman of his dreams, with a child and another on the way, the last I heard. He seems to have it all together, despite his checkered past.

"For all that it matters, I'm with you." Edward slides his hand into his pocket. "I thought I believed in love, but it didn't believe in me. You have to be fortunate for it to find you, and when it does, don't let go."

I take in his resigned features. "You don't think you'll fall in love again?"

"Lighting doesn't strike twice." He narrows his gaze on me. "I have other passions in life. Love isn't for me. It's understandable if you feel the same."

I draw in a sharp breath, then square my shoulders. "And if I don't?"

59

Gio

"Go, Stone!" I press my fingers into the plexiglass close to the bench of the Ice Kings. On the ice, Rick scoops up the puck from Enzo, then throws it past the opposing team's goalie. Cheers erupt. They did it, they're through to the semi-finals of the League.

It's been two days since Grams regained consciousness from the operation.

Two days, during which I've barely seen Rick. He came to the hospital, and Grams was so happy to see him. She faded fast though, and we came home from there. That night, we fell asleep wrapped around each other.

The next morning, I made sure I was awake before Rick and left the house without seeing him. If I were there, he'd try to continue the conversation he started, and I don't want that. I'm not sure what he's trying to tell me, but whatever it is, it's going to spoil this...whatever it is that's developed between us, and I'm not ready for it.

Last night, I stayed out with the girls, and by the time I got home, Rick was asleep. I crawled into bed, and he turned to me in his sleep and pulled me close. I fell asleep surrounded by Rick.

This morning... I have a vague recollection of him kissing my forehead, then sliding out of bed, but by the time I woke up it, was time to head to work and then to the match.

I haven't been able to take my gaze off of my fiancé. Seeing his fluid moves, his commanding presence on the ice, the way he interacts with his team with a confidence that's so very Rick, lights a million tiny flames under my skin. Watching him score, I can't stop the smile from curving my lips. On the ice, Rick raises his fist. That's it. One fist pump is all he allows himself in celebration. Typical, understated Rick. Then he turns, and without erring, his gaze finds mine. For a few seconds, everything around me fades, and it's just me and him. I raise my right fist, mirroring his stance.

He begins to skate toward the gate, when the rest of the team on the bench jump onto the ice, joining the Ice Kings players who're already headed toward Rick. He must sense them coming, for he bends his head, tucks his stick under his arm, and races like the devil—or in this case, Ice Devils—are on his tale, which they are.

He makes it to the gate, and I'm sure he's going to get off the ice before the others. But the one right behind, Finn, throws himself on Rick, who hits the floor with Finn on his back. The rest of them follow Finn's lead, and it's one heaving mass of arms and legs and sticks held out to the side. I wince. Hope they didn't hurt Rick. Of course, they all wear protective gear, but I've seen how they block the opposition on the ice. I've also seen the various discolored patches and scars on Rick's torso—not all of which comes from his brief military stint. The ice is no less dangerous than the battlefront, and the way this team has been fighting back the last few games since the face-off with the Sentinels makes it clear, this is a life-and-death situation for them.

I hadn't realized how dangerous the game is; one wrong, misplaced step can result in serious injuries. Life-threatening injuries. I bite the inside of my cheek and peer through the glass at the heaving mass of men.

Then, Edward approaches them, his suit-clad figure incongruous among the jerseys. He's also strapped on skates. What the—? Does Priest know how to skate? He's the GM of the team, so it's not entirely surprising, but I haven't seen him wearing skates before. He grabs the first guy, and with a strength I didn't know he possessed, throws him off. Then the next guy. The third guy jumps off himself, then pulls the next guy off. The rest of them seem to get the memo, for they melt off.

I crane my head and see Rick's figure immobile on the ground. Oh, no, is he okay? I begin to head in his direction, when he moves. I blow out a breath and watch as he rises to his feet.

He shakes his head as if to clear it, then turns and holds up his right fist.

The guys on the team raise their own fists and cheer. Rick nods at Edward, then turns, and without hesitation, he finds me. All the noise, the yelling around me, the sight of everyone else fades. As if in a dream, I run toward the gate, reaching it at the same time as Rick. Without hesitation he scoops me up and throws me over his shoulder. The sound of cheering rises in decibels.

"What the—!" I huff, for he's tapped my butt. He didn't! And in front of everyone. I wriggle around, but his hold tightens, and then he's walking toward the steps. "Rick, let me go!" I bring down my fists on his compression pants-covered rear-end. Strands of hair come free from my bun and flow over my face. I have a fleeting impression of the aisle, of people crowding in on us, but Rick doesn't slow down. Then security guards fall into place and Rick picks up speed. He reaches the top of the aisle and takes a sharp left. The sound of the crowds fade away, Rick picks up speed, turns another corner.

"Let me go!" I cry out.

He doesn't stop. He's wearing his skates but that doesn't seem to slow him down. He turns another corner, moves up a long corridor, then turns again. He enters a room and the door slams shut with the security team on the other side. My heart jumps into my throat. I know this man, trust him, but he's not demonstrative. And carrying me over his shoulder in front of the entire world is very demonstrative and out of character for him. The hair on the back of my neck rises. My pulse rate speeds up until it feels like it's echoing the sound of someone running. The blood flows to my head, and I feel woozy. "Let me go, Rick, right now or else—" I gasp, for he's lowered me to my feet.

I take a step back, glance around to find we're in one of the VIP rooms overlooking the rink, only it's empty. Which is strange, because this is an important game. Unless… I shove the hair out of my eyes and glower at him. "Did you plan this?"

Through the gap in his helmet, his blue eyes flare. He doesn't reply, but I read the answer in the stance of his body. "I can't believe you planned this. Were you so sure of winning? So sure I'd be there in the stands waiting for you?"

He tips up his chin, then takes a step forward; I sidle back. He flexes his gloved hand and the threat in that movement shoots a shiver of excitement up my spine. I'm not turned on by the air of danger that clings to him, I'm not. But as he continues to close the distance between us, my entire body goes into a state of anticipation. I shuffle back until I hit the glass wall that looks down on the arena. Behind me, the sounds of the crowd rise. Music plays over the speakers. Then, an announcer reels off stats from the game.

"You need to be down there for the presentation." I swallow.

In reply, he moves one gloved hand over the other, tugs at the fastenings around the cuff, then pulls it off. The glove hits the ground, followed by the next. He flexes his big fingers, and I swallow.

I can't take my gaze off those thick, fat digits. Not as thick or as fat as his cock, but almost as lethal when it comes to wringing pleasure from my pussy. My core clenches. I squeeze my thighs together, then curse myself for not wearing pants. Stupidly, I came dressed in my tightest skirt and jacket.

As always, he seems to read my mind, for his gaze drops to the space between my legs. He reaches up and tears off his helmet, and when he drops it to the carpeted floor, the dull thud reverberates around the space.

"Rick, you're scaring me." I swallow.

He merely bares his teeth, and it's not a smile. Or a grimace. It's the sneer of a predator getting ready to claim his prey. He reaches up, tears off his skull cap, and his sweat-soaked hair falls over his forehead. My fingers tingle; I want to run them through the wet strands. He lets the cap drop to the floor, and when he cracks his neck, every cell in my body seems to stand to attention. His jaw tics, and his left eyelid twitches. He's pissed at me, I have no doubt about it.

"I-I'm sorry I've avoided you the last couple of days."

His grin widens. And oh god, that's scary. I've never seen him voluntarily offer a smile, so to see him grin is akin to watching a shark show its teeth. I gulp, push back against the glass. "Wh-what are you doing?"

In response, he reaches inside the pocket of his pants and pulls out a mask. A mask? He pulls it over his hair and face, and suddenly, it's not Rick, but a scarier, more monstrous version of him standing over me.

"I-I didn't know your hockey pants had a pocket." I attempt a smile, fail. "I-I guess you had them tailor-made?"

He cracks his neck, and the sound is like a bullet shot. My throat dries. My lower belly quivers. My nipples tighten until I'm sure they're going to tear through my blouse. What does it say about me that I find this entire situation erotic? Scary, too, but also, very, very arousing.

I look past him at the door, and even though I can't see his features, I swear, his smile widens.

"Umm, I'm not sure what you think you're doing, but I'm going to go now."

He steps aside and gestures to the door, all casual-like, and that sends another spurt of excitement up my spine. I sidle forward, and he gives me more space. His body is relaxed. The crowd outside screams in excitement. He jerks his head toward the glass partition. That's when I take off.

60

Rick

She leaps toward the door, and I give her a head start. Five, four, three, two…
I jump forward. Before she can reach the door, I plant myself against it.

She skids to a halt, chest heaving, hair undone and framing her face. "Let
me go," she pants.

I tap my fingers against my thighs.

"I don't know what your game is, Rick, but it's not funny anymore."

*It's not supposed to be. But I know your darkest secrets, baby. I know your filthy
dreams. I've read the scenes you've underlined in your spicy books, and I'm here to make
them come alive. One-by-one.* I roll my shoulders, and she swallows.

I move toward her, and she yelps, then turns and races away. I follow at a
leisurely pace, knowing she can't escape. I won't let her escape. Not until I've
made her come one last time. I may not be able to give her everlasting love.
But bringing her most secret fantasies to life, I can do. Pleasuring her so she
can enjoy the heights of ecstasy only I can take her to? That I can do for her.

She looks at me over her shoulder, then zig-zag's across the room. When
she realizes she can't evade me, she turns, grabs one of her heels and throws it
at me, and misses. The next one she lobs at me, I don't duck. It hits my forehead and bounces off.

"Oh my god," she gasps. "Rick, I—"

I close the distance toward her, grab her under the backs of her thighs, lift her, and plant her against the glass wall. The momentum pulls her hair free of its bun and the golden strands pour about her face.

Her features are flushed. The color on her cheeks is fucking gorgeous. Her skirt is bunched around her waist, and she stares at me with lust and a touch of fear, which ratchets my desire up to fever pitch. I reach down and tear off her panties. She cries out.

I shove the piece of silk inside my pocket, and she swallows. Her gaze grows heavy with lust. Then she gasps when I shove my hand down my pants. I wince as I yank off the codpiece and toss it aside, then pull out my cock and position myself at her entrance. I stare into her sun kissed eyes waiting… waiting for her to indicate it's okay. I hold her gaze and lean in until only a hair's breadth of space separates us.

She swallows, and her pupils dilate. Then she leans in and presses her lips to where they're painted on my mask. I feel her scented breath, can imagine the honeyed taste of her lips. She throws her arms about my neck and whispers, "Fuck me, Stone."

Before the words are out of her mouth, I kick my hips forward. I bury myself to the hilt, and she cries out against my mask-covered face. She locks her ankles about my hips as I stuff myself inside her again and again and again. I tilt my hips, balance her at the right angle. The next time I thrust into her, I hit that spot only I know about, and she cries out. She throws her head back, and her inner muscles clamp down on my cock as she orgasms. It's so fucking hot, so perfect, with a roar of possession I empty myself inside her. When she begins to slump, I pull her close, then reach up and tear off my mask.

I push my forehead against hers, then swallow. "Goldie? We need to talk."

She shakes her head, her throat moving as she swallows. "I prefer fucking to talking any day."

"Once we talk, you might not want me to fuck you again."

She stiffens, then leans back enough to glance up into my face.

"Diana?" she whispers.

"Diana." I pull out of her and miss her warmth, the clasp of her pussy around my shaft, the feel of her curves pressed against mine. I press a kiss to her forehead, then lower her to the ground. When I know she's steady, I tuck myself inside. I grab some napkins and clean her up. Then, I pull out a fresh pair of panties for her from my other pocket, and once she's stepped into them, I straighten her clothes.

"I should be surprised you carried a pair of my panties on you while you were on the ice, but somehow, I'm not," she murmurs.

"When it comes to you, I know I won't be able to control myself, so I'm prepared." I ball up the napkins and flick them into a basket. I brush her hair behind her ear, then bend and pick up her hair-tie which fell off earlier and offer it to her.

I watch as she puts up her hair with practiced ease, then lowers her arms to her sides. "Your sister... Did I ever meet her?"

I take a step back, then another. I need to put distance between us. I also want to hold her while having this conversation, but that would be wrong. That wouldn't be fair to my little sister.

I firm my shoulders, then meet her gaze. "She moved to L.A. to try to make it in Hollywood. I knew she was struggling, but I didn't realize how much until later. My sister had a complex personality. She could be obsessive when she set her mind on something."

"Like you?" she asks in a wry voice.

"Yeah—" I half smile. "We are, *were* similar in our ability to focus. She told me she'd found her muse. She'd written a screenplay with a famous celebrity in mind. He was perfect for it. She was going to arrange to meet him and when he read the screenplay, she knew he'd want to make the movie. I didn't hear from her for weeks after that. Then I was away on an NHL tour. When I returned, I found my sister had committed suicide."

She gasps, "I'm so sorry, Rick."

"She'd tried to meet the Hollywood star who had inspired her story. She'd tried to send him the script through his manager. When that didn't work, she broke into his house. She was captured by the security cameras, and the cops got to her first."

Her forehead furrows. "Why are you telling me this? Did I know her?"

"You were the assistant to the manager she tried to contact."

She shakes her head. "Do you know how many calls I'd get every day from hopefuls who wanted to get through to my boss? It was my job to be the gatekeeper."

"You did your job well. When she realized there was no hope of getting through to you, she stalked the star's social media and ended up breaking into his house. She was hoping to meet him and get him to read her script. Instead—"

"The celebrity was Declan Beauchamp..." She draws in a sharp breath. "I remember now. I was his PR manager's assistant at that time. Declan was away on a film-shoot. I'm the one who found her at his place and called the cops."

"She tried to apologize, to tell you what she'd done was wrong, that she'd never stalk Declan again, that it had been a temporary loss of reasoning on her part. She begged you not to call the cops because it would kill any possibility of a career for her in that town. All she wanted was for you to read the script."

She reaches for my hand, but I shake her off.

"You didn't listen to her. You turned your back on her."

"Rick, you have to understand. I was scared. I thought she was dangerous."

"My sister was harmless."

"Your sister broke into a well-known celebrity's home."

"If you'd heard her out, she might be still alive."

The blood drains from her features, leaving her so pale, so vulnerable, I almost reach for her again, but stop myself. This is about Diana. All of this is for Diana. It's the least I can do for her. I couldn't be there for my sister when she needed me most. This is the minimum I can do for her. I can punish the woman who put an end to her career and to her life.

"I was scared, Rick. I came across an intruder, and I did what anyone else in my position would have. I ran out of there, shut the door on her and called the cops."

"Your position was that of Declan's PR manager."

"I was the PR manager's assistant then. I became his manager later. You have to understand, I was young and inexperienced."

I raise my hand. "She begged you to listen to her, she tried to hand over the script to you."

Gio hunches her shoulders. "I was freaking out. Even if she didn't look dangerous, it's not like stalkers wear signs on their foreheads announcing who they are."

The plea in her eyes strikes me to my core. *She can't be held responsible for what my sister did, can she? No one is responsible for another's actions, and yet… If she had spared a few seconds to listen to her, if she'd accepted the script from Diana, if she'd been a little more sympathetic, wouldn't my sister still be alive?* I firm my jaw and thrust out my chest. "She tried to call you afterward. She tried for weeks on end."

She takes a step in my direction, and when I move back, her face falls. "I'm sorry for your loss, truly. But you have to know the impossible situation I was in. There are a lot of people who would try to reach my clients, and if they weren't known, they wouldn't get through the checks in place."

I hold up my hand. "Thirty seconds of your time. That's all that was needed to make a difference. If you'd listened to her, she'd still be alive."

"Rick, I can't tell you how sorry I am that my actions inadvertently led to your sister dying. But if she hadn't broken into his house, I wouldn't have found her, and it wouldn't have led to the string of events that happened."

A visceral sensation grips my body. The hair on the nape of my neck rises. Every logical thought in my head insists she's right. *Have I been wrong blaming her all this time? Was I mistaken for harboring a need for revenge all this time?*

"You can't blame me for her death, Rick, you can't."

I want to believe her, I do. Everything would be so much easier if I could. Everything would be... too easy. Too straightforward. And if anything seems too simple, it probably is. The line dividing right and wrong cuts through my heart, and who's going to risk cutting out their own heart? I'm paraphrasing some philosopher, no doubt, but what-fucking-ever. I've come too far to walk away without the satisfaction of seeing her as crushed as I was when I found out about my sister.

"You may not have meant to, but your actions caused her to lose hope in the future. With a criminal record, there was no way she was going to get hired in Hollywood. I lost my sister and I hold you responsible."

"You're being unreasonable," she cries.

"Am I?"

She scrutinizes my features, and whatever she sees there must bring home the depth of the anger I hold toward her. She draws in a sharp breath, and something shifts in her expression.

"Wait, did you know I was Declan's PR manager when you took on the role of his bodyguard? Is that why you always seemed pissed off with me and barely spoke to me then?"

I don't answer, but whatever she sees in my eyes makes her gasp. "It is, isn't it? So why didn't you confront me then? Why did you wait until I moved to London—hold on, did you manipulate things so I would move here and take on the PR for the Ice Kings so you could get me in a more vulnerable position?" She scans my features. "Did you arrange things so I'd have to share the room with you?"

When I stay silent, she rubs at her temples. Her features are pale, the hollows under her cheekbones pronounced. My chest hurts. A pressure builds between my eyeballs. If it weren't impossible, I'd say I'm feeling her pain as my own. But that's not possible. She means nothing to me, nothing. All of this was a plan to get my revenge. Right?

So why do I want to go to her and gather her close and apologize for the pain I'm causing her? Why am I this close to abandoning my scheme for retribution and falling to my knees in front of her and telling her I have feelings for her and—I curl my fingers into fists.

No, I can't do that. Not now. Not when I'm this close to getting retribution for Diana. I owe that much to my sister. I raise my hand toward her, then stop. *I can't do this. I shouldn't do this. Not if I want to be loyal to Diana's memory.* And if it means I get hurt in the process, so be it.

"You did maneuver events so we'd share a room." She nods slowly. "But what I don't understand is how you ensured I'd move to London? You couldn't have known I'd be cheated on. That I'd want to leave L.A. and move here because of that?" She bites the inside of my cheek and whispers, "Could you?" Her eyes glitter with unshed tears. She swallows, and when she speaks, her voice is hoarse, "Was everything you told me a lie?"

61

Gio

"What did he reply?" Mira cries.

I'm seated with my back straight on her couch. My hands are folded in my lap, and I'm trying to compose my features into a placid expression but failing, especially when my fingers brush the ring he gave me. *Grams' ring. Why would he give me a ring that's a family memento, if he didn't feel something for me?* It's a question that bothers me every time I look at it. It's a question I haven't dared ask him; I'm not ready for the answer.

"He didn't. He walked out of there."

I was too shocked to move. If Edward hadn't found me, I might still be frozen with my back against that glass wall. I should be grateful Rick made sure to clean me up and straighten my clothes before he left me.

Edward guided me to his car and dropped me at Mira's place. He also revealed Rick had sent him to check on me. Which confused me. *If he hates me, why be so chivalrous toward me? If he's out to get revenge, why be so concerned about me?*

"And he thinks you're responsible for his sister's suicide?"

I hunch my shoulders, then force myself to square them. I will not give in to this helplessness that gnaws at my insides. I will not allow this feeling of powerlessness to overwhelm me. I've survived so long on my own. Even when

I found my ex cheating on me, I didn't fallen apart entirely. Sure, I packed up my things and moved on, but that didn't hurt me as much as realizing Rick has been pretending this entire time.

So why does it seem like the entire world around me has changed in an instant? Why does it feel like I'm staring down at myself and watching this scene playing out? Why does it feel like my skin is going to break any moment and my insides are going to shatter into a million tiny pieces... All of which are going to call out his name? A teardrop rolls down my cheek, and I can't stop myself from sniffling.

"Oh, honey!" Mira rushes over and sinks down into the seat next to me. When she hugs me, I squeeze my fingers together even tighter.

Why is it so difficult for me to accept kindness from my friends? Why am I unable to express how I feel? Why do I feel so cold inside, like he destroyed my ability to feel? Why am I so dependent on a man for my happiness? Why can't I find a way to self-soothe and get out of this funk I've fallen into?

"Don't be so hard on yourself." Mira strokes my hair. "You demand too much of yourself, Gio. It's okay to fall apart sometimes."

I swallow. "If I do, I'm not sure I'll be able to pick myself up and move on."

"That's why you have friends—to help you when that happens. And if you don't allow yourself to fall apart now, when you finally suffer a breakdown, it'll be even worse," she warns.

"You're right, but I'm so used to being in control. So used to trying to manage everything, you know? But every-time my life feels like it's on track, something happens, and I feel like I'm back at the beginning."

"Which is why I don't plan at all. I prefer to be spontaneous. Life is what happens when you're busy making plans, so I prefer to focus on everything else but the plan. That way, I know I'm living life to the fullest."

I scrutinize her features. "It seems to have worked for you so far. You're one of the most happy-go-lucky people I know."

"It's all the time I spend with kids. Nothing like wiping runny noses, changing diapers, and constantly serving up juice boxes and snacks. Not to mention, entertaining two-year-olds all day long keeps you present in the moment."

"You love your job," I state.

"Wouldn't want to do anything else. I know it might seem like the height of being unambitious, but all I've wanted is to have kids of my own and take care of them. It's probably because I'm the oldest of four. I grew up taking care of my sisters and found I enjoyed it. Kids are so innocent, so present, so in the moment, it's rubbed off on me. I'd rather enjoy what I have than focus on the future and what I don't have." She chuckles. "I know it's all a bit woo-woo, but it works for me."

"I wish I could be a little more relaxed about my future, too." The only time I've let myself go is when I'm with him. It's because he makes me feel secure—because I thought he had my back, because I trusted him. Because I thought I'd found the man I'd spend the rest of my life with. I was so sure he was the one. Sure, even though we started this relationship under fake pretenses, he'd begun to fall for me, too. How could I have been so wrong?

She takes my hands in hers. "I know he's upset with you, but I think it's positive he came out and told you the truth."

"I would have preferred it if he'd told me this before I developed feelings for him." I pull my hands from her, then rise to my feet. "Maybe that was the plan all along—to make me fall in love and then tell me the truth so I'd feel every part of his betrayal."

"He told you before he married you, though."

I pause. "That's true." I begin to pace. "Why would he do that? Why not have gone through with the charade, then once we were married, tell me about it? It would have been so much worse that way."

"Maybe because he's also in love with you."

"Oh, trust me, he doesn't love me. You didn't see the hate and pain in his eyes when he told me about his sister. He holds me responsible for what happened to her. He's never going to forgive me. He—"

There's a knock on the door, and we look at each other.

"Maybe that's him," she murmurs.

My heart drops to my stomach. *No, no, no I don't want to see him, not right now. Now when I'm this vulnerable, this open, this broken, this everything I'd never want him to witness.* If he looks at me with those piercing blue eyes, I'm going to forget every promise I made to myself, and throw myself at him, and I can't do that. I can't, not after the way he decided I was guilty without giving me a chance to defend myself. Not after he told me he holds me responsible for something that's not my fault. *It's not.*

There's another knock on the door. "Goldie, I know you're in there," he calls out.

"Oh my god, I'm not ready, I'm not."

"Want me to tell him to leave?"

"Yes, no, I don't know." I glance around the space, then bound toward the bedroom door.

"Where are you going?"

62

Rick

"Gio, if you don't open the door, I'm going to break it down and—"

The door swings open. The woman who stands before me has her hands on her hips and a frown on her face.

"Mira, sorry about that." I hold up my hands. "I would've paid to get the door replaced if I'd broken it down."

"Hmm." She looks me up and down. "You here to apologize to her?"

I shuffle my feet. Fact is, I'm not sure why I'm here. All I know is, after I left her in that room, my entire body felt like I was weighed down. I struggled to put one foot in front of the other and move forward. Every inch of space I put between us felt like a mile. Every breath I drew hurt my throat and cut into my chest. Every beat of my heart felt like it was my last. Every muscle seized up and refused to cooperate with me.

My mind told me I had to keep going, my body refused to comply, and my heart? My heart felt like someone had reached into my chest, ripped it out, stomped on it, and left it laying on the floor at her feet. That someone would be me.

I haven't felt this fractured since I got the phone call about Diana and realized I'd failed in my duties as a brother.

I managed to head to the locker room and clean up, then walked out to the team bus, which was waiting to take us to a bar to celebrate tonight's win. Only halfway there, I jumped up and told the driver to pull over. My team-mates thought I was losing it. Only Finn realized something was wrong. He must have read something in my expression because he asked me if I'd broken up with Gio.

Wham, just like that—hearing him say the words aloud, the blood drained from my face. My breath came in pants, and it felt like my heart—which I honestly thought I'd left behind—was trying to cleave its way out of my chest. He handed me a bottle of water, made sure I drank it, then asked me what I was going to do about it.

When I was stumped, he pointed out I had to make things right. And he was right. Once I'd taken a few sips of the water, he took the bottle from me, then urged me to get off the bus and go to her.

I tried to call her, but it went to voice mail. I was sure she wouldn't go to the house; she wouldn't want to see me. I called Edward next, and he told me he'd dropped her off at Mira's place. I pulled the hood of my sweatshirt over my head, pulled on my sunglasses, then flagged down a cab and high-tailed it to her place.

I shouldn't have worried about being recognized, though. The cab driver was a cricket fan and gave me an earful of how Cade is the best captain the English team has ever had. Not that I begrudge Cade his fame. Ice hockey has its share of fans, and the media loves to write about us, but the game has yet to catch up with cricket and footie when it comes to popularity in this country. The drive gave me the chance to gather my thoughts, and by the time I reached Mira's apartment, I knew what I had to do.

"I want to put things right with her," I admit to her.

She folds her arms about her chest. Her features are set in hard lines. "I don't think she wants to see you."

I look past her but can't see Goldie in the living room. It feels like a freight truck rammed into me. I sway and have to grab the frame of her door to stay upright. Fucking hell, I can face down a hockey team of six-foot five-inch men who each weigh more than 200 pounds, but the thought of not being able to see her again reduces my knees to pulp. I open my mouth to speak, but no words come out.

"You okay?" Mira frowns.

I'm not okay. I don't think I ever will be. Not until I can explain things to her; not until I put things right with her somehow. I shake my head. "Can I come in?" I manage to say through gritted teeth.

She glances over her shoulder, then back at me. "Umm, I'm not quite sure."

"Please, I need to talk to her, is all. I *have* to talk to her. You understand, right?"

"Why do you want to talk to her?"

"Because I said and did things that hurt her, and it hurt me so much more."

"You sound surprised."

I shake my head. "I'm not surprised. I knew it would be like stabbing myself with my hockey stick to cause her any pain. But the intensity of it, how horrifying it felt... How it felt like I was tearing off a part of myself, to realize I might never get to see her again... I wasn't prepared for that," I concede.

She puts her hands on her hips. "I repeat, why do you want to see her?"

"To apologize to her."

"And if she isn't appeased?"

"Then I'll do anything, *anything*, to make it up to her."

She purses her lips, then a look of surprise dawns on her feature. "You do mean it, don't you?"

"Of course I do."

"You'd better grovel hard enough to make it up to what you did to my girl. You broke her heart."

"I broke mine, too." I roll my shoulders. "Please, let me talk to her. That's all I ask."

She draws in a breath, then nods. "She's in the bedroom." She steps aside.

"Thank you." I take a shaky step forward, and when my knees seem to hold up my weight, I manage to make it across the floor and to the bedroom.

"Don't make me regret it," Mira calls out from behind me.

I glance back in her direction. "I won't," I promise. I pause at the door, then knock on it. "Goldie? Can I come in?"

63

Gio

"Goldie, please?"

I push my back into the door and squeeze my eyes shut. *I can't do this. I can't see him. I don't want to see him.* If I do, it'll only weaken me, and I can't let that happen. Not after how he strung me along. And I thought he had feelings for me. I was sure I saw the tenderness in his eyes. Glimpsed affection, perhaps even, a liking... maybe, love for me. I was sure he'd never hurt me.

I was wrong. Again. I really know how to pick 'em, huh? I had my heart broken and dared to believe in love. And now, I'm paying the price. How am I going to recover from this? How?

"Goldie, give me a chance, please. One chance to make it up to you. That's all I ask."

I hear the plea in his voice, and something knotted in my chest begins to loosen. I steel myself against the barrage of feelings that pour through my veins. I can't let myself soften toward him, I can't, no matter that he's apologizing. If I did, I'd never forgive myself. I'd never look at myself in the mirror with self-respect again. And will I forgive myself if I don't give him a chance?

"Goldie?"

A ripple squeezes my insides. He must have placed his palm against the door, for I swear, I can feel the imprint on the small of my back.

"Please?" He lowers his voice to a hush, and my nerve-endings spark.

"You're not playing fair," I manage to choke out. "If you use that tone of voice, you know I'll obey you, and I don't want to. I don't."

"Then open the door."

"Why should I?"

"I need to see your face. Please, baby."

"Don't. Don't call me by any endearments you don't mean."

"But I do. It's true I was angry with you. That I was holding onto a grudge against you. That perhaps, a small part of me still holds you responsible for what happened with my sister. But I'm trying, Goldie. I promise, I am."

"Was everything you told me a lie? The way you fucked me—"

"Made love to you," he corrects me.

"Fucked me. You held my gaze as you fucked me, and I thought I glimpsed the truth of us in your eyes—"

"And you did, I promise. I was conflicted about what I was doing. I knew I was falling for you, and I hated myself for it. It wasn't supposed to happen this way. I wasn't supposed to develop emotions where you were concerned. It was supposed to be an arrangement, that's all."

I wince. "If you're trying to sell me on an apology—"

"I'm not. I mean, I'm not trying to sell you. And I'm doing a piss poor job of apologizing to you, too. Gio, open the door, I beg you. Let me look at you while having this conversation, at least."

I shake my head. "You turned your back on me and walked away. And you never told me about your sister. You had the opportunity—"

"I tried to tell you many times, but I knew if I did, it would change everything between us."

"So, you let me believe that you were developing feelings for me?"

"I was! That was the entire problem." He groans, then I hear a thump against the door, and while I can't see him, I know he's pushed his forehead into the wood. I turn and place my palm against it, then lean my forehead into the door.

"I don't believe you," I say softly.

He must hear me, for he growls, "Better believe it. We wouldn't be having this conversation if I didn't feel something for you. It's because I was falling for you, I decided to tell you the truth about Diana. I couldn't have married you without you knowing the reality. It's why I had to tell you."

"And I'm asking myself, why you didn't pretend to marry me and then tell me the truth. Wouldn't it have hurt me more that way?" *Why does it matter? Why am I asking him these questions, when nothing he says is going to change the fact that everything between us was a lie.*

"You're right, and I know it would have hurt you even more if we'd gotten married—"

"Fake married—"

"Married." His voice turns hard. "We're in love, and we are getting married."

"No, we're not." I shake my head.

"Goldie!" His tone turns glacial enough, if words were weapons, he would have torn down the door with them. "We have to get married. Grams expects it."

"First your sister, now your grandmother." I throw up my hands. "Once again, you're placing responsibility for the health of one of your family members on me. It's not fair. You can't do this. You can't manipulate me into doing something I don't want to, you—"

As if on cue, my phone rings. I pull it from the pocket in my jacket and look at it. *Oh, no, it's Grams calling.* I stare at the screen as her name flashes there. I hold the phone until it stops ringing, only for a buzzing from the other side of the door to start.

"Fuck!" Rick exclaims, but he doesn't answer the phone, either. The buzzing sound continues, then cuts out.

A few seconds later my phone starts ringing. It's her again. I glance up at the door then at the phone. Then, before I can change my mind, I answer the call, "Hello, Grams!"

"There you are," Grams coughs. "I can't reach my grandson, but that's fine. I'd rather talk to you anyway."

"Why are you on the phone, you should be resting."

"Oh phsst"—I can imagine her wave her hand in the air—"I'll rest when I'm dead."

"Don't talk about dying, please." I swallow.

"It's inevitable. We're all going to die, Giorgina, some of us sooner than others. It's why I want the two of you to get married right way."

"What?" I burst out.

"The two of you *are* getting married, aren't you?" She sounds uncertain. When I don't answer, I hear her sniff. "Has that fool of my grandson done something to upset you? Are the two of you fighting? Is that why neither of you is answering my phone call?"

I stay quiet. The silence stretches, then I hear Grams swallow over the phone. "Is... is everything okay between the two of you? My Rick can be a little hard-headed, but he has a good heart. I hope you won't hold his stubbornness against him?"

The vulnerability in her voice reaches into me and twists that part of me I've tried to protect for as long as I can remember.

I've put up barriers against the world, so I wouldn't be hurt. Every time I've let someone through, they've only hurt me. I was wise enough not to let my guard down against Dennis. But with Rick, he bulldozed it all without trying. He crawled under my skin and imprinted his scent in my cells. He wrote his name on my heart. And any remaining resistance I might have had was knocked down by the sadness in Grams' voice.

I never met my grandparents or my father, and my mother wasn't known for her maternal instincts.

It's why I learned to be independent at such an early age. It's why, when I met Grams, I fell for her as much as I had for Rick. She's been more loving to me than my own parents had ever been. She's the closest I've come to having a family. It's why I have to do this. "Sorry we didn't answer the phone, Grams. Rick is with me."

I open the door, and his cerulean gaze locks with mine. The helplessness, and the anger, and the frustration I'm feeling is mirrored in his eyes. It convinces me, this is the right thing to do. "As soon as the paperwork is arranged, we're getting married."

64

Rick

"You may kiss the bride." The registrar from the local town hall agreed to come to Grams' place to wed us, and I managed to get him in without arousing the interest of the paparazzi.

After a week in the hospital, as soon as Dr. Kincaid gave his all-clear, Grams, herself, insisted on being discharged. For someone with three stents in her heart, she's chipper. If the doc hadn't updated me on the operation, I'd be sure she pulled this entire stent—I mean, stunt—of being unwell to get me married and settled down. Okay, I'm being uncharitable. Though Grams is savvy enough to try something like this, in this instance, she really was unwell. Although…she did use the condition to coerce me into getting married.

In a way, I need to thank her for bringing Gio into my life, and for ensuring she agreed to marry me. The same Gio who moved out of the room we shared and into Mira's place. The same Gio on whose finger I slid a wedding ring which had belonged to my mother and which compliments the engagement ring she already had on. The same Gio who offers me her cheek when I lean in toward her.

"If you think you can deprive me of what's mine, you're mistaken," I whisper.

She stiffens, but before she can reply, I wrap my fingers around the nape of her neck and tug with enough pressure that she has to turn her face in my direction. There's a mutinous expression on her face. Her lips are pursed.

"All the better to kiss you with." I close my mouth over hers.

I mean for the kiss to be hard, to show her who's in charge. To show her I'm as pissed off as she is at the turn of events. This was supposed to be my revenge, but somehow, the tables have been turned. I'm the one who should be pissed at her for how her actions affected my sister. Instead, she's pissed at me —and she has reason to be. I realize now, I can't lay the blame for my sister committing suicide on her shoulders. It was my sister's actions that led to what happened.

And if I'd been there, I'd have stopped her. If I'd known what she was going through, I'd have helped her. So, really, I'm the one responsible for what happened. The buck stops with me. But no part of this realization is going to bring my sister back. Anger squeezes my guts. My shoulder muscles bunch. I tighten my hold on her, tilt my head, and lick up the seam of her lips. She parts them on a groan, and I plunge my tongue inside her mouth. The taste of her goes to my head, the scent of her sinks into my blood, and as always, my cock is erect and ready for action when she's involved. *Why am I so in thrall to this woman?* She can make me do anything she wants. Does she know that?

And now I have her where I want her—in my arms, married to me, she's my wife. *My other half. Mine.* The realization sweeps through me. The knots inside of me she's unloosened dissolve completely. A quiver undulates my spine. I soften my lips, gentle my kiss, and she melts into me. I wrap my arm about her waist and draw her close. She moans against my mouth, I absorb the sound, then haul her up to her toes, bringing her closer.

"Look at me while I kiss you, wife," I demand against her mouth.

She raises her heavy eyelids, and the gold in her eyes lightens to silver. She's aroused, alright. She might want to hate me, but her reaction to me tells the true story. She swallows, a look of helplessness seeps into her eyes, and my heart stutters. And when she beseeches me without saying a word, I understand her frustration, her pain, her need for me, and the self-recrimination she levels against herself for feeling the way she does. It mirrors the contradictory emotions that crowd my mind, my heart, every cell in my body. The need to continue kissing her, yet to release her. The need to claim her, knowing she'll never love me the way I already love her. Knowing I'll never confess how much I want her and what she means to me, for the ghost of my sister will always be in the background, making me feel guilty.

Once more, I turned my back on her. Once more, I failed her. I release my wife, and she stumbles. A flash of satisfactions zips through me. I kissed all thoughts from her mind. I ensured she couldn't think, couldn't feel anything but the sensation of my lips pressed to hers, my fingers on her skin, the hard lines of my torso digging into her curves, my palm-prints imprinted into the dip of her waist, marking her as mine. Too bad I'm not going to follow through on the satisfaction my kiss promised her.

I squeeze her shoulder until I know she's steady, then step back. Her forehead scrunches, a look of confusion on her features, and I want to soothe her and reassure her and tell her it's okay. Only, I'd be lying. We're married, my grandmother is on her way to recovery. Now, all that remains is to ensure her ex never lays eyes on her again, and my work will be done.

I wrap my arm about her and turn to face Grams. "Happy?" I ask her.

"Very." She rises to her feet and walks over to us. Her steps are slow but steady. She's lost weight since the operation, but the paleness on her features is slowly fading. She's still weak, but she wouldn't hear of us waiting another day. Her eyes are bright, her face wreathed in smiles as she leads Tiny over to us. She's insisted on having him by her side every second since she came home.

The Great Dane, for his part, has been very gentle with her. He slept by her bed, and dogged her footsteps, and never barked once in her presence. It's as if he knows not to do anything that would put any additional strain on her heart. I checked with Doc Kincaid about it, and he said, if the mutt helps calm her, then there's no reason she can't spend time with him. Now, Tiny looks from me to Gio to me. Then, of course, he brushes his head gently against her.

Goldie pats his head, and Tiny makes a purring sound. One touch from her has turned him into a cat, apparently.

Grams giggles, then claps her hands and looks between us. "I'm so happy!" She turns to me. "I can't believe you're married."

Me neither.

"She's too good for you, obviously." Grams sniffs. "And if you do anything to upset her, you'll have me to contend with."

Too late.

"Whose side are you on?" I frown.

"Giorgina's, of course," Grams chuckles.

Tiny wags his tail in agreement.

My entire family has turned against me. Not that I blame them. Given a choice, I'd take Gio's side over mine, anyway.

"I'm sure you'd like to spend time with my bride, but—"

"You're taking her on a honeymoon, I assume?" Grams arches an eyebrow at me.

I shift my weight from foot to foot. "I —"

"I don't want one." Goldie bends and takes Grams' hand in hers. "We're in the middle of the season, so neither Rick nor I can get away. It's a miracle the paparazzi haven't found out about this ceremony. We want to take advantage of that and keep things quiet. In fact, we decided not to tell our friends or the team, either."

"We did?" I scowl.

We didn't discuss it, and I've been too focused on my daily practice to mention it to anyone. Then, there's the fact that I've missed her presence. Something which took me by surprise, even though it really shouldn't.

It's why I've begun working out every evening. So, when I stumble into bed, I fall asleep at once. Of course, then I awaken before dawn and reach for her, find she's not there, and admonish myself. I'm the first to turn up at practice, and the last to leave. And of course, I've gotten knowing looks from my teammates and Edward, who noticed she'd moved out.

Edward asked me if everything was okay, when I said it was, he didn't push the subject. It had been my idea she move into the house, to foster team-spirit, so it was no surprise he didn't have an issue with her moving out.

Gio didn't turn up for practice last week, but that wasn't a surprise. I told the team she had some personal things to take care of, which was why she was staying with Mira, but we were still together. Edward wasn't buying it, but as long as we kept the PR story alive, he was good. My teammates didn't pry into it. That is, except Finn, who asked me how things had gone with Gio? I lied and said everything was okay.

So no, we didn't decide *not* to tell our friends and team about our wedding, but we also hadn't mentioned it to anyone, yet.

"Don't you remember?" She widens her gaze at me, "You suggested we keep it quiet, lest it takes away from the excitement around the finals."

I glare at her. She pales, and tries to pull away, but I tighten my arm about her. I bend and pretend to kiss her forehead. "We had no such conversation, baby."

"It's the right thing to do, don't you think?" She rises up on tiptoe and whispers so Grams can't hear her, "This marriage is a farce; there's no need to go shouting about it to everyone. The less people who know, the easier it will be when we break up."

65

Gio

"So you guys are breaking up?" Mira asks me.

I got married, then made an excuse about getting back to work. Grams was surprised but she didn't try to stop me. She kissed me on my cheek, told me how happy she was to have me as her grand-daughter-in-law, then insisted I take Tiny for company. When I protested, her lips drew down. "Tiny loves being with the both of you."

Rick interjected, "But Grams, he's not strictly my dog. He's Liam and Isla's. Since they're away, the rest of us have been taking turns dog-sitting, and I thought you could do with some cheering, so—"

"And I'm all cheered up. Besides, he wants to go with the two of you," Grams insisted.

"He does?" I glanced doubtfully at the Great Dane, who looked up at me with his melting black eyes. Something in my heart shifted. Or maybe, it was simply that I was still getting used to the fact I was married and would be divorced soon. I was going to be on my own again. For someone who sworn never to get married in a hurry, I sure crossed *that* one off my list fast. The thought was beginning to sink in, leaving me with a sense of despondency, when Tiny made that whine he does, and my heart completely melted. I patted him, and the big dog pushed his head into my palm. Suddenly, I didn't feel alone. It felt right to bring Tiny back with me. So, without a second glance at my husband, I hurried Tiny out.

Rick followed me and insisted on driving me to Mira's. I told him I was keeping Tiny, and he agreed. Of course, I texted Mira, and she confirmed it was fine by her; pets are allowed at her apartment building. When Rick dropped me off, he confirmed he'd pick me up tomorrow, the day of the final match between the Ice Kings and the Sentinels.

I said no, but he simply brushed aside my protests. Then, Tiny pushed his big head between us from the back seat where he'd been strapped in, and that put an end to the argument.

Rick parked the car and carried Tiny's food and necessities that Grams' companion had packed to the door of Mira's apartment. He rang the bell and stayed until Mira opened the door. Then, he nodded his goodbye and left.

"I'm very confused. You two got married, and now you're breaking up?" Mira takes a sip of her wine. She makes a huge fuss over Tiny, who laps up all of the attention.

"Apparently." I turn away, not wanting to face the questions she has for me. I throw myself onto the settee and have no intention of moving. Tiny parks himself next to me; he seems to sense my despondency. He places his head on the edge of the sofa and is looking at me with his melting eyes. "Are you hungry?" I drag my fingers through the fur on his big head.

He thumps his tail.

"Oh, come here, sweetie. Let's get you some food." Mira jumps up.

Tiny whines again. Only when I nod my head, does he bound up to his feet and follow her into the kitchen. Her voice reaches me, "I know about your love for Champagne and you're not getting any from me."

Tiny sighs so loudly, I can hear him all the way in the living room. I can't stop myself from chuckling.

"No, no, don't think you can turn those big melting eyes on me and plead with me," she admonishes him.

Tiny woofs in response.

I hear her continue to baby talk to him and realize I have a smile on my face. Tiny seems to have that softening effect on people. When he's around, there's never a dull moment. No time to feel sorry for yourself, for your attention is taken up with him. Maybe that's why Grams asked us to take care of him? But did Grams know I'm not staying with Rick and that I'd end up keeping Tiny? Dogs aren't allowed in the house we share with the rest of the team. I hadn't mentioned anything to Grams, and neither had Rick, but Grams must have sensed something, to ask me to take care of Tiny. Or maybe it was a test, and I failed it? The doorbell rings.

"Will you get it?" Mira calls out from the kitchen. I hear the sound of Tiny's chomping as I head for the door, and when I throw it open, I gasp. My heart jumps in my chest. A thrill of pleasure runs through my veins. I tilt my head all the way back and take in that square jaw, that mean upper lip, that pouty lower lip, that hooked nose which lends him an air of always being in control.

"What do you want?" I cross my arms over my chest.

"I wanted to see you," my husband murmurs.

"You saw me less than an hour ago."

"I wanted to make sure you don't lack for anything."

"Why would you do that?" I frown.

"You're my wife," he reminds me.

"Not for much longer."

His lips thin. "You are my wife. End of story." He pulls something from his pocket and holds it out.

I glance at the rectangular card in the palm of his hand, then up at his face. "What's that for?"

"It's a bank card. You'll have access to all of the funds in my account with this."

"I have enough money of my own."

"Call me old-fashioned, but I'd prefer to provide for my wife," he growls.

"We've only been married a few hours, and you're already asserting your rights?"

"Oh, I haven't even started." His shoulders bunch, and the tendons of his throat stand out in relief. He looks like he's about to tear off my clothes, throw me on the ground and mount me and... *Would that be so bad?*

Heat flushes my skin. My heart descends to the space between my thighs. That familiar flip-flop of my stomach draws attention to the fact I'm utterly in his thrall. I try to look away from him, but those laser-sharp eyes of his hold me captive.

"Rick," I swallow. "Please, Rick." I'm not sure what I'm asking for, but he seems to understand.

"You're my wife. You should be with me, at my side."

"It's a farce, Rick. This was for Grams' benefit, and now she's happy. That's all that matters."

"If it's a farce, why are you wearing your ring?"

I glance at my left hand where the antique engagement ring, as well as the accompanying wedding band he placed there mock me. I curl my fingers into a fist and lower it to my side. "I forgot to take it off, is all."

"I didn't forget you, not for one second since I left you here. Come back with me, Goldie. The bed is too big without you, the room is too empty without you and I... I'm nothing without you."

Pressure builds behind my eyes. "I can't, Rick. Not after what you did to me. Everything you told me was a lie. Even getting me to share your room and your bed. All of it was a lie. There's nothing real between us, not even our marriage, so there's no reason for us to be together."

"But there is,." He reaches for my hand then turns my palm face-up and places his bank card on it. "I'm rich, Gio."

"So?"

"I'm very rich."

He's never flaunted his wealth, but given he's the captain of the hottest hockey team in the country, not to mention Grams lives in a townhouse in the most expensive borough in the city, somewhere along the line, it had registered with me that Rick was definitely well-off. Hold on, I frown. "If you think you can pay me—"

"I wouldn't dare." His eyes gleam.

I scowl. "Are you laughing at me?"

He shakes his head.

I squint down at the card. "Why would you give me your bank card instead of a credit card?"

"Because what's mine is yours. Because I trust you. But I betrayed *your* trust. I hurt you. I need to pay for betraying you, and I couldn't think of a better way than by placing my fortune in your hands."

66

Rick

"It's a start, but it's not enough." Edward leans a hip against the counter in the kitchen, where we're sharing a beer. After giving her my bank card, I turned and left. And that's only because if I stayed another second, I'd have thrown her over my shoulder and marched out of there. I wouldn't have regretted it, either. But... I promised myself to give her space, to let her come around, to act in a fashion that would show how remorseful I am for what I did to her. And I'm full of regret, mostly.

A part of me can't shake the thought that maybe, just maybe, she could have done a little more to prevent what happened to Diana. I've tried to push aside the notion, but it keeps circling around the corners of my mind. And damn, if that isn't driving me crazy.

My phone pings. I take in the notification, then blink. Some of the blood must drain from my features, for Edward narrows his gaze. "You okay, Stone?"

I show him the message on the phone screen. He takes a look, then whistles. "Is that—"

"A million dollars? Yes."

"And she transferred it out of your account?"

"Into that of Children's Futures."

"That's a charity the Seven started."

"It is?" I ask surprised.

He nods. "They're the best when it comes to supporting vulnerable children around the world. She picked well."

Another message pops up on screen, then another, and another. Ten messages come back-to-back, each showing a number with seven zeros. All of them are to different charities, most supporting causes related to women and children.

With each message, the warmth in my chest blooms, until it seems to permeate my entire being.

Edward whistles. "Your woman has a big heart."

I can't stop the smile that curves my lips.

"For someone who's net worth dropped by the millions, you're ridiculously happy," he remarks.

I crack my neck. "Between my NHL earnings and my grandmother's estate I'm a multi-billionaire—and you know what? She can transfer my entire fortune to causes she supports, and even that won't make up for what I did to her."

Silence descends. I glance up to find Edward looking at me with an expression I can only describe as not surprised.

"You guys knew?" I ask with resignation. I'm not surprised. Between the combined power that the Seven and the Sovranos weld, there's not much that happens that they can't find out about.

"Your sister. We're aware you wanted to avenge her."

I rub the back of my neck, continuing to stare at the screen. The messages have paused, but I have no doubt, it's a temporary lull. I hope it's a brief pause. I wasn't lying when I said none of my material possessions don't have her by my side. I'd gladly give up everything if it meant it would make her feel better.

"Gio was the person who called the cops on my sister. She was doing her job. Anyone in her position would have done that. I realize that my sister was in the wrong to have broken into Declan's house."

"Your sister had a fixation on Declan, enough to write a script with him in mind, then break into his house and wait for him, so she could talk to him in person." Edward leans forward on the balls of his feet. "But you don't hold Declan responsible for what happened to her?"

I shake my head. "I confronted him when I was his bodyguard. I took on his security detail so I could have this conversation with him. But Declan had no idea about the incident. He didn't know Diana was stalking him, let alone that she'd broken into his home. He doesn't manage his social media or his PR. Gio was his PR manager's assistant at that time. She's the one who monitored his social media and picked up Diana's messages."

"She's the one who discovered Diana when she broke into his home. She's the one who didn't listen to Diana, who called the cops on her. A part of me understands why she did it, and yet"—I crack my neck— "yet, I can't help wondering, what if Gio had given Diana a few seconds of her time? What if she'd taken the script from her and told her she'd give it to Declan. Even if she hadn't, my sister would have felt heard. It would have made her feel like there was a chance for her. It might have bought her a little more time. Enough for me to have met with Diana and understood her frame of mind. I could have helped her. My sister would still be alive." The pressure drums against my skull. I grab tufts of my hair and tug. "Fuck!"

Edward scrutinizes my features. "Are you upset with Gio, or are you using this as an excuse to not blame yourself?"

"What?" I flinch.

"I'm not the best when it comes to understanding relationships but what I have is perspective. I can't claim to know how it feels to be in your shoes, but it certainly seems obvious that you're avoiding the real issue here."

"The real issue?" I manage to keep emotions out of my voice, not that it fools Priest, for he tilts his head.

"You married her and didn't inform the rest of the team."

"Fucking hell." I throw up my hands. "I should have known you guys would find out about it."

"And you're entitled to your privacy, but if you loved this woman and intended to spend your life with her, you'd have announced it to the world."

Anger squeezes my chest. "My not announcing to the world that she's my wife has nothing to do with my sister's suicide."

"Hasn't it?" He meets my gaze with a challenge in his eyes.

I look away, then back at him. "Our marriage is a farce. I proposed the arrangement so I could get my grandmother to go through with a life-saving procedure and so she could get revenge on her douche ex."

His gaze stays steady. He doesn't seem surprised by my revelation.

"What?" I scowl.

"I've heard that before," he drawls.

"You're not making sense."

"It seems to be a common theme where my friends are concerned. Men who conveniently use the front of a 'fake relationship'"—he uses air quotes

—"to deny their feelings for their woman, until they come to their senses and realize their mistake. And then need to grovel non-stop, and sometimes, that isn't enough to make things up."

"Is that what happened to you?"

"Me?" His expression turns bleak. "I never got that far. She decided I wasn't the one for her. And she was right. I would have made a poor life partner. I hadn't sorted out the stuff in my own head. How could I focus on anyone else? How could I fulfill her needs when my own were so twisted out of shape?"

"And now?"

"I know I made the right decision. I've loved and lost and realized, it's not for me. I'm better off focusing on other things. Things that impact a wider number of people."

"Hence, you took on the role of the General Manager?"

"I did it because I could." He hesitates. "Because it gave me the sense of purpose I was looking for. Because I could give direction to the team, and I hoped it would help me find my own direction."

I chuckle. "You always this philosophical?"

"If that's what's needed."

"Is that what I need?" I can't stop the skepticism from creeping into my tone.

"Isn't it?" His lips quirk. "You need to man up to your feelings. You've used every possible excuse to stop yourself from committing."

"My sister's suicide is not an excuse," I bite out.

"It's not. I can only imagine how difficult it must be to be in your shoes right now. You're blaming yourself for what happened to your sister. You're taking that out on Gio."

"I'm not."

A knowing look enters his eyes, "You're filled with guilt about your sister's death. You think you could have prevented it if you were there. And now you're trying to hang the guilt on Gio so you don't have to blame yourself. You need to confront your feelings."

"Feelings? I'm Stone, I don't have any feelings or emotions, remember?" I scoff.

Edward frowns. "Surely, you're not going to take your reputation to heart? Being Stone, the controlled one, the cool as ice man, who plays on ice is a myth that belongs in the rink. Off it, you're human. A man who's susceptible to making mistakes. A man who's been beating himself up for being away when his sister needed him. A man who's denying his love for his woman in the hope of punishing himself. You don't want to commit to Gio because she is a living reminder of the fact your sister is dead. So you've decided you need to punish her as much as yourself."

My heart slams against my ribcage with such force, I'm sure it's going to break out of my chest. My pulse crashes against my temples. Sweat breaks out on my forehead, and my vision wavers.

Edward must notice my reaction, for he touches my shoulder.

I shake it off. "What gives you the right to analyze me, huh? What makes you think you have the answers to the challenges I'm facing?"

He lowers his arm to his side, and a bleak look comes into his eyes. "I don't." He looks away, then back at me. "But I've been where you are, and I stumbled. I lost the woman I loved, and my life has never been the same. I don't want any of my friends to go through what I did. It's why I'd rather risk pissing you off and telling you what you need to hear now than not."

I scowl at him. He looks at me with a steady gaze—one in which there's pain, but also determination.

"I'd tell you to piss off, but I know you have my best interests at heart," I say slowly.

He nods. "I'm the General Manager of the team, but also your friend.

I never met your sister, but I'd wager, she wouldn't be happy that you're beating yourself—or anyone else—up over her choices. You're stopping yourself from moving on with your life, and that's doing you and the people around you—that includes your wife, your grandmother, and your team—a disservice."

My stomach heaves. Acid laces my throat. He's right. There's a ring of truth to his words I can't deny. If only I could do the right thing moving forward.

"It pains me to admit it, but you're right."

"I am." His lips curve slightly.

"Doesn't negate the fact it's fucking easy to be the one giving advice." I drag my fingers through my hair. "I can't wait to return the favor."

He laughs. "A situation I'll never find myself in. My path is set. There's no room for love."

I shake my head. "You're right about perspective. It's easy to spot the problem when you're not caught up in it."

He seems taken aback, then slowly nods. "Which is why you know I'm right when I tell you to stop pissing about and confront the fact that your life is not your own anymore."

67

Gio

Stonehole: Woman, you realize you've given away the
equivalent of the economy of a third-world country to
your favorite charities?

I read his message and allow myself a small smirk. I gave away close to a billion dollars, by my count. And yep, I settled for calling him by that name in my contact list. Bosshole or even Alphahole seemed too tame. Stonehole seems more apt. He is a stone, and I need him like I need a hole in the head. More like I need him to fill my holes, a-n-d, nope, not going there. I slow down my pace and message him back.

Me: Are you complaining?

Stonehole: I have no problem if you give away my entire fortune, all I ask is you spend some of it on yourself!

Me: I don't need your money

To which he doesn't respond. There isn't even the jumping around of dots on the screen to tell me he was even contemplating a response. Typical Rick. It's like he slammed that stone wall down, and now, I have no idea what he's thinking.

"Was that him? What was his reaction to the card charges?" Mira pants as she tries to keep pace with Tiny, who's walking fast enough to force us to trot to keep up with him. The big dog needs his exercise, so the two of us set off on a walk first thing in the morning. I reach for my bottle of water and take a swig.

"Not what I expected." I look up at her with a frown on my face.

"So he wasn't angry?"

"He seemed to expect it. In fact, he almost seemed thrilled about the money I've spent." I bite the inside of my cheek. "His only question was why I haven't spent any of the money on myself."

"It's a question I have, too. Anyone else would buy themselves designer clothing and shoes. Given your love for designer brands, you could buy out half of Selfridges and still not run out of money, but you chose to give it to charity."

"Does that make me a loser?" I shuffle my feet. "It's not that I didn't think about buying clothes or shoes or going out to a fancy restaurant, but the gestures have begun to seem empty. I don't feel the need to spend his money on myself. I have enough of my own to take care of my needs." I raise a shoulder. "Maybe I'm not like other girls. Maybe that's why I went from one man who betrayed me to another who also betrayed me."

Tears crowd the back of my eyes, and I blink them away. *I am not a loser. I am not.* So what if I'm in a marriage that doesn't mean anything? It's been a week since I moved out of Rick's room, a week since he reveled of the reason why he'd asked me to marry him, a week since I married him anyway.

I shake my head. I'm working from home today. A suggestion Edward green-lit, but which was met with stony silence from Rick on the call today, given I hadn't informed him of it. I figured he was going to find about it anyway, so there was no need for me to tell him. Throughout our conference call, Rick didn't say a word. His disapproval was a sheet of glacial ice that loomed high over my updates.

Edward pretended not to notice, so I followed his cue and addressed all of my comments toward him. Except at the end, when he said congratulations. I faltered then. Edward gently chided me on not keeping him updated on the step Rick and I had taken. My husband still didn't utter a word.

Argh, my husband. It feels strange to think of him that way. It doesn't seem real to me. Maybe because I haven't told anyone else—certainly not my mother, who wouldn't have cared either way. I'm wearing my engagement ring but took off my wedding ring after that run-in with Rick. I don't want to risk running into anyone else while wearing it. It would raise a lot of questions, most of which I have no answers to.

Tiny must sense my distress, for he slows down and bats his head against my side.

"Hey baby." I bend and hug him. He immediately nestles his head into my neck. I giggle. "Ooh, Tiny, that's tickles."

"He's making the most of having two women at his beck and call." Mira rubs his side, and he makes a purring noise. I chuckle, then straighten and tug at his ears. His eyes roll back in his head. Both of us burst out laughing. Tiny pants a little, and his tongue lolls down one side of his mouth. The dog definitely has a smile on his face.

"So that's why Grams insisted I take him. She knew I was feeling down and Tiny would cheer me up."

"She seems like a wise woman."

"She is." I nod.

"I'd love to meet her."

"I'd love for you to meet her, too, but I'm not sure that's wise, considering the situation between me and Rick." I raise a shoulder.

"I'd think your relationship with his grandmother is separate from your relationship with him."

"You're right, of course. It feels weird, is all, considering I met his Grams through him, and now he and I are not exactly on speaking terms. And it would be hard to keep that a secret from her."

"Maybe you should speak to him and sort things out. Especially since you're going to have to face him sooner or later."

I wince. "Hopefully, it's later." I've managed to avoid him, for the most part. But with the League finals coming up, and with the Ice Kings having made it to the final round, the media attention around the finals is at an all-time high, too. I have my work cut out for me. I simply have to find a way to make it through without running into him.

"You're going to have to meet him, at some point." She looks past my shoulder and her gaze widens. "A point which might be sooner than not."

"If you see him coming yell 'alphahole,' will you?" I murmur.

"Alphahole," she mumbles.

At the same time, Tiny barks, then strains at his leash with enough force that he pulls it out of Mira's hand.

"Tiny!" Without even thinking about it, I pivot and begin to follow him, then stop when I take in the gorgeous man, clad in shorts that mold to his thighs and a T-shirt that shows every hard plane and divot of his delicious chest, grab his leash, before petting him. *I will not drool. Will not drink in the sight of his familiar features which send a burst of happiness and arousal coursing through my veins.* I tip up my chin, then fold my arms across my chest. "Are you following me?"

68

Rick

"Are you avoiding me, you—" I wince because Tiny plants his paws on my chest. He's a well-behaved dog, but the excitement of seeing me has made him forget his training. Is it crazy to think he's punishing me for what I did? That he's putting his weight on me to send me a message? He presses down on the parts of me that haven't yet fully mended. Then, rising up to his full height, he unfurls his tongue and licks my face. "Ugh, Tiny." He pants, and doggy breath swirls over me like a cloud of exhaust. I cough, then tug on his leash. He manages to lick my face with his dinner-plate-like tongue before I step back and urge his front legs down. He pants and looks at me with that smiling face of his. Too bad my woman doesn't feel the same.

Goldie scowls at me. She doesn't come closer, either. As if sensing the tension between us, Tiny woofs. Then he strains at his leash. It's either let him go or follow him… I choose the latter. He closes the distance to Goldie, and when he reaches her, he rubs his big head against her side. Her features soften. She rubs him behind his ear, and he makes that purring sound that's so incongruous, considering it's coming from a two-hundred pound dog.

Mira chuckles. "Jeez ,Tiny, you need to be more dog."

"And *you* need to be gone," Goldie says without looking at me, derision evident in her tone.

"You need to give me a chance."

"I don't *need* to do anything. Anyway, I gave you a chance. See how that turned out?" she says in a low voice.

I wince. A stabbing sensation pierces my chest. "I'm sorry for what I did, Goldie. Truly. Haven't you punished me enough?"

"All you've paid for it with is your money, so far." She tosses her hair over her shoulder. "And that means nothing."

"Especially not when you haven't spent it on yourself."

"I told you, I can do without your money." She fastens her fingers around Tiny's collar. The skin around her knuckles stretches. She seems to be using him for support. I'm glad she has him during this time, but I'd rather she depend on me.

"What else can I do to make it up to you? Tell me, Goldie. Please? Do you want me on my knees? Because—" I bend one knee then the other.

She gasps.

"—here I am, on my knees, asking you to forgive me."

An older couple jogs by. The woman makes an 'awww' sound, and the man nods in my direction. "Looking good, mate." He flashes me a thumbs-up sign.

Tiny takes it as a signal that we are playing, for he barks and dances closer to me, brushing against my shoulder with enough force that I have to grab him and hold on for support.

"I'll take Tiny for a walk." Mira grabs his leash and tugs at him. "Come on, Tiny, I'll buy you a doggy breakfast."

His ears perk up. I swear the dog is half human. He barks at me, then at Goldie, as if to say, "Catch ya later," then allows Mira to lead him away. In the silence that ensues, a soft breeze blows her hair across her features.

"You wore your hair down," I murmur.

"I was in a hurry to leave the house." She searches in the pockets of her yoga pants, which cling to every curve of her thighs and outline her shapely calves. "Damn, I forgot my hair-tie."

I love it when she wears her hair down, but I know she prefers to put it up. And I want her to be comfortable. "Here." I pull one from my pocket and hold it out.

"You carry hair-ties?" She takes the band, and squints at it. "Is this mine?" She scoffs, glances up to see the look on my face and says, "Have you been carrying it around with you?"

I ignore the question and take in her left hand. "You're not wearing your wedding ring." My voice comes out harsh, and I struggle to keep the anger off my face. I didn't plan to be here, but after a night of missing her and being unable to sleep, I grabbed the pillow from her side of the bed and buried my nose in it to drag in any remnants of her scent. I finally managed to fall asleep, and woke up with an aching heart, and balls so heavy with need for her, I knew I had to see her. I told the team I'd meet them at the arena, then driven here.

"Neither are you."

"You're my wife. It's important you wear my ring, so everyone knows you're taken," I snap.

"Wow." She gapes. "You didn't say that. Of all the chauvinistic, sexist sentiments—"

"I'm on my knees, aren't I?" I shift my weight, ignoring the stones digging into my skin.

"Please get up. You're making a spectacle of yourself." A female jogger runs by, then does a double take. She stumbles, rights herself, then keeps going, casting looks at us over her shoulder.

"Please, Rick, get up."

"Only if you forgive me."

"This is blackmail."

"I haven't even started."

She firms her lips. "I'm not sure if you came here to apologize or to make things worse."

"Clearly, this is not one of my talents," I concede. "Also, I refused a wedding ring because I had something more permanent in mind." I hold up my left hand, with the back toward her.

She stares at my left ring finger, and her gaze widens. "What... What is that?"

I spread my fingers out for her perusal.

She takes a step forward, and another, until she's finally, *finally* standing in front of me. The wind changes direction, and a whiff of her honeysuckle scent wafts over me. I inhale deeply, and my muscles unwind. I missed her more than I realized. I missed the feel of her skin against mine, the swell of her hips as I spoon her at night, the sound of her voice, the spark in her eyes when she's animated, the curve of her lips—my favorite kind of curve about her—when she smiles.

She stares at my ring finger, and a stunned expression flits across her features. "That's— That's—" She swallows. "You have a wedding band—"

"Tattooed around my ring-finger."

She draws in a sharp breath. Then, as if unable to help herself, she bends and peers at the design. "Is that—?" She shakes her head. "No, it can't be."

"It is."

"It can't be my name," she says.

"It is," I repeat.

She shakes her head. "You tattooed my name around your ring finger?"

I allow myself a small smile. "It's the least I could do. I wanted something more permanent than metal."

"Did it hurt?" Her forehead creases. "Will it impede your ability to play hockey?"

"It didn't hurt enough, and if it does, it'll be worth it."

"Rick..." She raises her gaze to mine. "Why are you doing this?"

"Doing what?"

"Why are you trying so hard?" She reaches out and touches the still-new tattoo. A whisper of pain flickers over my nerve-endings. It adds to the agony of having her so close, yet not being able to touch her. I will not touch her; not until she's forgiven me. It's the least I can do after what I put her through.

"I haven't even started."

She traces her name etched into my skin between the honeysuckle flowers.

"My favorite flower," she whispers.

"It's what you smell of. Honeysuckle and hope and the spaces between things that matter most, the light between the stars, the heat in the circle of a fire that burns brighter with each day. You're my dream, my desire, the one thing I will always want, the one thing I will never forget, the one thing that occupies my mind day and night and in the time between. I want to wake up with you and fall asleep with my body curled around yours. I want to hear you laugh, make you smile, see the tears of joy shine in your eyes. I want your everything. I want to be your everything. Keep you safe from the world. Keep you happy. Make your desires come true. I want you in my life."

Her lips quiver, and her chin wobbles. Her breath comes out in little gusts of emotion. She feels the intensity of my words, knows I'm serious, understands what I'm trying to convey. She does. She must. She has to forgive me, even though I'll never forgive myself.

Her features soften. She seems to melt in my direction, and I open my arms to gather her close, when... She straightens. A tear runs down her cheek. "You had me, Rick."

69

Gio

"He tattooed your name into his skin?" Mira side-eyes me.

We're in the main VIP room overlooking the home rink of The London Ice Kings. It's the finals where they take on the Manchester Enforcers. The stands are full, the crowds steadily growing over the last few hours. The sound of their excited cheering echoes off the walls of the space. The atmosphere is electric, and even sealed off as I am in this room, the exhilaration seeps through the glass walls.

"Well, aren't you impressed by it?" she prompts.

I shrug.

"Not even a little bit?"

"Maybe a little, but it's a stunt to get my attention, no doubt."

"And he succeeded," she cries.

"Whose side are you on?" I frown as the opposing team glides onto the ice.

"Yours, babe, always yours. But I do believe the man loves you."

"He betrayed me."

"It's what brought you to his notice in the first place. Maybe he fell for you as soon as he saw you, but felt he had to be loyal to his sister's memory."

"Still doesn't forgive what he did." The Enforcers skate around the rink, and their supporters, who fill one side of the arena rise to their feet. The home supporter's boo. The players complete their circuit, then line up to face the entrance.

"What are you waiting for, Gio? You spent a million dollars of his money—"

"A billion, actually."

"What?" She cries out. "You spent a billion dollars of his money?"

There's silence behind us. I turn to find the rest of the wives and girlfriends of the Seven and the Sovranos looking at us. Yep, I was invited to watch the finals by Knight's wife Penny, and I couldn't refuse. It gave me a valid excuse not to be down at the stands. It also meant we could bring Tiny along.

Mira flashes a smile at the group, before turning back to me. "Holy shit. Tell me you didn't do that."

"I did. Plus, it's not like he noticed it. It barely made a dent into his enormous fortune—his words, not mine." I train my gaze on the rink below. *I am not looking for him. I am not looking for him. Am not.* A cheer goes up.

The Ice Kings glide out. I spot him at once, in the jersey with the number thirteen on both sleeves and on the back of the jersey, with 'Mitchell' centered above it. He pauses halfway to the center and turns. He tips back his helmet-covered head, and even across the distance, he spots me. I can't see his face, but the buzz that jolts up my spine confirms his gaze is on me.

My mouth dries, and my nipples pebble. My pussy flutters. I ache for his touch, to feel the stab of his cock inside me. To have his arms wrapped about me, his breath on my cheek, the thud of his heart against mine as he impales me. Pressure squeezes my chest. My heart vaults into my throat before sinking to that space between my legs. I squeeze my thighs together to clamp down the yawning emptiness between my legs.

"Holy hell, I can feel the sparks flying between the two of you across the distance," Mira gasps.

I press my palm into the glass and meet his gaze. No one in the crowd knows I'm here, and this might be the last time I see him play live. I swallow, and a tear spills down my cheek.

"You love him," Mira breathes.

On the ice, he raises his right fist without breaking our connection. It's a war-cry, a promise, an assurance, an oath... He'll never let go of me. Not as long as he's alive. He'll haunt me from the afterlife. He'll never relinquish his claim on me.

Moisture bathes my channel. Desire hums under the surface of my skin. It's the most incredible gesture of ownership anyone has ever shown me, and it turns me on and pisses me off in equal measure. Okay, fine, it turns me on more. Happy?

"I have to leave this city." I deliberately look away from him. "I have to." I grasp Mira's hand in mine. "If I stay here, if I see him again, I'll give into him."

"Would that be so bad?" She searches my features. "Would it?"

I nod. "I trusted him. I was ready to commit, to give him everything. Despite the fact my previous relationship showed me how much I couldn't trust another man. Despite the fact I'd been betrayed once. I took the chance. I gave him my heart. He trampled over it."

She swallows, then nods. "I can't claim to know how you feel, but if this is what you want…"

"It is."

"Then stay until the game is over. You owe your professional career that much."

I already told Edward I was resigning after this game. Regardless of the outcome, I've have completed the project of seeing the Ice Kings through to the finals of the League. I reached out to my contacts in L.A., and have a job lined up there. It's time to leave this city, to put him behind me. *Except you won't. You'll carry him around in your heart, in your soul, in the secret corners of your body which only he has traversed. You'll forever have his name imprinted in your cells, in your every breath… And you'll learn to live with it. You have to.*

I turn my back to the game and walk toward the group of women who're talking to each other. Tiny gambols up and brushes against me. Max, Sinclair and Summer's whippet is on his heels. They're followed by Andy, Michael and Karma's cat. The animals dance around me, then Andy clambers onto the Great Dane's back. O-k-a-y then. Tiny takes off with Max right behind. They tear around the room with barks and woofs, Andy digging his claws into Tiny, but the Great Dane seems unphased.

"Andy thinks he's a dog." Karma pats her tummy. Her features wear a surprised expression.

"There's a mutual admiration society between the critters," Summer laughs.

"They do get along better than when the men first met." Penny taps her cheek. "The alphaholes have a lot more posturing happening among them."

"Alphaholes?" I snort out a laugh despite myself. "So, I'm not the only one who uses that word in reference to these men?"

"Nope," Summer chuckles.

"Of course not." Penny rolls her eyes.

"The first word that came to mind when I saw Michael." Karma wheezes, then turns pale.

"Are you okay?" I grip her arm.

Summer holds her other. "You need to sit down, sis."

Together, we guide Karma to one of the settees. She sinks down into it and manages a smile.

"Have some water." Penny uncaps a bottle and offers it. Karma takes a few sips.

"I'm going to get Michael."

The guys are in the VIP room down the corridor. Mira turns in the direction of the door, but Karma grabs her arm. "No, don't, please. It'll only worry him. I'm okay now."

I scan her features. She does look better. There's more color on her cheeks. She hands the bottle back to Penny.

"I'm okay. Please, don't let me distract you from the game." She sits up.

Summer scoots closer and cups her cheek. "You sure, little sister? Maybe you shouldn't have come today."

"And miss all the excitement?" She rolls her eyes. "I'm pregnant, not sick."

"It puts so much more strain on your heart." Summer bites down on her bottom lip. "I'm surprised Michael agreed to have a second child."

"Oh, he didn't."

"He didn't?" I ask surprised.

"You could say I tricked him. Not that it took much convincing to do the deed." She nods.

Mira cackles. Penny chokes out a laugh.

I can't see the mean ex-Mafia Don being tricked into doing anything, let alone having a child with the woman whose life might be in danger now that she's pregnant. I heard from Penny how Karma suffers from a heart-condition which resulted in a complicated first pregnancy. Being pregnant again could be a major health risk for her. So it stands to reason her husband would be concerned.

"Are you sure you're okay?" I lower my chin.

She meets my gaze and half smiles. "Truth is, I am not okay. I was aware of the risks when I decided to get pregnant. Aware that my husband would not be happy because I went against his wishes without telling him. But I wanted this child." She places her hand on her stomach. "And I know he wanted a second child, too. Of course, not at the risk of my health, but Michael deserves a larger family, and I can give it to him."

"You're putting yourself in danger," I warn her.

"I'm aware." Her smile grows. Her expression is serene. "But it's worth every chance, every unpredictability, every precariousness along the way. What's life if you don't live it to the fullest, eh?" She laughs.

She's right, if only I could be more like her. If only I could look past everything he did and be with him again, because without him, my life is far from full. My every day is incomplete and the nights... unbearable.

"I wish you weren't this stubborn." Summer takes her other hand in her own. "If something were to happen to you —"

"It won't. And if it does, I'll make arrangements to ensure Michael and the children are taken care of."

"Oh, Karma." Summer throws her arms about her sister.

The rest of us look at each other. These women are such an amazingly tight-knit group. They come from all walks of life, and the fact that Karma and Summer are sisters puts them at the core of this ever-growing tribe of wives and girlfriends who've given me such a soft landing in London. Leaving here means leaving all of them, too. I'm going to miss them. I grew up in L.A., come of age there, started my career and progressed, but I never managed to form connections the way I've done here, in just two months. I also forged an attachment of the heart here... And now, I'm going to break it.

70

Rick

I gain control of the puck and carry it up the right wing. Spotting Caspian streaking toward the net from the opposite side of the ice, I pass it across to him. Caspian receives the pass as he enters the left side of the crease. He outmaneuvers the Enforcers defenseman, and when he's attacked by another, he shoots it back to me. I manage to redirect the puck, and it sails past their goalie and into the back of the net. The crowd yells in delight. My teammates erupt. It's a 3-2 victory for us, and our first League win. Bloody hell, we did it.

I raise my fist in victory. Adrenaline pumps through my blood. My heart pounds in my chest with such force, I'm sure it's going to break through my ribcage. I point my finger at Caspian, who raises his stick over his head in response. A huge grin wreathes his features. Jagger throws his head back and roars. The crowd's decibels rise, mirroring him. Enzo pounds on the glass separating him from the crowds. Finn extends his arms, stick still clutched in one hand, and skates to the center of the ice. From the corner of my eye, I spot those on the bench spilling onto the ice. Their shouts of exuberance rise into the air. They glide toward me. Caspian, Jagger, Enzo and Finn in the lead.

Like a swarm of locusts, they descend upon us. The tension that's gripped me for months begins to fade away. It's replaced by relief, a burst of happiness, a sense that I've vindicated myself. I allow myself a grin, then grunt when Finn jumps on me. I hit the ice. Enzo, Jagger, and Caspian swarm over me, followed by the rest. The men are laughing, crying, yelling, a mixture of noises that drowns out my groans as their weights press in on me, a second, another, then the pressure is lifts. I draw in a deep breath as the guys spill off me and onto the ice, where they lay panting.

"You okay, buddy?" Edward holds out his arm. I grab it, and he hauls me to my feet. I take in the three-piece suit he's wearing, combined with the skates on his feet, and the helmet he's pulled on. He resembles a medieval knight.

"Thanks." I glance up toward the stands, scan the space where she normally would be on the front row behind the plexiglass. When I can't see her, I look toward the balcony outside the VIP rooms, but there's no one there who resembles my Goldie.

"She's leaving."

"What?" I continue to scan the bleachers, but I can't find her.

"Gio. She quit her role. She said she's returning to L.A." He's close enough that I hear him over the roar of the crowds and our team.

"What?" I swing my head in his direction. See the finality in his expression through the cage. "She can't do that." I brush past him. Jagger steps forward; I skate around him. Enzo grabs my shoulder, but I shake him off. Finn plants his body in my path, and I shove him aside.

"Not now." I race toward the exit, but he keeps pace.

"Captain of the winning team for one minute, and already, you've forgotten your teammates and—" He must glimpse something on my face for he sobers. "Shit. What's wrong?"

I shake my head, reach the exit doors and step off the ice.

"Bro, tell me. Whatever it is, I can help you."

"In this, you can't." I walk up the pathway, cursing the skate boots which impede my progress.

"Is it Gio? If so, I overheard her tell Edward she's taking the night flight to L.A., but she hasn't left the arena yet."

"How do you know?" I turn on him. "You keeping tabs on my wife, asshole?" I grab the front of his jersey and haul him to his toes.

"Relax, Gio's the sister I never had." His expression reveals he noticed I called her 'wife,' but he doesn't comment on it. "She realized I knew about her plans and begged me not to tell you."

"But you did anyway?" I ask slowly.

"Of course I did. I also negotiated with her. I told her I wouldn't breathe a word to you during the game, provided she came to watch it."

"You broke your word to her?" I scowl.

"The game is over." He raises a shoulder. "I reckon, she's headed toward the car that was called to take her to the airport. A car which is, conveniently, 'stuck in traffic' and not yet here." He winks. "So, if you hurry, you might—"

Before the words are out of his mouth, I rush up the aisle. I almost trip in my haste—goddamn skates—when Knight appears. He steps past the security folk and drops my trainers on the ground. "Here."

I throw him my stick and tear off my skates. Then pause, long enough to unhook my pads, my gloves, my helmet and the protective gear I'm wearing. The laces of the sports shoes are already knotted, so all I have to do is stuff my feet into them. Then I'm off, up the players tunnel, dodging fans who've evaded security and are blocking my path. Right, then left, then right again. I pause then rush up the stairs. I reach the VIP room, dash in and grab Tiny's leash. I need all the help I can get, and that woman loves this mutt. Perhaps, it'll soften her heart and make her listen to what I have to say?

Mira jumps up from the seat next to Tiny. "Gio, she's—"

"I know."

"You need to go to her."

Without replying, I turn and dash for the door, past the others in the room who gape at me. Tiny keeps pace as I take the steps two at a time, reach the first floor, run up the hallway, and pass the men milling around in the reception arena.

"*Hey, isn't that Rick Mitchell?*"

"*It is Rick Mitchell.*"

"*Rick!*"

Their excited voices follow me. I speed up, shoulder open the doors to the arena, then race down the steps. I briefly notice the group of girls who're watching me, open-mouthed. To my right, a family with a teenaged boy and girl is walking away. A group of men hail me. "Hey, Rick, great win."

Someone comes up behind me and claps my back. "You were amazing, Stone."

I ignore them and keep walking, Tiny in the lead.

Where could she be? If she's waiting for a pick-up, then— I break into a run toward the area where cars pick up and drop off people. Past more people who stop and gape. Past the bicycle parking space, more security checkpoints, toward the drop-off points, and there she is. I slow down, but don't stop until I'm a few feet from her. That's when she turns, spots me, and in the light that pours down on us from the streetlamp, I see her pale.

"You..." She swallows. "What are you doing here?"

71

Gio

"What do you think I'm doing here?" He comes to a stop in front of me. Tiny ambles forward and plants himself on his haunches between us. I reach forward and rub his big head, and he looks at me with adoring eyes. My heart melts a little.

"Look at me, Goldie," Rick orders.

I shake my head and continue to pet Tiny.

"Goldie. Look. At. Me." Rick lowers his voice to a hush and goosebumps flutter over my skin. Before I can stop myself, I lower my hand and tilt my head back, and further back, to see his face.

In the lengthening shadows, he seems bigger, taller, broader—and not only because he still has shoulder pads on under the jersey. I refuse to meet his gaze, instead focusing on the cords of his neck that stand out in relief, the width of his chest which seems to have expanded until it's twice the size it was, down to where his thigh muscles are so tense, they strain the hockey pants he's wearing. His legs are braced apart, and I'm aware the bulge in between his thighs is caused by his jockstrap—yet, I can vouch that when he's aroused, it looks bigger.

"Remembering how my cock feels inside of you?" he growls.

I blush to the roots of my hair and jerk my chin up. His cerulean blues bore into me, and I take a step back. He moves toward me, and I throw up my hands. "Stop, please."

He does. But every inch of his body is wound up like he's spring-loaded. Waves of tension vibrate off of him.

"Where are you going?" His voice is hushed, but the tone feels like a whiplash across my skin that's sensitized to his every mood.

"You know where." I look away, unable to see the truth in his eyes. That he knows exactly why I'm standing here.

The breeze blows a strand of hair in my face, and I tuck it behind my ear.

Tiny looks between us, his body on alert. He, too, senses the tension in the air.

For a few seconds, we stand there, not talking. The sounds of the crowd cheering reach us. Footsteps approach, then stop. I don't dare look past him. I'm sure we're making a spectacle of ourselves, sure there are paps around who're going to photograph us together, and yet… I can't bring myself to turn my back on him.

This might be the last time I see his beautiful face, take in the solidity of his presence, and sense that shiver of security that sinks into my bones whenever I'm in his presence. I'll never again feel my heart expand with those sensations that crowd my chest only when I see him. I'll never feel this way with anyone else. Never, has my breath stuck in my throat or my stomach fluttered at the thought of anyone. I'll never need to squeeze my thighs together at the thought of someone else. Only him. I'll never fall in love again. The only man who'll make me feel like this is him. And he betrayed me. He doesn't care for me. He can't, not after what he did to me.

"I need to leave," I choke out.

"No," he growls.

"You don't have a say in what I do. You lost that privilege when you made me fall in love with you under false pretenses. When you knew you were setting me up, just so you could break my heart."

"I'm sorry, Goldie. I know, however much I apologize, it won't be enough to right what I've done, but you can't leave me. You can't." His voice cracks and the anguish I hear… The expression in his eyes is so intense that it hits me square in the chest. My heart stutters, I feel something inside of me begin to give in, inch by inch, and —

I shake my head. *I can't do this. I can't forgive him. Not after how he hurt me. How can I trust him again, knowing he'd purposely set out to destroy me?*

"Do you know why I left the NHL?"

I shake my head.

"It was in the finals of the Cup that I found out that Diana had committed suicide. She was nineteen, only a year younger to me, but I'd been her protector. Her big brother. I should have been in L.A. with her, looking out for her, but I was too busy building my career. I got the news during half-time."

"Oh, my god, Rick." I cover my mouth with my palms.

He hasn't told this to anyone. It's not in his PR file, not in any news story. He's choosing to share it with me because he wants to show me he trusts me. And I want to take that step toward him, I want to meet him halfway, want to close the distance to him and throw myself in his arms and comfort him, but something inside me doesn't let me. So, I stand there and watch the man I love hunch his shoulders. He closes his eyes and swallows, and when he opens his eyelids, a tear rolls down his cheek.

Tiny whines.

"She was so young, and she'd already written a film script?" I wrap my arms about my waist. "She must have been very talented."

He nods. "She was also bipolar. A diagnosis she insisted Grams keep from me so it wouldn't interfere with my NHL career. One I only found out when it was too late. If I'd known, I'd have prioritized her before my NHL games. She knew it and insisted Grams not bother me with it."

Emotions flash across his features. It's a shock to see how much grief and anger there is in him. But it's also a welcome surprise to see he's hurting. That he's as human as me. I don't want to see him in pain, but it's also confirmation he's not as much in control as he'd like the world to believe.

"It explained her mood-swings, and also, her genius when it came to making up stories," he says with a far-away look in his eyes. "Even as a little girl, she loved to weave scenarios, first in her head, then on paper. Grams bought her a video camera, then a high-end smartphone, and she was always making short movies and editing them. She was gifted. I always thought she'd win the Academy Award before she was thirty."

He swallows and glances away.

"So when coach told me she was gone, I couldn't believe it. He later told me, he'd debated with himself before telling me, but he said he knew it wouldn't be fair if he didn't let me know. He said he wouldn't blame me if I left right then to fly to her. In fact, he recommended I should. But you know what I did? I went on playing. I wanted to complete the game. I'd played so hard to get that far, to find a place for my team and for myself in the finals. I wasn't going to leave without seeing it through. I couldn't tear myself away from the game, even when I found out my sister was dead." He chokes on the last word before he continues. "I went back on the ice… Only, I wasn't fully there. I lost my focus, kept making errors, got so angry with myself that I hit the referee."

"The charges against you were dropped," I murmur.

Tiny whines again. This time, Rick pats him, his action absentminded. "But the damage was done. I knew I was in the wrong. For everything. I knew it was my fault she was dead. And I remained selfish to the end. It was because I thought the game was so important that my attention was divided. I put my career before her, and I decided I didn't deserve to play again."

"Then you joined the Royal Marines?"

"I did. It was Grams who suggested it. She saw how badly I'd taken Diana's death. I returned to London, ended up getting drunk and into bar fights. I was unable to get a hold of myself. She realized I needed a purpose and suggested the military. I barely remember signing up for it. The next thing I knew, I was in training and being pushed around by the Commandant in charge."

"That's how you found an outlet to your anger?"

He laughs, the sound uneven. "And how. I got into fights and was disciplined, which made me madder and pick up even more brawls, until the Commandant sat me down and told me I was better off channeling my emotions into the training. After that, I pit myself against the challenges of the training course. I found myself acing the Commando training, then the King's Squad. As part of the Special Forces, I fought on the front. And that was my wake-up call."

"Wake up call?" I tilt my head, absorbing what he's telling me. For so long, I've wanted to find out everything about this man, and now that he's sharing his past with me, I want to make sure I don't miss anything. "It must have been difficult being on the front line."

"Not at first. I didn't give a shit about my life. It's when I saw the men in my team get wounded and die that I woke up. I realized Diana was gone, but I was still here. And she'd be pissed if I joined her up there that quickly."

"So what did you do?"

"What could I do? I focused on making sure I got the enemy before they did me or any of my brothers-in-arms. I found I was good at it too. Ended up serving the military for five years before I retired and moved to private security."

"And throughout that time, you continued to play hockey?"

"Spending all that time in the desert, which is where I was always shipped out, made me appreciate how much I loved being on ice. Whenever I was home, I made sure I played."

"And being assigned to Declan Beauchamp's security, How did that come about?"

"Initially, I blamed him for Diana's death. Which is why, when the position of his bodyguard came up, I took it. Soon, I found out he wasn't in the country when it happened, that it was you who called the cops. But before I could plan on how to make you pay, you'd left the country."

I swallow. I know he holds me responsible for what happened to Diana, but every time he says it aloud, it makes me want to scream. *Can't he see how unreasonable he's being?*

I draw in a breath, get my emotions under control. "And you followed me?'

"I did." He sets his jaw. "I didn't have anything lined up. Knight had offered me the job as Captain for the team. I told him no, several times. Then I found out you were taking on the role of the PR manager."

"And you realized the best way to get close to me was if you accepted the role of the captain?" I swallow.

"Yes and no. I still didn't know how I'd get my revenge, but when I was with you, I felt an indescribable pull to get closer. And the mere thought of anyone else working with you"— his nostrils flare—"no way was I going to tolerate that. So, when I agreed to the role, it was spontaneous. Once I'd committed, the plan fell into place." He raises a shoulder.

It feels like a wall has collapsed on my chest. I can't breathe. I knew he'd strategized and set things up to lead me into a position where I'd find myself falling for him. And yet, hearing the details of how he did it only makes things worse.

I rub the back of my hand across my mouth. "And now, you're confessing so you can get it off your chest? In the hope that I'll forgive you and be with you again?"

"I'm telling you everything because the only way for us to move on is if I come clean on everything."

"There is no us." Even as I say the words, it feels like I'm being cleaved in half. The pain in my chest intensifies. Every inch of my body hurts. My phone buzzes in my handbag; I ignore it.

"There can never *not* be an us," he says in a low voice. "You're my wife, Goldie."

Tiny huffs. I reach for him at the same time as Rick. Our fingers brush, and a shiver runs up my spine, adding support to his words. I shake my head, trying to negate the truth, but there's a part of me, deep inside, that acknowledges he's right. I'll always be his wife. I'll always be…his. I lower my hand to my side. Rick pats Tiny, then turns to me.

"When I was playing in the finals today, I realized I couldn't let my team down. I couldn't let you down. You're the PR manager for this team. A win for us would boost your career. This time, I wasn't playing only for myself. I was playing for you and for my teammates. And now we've won the League, but it means nothing if I don't have you at my side. Everything loses importance, unless I can call you mine."

My phone stops, then starts buzzing again, but I shove aside the intrusion. "Don't, Rick. Don't do this." I swallow around the ball of emotion in my throat.

"I have to. I can't let you go, Goldie. You're mine. Mine to hold. Mine to own. Mine to love. To cherish and protect with my life. To spend the rest of my life striving to make up for what an asshole I was. To spend every day proving to you how sorry I am. For better or for worse, Goldie, you are mine. Only mine. And I'm yours. Only yours."

My phone stops, then starts again. This time, I pull it out to decline the call when I notice the caller ID. "It's Grams."

"Grams?" He frowns. "I tried calling her before the game, but she didn't pick up the phone."

I raise the phone to my ear. "Hello, Grams?" I listen, then feel the blood drain from my face. I sway. The next moment he's there.

He grips my arm. "What's wrong?"

72

Five days later

Rick

"I'm sorry for your loss." The old woman squeezes my hand. Her skin is soft, her fingers so thin, I worry I might crack them. I gently place one of my much bigger, broader paws over hers.

"Thank you." I swallow.

They say the pain gets better with every passing day, but it's only grown bigger and wider, filling up, first my chest, then my belly, spreading to my legs, where it weighs down every step I take. Grams had been watching the game on TV with India when she fell asleep. She never woke up. India said she'd begun cheering when the Ice Kings had won, then turned to share the excitement with Grams and found she had her eyes closed. She called her name and there was no answer. That's when she realized something was wrong. She touched Grams' hand which was still warm, but Grams wasn't breathing. She grabbed Grams phone which was next to her—unlocked, because Grams didn't believe in passwords—and called, first Dr. Kincaid, then tried me. When I didn't answer, she called Gio.

Gio's car drew up as she disconnected the call. We took it to Grams' place, where Dr. Kincaid gave us the news. Grams didn't die of heart failure. She simply stopped breathing. It's as if she waited until I'd won the League, and then passed. I couldn't believe it. Grams, who was so full of life, so happy that we'd gotten married, who'd been making plans to go on her next cruise. She was content, India said. And the happiest she'd ever seen the old woman.

I set out to get revenge for my sister, but I ended up ensuring Grams' last few weeks were joyful. I owe that to Goldie. It's because of her that Grams believed our marriage was real. Perhaps, I should feel some guilt for the charade and for having deceived Grams, but having a conscience isn't one of my strong points.

No, I don't regret it. I don't regret the smile I put on Grams' face, the contentment when she saw me and Goldie together. No, I don't feel contrite for what I did. I may have set out to get revenge, but I fulfilled Grams' wishes along the way.

The reason I wanted to make Goldie suffer receded, too. It became less and less important that I thought she was responsible for what happened to Diana. I knew it was irrational to think she was the catalyst for Diana taking that final step. But my ego wouldn't let me admit it. I couldn't face the reality that I was more to blame than she was.

It wasn't until I faced the prospect of losing Goldie, as well, that I was willing to confront my own guilt and my misguided attempts to shift the blame away from myself. And I want to tell her all this. I want to open my heart to her, to share the feelings I have for her. To declare my love for her, but every time I try, the coldness in my chest stops me.

Losing Grams hit me with the kind of gut punch that pushed all feelings out of my body. I feel like I'm looking down at the events unfolding around me. I must have said and done the right thing, though, for there was only sympathy on Dr. Kincaid's face. Goldie tried to talk to me, but I shut down and refused to answer.

I saw the hurt on her face, felt a twinge in my belly, but was unable to act on it. With the win at the League, there was no need to share the house with the team anymore. I didn't attend the presentation ceremony, and Finn, as the alternate captain, received the cup along with the rest of the team. When he and the team found out what had happened, they wanted to come over, but I dissuaded them. I also asked Edward, Knight and my other friends to give me space, and so far, everyone has acceded to my wishes.

But today's the day of the funeral, and there's no stopping them. Edward insisted on driving Goldie and me to the cemetery where Grams' friends are in attendance. She was popular with the community, with the result that her living room is overflowing with all those who came by to offer condolences. People like this old woman, who wipes a tear from her face as she tells me she was Grams' bridge partner. Then, there's the man who runs the corner shop, who shares how Grams put his kids through school. The delivery guy, who dropped off her groceries from Waitrose and whose citizenship application Grams sponsored. And her book club friends, those who attended the senior citizens' weekly ballroom dancing classes with her over the last decade, her golfing gang... Yeah, Grams led a long and happy, and fulfilling life.

She made the most of every moment. She was gutted when my parents passed and fell apart when Diana died but managed to pull herself together and comfort me. She was insistent Diana's suicide wasn't my fault, even though I refused to believe her. She warned me I needed to move on, then pushed me into getting married. I owe having met my wife to her. My wife, who I haven't been able to look straight in the face since she moved into the guest bedroom of the apartment I've been renting since before I became the captain of the team. She put off going to L.A. by a week, then took charge of all the arrangements related to the funeral.

I, on the other hand, have taken to running day and night and working out. It's the only thing that helps me get through the days. The nights are the worst. My insomnia is back in force. If I get a few hours of shut-eye, I'm lucky. Every time I close my eyes, my family's faces crowded in on me. Did I fail them all? I spent so much of my life pursuing my own goals, then running away from my demons, I missed the opportunity to be with those I loved.

You'd think I'd learn from the mistakes of my past, but here I am, still turning away from sharing the depth of my feelings with the woman who means so much to me. I tried to show her how sorry I am for what I did, but I know that's not enough. I needed to find a way to make things up to her, but it feels like I'm caught in a limbo where my thoughts don't quite make sense, even to me.

We've spent the days in a strange silence which she's tried to interrupt, but I haven't reciprocated. To her credit, she hasn't given up. She also started wearing her wedding ring, probably because it made things easier when she was dealing with the arrangements. Every time she introduces herself as Rick Mitchell's wife, a jolt of sensation pierces the fog that seems to envelop me. It's the only time something close to hope ripples under my skin. The only time I sense cracks in the wall that seems to be closing in on me. It's akin to green shoots breaking through the hard winter ground, or the growing pains of a teenager who grew so quickly, his bones stretched and hurt and the rest of him scrambled to keep up.

I'm finding my way through the darkness, and she's the glimmer of light beckoning me. Only I don't acknowledge her. I see her, but I don't tell her how much it means to me that she's there. It's like I'm trapped behind glass of my own making, and no matter how much I scream, she can't hear me. She doesn't even know I'm there.

I wake up in the middle of the night and go into her room to watch her sleep, her hand flung out, the dark shadows under her eyes telling me this is as difficult for her, but I don't let on that I see it. I don't once open my mouth and tell my wife how much I appreciate what she's doing, how I couldn't have done this without her, how I need her to make sense of this world, how when I look into the future, I see her. How...

I love her so much, it feels difficult to put into words the ferocity of my feelings. How... I know I should share my thoughts with her, but I can't. So, I settle for doing what's needed to ensure I give Grams a good sendoff, which includes inviting all her friends to the house for a gathering after the funeral.

Each of them comes up to me, shakes my hand, and offers their condolences. And with each commiseration, that wave of emotion in my body solidifies, until it feels like I've turned into the Stone which is my nickname. I grit my teeth, manage to say and do the right things, and get through it. I know Gio's making sure the food and drinks keep coming, but I don't thank her for it. I want to. God, how I want to pull her into me and bury my face in the crook of her neck, and inhale and stop the walls from building up between us, but I can't.

I keep the mask of polite interest on my face until, one by one, Grams' friends begin to depart. The Ice King team follows. They turned up in suits, bringing the press to my door—something else my wife managed with great finesse.

Fuck, if I don't admire her. Fuck, if it doesn't convince me further—I can't do without her. Fuck, if it doesn't affirm she's too good for me.

Not that I share the decision I arrived at with my closest friends. I don't need to, though. These men know.

Finn scowls. "You need to grieve. Holding it in is going to turn you into the man you were before she came along," Finn warns before he leaving. *Thanks for nothing, asshole. It's not like the thought hasn't crossed my mind.*

JJ takes one look at me and wipes the smirk off his face. "Don't do it," he warns. "Whatever it is, don't make decisions when you're in emotional distress." *Good advice. A little too late, though.*

Sinclair sets his jaw. "You're grieving, but that doesn't excuse making poor choices." I bare my teeth. He arches an eyebrow, then growls, "I hate having to pick up the pieces when my friends are hell bent on burning bridges to the lifeline they have." Then he spins around and leaves with Summer.

Michael doesn't waste his breath on words. He points his forefinger and middle finger toward my eyes, then back at his. *Yeah, yeah, like that scares me.* I've made up my mind. And I'm doing it for the good of both of us.

Edward's the last to leave. Under the guise of hugging me, he squeezes my neck so tight that my vision blurs. "If you hurt her any more, I'll fucking kill you."

Take a ticket and get in line, mofo. And the temporary hurt I'm gonna cause her is better than the lifetime of hurt she's setting herself up for if she stays with me.

Tiny, though… That mutt is something else. He runs between me and my wife all evening. Back and forth, back and forth. As I put distance between us, he traverses it faster. He knows something's up. He's trying his best to keep us together. And if he stayed, he'd know what I'm about to do is unforgivable. That I deserve all the hate my friends and hers are going to pour on me. If he stayed, I'd lose my nerve.

Grams set up India for life in her will. She wants to go traveling and is leaving tonight. So, I push Tiny's lead into Edward's hands. "Will you dog-sit him? Just until Liam and Isla return?"

Edward looks at me strangely. I'm sure he's going to refuse, but then he nods and begins to lead Tiny away. The dog whines and pulls Ed toward Goldie. She pats his head and coos to him. Tiny brushes his head against her side very gently in goodbye, then the mutt turns and glares at me—no, I'm not kidding, he does. Then, he prowls over and bumps into me so hard, I almost fall over. It's a warning, I'll have him to deal with him if I cause Goldie any further sadness.

It's only temporary, though. She deserves better. Someone who doesn't come with so much baggage. Someone who'll love her the way she should be loved. Someone who'll be there for her every step of the way. Someone who didn't betray her. Yeah, she needs such a man.

But I'm not that man. She deserves so much better. She deserves someone who will treat her better than me. Someone better than me. It's why I'm doing this—for her good. It's why, when the last guest has left, and it's only my wife and me, and the remnants of the feast she laid out for them, I turn to her and say, "Thank you for your help this week. I won't forget what you did for me. But I don't need you anymore; you can leave."

73

Three months later

Giorgina's To Do List

1. ~~Wake up at 5 am, meditate for fifteen minutes.~~ Not even going to pretend to try. I miss him. Why do I miss him? I shouldn't miss him after what he did to me. But still, I miss him.
2. ~~Go to the gym at 5 am - half an hour workout.~~ => I have no motivation to work out and it's all his fault.
3. ~~Healthy breakfast = oats? Croissant.~~ Chocolate croissant. => I have no appetite, for the first time in my life. That's good, right? So why doesn't it feel that way? Why do I feel like someone put their fist down my throat and is squeezing my chest?
4. Get to the office by 8 am and get through all emails by 9 am. => I hate L.A. traffic. Hate it. What I wouldn't' give to get on the tube in London, which I hated while I was there. But everyone is polite and distant and gives me my space there. Here, I have to pretend to be in good spirts, and greet everyone, and bah! It's not just London. I miss him. There, I said it. Again.
5. Avoid thinking about the Dick and his big dick. Avoid, avoid.
6. Lunch – started the grapefruit diet and I hate it.

7. No need to shave legs, and other parts. He's not here. ~~And no I didn't do it for him.~~ I totally DID do it for him.

8. Hello, Steely Dan. You are no compensation nor competition for the Dick. But if you're all I have...

9. ~~Read/listen to 110 spicy books this year. 51 down, 59 to go~~ => I give up. All the detailed scenes remind me of him.

10. ~~Put this down for the satisfaction of crossing it off the list. There, happy? Not really.~~

74

Three months later

Gio

"Thank you, Gio, I couldn't have done this without you." Violet, the owner of The Sp!cy Booktok, a small Indie bookshop specializing in spicy books—you heard that right—in L.A., throws her arms around my shoulder and hugs me.

"I didn't do anything," I protest.

She snorts. "Since you started doing the PR, the number of people coming to the shop has more than doubled. And this is the first time we've had all of our new arrivals fly off the shelves. It has everything to do with you."

Heat flushes my cheeks. It's not the first time I've been complimented on my work. But coming from Violet, and knowing I helped a small business owner like her become successful, is much more satisfying than doing publicity for world-famous personalities.

Not that my stint with the London Ice Kings wasn't exciting. I loved building up the profile for the team in the media. Almost as much as I loved doing the PR for #Declene, a.k.a. Declan and Solene, before that. Although, this is why I ran into Rick's sister.

Deep down, I know it wasn't my fault that set off the chain of events that complicated my relationship with Rick. I also know he wants to get over holding me responsible for it. Logically, he knows what happened to her wasn't my fault. We're each responsible for our own actions. It's been the motto of my life. And while I admit, my resolve faltered in the face of how angry he was with me, the fact that he also tried to make up for it showed me he was reconsidering his initial assumptions. So, when he told me to leave, I was shocked. Speechless.

The days following Grams' death, he turned cold, almost unfeeling, more Stone than he'd been when I first met him, rather than the tender man I knew existed behind that wall he liked to throw up against the world. I cut him some slack due to Gram's passing away. He took it badly, not shedding one tear since we rushed to her place and found her sitting up in her chair. She seemed to be sleeping, her features serene. He knelt next to her, took her hand in his, and kissed it with such tenderness, tears slid down my cheeks. I wiped them away.

When we'd found Grams Tiny had padded over and laid down at her feet. He didn't move until I sniffed. Then, he rose up and padded over to me. I placed my hand on him, and he rubbed his head against my side. Then, the mutt stiffened. He lifted his head, sniffed me, and made that same purring sound at the back of his throat. Guess he was trying to console me.

The dog didn't leave my side over the next few days. He insisted on coming with us when we moved into Rick's flat. He slept on the floor next to me at bedtime. And he continued to sniff me at intervals, making that purring noise at the back of his throat. After Grams' funeral, as the crowd in the house thinned out and we were almost alone, he kept running between Rick and me, over and over again. I have a feeling Tiny sensed Rick was going to tell me to leave before he did.

Strange, how much I miss Tiny. Almost as much as I miss Rick. There were occasions in the days leading up to the funeral when I looked up from the phone to find Rick staring at me with a strange look on his face—a mixture of confusion and frustration, and an emotion I can only label as love. The alphahole loves me, I'm sure of it. But he never came out and said it. Not even when he was apologizing for what he did. Of course, if he hadn't asked me to become his pretend wife, I'd have never met Grams. Never known what it means to feel the warmth and love of parents.

In a weird way, I almost understand why Rick was so upset with me and why he held me responsible for his sister's suicide. He was grief-stricken, no doubt about it. He loved his sister in a way that makes me jealous. I never had a sibling's love, never felt that sense of family, all of which Rick once had. If I were in his shoes, maybe I'd have done the same thing. It doesn't mean I've forgiven him for what he did. For how he coerced me to marry him and fall in love with him with the intention of breaking my heart. And yet... I can't forget that he fell into his own trap and fell in love with me too—even if he doesn't want to admit it—and broke his own heart. I truly believe that. He made me feel more intensely than I ever have before. And for that, I'm grateful. Also, for introducing me to the circle of friends in London, who I'll always cherish.

Friends who were concerned when I left so abruptly and have been calling me every day. I've spoken to Mira and Summer and Karma and assured them I was fine. Not that they believe it. I didn't told them what had transpired between me and Rick, but they guessed. Mira was all set to tell him off, until I begged her not to. I told her this is between Rick and me, and we have to work it out in our time... Or not. My throat closes, my heart flutters, a flip-flopping sensation twists my insides, and I sway.

"Hey, you okay?" Violet grips my arms and guides me to a chair. "Here." She hands me a bottle of water, and I chug down some of it.

"Better?" She scans my features.

"Better." I manage a smile. "Sorry, I don't know what happened."

"When was the last time you ate?"

I glance away. I've lost my appetite since moving to L.A. The very thought of food makes my insides churn. The few times I've managed to eat I've thrown up—and it's not because I made myself.

Overall, I haven't been feeling like myself, haven't even been able to consume coffee, which is strange. Guess all the events of the past few months are catching up with me.

All of the changes—moving to London, moving back, changing jobs for the third time in as many months... Not to mention, falling headfirst into love and getting married. I touch my thumb to my empty ring-finger. I took off both the engagement ring and wedding ring and put them aside. This way, there won't be so many questions asked. It hasn't stopped me from looking at them every day or missing the weight of them on my finger.

And I miss him. So much. More than I'll admit aloud. I miss his weight on me, in me, miss his touch on my skin, the scent of him, and especially how he spooned me at night. The feel of his body curved around mine was as erotic as the thickness of his cock stretching me, and the heaviness of his body pressing me into the bed. I miss it all. I miss the life I created in London for a very short time. I even missed the weather... and that...is saying something. L.A.'s sunlight mocks the gloom in my heart.

"You're thinner than when I first met you," Violet frowns.

"I'll be fine." I rise to my feet, but my head spins and I sit down again. "Whoa." I shake my head, manage a laugh. "That was strange."

"Okay that's it, you're going to a doctor."

I shake my head. "No, I'll be okay, really."

Violet's frown deepens. "But Gio, you—"

"Gio, I've been looking all over for you." I look past her, and my gaze widens. "You?

Rick

"The fuck you guys doing here?" I step back as Finn shoulders his way into the apartment. On his heels are Jagger and Caspian. They wander in and survey the remnants of what was once a pristine space.

"I see you've been busy?" Finn gestures toward the various pizza boxes that grace the coffee table. He moves toward it, and his foot hits an empty whiskey bottle. It rolls toward the kitchen island on which are more take-out boxes, most of them half full. And more empty bottles.

Jagger sniffs the air and makes a face. "Smells like old socks and ass."

"That'd be his favorite scent." Caspian stabs his thumb in my direction.

"Speak for yourself," I drawl.

They take up position in different corners of the room, and I realize I'm surrounded. I flick my gaze to the door when Finn growls, "Don't even think about it."

I scratch my chin. "What do you all want?"

"We haven't seen you at practice," Jagger rumbles in a voice that could emerge from between the jaws of a meat-grinder.

"The season's over, didn't you get the memo?" I raise a shoulder.

"We're still practicing—together," Caspian reminds me.

"I'm not." I yawn.

"The team sticks together through thick and thin," Jagger reminds me.

"I'm not part of the team anymore."

"The fuck you mean?" Finn turns on me. "We won because of you."

"I agreed to lead the team into the finals and win the League. I did it. Now, it's time for me to move on."

"You talking about the team or about her?" Caspian drawls.

"Don't fucking talk about her."

His lips curve. "So there's some fight left in you yet, old man."

I open my mouth to protest I'm not old, then firm my lips. I am old. I feel like a thousand years old right now. Since I asked her to leave the light has gone out of my life. The music out of my every day. The taste from my food. The scent from — No, not true.

I started sleeping in my guest room because I could smell her on the sheets. I was finally forced to wash them, but if I close my eyes, I can still smell her scent. I imagine I can almost feel her in my arms. Yep, that's the sad state I'm in. Plus, her room is the only one that's in any semblance of order.

My own room has become a closet. I grab fresh clothes—when I remember to shower—and throw my used ones on the bed in my room. I'm living like a frat boy on a bender, and it's not what I want, but I don't have the energy to get up from sleep every day, let alone clean the space. The trip from her bed to the couch this afternoon—that's right, I'm spending most of my time in bed—wore me out. If I didn't have my phone on speed dial to get food delivered, I might have starved by now. When your pizza delivery guy—who's the only living person I've seen in the months since she left—mentions he's worried about you, perhaps, that's an indication your life has gone off the rails.

I brush past Finn, head to the oven and pull open the door, before straightening with a bottle of whiskey. I uncap it, and am about to take a sip, then hold it up. "You guys fancy a drop?"

Finn frowns. "You don't need that."

I scoff, "You have no idea what I need."

"You need her," Jagger says in his gravelly voice.

I chuckle. "Thanks, but you're the last people I'm going to take advice about my love life from."

"'Love life?'" Caspian makes air-quotes with his fingers.

"I mean, personal life." I narrow my gaze on him.

"You said 'love life,'" Jagger admonishes me.

"Admit it, you love your wife," Finn snaps.

I stiffen. It's no secret Gio and I are married. The team knows. The Seven and the Sovranos know. All of my friends know, but not a word had appeared in the press about it. That's how loyal these guys were. Luckily, the end of the season meant things quieted down on the media front. Not to mention, we don't have a PR manager to keep the press fed with information. Knight told me he's not going to hire a PR manager until the season starts up in September.

Not that I care, either way. I'm done with the game. It's too painful to play on the ice when my memories of the game are so intertwined with her. Apparently, she replaced the one passion I had in my life.

When I played for the NHL the first time, hockey was all that occupied my mind. During my time in the military, and then in my stint in private security, even though I swore I wouldn't play the game again, I wasn't able to get the thought of it out of my mind. Later, I agreed to become the captain of the team only so I could take revenge for Diana's death.

Little did I realize it would not only win me my first championship but also result in my love for the game being overtaken by the love I feel for her. It's why I told her to leave, after all. So I wouldn't have to face my feelings for her.

"I'm not admitting anything." I look between the men. "This is a personal matter."

"Too-fucking-bad," a new voice drawls. I turn to find Edward in the open doorway. He prowls in, followed by JJ, Michael, and Sinclair. The men take up positions, cutting off any hope I might have harbored of making a quick getaway. I look from my team on one side to my friends on the other. "Since when did the lot of you join forces?"

"Since you buried your head up your arse and decided you were going to hide away from the world," Sinclair answers.

"I'm not hiding." I fold my arms across my chest.

"Oh?" JJ glances about the space, then back at me. A flush creeps up my neck. I'm ex-military, for fuck's sake. And I broke the cardinal rule any serviceman lives by. Tidiness reflects the attention to detail needed to run military operations. I've strayed as far as I could from the only other stabilizing force in my life—the military.

A sense of clarity overcomes me with such speed, it's almost a physical blow. I turned my back on everything that created the man I am, because I'm a coward. I've been unable to admit I was wrong in holding her responsible for Diana's suicide. I shouldn't even be holding myself responsible, as Grams told me so many times. Instead, I let that guilt bleed into every aspect of my life. I've held it close to me like a shield. I can't let myself accept the gut-wrenching impact she had on my life. Can't bring myself to acknowledge the feelings I have for her.

"You're the first of my friends I've been tempted to shoot at." Michael brushes his fingers against his side.

Is he carrying? Naw, he's a family man now. True, he's an ex-Mafia Don, but he gave up his career in crime. Right? I take in his bared teeth and I'm not so sure now.

"This is your last chance to make amends," JJ warns.

I crack my neck. "Whatever you guys are here to tell me, I don't care."

The men exchange looks, then seem to direct their gazes on Edward.

"What?"

He pulls out his phone, walks over and shows me the screen. It's a video of her with a man I don't recognize. They're engaged in conversation, then he places his hand on her shoulder.

"Motherfucker!"

75

Gio

"You're wasting your time." I pull my hand out from under my date's. Violet set me up with him, and I didn't have the energy to say no. He turned out to be pleasant enough...and polite and boring. There was no connection, no chemistry. And he didn't try to kiss me goodnight. Which is probably why I agreed when he asked me out again.

Or maybe I'm lonely and miss Rick. Only, he hasn't called me or texted me. Not once in these three months. And if sometimes, I felt I was being watched, that was only a figment of my imagination, right? Rick has forgotten me. No matter that we're married. It doesn't mean anything to him. And while he might have been regretful for how he'd made me fall in love with him, all of that was pushed aside when he told me to leave. He didn't want me in his life.

I've managed to stay off his social media feeds and told Mira and my other London friends not to give me news of him. As a result, I have no idea what he's up to. He's probably moved on to other women.

He was genuinely broken up at Grams' death, and without Tiny there to keep him company, he's definitely turned to someone else for solace. He's probably been fucking the puck-bunnies who lined up outside the dressing room after every game. He didn't play in the last exhibition match the Ice

Kings participated in. I only know this because I chanced upon a news item on my phone. I clicked out of it, but not before the announcer said Rick Mitchell was not playing. Probably too busy with whoever the new woman in his life is. The fact that he's married doesn't matter to him. I'm nothing, and it's time I realize that and move on.

"Gio?" My date's voice cuts through my thoughts.

"Sorry, what did you say, Calvin?"

"It's Kevin." He regards me with a half-patient, half-frustrated look. "I said, do you want to go dancing tonight?"

"Umm, not really, Devin." I toy with my fork and regard the full plate of food in front of me. The smell of the fish and chips—which I ordered in a fit of nostalgia over my time in London— makes me queasy. I let the fork fall to the plate with a clatter.

"I'm sorry I'm not better company, Levin," I murmur.

His cheeks redden. "My name is Kevin, with a K."

"Isn't that what I said?" I frown.

"No, you didn't."

Oh." I swallow. For some reason tears prick the backs of my eyes. "I'm so sorry." I swallow down the ball of emotion in my throat.

He searches my features. "You don't look great."

"I don't feel great," I confess.

"You look like you want to be anywhere else but here."

I half laugh. "Sorry, it's not you. Honestly. I'm...not in a good space, is all."

"Whoever he is, I hope he knows how lucky he is," he murmurs.

"Not likely," I mumble. I glance away. I doubt Rick has spent any time thinking of me, at all. I need to stop trying to date other men. This pretense that I'm not married is not working. I might try to convince myself I'm over Rick, but the fact is, I fall asleep every night with his name on my lips. And dream of him. And wake up from some very X-rated dreams, horny and sweating.

"Would you like some dessert? How about some chocolate cake?" Kevin asks.

My stomach protests. I shake my head, then jump to my feet. "I have to use the ladies' room. I'll be back."

He opens his mouth to say something, but I rush past him, across the floor of the restaurant, up the short hallway and into the ladies' room. I pause in front of the sink, grip the edge, and take a deep breath.

I can do this. I can move on from Rick.

I stare at my reflection in the mirror—hollowed out cheeks, dark circles under my eyes. My hair flows down about my shoulders, but it's lost its luster.

My life has lost its luster, Grams. I knew you for such a short time, but you became my family. What little time I spent with you showed me what it was to have someone who loves you. If only your grandson felt the same way. I'm sorry, I couldn't make it work with him...

No... I wasn't the one who couldn't make it work. That's on Rick. But you know this already. You know what he did to me. You know how he tried to apologize, and I might have even forgiven him. I was so close to making a fresh start with him, but he decided he didn't want it. He didn't want me, Grams. And you weren't there to knock some sense into him, either, so—I raise a shoulder. *So...*

The pressure builds behind my eyes. My stomach creases in on itself, bile boils up, and I swallow it away. And now, to top it all off, I feel sick. Just great. I run water over my wrists, and splash some on my face, not caring about my makeup. I pull out some paper towels and pat my forehead and hands.

The door opens, I glance up then pale.

"Dennis?"

He bares his teeth, then deliberately shuts the door behind him and locks it.

"Getting a little repetitive, aren't you?" I manage to infuse a bored tone into my voice.

His smile widens. "Your fiancé, or should I say, your husband is not here to save you this time."

Adrenaline laces my blood. My pulse booms at my temples.

He moves toward me. I watch him approach, and force myself to breathe, breathe. I *am not helpless. I am not. I will not let this asshole touch me.*

When I flutter my eyelashes at him, he blinks. When I lick my lips, he comes to a stop, mesmerized. And when I bring up my hands and squeeze my breasts, the asshole pants. This...is true power. To take things in your own hands.

I meet his gaze in the mirror and aim a sultry smile at his reflection. "You need to come closer," I say in husky voice.

He steps forward, stopping at what I gauge is the right distance. That's when I turn, grab his waist, fold my knee and swing it up. It connects with his crotch with a satisfying thunk.

"What the fuck?" he yells.

I release him, then brush past him, only he grabs my hair and tugs.

Fire races across my scalp, and tears squeeze out from the sides of my eyes. "Let go of me."

"Not until I've taught you a lesson, you tease." He shoves me with enough force that my hipbone smashes into the edge of the sink. Pain slices through me, but I refuse to let a groan escape me. I will not give him the satisfaction, will not.

"Release me, or I swear, my husband will kill you." As I say it, I know it's true. Regardless of the fact he asked me to leave, Rick would never let any man who touched me live to see another day. A calmness descends. "You'd better let me go, if you want to keep your sorry life intact."

He scoffs, "Your husband's not even in the country. By the time he finds out, I'll be long gone. He—"

The door crashes open. The next moment, Rick lunges into the room, grabs Dennis by the shoulder, tears him off me, and throws him against the wall with a crash that echoes around the space.

There's a stunned look on Dennis' face, then he bares his teeth, straightens and rushes forward. Rick blocks him, then punches his face, then his shoulder, then his stomach. Dennis squeals, then staggers back. Without waiting for him to recover, Rick swings at him again. This time, Dennis sidesteps him. Rick's fist connects with the wall—which cracks. Bits of plaster rain down from the ceiling.

There's a commotion outside. I step up to the door, and lean my back against it, shutting it. I might not be the PR manager of the Ice Kings but I'm not going to let anyone get pics of what's happening in here. The last thing the team or Rick needs is more notoriety.

This ends here, today. It has to. Rick spins around and kicks Dennis' legs out from under him. He hits the floor and lays there, stunned. Before he can recover, Rick kicks him in the side, once, twice, thrice, then plants his foot on Dennis' throat. His gaze widens, he brings his hands up, grips Rick's leg, but Rick must apply pressure, for his entire body shudders.

"You dare touch her, motherfucker? You dare touch my wife? I'm not going to let you live, this time." He leans forward.

Dennis' features pale. His arms lose their hold, and his entire body jerks.

"Rick, don't do it," I yell.

He doesn't answer.

"Rick, stop, please!"

He blinks, then glances up at me. "You know, I can't let him go now. He came after you, and after I warned him. I have to kill him."

"No, you don't."

He glares at me.

"But you can punish him, so he never forgets."

He stares at me for another second, then bends, grabs the other man's arm, and twists. There's a sickening crack and a gurgling sound emerges from his throat. Rick removes his foot, then grabs his other arm. Dennis's gaze ping-pongs from his still intact arm to Rick's face.

"No, no, please," he cries.

Rick lowers his chin. "This is for collateral."

That's when there's a banging on the door, then Edward's voice reaches us, "Rick? Gio? You guys in there?"

76

Rick

"You all right?" I glance sideways at Goldie's profile.

"What took you so long to get here?" She wraps her arms about herself but refuses to look at me.

I'll never forgive myself for not reaching there before he could threaten her again. Sinclair offered me his private jet, and I jumped on it so I could get to her before she decided to go out with anyone else. Seeing her talking to another man on that video Edward had shown me had sent a jolt of anger and jealousy—and yes, fear—through me. It all became clear in that moment. I couldn't lose her, and I was a fool to think that a ring would be enough to ensure she was mine. What was I thinking? I could send her away and expect her to remain in some state of limbo, waiting for me to pull my head out of my arse?

Edward insisted on accompanying me, as did Finn, and I was unable to dissuade them.

Gio opens the door, and they step into the restroom, telling me to leave with Gio. They'd take care of Dennis, as well as any footage from the security cameras which might incriminate me.

Sadly, their arrival also stops me from breaking his other arm. More the pity. I'm not convinced the douche has learned his lesson. I tried and failed, and now I'll have to do things the old-fashioned way. Why else would one have friends in the Mafia, if not for situations like this, hmm?

I carry Goldie to the car—she protests, of course, but I plead with her, and she'd finally allows it. She hasn't met my gaze once—not when I place her in the passenger seat and buckle up her seatbelt, and not as I slide into the driver's seat and ease the car out. She also hasn't spoken on the journey so far. I glance sideways at her. She's staring straight ahead, her features pinched.

"I'm sorry Goldie. Sorry I didn't stay in touch. Sorry I let you go." I lower my voice. "Sorry I told you to go."

She swallows, but still stays silent.

"I'll do anything to make up for what I put you through. There hasn't been a day since I asked you to leave when I haven't berated myself. I'm an arse for how I treated you. I was running scared. I didn't want to face up to my feelings for you. I was angry at the depth of how much I felt for you. I—"

"Stop." She bursts out, "Don't say things you don't mean."

"But I do mean it. How can I convince you that I missed you?"

She locks her fingers in her lap. "I don't know. Do you have a time machine? Can you go back and change what you did to me?"

I sigh and look away. "I wish I did, Goldie. God knows, I wish I did. I really am sorry."

She scoffs, "You have a fine way of showing it."

"If you mean not keeping in touch with you—"

"That's exactly what I mean. No phone, no email, no messages. Nothing. Not even updates on your social media accounts."

"You checked my social media?"

She tosses her head. "I didn't mean to. I was scrolling and chanced upon it and—" She jerks her chin in my direction. "Are you pulling my leg? You know what my job requires."

I allow myself a small twitch of my lips.

"Oh my god, you *did* make a joke."

"I'm trying…for you."

She gnaws on her lower lip but doesn't reply.

I focus on the road and grip the wheel. "You should have let me take out that motherfucker," I say in a low voice.

"And let you spend the rest of your life behind bars?" She snorts.

I raise my shoulders. "I know enough people in the right places."

She glances out the window. "I forget you were a soldier, so killing isn't a stretch for you."

I steer the car off the highway, continuing to focus on the road. "I'll do anything to keep you safe, Goldie."

"Including letting me go?"

I swallow. *How do I reply to that, especially when she's right?*

"Or is it that you see another man putting his hand on me and you can't bear it? I can't be yours, but you don't want me to be anyone else's, either." Her chin trembles.

"Goldie, please, don't." My chest feels too tight, my skin too prickly. "I can't bear to see you like this."

"I'm not sure what you want from me. Why are you even here?" She stiffens, then turns to me. "How did you get here? How did you know where I was?"

My neck heats. If I tell her I had her followed, she's bound to hate me. If I don't tell her… No, that's not an option.

At some point on my way here, I decided I was going to do things the right way this time. Which means, no more hiding, no more secrets. Which means, being open and honest and letting her see who I am. If I want a relationship with her, if I want her in my life, if I want to keep my wife happy and keep her by my side for the rest of my life, it means swallowing my pride and being upfront with her and letting her see my shortcomings. It means, letting her decide for herself if she wants to be with me. It means… Giving her the freedom to decide. And that's the most difficult thing of all, when all I want to do is tie her to me and never let her go. It means telling her: "I had eyes on you."

"Excuse me?" She gapes. "Did you say—"

"You didn't think I'd let you leave and not make sure you were safe?"

She opens and shuts her mouth. "So all this time, since I've been in L.A.—"

"I hired the security agency I used to work for. I told them to follow you at a safe distance and in a way that wasn't intrusive at all. I only asked them to protect you and notify me if you were in danger."

"So, that's why I had the feeling I was being watched," she bursts out.

"I didn't mean to make you feel uncomfortable. I wanted to make sure that douchebag ex of yours never came near you."

"You failed." She grips her fingers tighter in her lap.

"I'm sorry, I asked you leave. I was hurting from Grams' death. I knew it was inevitable, but when I lost her, I wasn't prepared for how it would make me feel. It was like losing my parents and my sister all over again. I was an orphan this time, in the true sense of the word. My whole family was gone. I—"

"You had me," she says so softly I almost miss it.

"You're right, I had you. But I was in so much pain, I missed it, and I took it out on you. I truly am sorry for hurting you."

No answer. I risk a look in her direction to find she's staring through the windshield with a pensive look on her face. "What are you thinking?"

"Would you forgive me if you were in my shoes? After how you set out to make me fall in love with you, only to tell me you did it all to hurt me. Then, you try to make it up to me. Except, when I start imagining a possible future together, you ask me to leave you?" She glances in my direction. "What would *you* do if our roles were reversed?"

My guts churn. My muscles bunch. A throbbing sensation pushes down on my eyeballs. What *would* I do, if the tables were turned? What would I do if I were in her position?

I swallow, then square my shoulders. "I would forgive you, but not easily. Not until I was convinced you were genuine in your efforts to make things up to me. That you truly loved me. That you would make me happy. That you would give me everything I want. That I was one-hundred percent sure you were the woman I want to spend the rest of my life with, that I knew, without a doubt, you were the woman for me."

I turn onto the exit for Venice Beach. "And I intend to convince you to do so, even if it takes me the rest of my life. Because a life without you is no life at all."

We drive for another ten minutes, then I ease the car to a stop in front of her home.

She doesn't comment or seem surprised that I know where she lives. She pushes her door open, leaving me to follow her up the path that leads to her place. I follow her up the steps, past the porch of the brightly colored two-story house and into her home. She drops her keys into her bag and walks past the living room into a kitchen where she places her bag on the island. She walks around to the sink, grabs a glass and fills it up. She takes a long drink from it, then places the glass aside. She walks over to a shelf at the far side of the kitchen and takes down a first-aid box.

Then, she walks back to the island to place it there before busying herself filling a bowl with warm water and grabbing a fresh washcloth. She places the items next to the first-aid box and gestures to the bar stool.

I follow her lead, and when I sit down, she takes my hand in hers. Dipping the cloth in the water, she presses it to the torn skin of my knuckles. Pain whispers across my nerve-endings, but it's nothing compared to the ache that bubbles up in my belly. I've been so wrong in how I treated her. My sister's actions weren't her fault.

"I don't regret asking you to share my room or using Grams' condition and your douche ex as a reason to make you marry me."

"You don't?" She scowls up at me. "And here I thought, you were finally going to apologize."

"I did, too. But then I realized, I'm not sorry for what I did because it brought you into my life."

She opens her mouth, but I shake my head. "Please, hear me out. I regret hurting you. The anguish I caused you. The months of your thinking I didn't have feelings for you, when I do. I love you, Goldie."

77

Gio

"When I say I want you, I am more serious than I have ever been before. I won't pretend to know how you're going to react to this, or if you'll every truly forgive me, but I have to tell you, I've lived the last few months without you, and it's been the worst experience of my life. More traumatic than watching my friends die on the front. More agonizing than leaving the NHL. More heartbreaking than losing Grams. You're what's most important to me."

He peers between my eyes.

"I never want to wake up without seeing you next to me. I never want to be in a position where you're not in my life by my side. Where I can't see you every day, where I can't hold you and touch you and kiss you and take care of you. My life is empty without you. Nothing I do can make up for what I did to you. Nothing can erase the pain and the anguish I caused you, and maybe —" He swallows. "Maybe you'll never forgive me. If that's the case..." For the first time since I've known him, an uncertain look comes into his eyes. "I know it's what I deserve. But if that's the case, I am going to spend the rest of my life, and if there's an afterlife, making it up to you. I'm going to wait weeks, months, years, until the end of time, until you do."

My heart thrums, and my pulse oscillates. Heat flushes my face, but I push all that aside. I look away, then back at him. "And if I still don't?" I hold his gaze. "What then?"

He swallows, and a shadow creeps into his eyes. He turns his big hand palm up, so he's cradling mine. "I'll never stop trying, Goldie. There'll never be a moment when I'm not making it up to you in every way possible."

A knocking builds between my eyes.

"The world around us can collapse, temperatures can shoot up, all the ice can melt so we end up playing hockey on dry land, and I'll still be trying to make it up to you."

The pressure at my temples rockets up. My eyelids feel like I'm trying to hold in a dam, so I look up so gravity will force them back down. I sniffle. *I will not cry. Will not.*

I try to pull away, and to my surprise, he lets me. Which, in itself, makes me pause. This man… He's different from the one I left behind three months ago. He's more open. He seems to be trying. Unlike the last time, his words are more heartfelt. But is that all they are? Just words? "So you ask me to forgive you, and I should? You say, 'I love you,' and I should believe you?"

His shoulders deflate. His chest rises and falls. "Before I met you, I felt no fear. I was angry when my parents died in a car crash. I was enraged when Diana took her own life. Upset enough to spoil my chances in the NHL. I was so filled with fury, it propelled me all the way to joining the Royal Marines. I faced down every physical trial thrown my way, looked the enemy in the eye, dodged bullets, killed men—all without fear. I took on the challenge of captaining the Ice Kings, jumped back on the ice, crashed with rival teams, men younger than me, fitter, faster, and I still, knew no fear.

"Even when Grams died, all I felt was a lack of feeling, an awakening to the reality that life is not infinite, but facing you now, knowing I might never be able to win you back…knowing all of my happiness rests on being with you…knowing if I can't convince you to look past what I did and give me another chance…then"—a muscle jerks at his jawline—"then all I feel is fear. For the first time in my life, I'm afraid. For the first time, I can't see a way forward, can't see through the darkness… For you are my light."

"Stop." I slap the wet cloth, now stained with his blood, on the island. "You don't get to make these fancy declarations of love, which feel so heartfelt that I know they're genuine, and expect me to take you back into my life. How can I, when I don't know if the next moment you'll decide you don't want me anymore?"

He jerks as if I've physically slapped him. And when I dare to look at him, his expression is one of anguish. "Goldie, I am so sorry, baby." The tendons of his throat stand out in relief. "I know I haven't come through for you in the past."

"Well"—I manage a small smile—"to be fair, you were there both times my jerk of an ex tried to get stupid with me."

"I'll always be there for you, Goldie." He looks between my eyes. "And I'm going to prove it to you, I—" He winces. The color fades from his face.

"What's wrong?" I scan his features and notice the pain that clings to the edges of his eyes. "Are you hurt?"

"It's nothing." He sets his jaw.

For the first time, I take a closer look and realize he's holding himself stiffly. Also, there's a growing patch of blood at the side of his sweatshirt.

"You're hurt," I exclaim.

"I'll heal."

"Take it off." I gesture to his clothes.

"I've been dreaming of you saying those words." He begins to smirk, but it comes out as a groan.

"Okay, that's it, you need to get out of what you're wearing so I can see the damage."

"It doesn't hurt at all." He sets his jaw.

I roll my eyes. "Can you stop being so stubborn and let me clean your wound."

He tucks his elbow into his hurt side and stifles another groan. "I'm fine."

"You. Are. Not. Fine." I tug on the sleeve of his sweatshirt, and he hisses in pain. I glower at him. "Take it off, right now."

He stares at me, then a small smile curves his lips. "Bossy, huh?"

"You have no idea. Also, stop trying to charm me with your smile."

"You think my smile is charming?" he asks with interest.

I huff. "Hasn't your ego been stroked enough already?"

"Other parts of me haven't been stroked in a long time, unless you count my hand, but I don't." His mouth curls.

"Okay, I've had enough of this." I grab the neckline of his sweatshirt, but he curls his fingers around my wrist.

"You don't want to do that."

"What do you mean?"

"I mean, you don't want me to take off my shirt."

"Umm, I do. I need to clean your wounds and stop more blood from flowing."

"You sure?" He looks between my eyes.

I frown. "O-k-a-y, this is getting weird, but since you ask, yes, I'm sure."

"Okay." He slowly raises his arms, wincing as he does.

"Okay." I manage to tug his sweatshirt off. He flinches.

I drop it on the counter, then pull off the thin T-shirt he's wearing underneath.

"You need to take off your jeans."

"Eh?'

"Your jeans." I gesture to where blood stains the fabric over his left thigh.

"You sure about this?"

I roll my eyes. "Nothing I haven't seen before, remember?"

His cheeks flush. "I think it's better I keep them on."

I stare at him. "Okay, this is really weird. And now I'm curious. Also I can't tend to your wounds unless you undress."

He searches my features, then gives a resigned nod. "Okay, but don't say I didn't warn you." He unfolds his length, grimaces, then toes off his boots, before lowering his zipper and shoving down his jeans. He kicks them aside — keeping his boxers on — then straightens.

My breath catches. I've dreamed of this man on me, inside me, all over me but the impact of his almost naked body is a force that slams into my chest and sends my pulse-rate shooting. *Focus. Focus. You're not here to gawk at him; you're here to take care of his wounds, remember?* I square my shoulders, take in the massive expanse of his chest, and the blood that dots the cut in his side.

I'd be lying if I said I don't ogle those cut abs, the smattering of hair between his pecs, the ridges of his eight pack, which are more defined than when I last saw them, the moon-shaped tattoos he must have recently added on his shoulders and at various points across his torso.

I jerk my chin toward the markings. "What's that?"

78

Gio

"Tattoos..." He says this as if he's goading me to ask more, so I do.

"I can see that. What I don't understand is what or why." I take in how my fingertips fit perfectly in the circular marks on his torso and his shoulders, presumably where I've dug my fingernails into him in the throes of passion. Some are smaller than the others, in the shape of a string of quarter moons. They look like bite marks. "Are those..." I tip up my chin in their direction. "Are those also mine?"

He nods.

I swallow. "When did you do this?"

"After the last time we made love, I knew I was falling for you. I knew I had to tell you why I married you, and it was not only about Grams or to help you get back at your douche-ex. I knew I was going to break your heart... and mine. I couldn't see a way out. I was at war with the need to stay true to the memory of my sister and yet...and yet"—he curls his fingers into fists at his sides—"I knew you were my future. That what I was feeling for you was something more powerful, more monumental than anything I'd ever felt in my life. More all-consuming than the need for revenge that had engulfed me since Diana's suicide. More compelling than the grief that gripped me when my parents died. More forceful than the disappointment in myself for not making it to the finals of the Cup in the NHL.

"When you touch me, I feel it in every part of my body. When I kiss you, it's as if my heart absorbs every sensation, my skin drinks in every whisper of your breath, and every part of me feels more alive than ever before. And when I'm inside you, I know I'm home. When I'm with you, I—"

"Stop." I jump to my feet. "You're killing me with your words. You're slicing me to pieces, and I'll never find a way to put myself back together. You're changing me by what you're saying, and I can't stop it, I can't."

He cups my cheek. "I don't want to cause you any further grief or upset you…or unduly influence you. It's why I didn't want to take off my shirt or my jeans."

"Too late," I mutter. There's a thread of bitterness running through my tone, and he hears it for his gaze narrows.

"I am so sorry for everything I did. And I promise you, I got the tattoos for myself. I want to wear your touch on me for every second I'm alive. I want to feel you close, want you to become a part of me. I needed to ink your touch into my skin so I could carry you in me forever."

A shudder grips me. Something hot coils in my chest. Every part of me insists I lean into him, melt into him, fuse our skins together and become one with him, and yet… *I can't. I can't.* I shake my head, take a step back, then stop. He's bleeding, I need to focus on his wounds. I'm not curious where else he had himself tattooed. I'm not.

He looks at me from under his thick eyelashes. His jaw is tense, and his muscles are coiled. He holds my gaze, and the air between us shimmers with unsaid words, emotions, and that chemistry which slithers down to coil in my lower belly. Even hurt, the power of his presence doesn't lessen. If anything, it adds to his appeal. He shifts his weight from foot to foot. He's in his underwear, but the power inherent in every dip and jut of his body turns him into someone who's not quite mortal. Someone who's larger-than-life.

Someone I can't stop loving, no matter how much I try to convince myself otherwise.

I retrieve another clean washcloth, then walk over to the sink and wet it. I return and press it into the wound at his side. I don't intend to be rough in my actions. Well, maybe subconsciously, I do want to punish him for everything he's done. Either way, I must hurt him, for he hisses. I glance up to find sweat beading his brows. Pain clings to the edges of his eyes, but he doesn't make another sound.

"It's okay to show you're in pain," I say around the ball of emotion in my throat.

"I can't bear to see you in pain." He raises his palm, and I know if he cups my cheek or touches me, or shows me any tenderness, I'll fall apart. And I don't want to do that. Not now. Not when I'm trying to figure out what I want to do with the feelings I have for him.

"Don't." I put a little distance between us, but not enough that I can't tend to him.

His jaw tics. His eyelid twitches. It's a clue that he's not as much in control as he'd like me to believe. Funny how I know his every tell, his every expression, his every gesture of tenderness, of anger, of dominance. I know him almost as well as I know myself and that...is not a surprise.

I wipe away the blood, plop the washcloth on the counter, then reach for the antiseptic. I smear it across the wound, and his breath catches. It must burn, but he doesn't say a word. He's back to being his namesake—that damn Stone I hate so much.

I want him to say something, do something, anything that will reveal he's suffering as much as I am. I finish dressing the wound, and he still hasn't said anything. He hasn't stopped watching me, either. I glance up at his features, then flinch when I see the turmoil in those cerulean eyes. Apparently, he's not the Stone I knew anymore. He holds my gaze and I see the plea in them. The apology. The longing. My heart knocks against my ribcage. *I can't forgive him. I can't.... Can I?*

I look away then back at him. "Did you tattoo yourself anywhere else?"

"On my back," he offers.

"Your back?"

He turns around and I sweep my gaze across the solid expanse. Sure enough, the same half-moons—which is where I'd dug my fingernails into his skin—dot the top of his shoulders with a few tracking across his shoulder blades.

"Is that it?" I clear my throat. "Any more I should know about?"

He turns back to face me. "You sure you want to know?"

"I wouldn't have asked if I didn't."

"You don't have to see this. I don't want you to feel obliged to—"

"Forgive you? Want to take you back? Fuck you?" I burst out.

He doesn't smile. "All of it. I want to earn back the right to be in your life. These tattoos are not a quick fix for that, I promise."

"Okay." I lock my fingers together. My heart rate kicks up, and my pulse points turn into pockets of quicksand absorbing all my feelings and amplifying my nervousness. Why am I so nervous about what he's going to say or do next? It's only a tattoo, a tattoo of where I dug my fingernails into him, where I bit him, where he's forever etched the evidence of my passion into his skin. Where he's marked his flesh with the proof of how I lost myself in him. How we lost ourselves in each other.

He reaches for the waistband of his briefs, then stops. "I don't think you should see this, and —"

"Okay, enough already." I push his hand aside, then tug down his briefs. His cock springs free, massive, huge, bigger than I remember it. And on the skin that sheaths his length are a row of tiny quarter moons. He had them tattooed into the most sensitive part of him?

I push my knuckles into my mouth to stop myself from crying out.

"Why, how… Oh my god, this is unbelievable. Why did you do it? What made you do something this crazy?" I shoot out my fist until it connects with his chest. "You're crazy, certifiably insane. How could you —" The rest of the words are lost against his chest, for he pulls me in close.

"Shh, baby, it's okay."

79

Rick

"No, it's not. You marked yourself, not only all over your body but also on the most important, most intimate, most sensitive to pain part of you, and I can't understand why you did it. Why did you, Rick?" She looks up at me. "Tell me why."

"I wanted to look at it and remember you. I wanted to see myself in the mirror and see how you'd marked me forever. Somewhere along the way, I realized how important you were, and I wanted to find a way to show it. I needed to declare to myself that you come first. Not my ego, not my needs, but yours. *You* are what matters. You were my love at first sight, at last sight, and every sight in between, and I wanted a way to show it. I knew it wouldn't be easy for me to tell you this, but I could do this. I could show you I loved you, if not by words, then by my actions."

"By tattooing the imprint of my bite marks on your cock?"

"By tattooing how much it meant to me to have your mouth on my cock. By tattooing your touch permanently into my skin. By etching into me those moments when you clung to me in ecstasy, capturing those seconds when we were one."

Her eyes dilate, and her cheeks flush deeper. She looks at me like she wants to slap me then kiss me, or both at the same time. "I can't believe you did it and I wasn't even aware of it."

"I marked them out with permanent ink, then went straight to a tattoo artist I trust."

"What about the ones on your back?"

"Finn helped with those."

She seems taken aback. "So, he knows—"

"That I tattooed your marks on my skin? He didn't ask; I didn't tell."

She nods slowly. "Did it hurt?" She laughs, her tone self-deprecating. "Of course, it must have hurt, especially"—she curls her fingers around my cock and all the blood in my body drains to my groin—"here."

"Not as much as it hurt me to see the shock on your face when I told you to leave."

She squeezes down, and fire zips up my spine. My cock extends, and my groin tightens. A groan rumbles up my chest but I swallow it.

She looks up and into my eyes. "I still don't understand. Why did you do it?"

I hold her gaze. "I convinced myself I didn't deserve you, that there was someone better for you, someone who would treat you the way you deserve."

"And now?"

"Now, I know you make me a better version of myself. That I couldn't bear to see you with anyone else. That I was yours from the moment I met you. That I'm going to spend the rest of my life making things up to you."

I wrap my fingers over hers and swipe our joined hands to the crown then back to the root. My shaft instantly thickens.

"Oh,"—she breathes—"you're bigger than I remember."

"And I'm always aroused when I'm near you. And when I think of you, I can't stop my body from reacting to how it would feel to be inside of you."

The pulse at the base of her throat tics up, and her lips part. The air around us grows dense, presses down on my chest, and pushes out the words I've been unable to tell her so far. "I love you, Goldie."

She swallows. "I—"

I place my fingers on her lips. "Don't feel compelled to tell me. Don't feel coerced into telling me those three words because I have your touch tattooed on my body."

She flicks out her tongue and licks my digit, and my heart thuds in my chest. She must notice my reaction for her eyes gleam. "Sorry," she says in a voice that implies she isn't. "Also,"—she widens her gaze—"who are you and what have you done to the Stone who barely showed emotions on his face, let alone put his feelings into words?"

"I've had a few months to practice what I'd say when I saw you again, though"—he shuffles his feet—"I might have been coached by Edward."

"Priest?" I ask, surprised.

"He might not come across as eloquent in everyday life, but his former life as a priest qualifies him when it comes to giving life advice. More than me, at any rate."

She squeezes down on my shaft, and a growl rumbles up. "You don't know what you're doing to me," I say through gritted teeth.

"I think I might have an idea." She brings her other hand down to cup my balls and a shudder rips through me. "Fuck, Goldie, you're playing havoc with my good intentions."

"Which were?"

"To take it slow with you, to show you how much I love you, to prove to you, and to me, that I'm a man worthy of you."

She looks between my eyes. "I always knew you were, but—"

"But?"

"A few reassurances might not be amiss." She bites the inside of her cheek.

"You haven't lost your sass, hmm?"

"Never, and now that you're here with me, it emboldens me to go toe-to-toe with you."

"Hmm..." I lower my voice to a hush. "I've always wanted to be a brat-tamer."

Her jaw drops. "Did you say—"

"Brat-tamer." I nod slowly. "A relationship in which the dominant partner enjoys exerting their will over their submissive and shows them why their brattiness will not be tolerated."

She swallows. "Why does that sound so hot?"

"Because you love topping from the bottom, babe. But I'm here to show you how much pleasure there is when you finally let go and let me choose how I want to pleasure you."

A shiver grips her. She tightens her hold on my dick, and with her other hand gently plays with my balls.

"Fuck," I grit my teeth. Sweat beads my forehead. "I'm trying very hard to behave."

"Maybe I don't want you to."

"And I don't want to, but"—I manage to pry her hand from my cock, then with a tug, ease her fingers from their grip on that other important part of me.

I bring them up, then kiss each of her knuckles — "you need time to figure things out. You need a little space to work out if you want to be with me."

"But I do." She tries to pull her hands away, but I shake my head.

"You think you do, but I want you to be very sure."

She begins to speak, then changes her mind. "I don't know if I should be grateful to you or if I should jump you and insist that you fuck me right now."

Every part of my body goes on alert; all of my muscles tighten with anticipation. Hearing that four-letter word from her mouth brings visions of how it would feel to be buried inside her, to throw her down and rut into her, to turn her over on all fours and pound into her, to take her pussy and her arse, to kiss her mouth so deeply it feels like I am swallowing her up. To...love her with the kind of intensity she deserves, to make her come so hard she's floating on the endorphins in her body for days. To —

"Rick?" She tugs on my fingers, and when I release her, she rises up on tiptoe and frames my face. "That look in your eyes is turning me on so much."

"Which is why you need to go to bed." I bend, grip the tops of her thighs and lift her. She wraps her legs around my waist, twines her arms about my neck, then pushes her breasts into my chest.

Without breaking the connection of our eyes, I manage to make it to her bedroom. Then, I lower her onto her bed, turn her on her side, and climb in after her. I pull the covers over us, curve my body into hers, and pull her into my chest.

"You expect me to sleep?" she asks in a small voice.

"You *will* sleep." I kiss the top of her hair, then settle my arm about her waist.

She drags her fingers over my hand, and her fingertips brush against the slim band at my wrist. "You're wearing a hair-tie?"

80

Gio

"So you always have one when you need it. I'll never let you want for anything." His voice rumbles up his chest, and the vibrations embrace me from head to toe. The hardness of his body is a solid wall of comfort. The heat a blanket from which I never went to emerge. It's always been like this with him. He turns me on, but his presence also soothes me. I feel... secure, protected, cared for. I've always known I could trust him, which is why what he did hit me so hard... but... I forgive him.

In a way, I almost appreciate the fact he felt for his sister so much, he wanted to do right by her. And he did fall for me, even though it took him so long to admit it. Even though he hurt me again. But he was striking out, trying to protect himself.

Am I making excuses for him? If I forgive him, will he do this again? No, he won't. Those tattoos on his body change everything. He feels me deep inside the way I do him. He wants me as much as I want him. He does love me; he does. I love how he makes me feel in body, in mind and in my soul. I'm in love with everything he does to me. And I need to tell him. My eyes flutter shut.

When I wake up, I'm alone, and the covers have been tucked around me, almost burrito-like. I'm warm and toasty, and when I turn on my side and push my cheek into the pillow, I can smell that minty scent that is so characteristically Rick. I draw it into my lungs and snooze a little while longer. When I open my eyes next, I spot the letter he's left me. Not a text, but an old-fashioned note scrawled on the piece of paper and secured under my phone. I sit up, and read it:

Goldie,

*   I'm heading over to the hotel to grab a shower & change my clothes, & for a quick recon with Ed. See you later at the bookshop?*

*   Love, Rick*

Love, Rick? LOVE, Rick. OMG, he wrote that all casual-like but whoa, that word resounds in my cells, in my bones, sinks into my blood and in those secret crevasses of my body. I stare at it for a few seconds more, then jump out of bed. I need to get to the bookstore to meet my husband.

When I walk in, there's no one at the till. It's only eleven a.m. but already, there are a few customers browsing through some of the books on display. The only books *are* those on display because all the shelves are empty. *All. Of the shelves. Are. Empty. What the...?*

One of the customers walks up to me. "Do you know when there'll be a fresh consignment of books? The owner told us she's sold out."

"Sold out?" I squint at her. "She said it's all sold out?"

"Apparently." The woman shrugs. "Good to know people are reading. I thought I was the only one who likes to hold physical copies of my books in my hand."

"Oh, I'm like that, too, but I also like the convenience of my Kindle. That way,"—I lean in and whisper—"I can read two books at the same time, if I want."

The woman looks surprised, then cackles. "Your secret is safe with me."

"How many books have you read so far this year?"

"A hundred." She shrugs. "Maybe more."

"A hundred? We're only halfway through the year."

"I know, right? I was hoping to set a record, which is why I came to buy a few more books, but they're all gone." She gestures to the empty shelves. "I was hoping to leave my number so the owner could call me when she gets the next delivery."

"Oh, you can leave it with me. I do the PR for the store," I explain.

"Well, you're doing a great job if she sold out!" The woman looks around, then walks over to the till. She scrawls her name and number on a piece of paper and hands it over to me.

"Awesome, I'll make sure you're informed when more books arrive."

"Thanks." She waves, then walks off. The other customer also left, so the store is empty.

Violet hasn't made an appearance, so I walk around to the office at the back of the store. She's behind her desk and staring at her computer screen with a dazed look on her face.

"Violet, you okay?"

When she doesn't reply, I walk around and peer over her shoulder at the screen. "Whoa," I gasp.

"You see it, too, right?" She stares at the number with many zeroes in her bank account.

"Is that—"

"It is. Someone paid for all the books, then sent people over to collect them. He's going to donate them to libraries around the city."

"A little unusual, but you got the money, so it's good, right?"

"It's"—her chin trembles—"it's not just good"—she turns and grabs my hand, "it's amazing. Incredible. Crazy. I can't believe this is happening. Someone not only bought out all of the books in the shop, but they also bought out the shop."

"They did?"

Her eyes light up. "I've been wanting to sell this shop for a while. I wanted to move to Florida, and now I can."

"You're sure about this?"

"Umm, a little too late, considering I already accepted the offer, but yeah, I'm sure. It was too much for me to run this store on my own. And if it not for your help over the last few months, I'd have sunk deeper into the red. But now, I can pay off my debts and have enough money left over to retire."

"Retire?" I take in her hair which only has a couple of threads of silver woven through it. "You're not that old."

"I'm fifty-five, which is relatively young but—" She shrugs, "I feel ready to scale back on my responsibilities. I want to travel while I still can. I don't want to give up working completely, and chances are, I'll end up working in a bookshop there, too, but I don't want the headache of running my own business anymore."

I touch her shoulder. "You should do what feels right for you."

"This is right for me." She smiles. "It's not easy to make a living being a bookshop owner, even a spicy bookshop owner. I haven't managed to keep pace with the new ways of marketing and getting the word out, until you came a long."

"I enjoyed doing it." More than that, I loved it. After doing PR for celebrities, it was so much more fulfilling to work on something that felt so real, so me.

"I'm sure the person who's buying the shop will want you to stay on and help with the PR."

"I guess so," my tone is doubtful.

"I know so." She flashes me a confident smile.

"And how is that?"

"I told him the only way I'd sell is if you were allowed to keep the account and he said, absolutely. In fact, it's because of the publicity you generated that he noticed the store. So, I have you to thank for this." She waves a hand in the direction of the computer screen.

I lean a hip against her table. "Okay, well, if you're happy, I'm happy. Though I'm sure the new owner was only making the appropriate noises to appease you. He probably doesn't want me to stay on, and—"

"He does want you to stay on," a new voice says from the doorway.

I know that voice. Slowly turning, I allow my brain to begin piecing together the clues. Something does not compute. It has to be him, but why? My gaze meets his, and the best word my brain can supply is, "Huh?"

81

Rick

"Mr. Mitchell." Violet rises to her feet.

"Please, call me Rick." I walk over to grasp her hand.

"Thank you so much for the prompt payment. I still can't believe how quickly everything has transpired."

"Thank you for creating an amazing space." I squeeze her hand, then turn to face the woman who's darting daggers at me.

"You're buying this shop?"

"I already bought this shop. I was fulfilling a promise I made to Grams."

"A promise?" She scowls.

"Grams wanted me to use the money I inherited from her wisely. A portion of it was to go toward helping struggling bookshops—specifically, spicy book-shops—from going under."

"And this was the one you identified?" Her frown deepens.

"Among others." I nod.

"You know each other?" Violet looks from me to Goldie, then back at me. There's a look of speculation on her face. After several moments of silence, Goldie slowly nods her head.

"I know him from London. He's my..." She swallows. "He's my husband."

A ball of heat forms in my chest, and my pulse rate shoots through the roof. Her *husband*. She called me her husband. I wasn't sure I'd ever hear that again.

She locks her fingers together in a gesture that gives away her nervousness, and the light bounces off of the rings—both of them—on her finger.

That warmth in my chest deepens and grows until my entire body is suffused with heat. I feel like I've won the League all over again. No, this is more fulfilling than winning a cup, more personal than winning any match, more adrenaline inducing than being on the hunt for the enemy on the front line, more real, more personal, more everything. This is everything. She is everything, and more. She is my universe. Every breath I take belongs to her. I take a step toward her, then another.

As if from a long distance away, I hear Violet say, "I'll leave you two to catch up." The door shuts softly behind her.

I come to a stop in front of her, then notch my knuckles under her chin. "Hello wife," I say softly.

She swallows. "Husband." She tilts her head. "You are my husband."

"And you are mine." I search her features. "Aren't you upset about what I did?"

"You mean, keeping track of me enough to know where I was working?"

"You noticed?"

"You didn't think when you asked me to meet you at the bookshop, I wouldn't?" She tips up her chin. "Or the fact you decided to buy out the shop? I don't think I need to ask why you did it. I already know you found out the financial troubles she was having, and you took it upon yourself to help her."

"And you're not pissed off about it?" I ask carefully.

"I wanted to be." She half smiles. "I almost was, if I'm honest, but I realized you did it because you could."

I nod.

"Because you wanted to help her."

I nod again.

"Because you wanted to make an impression on me?"

"Well, that wasn't to make an impression on you."

"It wasn't?" She frowns.

I shake my head. "But I'm hoping this will. I bought the store so I could gift it to you, so you could run it and do what you want with it."

"What?" She gapes.

"You love reading spicy novels. Grams loved them, too. She often told me, after Grandad died, they were her solace. She found friends among the pages, felt herself healing as she read about the journeys of the characters. Then, she got a new lease on life when she made friends amongst the book community. Her book club was very dear to her. And I'm hoping you can run this bookshop in her memory."

Her chin trembles. "I'd love to, of course."

"Would you hate it if I told you I also bought out a bookshop in London, which I'd love for you to rebrand and take over? Make it into a chain, you know?" I say nonchalantly.

"London?" She bites down on her lower lip. "You want me to run a bookshop in London?"

"Yep, come up with a name, and brand the two shops, then manage them as a franchise?"

"So you want me to spend time between L.A. and London?"

"I want you to spend time with me." I take her hands in mine. "How does that sound?"

"It's something I need to think about."

"Of course."

"I don't make any decision without first thinking it over, doing my due diligence, if you know what I mean?"

"Whatever works for you." I run my thumb over her rings, and a fierce satisfaction grips me.

"You're very accommodating," she murmurs.

"I'm learning to be patient."

"Not that patient." She tugs her hand from mine then places her palm on my crotch. My already thickening cock extends. She squeezes down, and a growl rumbles up my chest.

"And here I'm trying to be good to you."

"The only way you can be good to me is by being very bad" —her smile widens— "in bed, that is."

"Your wish is my command." I place my hand over hers. With my other, I cup her cheek. "You're sure you're not angry with me?"

She shakes her head.

"Not upset at me anymore?"

She shakes her head again. "I see you, Rick." She places her hand over my heart. "I hear you. I sense the man you are. Sensitive inside, but with this hard countenance that you put up to protect yourself. A bit like a jackfruit."

"O-k-a-y?"

"All prickly with a stony skin, but once you saw your way through, you're met with all that juicy flesh."

"Are you saying my flesh is juicy?" I ask mildly.

"This part of you is all thick and juicy." She begins to massage my thickening arousal and a groan vibrates up my throat.

"Keep that up and I might come in my pants like a teenager."

"I'd have loved to have known you as a teenager."

"No, you wouldn't've. You think I'm bad-tempered now? You should have seen me then. All irritable and surly, and I spoke even less."

"And you were adorable. I saw the pictures at Grams', remember?"

The smile fades from my features. "I want us to move into Grams' place. I want you to help me renovate it, keeping the parts that she loved but also making it our own for our family."

"Our family." She swallows.

"I'd love to have children." I search her features. "Whenever you're ready."

Her brow furrows.

"And if you don't want children, I'm fine with that, as long as I have you."

Her features flush, and her eyes shine. "You're amazing, have I told you that?"

I allow myself to smile. "No, but I'm not complaining."

Her eyes shine. She looks up into my face. "I have something else to tell you."

EPILOGUE

A month later

Gio

"Let me help." I reach for my husband's cuff and toggle the cufflink until it snaps into place, then I tug on the sleeve. "You look so handsome." I step back and survey his features. "Very handsome."

His lips quirk, then widen into a smile which reaches his eyes. That icy-blue expanse of his eyes melts until they're a rich cobalt. Flickers of silver amongst them lend a glacial warmth, which should seem contradictory but is reassuring, for he reserves that look only for me. The complex layers of his personality are reflected in his gaze that touches on my features. His possession is mirrored in how he wraps his arm about my waist and draws me close. His love is in the jut of his chin, the leanness of his waist, the gradient of his shoulders that are firm under my fingertips. I dig them into his shirt, knowing under the fabric on his skin, he wears my markings. How much more primal, more satisfying can it be to know he holds me in his cells? My touch forever recorded on the canvas of his sinews, the tapestry of his flesh, the fibers of his very being locking in my imprints.

"You're the part of me I didn't know was missing. The breath I need to live. The speed on my skates, the bounce on my puck, the edge to my face-off, the luck in my hat-trick, the power in my play, the—"

"Stop." I clap my hand on his lips. "I don't know if I should be flattered with all the hockey romanticisms or overwhelmed by your word-play?"

"Neither." His smile fades away, and his sincerity shines in his eyes. "I'm telling the truth." He frames my face with his big palm in that gentle, yet erotic way only Rick can. "Which is that you are—my truth. You are my every hope, my every reason, my every second, you are my time, my energy, my space, the space between the spaces which are filled with so much color because you are in my life."

Tears prick my eyes.

"No, don't cry." He rubs his thumb under my cheek. "I never want to see you in any discomfort."

I mentioned my ongoing struggle with bulimia to Rick. He wasn't surprised. He said he'd suspected it when we were staying with the rest of the team in London. I seemed to lose weight despite eating all of my meals. He felt it was healthy that I'd been the one to raise it with him. He persuaded me to see a counselor. I agreed, and I've already begun my sessions.

Truth is, since Rick came back into my life, I'm more settled about food. That phase I went through in L.A. where I kept throwing up after eating has eased. I no longer force myself to puke after eating. It must be because I love sharing a meal with Rick. Also, I'm so secure in his love, I no longer pay attention to my weight. His every glance, every touch, tells me I'm perfect. I see the love in his eyes, feel it in how his gaze follows me around in a room. He settles something inside of me. He makes me content, so I don't feel like I'm fighting myself. I feel...in sync with myself.

"These are tears of happiness." I sniffle. "I didn't think I could be this at peace. This content. When I'm with you, I'm not running, not searching, not seeking. When I'm with you, I'm not looking outside anymore, for everything I need is right here in front of me. It's in you"—I place my hand over his heart—"and I see you even more clearly. I was always attracted to you, but now I see your faults, and—"

"And?" he asks, a note of caution in his voice.

"And I want you even more. I love you even more. I need you so much that when you're not with me, the loss of you is a physical ache that I can't bear. I used to think this kind of love could only be found in romance novels, but now, I know better. I used to think that having five orgasms in one night was something only book boyfriends could provide—"

"But?" His lips curl in a satisfied smile.

"But... I know my real-life, marriage-of-convenience husband turned love-of-my-life can do one better." It's true! His speed on the ice is matched only by his speed between the sheets. His thrust on the rink is overshadowed by the force with which he takes me every single time. The heat we generate could easily melt a sheet of ice. The glacier around his heart had no chance. A-n-d this is what happens when you're in love with an ex-marine who is first and foremost a hockey guy at heart; your metaphors get influenced by the game.

"I'll take that as a compliment…and a challenge." His smile grows wicked. "I'll have to do one better next time."

I pale. "What? No. As it is, one night with you and I can feel you inside me for the next few days."

"Only days?" His expression grows resolute. "Gonna have to up the ante to seven."

"Seven orgasms?" A bead of sweat runs down my spine. "Five's good. Honest."

"Eight then?" His smirk grows broader.

My pussy clenches, the still sensitive bud of my clit spasming in recollection. Last night, on the way here on his private jet, he wouldn't stop. He rubbed the most intimate parts of me, then hooked his fingers inside me, and demanded I come over and over again. And I did. Not that I had a choice. Moisture drips down my thighs, and my toes curl.

"No, please, I won't be able to."

"Nine," he drawls.

"Stop, Rick. I can't."

"You can, and I'm not gonna stop until we hit a flawless finish, a perfect ten. That's a good, round number, don't you think?"

"This isn't the Olympics, Rick," I chide him.

"Isn't it?" He winks.

Those fires under the surface of my skin, that are never too far away when he's around, instantly ignite. "I think you're going to wear me out."

"I'll be doing all the work. All you have to do is give in and enjoy. Surrender to my ministrations, allow me to position your body any way I want, let me touch you all over, and kiss you, and show you how much I love you. And then…"

"Then?" I whimper.

"Come when I command."

"Jesus." I press closer to him. "Who'd have thought the Stone had a penchant for poetic declarations of love, as well as for talking dirty?"

"It's your influence. Only with you, can I let go and show who I truly am."

"Same." I throw my arms around him and hug him. "I love you."

"I love you, Goldie." He tucks my chin under his head.

"We have much to thank your sister for," I murmur.

He stills. "We do?"

"It's because of Diana that we met."

He draws in a sharp breath. For a few seconds he stays silent, then I sense him nod. "You're right. It's thanks to Diana I found you, the love of my life. Maybe I was led to you, not so I could seek vengeance, but so I could find happiness. So I could release the guilt I've carried around for so long. It's as if, in bringing you into my life, my sister was providing me with the gift of hope. So I wouldn't focus on the misery of losing her. I think she, too, is letting go. Now that I finally opened up my eyes." I hear him swallow. "I think she's finally at peace."

I tighten my arms about his waist. "I *know* she is."

We stay wrapped in each other arms, enjoying the stillness, that calm when neither of us is compelled to speak aloud, yet our bodies and our souls commune in harmony.

He rubs his cheek against the top of my head. "Do we have to go out?" His voice rumbles up his chest. "Maybe they'll wait. Maybe we could—"

"You guys, everyone is waiting. What are you up to? Oh—" Mira's voice breaks off. "Umm, sorry, didn't mean to interrupt."

"You're not." I lean back in my husband's arms. We gaze at each other with that secret smile we've reserved only for each other.

"Ohh, you guys,"—Mira's voice wobbles—"you're so in love."

"Are you crying?" I finally turn, my husband tucking me into his side and walking forward with me.

"It's just…" She fans herself. "It's so beautiful to see the two of you together. You're so into each other that my heart hurts. The way you look at each other. It's clear you love… No, more than love… You *are* each other."

"Aww, thank you, Mira. That's a beautiful thing to say."

"I know, I'm a romantic, but to see a love story come together in front of my eyes re-confirms it for me."

She sniffles, and I find a tear sliding down my cheek. "You're making me cry."

"Oh no, no, no, you don't want to mess up your face, not before your wedding."

I laugh. "To be fair, we've already had one wedding ceremony." This one will be in front of our friends, in the new bookshop I renovated and opened in London. Somehow, my husband read my mind and knew how much I'd love to get married in a bookshop. So, he insisted we plan this. Plus, it's a chance to get all our friends together and have a party. Besides, the chance to look into his eyes and repeat our vows, this time, knowing it's for real and that he loves me? I wasn't going to miss this opportunity. "But this one is going to be special," I say softly.

"Very special."

I look up to find Rick looking at me with what I can only describe as a love-light shining in his eyes. I know the same is reflected back from me.

With the right man, no words are needed. Nor gestures. Nor grand gestures. Don't get me wrong. Those things don't hurt. But all you really need is a look, a very special look you know he reserves for you.

The air crackles between us, that sizzle of electricity running up my spine. My entire body is flush with anticipation, with the need for him, a throbbing zing in my veins, and—

Mira clears her throat. "Umm, everyone is waiting... But if you need a little more time—"

Rick shakes his head. "We're ready."

Rick

"I'm not ready." Edward tightens his fingers around his glass of water. Then, as if he's unable to stop himself, he tosses the contents into his mouth and swallows.

"You look like you need a drink, Priest," Finn drawls.

"You look like you're ready for a new adventure," Sinclair drawls.

"I'm ready for something, but it's not what my grandmother's asking of me." Edward's jaw tics.

"If it wasn't for my grandmother, I wouldn't have found my soulmate," I offer.

"Grams, may her soul rest in peace, was an extraordinary woman. She loved you. My grandfather, on the other hand..." He shakes his head. "In all honesty, I didn't know of his existence until a week ago."

"A week?" JJ frowns. "How's that?"

"Turns out, my father was estranged from him, but Grandad's taken it into his head he needs me in his life. I think he also sees it as an opportunity to bring my half-brothers in line."

"Thought you were an only child?" I search his features.

"Yeah, me too. Then...a week ago, I find out, not only do I have a grandparent I never met, but I also have a bunch of half-siblings...who hate me."

"Why do they hate you? They barely know you."

He reaches over and grabs a bottle of water, then twists open the cap and glugs down half of it before setting it down and staring at it as if for answers. "Grandad changed his will so I'm his main beneficiary. My half-bros are not happy about it."

"Not like you need the money," Sinclair drawls.

"Except, his fortune makes my father's empire look like a corner shop."

"I'm confused," Finn scowls. "Your grandfather changed his will so you'd get most of his money? In addition, he wants you to take over his empire?"

I nod.

"And your half-siblings? How do they come into the picture?" I ask.

Edward rubs the back of his neck. "Turns out my father is not my blood father."

"He's not?" Sinclair asks.

Edward sighs. "Ok… I warn you, this is very confusing and convoluted, and I will *not* be holding Q&A afterward." He takes a deep breath before continuing, "My blood father is the man my mother left for my father, who also happens to be his brother. She didn't realize she was pregnant, and by the time she did, she was already married to my adoptive father. My blood father went on to marry again and fathered my five half-brothers. My adoptive father fell out with his family—no surprise there—changed his surname to his mother's maiden name, and never spoke to them again. But when my grandpa realized I was the oldest of his grandsons, he wanted me to rejoin the family business. He wants my blood father to groom me to become his heir."

Finn coughs. Sinclair stares. JJ looks at him with a speculative glance.

"Your grandfather asked you take over the Davenport empire?" Michael rumbles.

Edward shoots him a disgusted look. "Of course, you'd know."

Michael shrugs. "It's my job to know about every deal, above and below the line."

"This is one deal I could do without knowing about," Edward mumbles under his breath.

"Maybe it's time you step back into a church; you look like you could use the prayers." Caspian snickers.

JJ whistles. The rest of us look at Caspian with varying degrees of exasperation. Bringing up the church with an ex-priest? Not advisable. The silence stretches.

Then Edward arches a brow in his direction. "Spoken like a true prick, Prick."

The rest of us propping up the bar chuckle.

"That fucking nickname." Caspian glowers at me.

"Don't complain. It's better than 2Dix." I nod toward the other end of the room where Gideon, one of our defensemen, is talking to one of Goldie's friends at the coffee station. Yep, there's a coffee and cupcake station, because the wife insisted on it. We're in her bookshop, and you need them as an accompaniment for hungry and thirsty readers, which most of her friends are. And there are wine and cocktails with innovative names like Dramanie, after the Dramione fan fiction that her friend Penny loves to read, and Sugar and Spice, because they love to read spicy books Then there's Cliffie, Five Chillies, G00d Girl, Booktail, The Pierced Eggplant, The HEA, and My Fave Trope, to name a few.

Most of the names are incomprehensible to me, but if it makes her happy, who am I to complain? I can't take my gaze off of my wife where she's talking to her friends. As if she senses my gaze, she looks up and flashes me a smile. Her golden eyes gleam, and her soft hair is a halo around her head. My golden girl, my angel, my redeemer, my rescuer. She kept me from falling into a dark place, she rescued me, gave me the happiness I didn't think I had the courage to grasp, but with her by my side I can do anything.

I touch my tongue to my lip, and her gaze grows heavy. Her cheeks flush, then she shakes her head slightly.

I widen my gaze.

She shakes her head again and sends me a pleading look, which I interpret correctly as meaning, *just a few more minutes; we owe it to our friends*.

They all turned out for our second wedding. The Seven, the Sovranos, as well as Knight and Penny, and Cade and Abby. Even #Declene, along with Hunter, the Prime Minister of the country, and Zara turned up to toast us. Then, there's the rest of my team, who are scattered around the room.

This is a closed-door event, but the press got wind and camped outside until my wife and I went out and briefly spoke to them. After which, Abby took over and promised to send them exclusive pictures. We withdrew, shutting the main doors and closing the shutters of the bookshop. Once they realized there would be no more sightings of the goings-on, the paps finally disbursed.

I can't wait to get out of here and take my wife with me. But she's right; we do have to stay on a little longer. Yep, I'm learning fast that the key to a good marriage is falling in line with the wife's ideas. Not that I would dream of doing otherwise. Keeping my Goldie happy is the most important job in the world, as far as I'm concerned.

There's a woof, and the clatter of paws. Sinclair and JJ immediately grab the champagne bottles and hold them out of reach. Tiny stops in front of us.

There's a look of disdain on his face. He eyes the bottles of bubbles, then makes that pleading sound in the back of his throat.

"Nope, not happening." Sinclair shakes his head. "This can't be healthy for you, ol' chap."

JJ reaches down and rubs Tiny's big head. "It's for your own good."

Tiny whines.

"That's what they say," Edward says bitterly. "For your own good." He grabs Tiny's collar. "Come on, boy. I know how you feel. Let's go get you something to eat."

He leads Tiny toward where Mira and Goldie are deep in conversation. Halfway there, Tiny breaks away. He gambols over to Goldie and comes to a stop in front of her. He plants his butt down, then sniffs at her stomach.

"Tiny, what?" Mira gapes.

Goldie looks down at Tiny with an exasperated look. "Shoo, boy."

Tiny sniffs at her belly, then woofs.

"Stop it, Tiny." Goldie scowls at the dog.

"Why is he sniffing your stomach?" Mira frowns.

Tiny woofs again, then wags his tail. He sniffs at Goldie, then turns around to glance at me. I kid you not. That mutt... He has an elevated soul.

Edward looks at the dog, then at Goldie, then turns to me. "Something you want to tell us?"

Goldie looks at me, then throws up her hands. "Should I? I mean we weren't going to."

I walk over to her, past Edward, past the annoying mutt who decided to give away our secret.

"You might as well." I pull her into my side.

She glances around the room, then a big smile fills her features. "We're pregnant."

"You're pregnant?" Mira yells.

Everyone turns their gaze on her.

She flushes. "I mean, you're *pregnant;* oh my god, *you're* pregnant." She takes a step forward and trips on Tiny's tail. The mug goes flying from her hand, the contents spilling over Edward before the cup bounces off his chest and hits the ground, then spins away.

"What the fuck?" He glances down at the coffee stain he's wearing across the front of his suit, over his shirt, and the front of his pants.

"Oh god, I'm so sorry." Mira removes the scarf from around her neck and dabs at his suit lapel, then at his thigh, then his crotch.

Edward's entire body goes rigid, but she doesn't seem to notice.

"I'm not normally like this. I mean, I can be a klutz, but I thought I was over tripping over my two feet, or in this case, Tiny's tail. But Tiny didn't mean to cause the accident, did you?"

Tiny woofs, then head-butts her with enough force, the momentum causes her to tumble forward. Edward catches her. For a second, they stare at each other.

The air around them grows heavy with unsaid emotions. Then Tiny barks, and both of them jump back from each other as if scalded.

"Sorry, sorry, oh my god, I am so sorry. And I sound like I'm a record, stuck on repeat. You do know what I mean by a record, right?" She peers up at him. "Of course, you do. You're much older than me—not dinosaur age, but close to it—so I'm sure you do."

Edward's already rock-hard jaw grows more rigid. All expression is wiped from his face.

Mira pales. "Gosh, I didn't mean to imply you were ancient. I mean, you're, what, twenty years older than me?"

Edward glares at her.

"Okay, fifteen, at least." She coughs. "Not that I don't like older men. I have a soft spot for them." She shuffles her feet. "No, no, not that kind of soft spot. I mean, I find older men so much more confident. You know what you want, and you don't hesitate to get it. You guys have your shit together, you know?"

Edward's glare intensifies.

"I don't mean I find *you* attractive. Not that you're not good looking. You have that whole tall dark and intense look going on, which I admit, is a turn on. Not that you turn me on." Spots of color stand out on her otherwise pasty complexion. "Oh my god, I didn't mean to say that. Also, whoa—you'll have to dry-clean your suit. I'll pay for it, of course."

There's utter silence in the room.

A vein throbs at Edward's temple.

Mira gulps. "At least, the coffee was decaf."

Summer titters, then turns it into a cough. Someone else—JJ by the sounds of it— chuckles, then manages to stifle it.

Mira's eyes grow bigger. She hunches her shoulders. "You're not saying anything. Why aren't you saying anything? Are you pissed-off? Oh god, you're pissed-off. I'm sorry, you make me nervous, can you tell? Haha, I also like to answer my own questions when the person I'm talking to stays quiet. As long as you don't insist I go to confession and own up my sins to the priest. Oops!"

I wince.

Edward's shoulders bunch.

Gio trembles at my side, trying not to laugh. I don't dare look at her.

A horrified look comes over Mira's face. "I didn't mean to talk about your past. I was warned not to. Not that I'm a gossip—okay, maybe a little." She holds up her thumb and forefinger. "And only because gossip is good for you. It helps to de-stress. You, on the other hand, look like you could use some de-stressing. I'll bet you keep it all locked up inside. Which makes you a prime candidate for a coronary. Not that it's any of my business. Oh my god." She closes her eyes. "I've done it now, haven't I?"

Edward stares at her with an expression veering between fascination, disgust and anger.

"Okay, that's it. I will not speak anymore. I'll wipe you down, and you can be on your way." She leans forward, brushing her scarf over his crotch again and again, and I'll be honest, at this point, even I'm finding it hard to maintain my signature Stone face.

"You done?" Edward asks through gritted teeth.

"It's not getting any better, is it?" she asks in a small voice. "No, it's not. Am I making it worse? Of course, I am." She slowly tips up her chin and meets his gaze. "Can I make it up to you?"

He sets his jaw and looks ready to refuse her, then a cunning look comes into his eyes. In a voice I have to strain to hear, he says to her, "How are you at obeying orders?"

To FIND OUT WHAT HAPPENS NEXT, READ EDWARD AND MIRA'S MARRIAGE OF CONVENIENCE, FORCED PROXIMITY, ONE-BED HERE

READ AN EXCERPT

Mira

"Orders?" I blink slowly. "What kind of orders?"

Not the kind you read in your smutty books. Definitely can't be those kind of orders.

The skin around his eyes tightens. "What are smutty books?" he rumbles. My never-endings spark. Oh my god, that caramel-velvet voice of his brushes up against my skin, and every cell in my body seems to come alive. Also, no, no, no, did I say the S-word aloud?

"I meant, slutty books." I cover my face with my hands. "I said that aloud, as well, didn't I?"

I peek through the gaps in my fingers in time to see him nod slowly. He doesn't say a word, though. He merely glares at me like I'm a puzzle to solve, or maybe, an annoyance, or an irritant, or a pest he'd prefer to swat away.

The silence stretches. Our gazes catch. The air between us crackles with awareness. The fine hairs on the back of my neck rise. A heavy feeling pushes down on my chest. I swallow, and my throat feels like it's lined with sharp glass. *What's happening to me?*

"Do you always say what comes into your mind?" he asks in a voice that's detached but also curious, in the way a scientist might be while observing an animal in the wild.

I frown. "Of course not." I wave a hand in the air, striving for casual. "Only when I'm nervous. Not that I'm nervous now. And do you make me nervous? Of course not."

"Also a liar." He drags his thumb under his lower lip, and my gaze is drawn to his mouth. Gorgeous mouth. Hard mouth. A mean upper lip that hints at the his authoritarian nature. That puffy lower lip that might signify his pursuit of pleasure. A hedonist. A savage. A fiend. He's all of them. Does that make him a heartless monster? Or a merciless lover? One who seeks gratification, but not in an instant way. This man would wait months...years, if needed. This man would pursue what he wants with a singular focus. And oh, to be at the receiving end of that intensity.

What I'm facing now is a tiny insight into how it would be if he were to get fixated on me. I shake my head. Fixated? I don't want that. Not at all. I don't know this man. All I know is the passing reference to him within the circle of my girlfriends, whose husbands he's a friend of. I've never seen him with a woman, though.

"I've never seen you with a woman." What the—! "Did I say that out loud?" I ask weakly.

His features harden until they could be carved from a diamond-hard material, whatever that's called.

"Oh, shit," Gio says in a soft voice from behind me.

Indeed.

"Umm, sorry? Did I say something wrong? Of course, I did. But why is it wrong? I have no idea. No one has ever seen me with a man before today either, so it's not odd not to be seen with someone of the opposite sex. By the same token, it's allowed for a woman to have friends who are men and a man is allowed to have woman friends. Besides, you're no longer a priest, so..." I swallow, for he's leaned forward on the balls of his feet.

It's a slight movement, but it brings him close enough for his scent—something spicy, with notes of dark wood— to crash over me. It's as if I've been bathed in a cloud of aphrodisiacs—oh wait, those are his pheromones! A-n-d my stupid stomach goes into free fall. "Sooo, what I'm trying to say is, it doesn't matter if you have women friends. Or girlfriends. Or ladyloves, as they called it in the regency era. I mean, you look stuffy enough to belong in an historical romance. All you need is a ruffled shirt…" I hum thoughtfully. "Yep, a white ruffled shirt, which would stand out against your skin and be the perfect foil to your cut-glass cheekbones. Does that mean you're good-looking? Of course not. I mean, if you smiled a little more… Now—"

"Smile?" he asks in that dark, dangerous voice, and that swirling sensation in my belly intensifies. My toes curl. Goosebumps pop on my skin.

"Smile," I say in a dazed voice. "You know, when the sides of your mouth curve up because your sense of humor is tickled, or when you feel the urge to show your appreciation of a situation like this." I project my most confident, school-picture-day smile. "Not that either of *those* have crossed your mind for a decade."

"How do you know that?" he asks in a curious voice.

"Oh, b-b-b-because your lips have been set in a firm line since I saw you earlier. And there's this wrinkle between your eyebrows which seems to have been etched in permanently, and then the frown-lines that radiate out from the corners of your eyes, which are, no doubt, because you're old—er,"—I cough —"older and distinguished. Anyway, you have that dark-cloud-brewing-over-your-head look that only adds to your charm. From far away. I mean, it's understandable you don't have a girlfriend or any significant woman in your life. You look like you're angry at the world, and there's an internal war going on inside, and you're all scowling and brooding and menacing. Which is all fine in a smu—I mean, romance novel. But in real life, no one wants to be around a man who's an alphahole."

"Alphahole?" He says the word as if he's trying it on for size, and it fits. Speaking of fits, from the looks of it, he'd need an XL condom, given the size of the resting-package at his crotch. A-n-d, my gaze slides downward. It… it's bigger than what it was earlier, so the tent under that coffee-stained fabric is… because he's aroused?

Tiny woofs. I jerk my chin up to find he's looking at me with a glint in his eyes.

"Was I caught in the act?" When he only raises an eyebrow, I continue, unabated. That's me, I keep digging that hole. "I was. So what?" I tip up my chin. "A man can stare at a woman's chest, but a woman can't ogle a man's package?"

One of my girlfriends—Penny?—gasps, before turning it into a cough.

"Hear, hear," Gio calls out.

Someone else titters, then the sound cuts off.

I don't dare look around the room, though. Can't take my gaze off those tawny eyes of his. Burnished gold, glistening copper, hard like topaz gemstones. They could sear me, look right through me to decipher my secrets. They could turn soft like melted butter which... is not me. He's an unfeeling brute, a vicious beast. The devil incarnate. The kind of man who'd be all wrong for me.

Besides, I don't like him. I don't like the fact I can't read him. I prefer someone who's open and honest with his feelings, who can be sensitive to my needs. This man... He'd break me down, then leave me. I'd be better off keeping my distance from him.

"Oh, look at the time." I raise my hand and pretend to gasp at my empty wrist—no, I don't wear a watch, but so what? It's the intent behind my gesture that counts, right? "I need to be someplace else, somewhere urgent. Nice meeting you Mr. Ex-priest who shares his name with the man who's side I was not on in Twilight."

I turn to leave, when he drawls, "Team Jacob, are you?"

I pause, then scowl at him over my shoulder. "Is that a problem for you?"

"Is it for *you?*" he shoots back.

"Of course not."

"Good." He nods with satisfaction. "Remember, you asked how you could make things up to me?"

I nod slowly.

"Marry me."

My jaw drops, "You're kidding."

"Am I?" His eyes glint.

My heart crashes into my rib cage. This is a joke—him asking me to marry him. Only it doesn't feel like that. His harsh features indicate he has not one funny bone in his gorgeous, sexy, chiseled out of granite, body. And to be married to him? This brooding, unfriendly, severe man, this... dark, handsome in an uncompromising manner man, who'd relish getting his way with me in bed... is... not something I want. Of course not.

I turn to face him. "Of course, you are."

When the expression on his face doesn't change, I swallow, spare a glance around the room and find no one willing to meet my eyes. "Aren't you?"

He tilts his head, "What I am, is offering you a job."

"A-a job?" I manage to choke out.

"I assume you need one?"

"What makes you think—" I shut up because there's a knowing look on his features. What gave it away? I am still a plus-size woman. Never mind, I've been surviving on dry ramen for the last week, ever since the kindergarten where I worked went bust—my body shows no signs of losing those stupid curves. Good thing Gio had already moved out of the apartment when I lost my job. There's no way I would have wanted to bother her with my problems or allowed her to buy my food. And I know she would have insisted. It's not that I don't want to burden her because I know money isn't an issue for her and Rick. Hell, most of my friends are married to rich men. I'm too ashamed to admit I need help. I need to do this on my own. But what hurts the most is not being able to see the kids I used to take care of.

Between my aching heart and my empty stomach, I've only managed to make it to two interviews, both for jobs I didn't get. I'm running out of options. And there's no way I'm calling up my family. My stepmother and stepsisters would be only too happy to tell me, again, I'm a failure. I had enough of that when I lived with them. I am not subjecting myself to that ordeal again. So yeah, I need a job.

He sees the expression on my face, and a flash of satisfaction fills his face before he schools his features back into a mask. He reaches into his suit pocket and pulls out a card before handing it to me. "Be at my office, eight a.m. tomorrow."

Edward

"You think she'll turn up?" Sinclair spots me as I bench press twice my body's weight. My chest squeezes down, my shoulders scream in protest, my biceps threaten to tear apart, but I ignore it. Breathe through it. In and out.

"She will."

"And if she doesn't?" He assists me as I push the barbell up and over my head.

"She will," I grunt.

"There's a chance she won't."

"If she doesn't, there are more fish in the sea, but she will." I lower the weight down to my chest, hold, then he assists me as I hoist the barbell up again. The tendons on my throat strain, and my triceps feel like they are being shredded. I push the barbell up and hold. And hold. Sweat runs down my temples, between my pecs. My stomach muscles harden, my thighs contract. I push my feet into the floor and brace. Brace. *You need to bear the weight. Bear the mistakes of your past. Bear how you were abandoned by your parents when you needed them most. Bear how she decided you were not the one.* Not that I blame her. Baron would be—has been—a better husband for her. And now, they had a child. A family. Moisture trickles out from the corner of my eyes, joining the beads of sweat on my face.

"You okay, mate?" Sinclair murmur.

"Why wouldn't I be?" I begin to lower the barbell down, and he doesn't let go. He helps me as I push up and through the pain again. *Work through it. Keep riding it. At some point, you'll find the calm in the center of the storm.* At some point, I'll figure out my life's purpose.

It's the only reason I took the meeting my grandfather. My father's father, who I never met before. Imagine my surprise when he called me and introduced himself. My father never spoke about him.

After the incident the communication with my parents broke down. They were at a loss for how to deal with what had happened to me. And I took refuge in whatever helped me find oblivion from the emotional pain I was carrying—am still carrying—inside. I almost hung up but he pleaded with me to meet him. Just once. Ten minutes of my time. I finally agreed because, why not?

Being the General Manager of the London Ice Kings has given me some focus. Working with Rick Mitchell, the captain of the team, we steered the team to victory in the League. From being the underdogs to one of the highest paid teams in the world, and in one season. It was unheard of. I'd accepted the position as a favor to Knight, the owner of the team. But in working toward a greater goal, I discovered some measure of satisfaction. You can take the priest out of the church, but you can't take the need to help people from him. It's also the reason I agreed to my grandfather's request.

"You've been through a lot in the past week." Sinclair helps me ease the bar onto the rack. I draw in a breath, feel my heart thunder in my chest, and the blood pounds in my ears, drowning out all thoughts for a few seconds. It's the main reason I work out. Pushing my body in a way I can't push my mind. Controlling how much I can lift in a manner I never can control my thinking.

All those restraints, the limitations I imposed on myself. I lived my life according to the direction of the Church. Found some modicum of peace in the routine, the daily prayers, the sermons… All the while, knowing the storm brewing inside me would break loose, and ignoring the warning signs. Until it did. I sinned. And punished myself by leaving the house of God.

Unmoored, I left everything behind. I travelled until I managed to ground myself. And by the time I returned, it was too late. She had turned to Baron. And they were happy together. And me?

The empty shell that constitutes me, Edward Chase, lives from moment-to-moment, not quite sure what I wanted out of life. I feel un-needed, unwanted, useless to everyone, even myself. Maybe that's why I grasped onto Grandfather's ask. I could be of help to someone, after all.

I don't need a shrink to tell me I'm going about this all wrong. I don't need a shrink to tell me the person I see when I look in the mirror is not the person I was. I don't need my friends to point out I'm on a one way trip to a crisis again. Hell, I'm living from one crisis to another internally. Every minute I get through without doing something I'll regret is a win. As is the deal I made with my grandfather. It gives me a reason to... keep going.

I sit up, then reach for my bottle of water and chug from it. I lower it and raise a shoulder. "I'll live."

"For how long?" he asks softly.

"For however long it takes, I assume."

He searches my features. "I'm worried about you."

I bark out a laugh. "Since when did you start going soft?" I raise a hand. "Forget I said that. All six of you are married, and most of you with kids... Who'd have thought?"

His mouth curves in a smile, the kind I never thought I'd see on Sinclair fucking Sterling's face. The meaner they are, the harder they fall, apparently. The seven of us were united by an incident that changed our lives forever. And each of my friends went through their journey and found their soulmates. It's not to be for me, and that's okay. I'm happy they're happy. All of them. Including Baron. He makes her happy, and in her happiness is mine.

"Speaking of,"—he tilts his head—"what time is your girl coming to the office?"

"Not my girl, merely a—"

"Cog in the wheel?" His smile grows sly. "A piece in the puzzle. A—"

"Stepping stone to my larger plan? Yes," I say dryly.

"Hmm." He grabs the bottle from me, drains in.

"The fuck does that mean?"

"Nothing. Why should it mean something?"

I frown. "No, of course not, but if you have something to say—"

He caps the bottle, then wipes his hand over his face. When he lowers his arm, his eyes gleam. "It would be lost on you. Ergo, you need to learn your lessons yourself."

"Thanks. And to think, I'm the one who gave the sermons."

"You know what they say? Even a doctor needs another when he's unwell."

I lower my eyebrows. "Are you saying—"

"Nothing. You do you, Ed. Find your way. I have every confidence that you will."

I snort. "What-fucking-ever."

He laughs. "The classic rejoinder of a man who's at a loss for words. Also," — he nods toward the clock on the wall — "you need to rush if you don't want to be late."

I *am* late but not for the meeting with her. I left instructions with my HR director to get her settled in. I'm on my way to a much more important meeting. When I walk into the conference room adjoining my new office, the five men in the room turn to glare at me. Once again, I'm the outsider, but I prefer it this way. They're brothers. Some of their blood runs through me, but I've never met them before today.

"Knox." I jerk my chin toward the man standing in the far corner. The sunlight streaming in casts his face in shadows. The other four are at strategic positions around the conference room. None of them are seated. And I'm sure their locations weren't chosen by chance. These five are united in a way that tells me I am the opposition. The enemy. The one who came in from the cold to take over their business. The one chosen by their grandfather to take over as the CEO of their company.

"Edward," — Knox tips up his chin — "or should I call you Priest?"

There's a challenge in his tone — one I don't rise to. I've come across enough men who've decided it's best to go on the offensive when they're backed into a corner, as my half-brothers, no doubt, are at this moment.

"Priest, I prefer Priest."

"Yet, you left the church?" This from Ryot who's standing closest to me.

"Funny how you only value something when you don't have it anymore," I murmur.

"Like your girl who's not your girl anymore?" Tyler, the brother standing on the other side of the table, drawls.

Anger squeezes my guts. My pulse begins to race. "Better than not knowing if your child is your own or not." The moment the words are out of my mouth, I regret it. I raise my hands. "Sorry, that was a low blow."

Tyler's jaw tics. A nerve pops at his temple. He folds his fingers into fists and takes a few steps forward, as if he's about to jump over the table and hit me.

But the brother standing near him — Connor — moves forward and touches his shoulder. Tyler seems about to shake it off, but the other man says, "Don't. William won't be happy if you fuck up this meeting."

William. So they do refer to our grandfather by his first name? He's the chairperson of the company, so it stands to reason it's easier for all concerned to call him any other name at work, and he'd asked me to do so the one and only time we'd met. But I'd have thought when they were among family they'd refer to him as Grandpa? Or Grandad? Not that he looks like either of those.

Tyler lowers his arms to his sides but continues to glower at me.

The fifth man who, so far, stands in one corner of the room reading, looks around, then snaps his book shut and walks over to the table. From my research, I know that Brody is the quietest of the five, and the one I know the least about. He keeps to himself and does not participate in the day-to-day running of the company. The only reason he's here is because William asked him to come.

Brody pulls out a chair, turns it around and straddles it. The rest of the brothers look at him, their expressions ranging from anger to frustration. All of their gazes are tinged with stubbornness. Do I really want to take over the company and deal with their egos, not to mention, the roadblocks they'll put up to block any plan I want to execute?

If it's challenge I'm looking for, being the GM of the London Ice Kings provides me plenty — or rather, did provide me plenty — right until the time they won the League, and on their first attempt. I played a role by helping to put the team together, but the glory belongs to the players. And they won the championship.

I have the option to continue as GM, but I'm ready to hand that off. I paved the way for someone else to take over and build on the foundation I set up. That's me. I prefer to do the hard work, the dirty work, the work that requires the most obstacles to be overcome. And once that's done, I moved on.

The only time I stayed consistent was when I was part of the church. The routine, the discipline, and the regulations ensured I could focus on the only thing which mattered — my devotion to the Lord. And then I left it behind, and with it, my ability to have a focal point in my life. I hoped being the GM of the Ice Kings would provide me with that anchor, and it did. Briefly. But something was missing. The position always felt temporary. I loved building something with the team, but like I said, something was missing. Something I hope I'll find as the CEO of the Davenport group of companies.

It's why I accepted William's offer to take over this role. The fact that it means working with my half-siblings is something I've both been looking forward to while also dreading. It's not every day a man finds out he has an entire blood family he never knew anything about.

I glance about at the faces of my half-brothers, then pull out the chair at the head of the table and drop into it. The men stiffen. None of them move for a few seconds. Then, Knox steps forward into the light. I take in the scars on his face as he crosses over to the chair at the other end of the table. He sits down, and his brothers follow suit.

Then, Knox leans forward in his seat. "You have something to tell us?"

To find out what happens next, read Edward and Mira's marriage of convenience, forced proximity, one-bed romance HERE

For your exclusive bonus epilogue of The Ice Kiss – featuring Rick, Gio, Edward as well as Sinclair and Michael, click here

Read Summer & Sinclair Sterling's story HERE in The Billionaire's Fake Wife

Read an excerpt from Summer & Sinclair's story

Summer

"Slap, slap, kiss, kiss."

"Huh?" I stare up at the bartender.

"Aka, there's a thin line between love and hate." He shakes out the crimson liquid into my glass.

"Nah." I snort. "Why would she allow him to control her, and after he insulted her?"

"It's the chemistry between them." He lowers his head, "You have to admit that when the man is arrogant and the woman resists, it's a challenge to both of them, to see who blinks first, huh?"

"Why?" I wave my hand in the air, "Because they hate each other?"

"Because," he chuckles, "the girl in school whose braids I pulled and teased mercilessly, is the one who I — "

"Proposed to?" I huff.

His face lights up. "You get it now?"

Yeah. No. A headache begins to pound at my temples. This crash course in pop psychology is not why I came to my favorite bar in Islington, to meet my best friend, who is — I glance at the face of my phone — thirty minutes late.

I inhale the drink, and his eyebrows rise.

"What?" I glower up at the bartender. "I can barely taste the alcohol. Besides, it's free drinks at happy hour for women, right?"

"Which ends in precisely" he holds up five fingers, "minutes."

"Oh! Yay!" I mock fist pump. "Time enough for one more, at least."

A hiccough swells my throat and I swallow it back, nod.

One has to do what one has to do… when everything else in the world is going to shit.

A hot sensation stabs behind my eyes; my chest tightens. Is this what people call growing up?

The bartender tips his mixing flask, strains out a fresh batch of the ruby red liquid onto the glass in front of me.

"Salut." I nod my thanks, then toss it back. It hits my stomach and tendrils of fire crawl up my spine, I cough.

My head spins. Warmth sears my chest, spreads to my extremities. I can't feel my fingers or toes. Good. Almost there. "Top me up."

"You sure?"

"Yes." I square my shoulders and reach for the drink.

"No. She's had enough."

"What the—?" I pivot on the bar stool.

Indigo eyes bore into me.

Fathomless. Black at the bottom, the intensity in their depths grips me. He swoops out his arm, grabs the glass and holds it up. Thick fingers dwarf the glass. Tapered at the edges. The nails short and buff. *All the better to grab you with.* I gulp.

"Like what you see?"

I flush, peer up into his face.

Hard cheekbones, hollows under them, and a tiny scar that slashes at his left eyebrow. *How did he get that?* Not that I care. My gaze slides to his mouth. Thin upper lip, a lower lip that is full and cushioned. Pouty with a hint of bad boy. *Oh!* My toes curl. My thighs clench.

The corner of his mouth kicks up. *Asshole.*

Bet he thinks life is one big smug-fest. I glower, reach for my glass, and he holds it up and out of my reach.

I scowl. "Gimme that."

He shakes his head.

"That's my drink."

"Not anymore." He shoves my glass at the bartender. "Water for her. Get me a whiskey, neat."

I splutter, then reach for my drink again. The barstool tips in his direction. This is when I fall against him, and my breasts slam into his hard chest, sculpted planes with layers upon layers of muscle that ripple and writhe as he turns aside, flattens himself against the bar. The floor rises up to meet me.

What the actual hell?

I twist my torso at the last second and my butt connects with the surface. *Ow!*

The breath rushes out of me. My hair swirls around my face. I scramble for purchase, and my knee connects with his leg.

"Watch it." He steps around, stands in front of me.

"You stepped aside?" I splutter. "You let me fall?"

"Hmph."

I tilt my chin back, all the way back, look up the expanse of muscled thigh that stretches the silken material of his suit. *What is he wearing? Could any suit fit a man with such precision?* Hand crafted on Saville Row, no doubt. I glance at the bulge that tents the fabric between his legs. *Oh!* I blink.

Look away, look away. I hold out my arm. He'll help me up at least, won't he?

He glances at my palm, then turns away. *No, he didn't do that, no way.*

A glass of amber liquid appears in front of him. He lifts the tumbler to his sculpted mouth.

His throat moves, strong tendons flexing. He tilts his head back, and the column of his neck moves as he swallows. Dark hair covers his chin—it's a discordant chord in that clean-cut profile, I shiver. He would scrape that rough skin down my core. He'd mark my inner thighs, lick my core, thrust his tongue inside my melting channel and drink from my pussy. *Oh! God.* Goose-bumps rise on my skin.

No one has the right to look this beautiful, this achingly gorgeous. Too magnificent for his own good. Anger coils in my chest.

"Arrogant wanker."

"I'll take that under advisement."

"You're a jerk, you know that?"

He presses his lips together. The grooves on either side of his mouth deepen. Jesus, clearly the man has never laughed a single day in his life. Bet that stick up his arse is uncomfortable. I chuckle.

He runs his gaze down my features, my chest, down to my toes, then yawns.

The hell! I will not let him provoke me. Will not. "Like what you see?" I jut out my chin.

"Sorry, you're not my type." He slides a hand into the pocket of those perfectly cut pants, stretching it across that heavy bulge.

Heat curls low in my belly.

Not fair, that he could afford a wardrobe that clearly shouts his status and what amounts to the economy of a small third-world country. A hot feeling stabs in my chest.

He reeks of privilege, of taking his status in life for granted.

While I've had to fight every inch of the way. Hell, I am still battling to hold onto the last of my equilibrium.

"Last chance—" I wiggle my fingers from where I am sprawled out on the floor at his feet, "—to redeem yourself…"

"You have me there." He places the glass on the counter, then bends and holds out his hand. The hint of discolored steel at his wrist catches my attention. Huh?

He wears a cheap-ass watch?

That's got to bring down the net worth of his presence by more than 1000% percent. Weird.

I reach up and he straightens.

I lurch back.

"Oops, I changed my mind." His lips curl.

A hot burning sensation claws at my stomach. I am not a violent person, honestly. But Smirky Pants here, he needs to be taught a lesson.

I swipe out my legs, kicking his out from under him.

Sinclair

My knees give way, and I hurtle toward the ground.

What the—? I twist around, thrust out my arms. My palms hit the floor. The impact jostles up my elbows. I firm my biceps and come to a halt planked above her.

A huffing sound fills my ear.

I turn to find my whippet, Max, panting with his mouth open. I scowl and he flattens his ears.

All of my businesses are dog-friendly. Before you draw conclusions about me being the caring sort or some such shit—it attracts footfall.

Max scrutinizes the girl, then glances at me. *Huh?* He hates women, but not her, apparently.

I straighten and my nose grazes hers.

My arms are on either side of her head. Her chest heaves. The fabric of her dress stretches across her gorgeous breasts. My fingers tingle; my palms ache to cup those tits, squeeze those hard nipples outlined against the—hold on, what is she wearing? A tunic shirt in a sparkly pink... and are those shoulder pads she has on?

I glance up, and a squeak escapes her lips.

Pink hair surrounds her face. *Pink? Who dyes their hair that color past the age of eighteen?*

I stare at her face. *How old is she?* Un-furrowed forehead, dark eyelashes that flutter against pale cheeks. Tiny nose, and that mouth—luscious, tempting. A whiff of her scent, cherries and caramel, assails my senses. My mouth waters. *What the hell?*

She opens her eyes and our eyelashes brush. Her gaze widens. Green, like the leaves of the evergreens, flickers of gold sparkling in their depths. "What?" She glowers. "You're demonstrating the plank position?"

"Actually," I lower my weight onto her, the ridge of my hardness thrusting into the softness between her legs, "I was thinking of something else, altogether."

She gulps and her pupils dilate. *Ah, so she feels it, too?*

I drop my head toward her, closer, closer.

Color floods the creamy expanse of her neck. Her eyelids flutter down. She tilts her chin up.

I push up and off of her.

"That… Sweetheart, is an emphatic 'no thank you' to whatever you are offering."

Her eyelids spring open and pink stains her cheeks. Adorable. Such a range of emotions across those gorgeous features in a few seconds. What else is hidden under that exquisite exterior of hers?

She scrambles up, eyes blazing.

Ah! The little bird is trying to spread her wings? My dick twitches. My groin hardens, *Why does her anger turn me on so, huh?*

She steps forward, thrusts a finger in my chest.

My heart begins to thud.

She peers up from under those hooded eyelashes. "Wake up and taste the wasabi, asshole."

"What does that even mean?"

She makes a sound deep in her throat. My dick twitches. My pulse speeds up.

She pivots, grabs a half-full beer mug sitting on the bar counter.

I growl, "Oh, no, you don't."

She turns, swings it at me. The smell of hops envelops the space.

I stare down at the beer-splattered shirt, the lapels of my camel colored jacket deepening to a dull brown. Anger squeezes my guts.

I fist my fingers at my side, broaden my stance.

She snickers.

I tip my chin up. "You're going to regret that."

The smile fades from her face. "Umm." She places the now empty mug on the bar.

I take a step forward and she skitters back. "It's only clothes." She gulps. "They'll wash."

I glare at her and she swallows, wiggles her fingers in the air. "I should have known that you wouldn't have a sense of humor."

I thrust out my jaw. "That's a ten-thousand-pound suit you destroyed."

She blanches, then straightens her shoulders. "Must have been some hot date you were trying to impress, huh?"

"Actually," I flick some of the offending liquid from my lapels, "it's you I was after."

"Me?" She frowns.

"We need to speak."

She glances toward the bartender who's on the other side of the bar. "I don't know you." She chews on her lower lip, biting off some of the hot pink. How would she look, with that pouty mouth fastened on my cock?

The blood rushes to my groin so quickly that my head spins. My pulse rate ratchets up. Focus, focus on the task you came here for.

"This will take only a few seconds." I take a step forward.

She moves aside.

I frown. "You want to hear this, I promise."

"Go to hell." She pivots and darts forward.

I let her go, a step, another, because... I can? Besides it's fun to create the illusion of freedom first; makes the hunt so much more entertaining, huh?

I swoop forward, loop an arm around her waist, and yank her toward me.

She yelps. "Release me."

Good thing the bar is not yet full. It's too early for the usual officegoers to stop by. And the staff...? Well they are well aware of who cuts their paychecks.

I spin her around and against the bar, then release her. "You will listen to me."

She swallows; she glances left to right.

Not letting you go yet, little Bird. I move into her space, crowd her.

She tips her chin up. "Whatever you're selling, I'm not interested."

I allow my lips to curl. "You don't fool me."

A flush steals up her throat, sears her cheeks. So tiny, so innocent. Such a good little liar. I narrow my gaze. "Every action has its consequences."

"Are you daft?" She blinks.

"This pretense of yours?" I thrust my face into hers, growling, "It's not working."

She blinks, then color suffuses her cheeks. "You're certifiably mad—"

"Getting tired of your insults."

"It's true, everything I said." She scrapes back the hair from her face.

Her fingernails are painted... You guessed it, pink.

"And here's something else. You are a selfish, egotistical jackass."

I smirk. "You're beginning to repeat your insults and I haven't even kissed you yet."

"Don't you dare." She gulps.

I tilt my head. "Is that a challenge?"

"It's a..." she scans the crowded space, then turns to me. Her lips firm, "...a warning. You're delusional, you jackass." She inhales a deep breath before she speaks, "Your ego is bigger than the size of a black hole." She snickers. "Bet it's to compensate for your lack of balls."

A-n-d, that's it. I've had enough of her mouth that threatens to never stop spewing words. How many insults can one tiny woman hurl my way? Answer: too many to count.

"You—"

I lower my chin, touch my lips to hers.

Heat, sweetness, the honey of her essence explodes on my palate. My dick twitches. I tilt my head, deepen the kiss, reaching for that something more... more... of whatever scent she's wearing on her skin, infused with that breath of hers that crowds my senses, rushes down my spine. My groin hardens; my cock lengthens. I thrust my tongue between those infuriating lips.

She makes a sound deep in her throat and my heart begins to pound.

So innocent, yet so crafty. Beautiful and feisty. The kind of complication I don't need in my life.

I prefer the straight and narrow. Gray and black, that's how I choose to define my world. She, with her flashes of color—pink hair and lips that threaten to drive me to the edge of distraction—is exactly what I hate.

Give me a female who has her priorities set in life. To pleasure me, get me off, then walk away before her emotions engage. Yeah. That's what I prefer.

Not this... this bundle of craziness who flings her arms around my shoulders, thrusts her breasts up and into my chest, tips up her chin, opens her mouth, and invites me to take and take.

Does she have no self-preservation? Does she think I am going to fall for her wide-eyed appeal? She has another thing coming.

I tear my mouth away and she protests.

She twines her leg with mine, pushes up her hips, so that melting softness between her thighs cradles my aching hardness.

I glare into her face and she holds my gaze.

Trains her green eyes on me. Her cheeks flush a bright red. Her lips fall open and a moan bleeds into the air. The blood rushes to my dick, which instantly thickens. *Fuck.*

Time to put distance between myself and the situation.

It's how I prefer to manage things. Stay in control, always. Cut out anything that threatens to impinge on my equilibrium. Shut it down or buy them off. Reduce it to a transaction. That I understand.

The power of money, to be able to buy and sell—numbers, logic. That's what's worked for me so far.

"How much?"

Her forehead furrows.

"Whatever it is, I can afford it."

Her jaw slackens. "You think... you—"

"A million?"

"What?"

"Pounds, dollars... You name the currency, and it will be in your account."

Her jaw slackens. "You're offering me money?"

"For your time, and for you to fall in line with my plan."

She reddens. "You think I am for sale?"

"Everyone is."

"Not me."

Here we go again. "Is that a challenge?"

Color fades from her face. "Get away from me."

"Are you shy, is that what this is?" I frown. "You can write your price down on a piece of paper if you prefer." I glance up, notice the bartender watching us. I jerk my chin toward the napkins. He grabs one, then offers it to her.

She glowers at him. "Did you buy him, too?"

"What do you think?"

She glances around. "I think everyone here is ignoring us."

"It's what I'd expect."

"Why is that?"

I wave the tissue in front of her face. "Why do you think?"

"You own the place?"

"As I am going to own you."

She sets her jaw. "Let me leave and you won't regret this."

A chuckle bubbles up. I swallow it away. This is no laughing matter. I never smile during a transaction. Especially not when I am negotiating a new acquisition. And that's all she is. The final piece in the puzzle I am building.

"No one threatens me."

"You're right."

"Huh?"

"I'd rather act on my instinct."

Her lips twist, her gaze narrows. All of my senses scream a warning.

No, she wouldn't, no way—pain slices through my middle and sparks explode behind my eyes.

READ SINCLAIR AND SUMMER'S ENEMIES TO LOVERS, MARRIAGE OF CONVENIENCE ROMANCE IN THE BILLIONAIRE'S FAKE WIFE HERE

READ LIAM AND ISLA'S FAKE RELATIONSHIP ROMANCE IN THE PROPOSAL WHERE TINY FIRST MAKES AN APPEARANCE, CLICK HERE

READ AN EXCERPT FROM THE PROPOSAL

Liam

"Where is she?"

The receptionist gazes at me cow-eyed. Her lips move, but no words emerge. She clears her throat, glances sideways at the door to the side and behind her, then back at me.

"So, I take it she's in there?" I brush past her, and she jumps to her feet. "Sir, y-y-you can't go in there."

"Watch me." I glare at her.

She stammers, then gulps. Sweat beads her forehead. She shuffles back, and I stalk past her.

Really, is there no one who can stand up to me? All of this scraping of chairs and fawning over me? It's enough to drive a man to boredom. I need a challenge. So, when my ex-wife-to-be texted me to say she was calling off our wedding, I was pissed. But when she let it slip that her wedding planner was right—that she needs to marry for love, and not for some family obligation, rage gripped me. I squeezed my phone so hard the screen cracked. I almost hurled the device across the room. When I got a hold of myself, for the first time in a long time, a shiver of something like excitement passed through me. *Finally, fuck.*

That familiar pulse of adrenaline pulses through my veins. It's a sensation I was familiar with in the early days of building my business.

After my father died and I took charge of the group of companies he'd run,

I was filled with a sense of purpose; a one-directional focus to prove myself and nurture his legacy. To make my group of companies the leader, in its own right. To make so much money and amass so much power, I'd be a force to be reckoned with.

I tackled each business meeting with a zeal that none of my opponents were able to withstand. But with each passing year—as I crossed the benchmarks I'd set myself, as my bottom line grew healthier, my cash reserves engorged, and the people working for me began treating me with the kind of respect normally reserved for larger-than-life icons—some of that enthusiasm waned. Oh, I still wake up ready to give my best to my job every day, but the zest that once fired me up faded, leaving a sense of purposelessness behind.

The one thing that has kept me going is to lock down my legacy. To ensure the business I've built will finally be transferred to my name. For which my father informed me I would need to marry. Which is why, after much research, I tracked down Lila Kumar, wooed her, and proposed to her. And then, her meddling wedding planner came along and turned all of my plans upside down.

Now, that same sense of purpose grips me. That laser focus I've been lacking envelops me and fills my being. All of my senses sharpen as I shove the door of her office open and stalk in.

The scent envelops me first. The lush notes of violets and peaches. Evocative and fruity. Complex, yet with a core of mystery that begs to be unraveled. Huh? I'm not the kind to be affected by the scent of a woman, but this... Her scent... It's always chafed at my nerve endings. The hair on my forearms straightens.

My guts tie themselves up in knots, and my heart pounds in my chest. It's not comfortable. The kind of feeling I got the first time I went white-water rafting. A combination of nervousness and excitement as I faced my first rapids. A sensation that had since ebbed. One I'd been chasing ever since, pushing myself to take on extreme sports. One I hadn't thought I'd find in the office of a wedding planner.

My feet thud on the wooden floor, and I get a good look at the space which is one-fourth the size of my own office. In the far corner is a bookcase packed with books. On the opposite side is a comfortable settee packed with cushions women seem to like so much. There's a colorful patchwork quilt thrown over it, and behind that, a window that looks onto the back of the adjacent office building. On the coffee table in front of the settee is a bowl with crystal-like objects that reflect the light from the floor lamps. There are paintings on the wall that depict scenes from beaches. No doubt, the kind she'd point to and sell the idea of a honeymoon to gullible brides. I suppose the entire space would appeal to women. With its mood lighting and homey feel, the space invites you to kick back, relax and pour out your problems. A ruse I'm not going to fall for.

"You!" I stab my finger in the direction of the woman seated behind the antique desk straight ahead. "Call Lila, right now, and tell her she needs to go through with the wedding. Tell her she can't back out. Tell her I'm the right choice for her."

She peers up at me from behind large, black horn-rimmed glasses perched on her nose. "No."

I blink. "Excuse me?"

She leans back in her chair. "I'm not going to do that."

"Why the hell not?"

"Are you the right choice for her?

"Of course, I am." I glare at her.

Some of the color fades from her cheeks. She taps her pen on the table, then juts out her chin. "What makes you think you're the right choice of husband for her?"

"What makes you think I'm not."

"Do you love her?"

"That's no one's problem except mine and hers."

"You don't love her."

"What does that have to do with anything?"

"Excuse me?" She pushes the glasses further up her nose. "Are you seriously asking what loving the woman you're going to marry has to do with actually marrying her?" Her voice pulses with fury.

"Yes, exactly. Why don't you explain it to me?" The sarcasm in my tone is impossible to miss.

She stares at me from behind those large glasses that should make her look owlish and studious, but only add an edge of what I can only describe as quirky-sexiness. The few times I've met her before, she's gotten on my nerves so much, I couldn't wait to get the hell away from her. Now, giving her the full benefit of my attention, I realize, she's actually quite striking. And the addition of those spectacles? Fuck me—I never thought I had a weakness for women wearing glasses. Maybe I was wrong. Or maybe it's specifically this woman wearing glasses... Preferably only glasses and nothing else.

Hmm. Interesting. This reaction to her. It's unwarranted and not something I planned for. I widen my stance, mainly to accommodate the thickness between my legs. An inconvenience… which perhaps I can use to my benefit? I drag my thumb under my lower lip.

Her gaze drops to my mouth, and if I'm not mistaken, her breath hitches. *Very interesting.* Has she always reacted to me like that in the past? Nope, I would've noticed. We've always tried to have as little as possible to do with each other. Like I said, interesting. And unusual.

"First," —she drums her fingers on the table— "are you going to answer my question?"

I tilt my head, the makings of an idea buzzing through my synapses. I need a little time to flesh things out though. It's the only reason I deign to answer her question which, let's face it, I have no obligation to respond to. But for the moment, it's in my interest to humor her and buy myself a little time.

"Lila and I are well-matched in every way. We come from good families—"

"You mean rich families?"

"That, too. Our families move in the same circles."

"Don't you mean boring country clubs?" she says in a voice that drips with distaste.

I frown. "Among other places. We have the pedigree, the bloodline, our backgrounds are congruent, and we'd be able to fold into an arrangement of coexistence with the least amount of disruption on either side."

"Sounds like you're arranging a merger."

"A takeover, but what-fucking-ever." I raise a shoulder.

Her scowl deepens. "This is how you approached the upcoming wedding… And you wonder why Lila left you?"

"I gave her the biggest ring money could buy—"

"You didn't make an appearance at the engagement party."

"I signed off on all the costs related to the upcoming nuptials—"

"Your own engagement party. You didn't come to it. You left her alone to face her family and friends." Her tone rises. Her cheeks are flushed. You'd think she was talking about her own wedding, not that of her friend. In fact, it's more entertaining to talk to her than discuss business matters with my employees. *How interesting.*

"You also didn't show up for most of the rehearsals." She glowers.

"I did show up for the last one."

"Not that it made any difference. You were either checking your watch and indicating that it was time for you to leave, or you were glowering at the plans being discussed."

"I still agreed to that god-awful wedding cake, didn't I?

"On the other hand, it's probably good you didn't come for the previous rehearsals. If you had, Lila and I might have had this conversation earlier—"

"Aha!" I straighten. "So, you confess that it's because of you Lila walked away from this wedding."

She tips her head back. "Hardly. It's because of you."

"So you say, but your guilt is written large on your face."

"Guilt?" Her features flush. The color brings out the dewy hue of her skin, and the blue of her eyes deepens until they remind me of forget-me-nots. No, more like the royal blue of the ink that spilled onto my paper the first time I attempted to write with a fountain pen.

"The only person here who should feel guilty is you, for attempting to coerce an innocent, young woman into an arrangement that would have trapped her for life."

Anger thuds at my temples. My pulse begins to race. "I never have to coerce women. And what you call being trapped is what most women call security. But clearly, you wouldn't know that, considering" —I wave my hand in the air— "you prefer to run your kitchen-table business which, no doubt, barely makes ends meet."

She loosens her grip on her pencil, and it falls to the table with a clatter. Sparks flash deep in her eyes.

You know what I said earlier about the royal blue? Strike that. There are flickers of silver hidden in the depths of her gaze. Flickers that blaze when she's upset. How would it be to push her over the edge? To be at the receiving end of all that passion, that fervor, that ardor… that absolute avidness of existence when she's one with the moment? How would it feel to rein in her spirit, absorb it, drink from it, revel in it, and use it to spark color into my life?

"Kitchen-table business?" She makes a growling sound under her breath. "You dare come into my office and insult my enterprise? The company I have grown all by myself—"

"And outside of your assistant" —I nod toward the door I came through— "you're the sole employee, I take it?"

Her color deepens. "I work with a group of vendors—"

I scoff, "None of whom you could hold accountable when they don't deliver."

"—who have been carefully vetted to ensure that they always deliver," she says at the same time. "Anyway, why do you care, since you don't have a wedding to go to?"

"That's where you're wrong." I peel back my lips. "I'm not going to be labeled as the joke of the century. After all, the media labelled it 'the wedding of the century'." I make air quotes with my fingers.

It was Isla's idea to build up the wedding with the media. She also wanted to invite influencers from all walks of life to attend, but I have no interest in turning my nuptials into a circus. So, I vetoed the idea of journalists attending in person. I have, however, agreed to the event being recorded by professionals and exclusive clips being shared with the media and the influencers. This way, we'll get the necessary PR coverage, without the media being physically present.

In all fairness, the publicity generated by the upcoming nuptials has already been beneficial. It's not like I'll ever tell her, but Isla was right to feed the public's interest in the upcoming event. Apparently, not even the most hard-nosed investors can resist the warm, fuzzy feelings that a marriage invokes. And this can only help with the IPO I have planned for the most important company in my portfolio. "I have a lot riding on this wedding."

"Too bad you don't have a bride."

"Ah," —I smirk— "but I do."

She scowls. "No, you don't. Lila—"

"I'm not talking about her."

"Then who are you talking about?"

"You."

TO FIND OUT WHAT HAPPENS NEXT READ LIAM AND ISLA'S FAKE RELATIONSHIP ROMANCE IN THE PROPOSAL WHERE TINY FIRST MAKES AN APPEARANCE, CLICK HERE

READ MICHAEL AND KARMA'S FORCED MARRIAGE ROMANCE IN MAFIA KING HERE

READ AN EXCERPT FROM MAFIA KING

Karma

"Morn came and went—and came, and brought no day…"

Tears prick the backs of my eyes. Goddamn Byron. His words creep up on me when I am at my weakest. Not that I am a poetry addict, by any measure, but words are my jam. The one consolation I have is that, when everything else in the world is wrong, I can turn to them, and they'll be there, friendly, steady, waiting with open arms.

And this particular poem had laced my blood, crawled into my gut when I'd first read it. Darkness had folded within me like an insidious snake, that raises its head when I least expect it. Like now, when I look out on the still sleeping city of London, from the grassy slope of Waterlow Park.

Somewhere out there, the Mafia is hunting me, apparently. It's why my sister Summer and her new husband Sinclair Sterling had insisted that I have my own security detail. I had agreed... only to appease them... then given my bodyguard the slip this morning. I had decided to come running here because it's not a place I'd normally go... Not so early in the morning, anyway. They won't think to look for me here. At least, not for a while longer.

I purse my lips, close my eyes. Silence. The rustle of the wind between the leaves. The faint tinkle of the water from the nearby spring.

I could be the last person on this planet, alone, unsung, bound for the grave.

Ugh! Stop. Right there. I drag the back of my hand across my nose. Try it again, focus, get the words out, one after the other, like the steps of my sorry life.

"Morn came and went —and came, and... and..." My voice breaks. "Bloody asinine hell." I dig my fingers into the grass and grab a handful and fling it out. Again. From the top.

"Morn came and went —and came, and — "

"...brought no day."

A gravelly voice completes my sentence.

I whip my head around. His silhouette fills my line of sight. He's sitting on the same knoll as me, yet I have to crane my neck back to see his profile. The sun is at his back, so I can't make out his features. Can't see his eyes... Can only take in his dark hair, combed back by a ruthless hand that brooked no measure.

My throat dries.

Thick dark hair, shot through with grey at the temples. He wears his age like a badge. I don't know why, but I know his years have not been easy. That he's seen more, indulged in more, reveled in the consequences of his actions, however extreme they might have been. He's not a normal, everyday person, this man. Not a nine-to-fiver, not someone who lives an average life. Definitely not a man who returns home to his wife and home at the end of the day. He is...different, unique, evil... Monstrous. Yes, he is a beast, one who sports the face of a man but who harbors the kind of darkness inside that speaks to me. I gulp.

His face boasts a hooked nose, a thin upper lip, a fleshy lower lip. One that hints at hidden desires, Heat. Lust. The sensuous scrape of that whiskered jaw over my innermost places. Across my inner thigh, reaching toward that core of me that throbs, clenches, melts to feel the stab of his tongue, the thrust of his hardness as he impales me, takes me, makes me his. Goosebumps pop on my skin.

I drag my gaze away from his mouth down to the scar that slashes across his throat. A cold sensation coils in my chest. What or who had hurt him in such a cruel fashion?

"Of this their desolation; and all hearts
Were chill'd into a selfish prayer for light…"

He continues in that rasping guttural tone. Is it the wound that caused that scar that makes his voice so… gravelly… So deep… so… so, hot?

Sweat beads my palms and the hairs on my nape rise. "Who are you?"

He stares ahead as his lips move,

"Forests were set on fire—but hour by hour
They fell and faded—and the crackling trunks
Extinguish'd with a crash—and all was black."

I swallow, moisture gathers in my core. How can I be wet by the mere cadence of this stranger's voice?

I spring up to my feet.

"Sit down," he commands.

His voice is unhurried, lazy even, his spine erect. The cut of his black jacket stretches across the width of his massive shoulders. His hair… I was mistaken—there are threads of dark gold woven between the darkness that pours down to brush the nape of his neck. A strand of hair falls over his brow. As I watch, he raises his hand and brushes it away. Somehow, the gesture lends an air of vulnerability to him. Something so at odds with the rest of his persona that, surely, I am mistaken?

My scalp itches. I take in a breath and my lungs burn. This man… He's sucked up all the oxygen in this open space as if he owns it, the master of all he surveys. The master of me. My death. My life. A shiver ladders along my spine. *Get away, get away now, while you still can.*

I angle my body, ready to spring away from him.

"I won't ask again."

Ask. Command. Force me to do as he wants. He'll have me on my back, bent over, on my side, on my knees, over him, under him. He'll surround me, overwhelm me, pin me down with the force of his personality. His charisma, his larger-than-life essence will crush everything else out of me and I… I'll love it.

"No."

"Yes."

A fact. A statement of intent, spoken aloud. So true. So real. Too real. Too much. Too fast. All of my nightmares... my dreams come to life. Everything I've wanted is here in front of me. I'll die a thousand deaths before he'll be done with me... And then? Will I be reborn? For him. For me. For myself.

I live, first and foremost, to be the woman I was... am meant to be.

"You want to run?"

No.

No.

I nod my head.

He turns his, and all the breath leaves my lungs. Blue eyes—cerulean, dark like the morning skies, deep like the nighttime...hidden corners, secrets that I don't dare uncover. He'll destroy me, have my heart, and break it so casually.

My throat burns and a boiling sensation squeezes my chest.

"Go then, my beauty, fly. You have until I count to five. If I catch you, you are mine."

"If you don't?"

"Then I'll come after you, stalk your every living moment, possess your nightmares, and steal you away in the dead of night, and then..."

I draw in a shuddering breath as liquid heat drips from between my legs. "Then?" I whisper.

"Then, I'll ensure you'll never belong to anyone else, you'll never see the light of day again, for your every breath, your every waking second, your thoughts, your actions... and all your words, every single last one, will belong to me." He peels back his lips, and his teeth glint in the first rays of the morning light. "Only me." He straightens to his feet and rises, and rises.

This man... He is massive. A monster who always gets his way. My guts churn. My toes curl. Something primeval inside of me insists I hold my own. I cannot give in to him. Cannot let him win whatever this is. I need to stake my ground, in some form. *Say something. Anything. Show him you're not afraid of this.*

"Why?" I tilt my head back, all the way back. "Why are you doing this?"

He tilts his head, his ears almost canine in the way they are silhouetted against his profile.

"Is it because you can? Is it a... a," I blink, "a debt of some kind?"

He stills.

"My father, this is about how he betrayed the Mafia, right? You're one of them?"

"Lucky guess." His lips twist, "It is about your father, and how he promised you to me. He reneged on his promise, and now, I am here to collect."

"No." I swallow... *No, no, no.*

"Yes." His jaw hardens.

All expression is wiped clean of his face, and I know then, that he speaks the truth. It's always about the past. My sorry shambles of a past... Why does it always catch up with me? *You can run, but you can never hide.*

"Tick-tock, Beauty." He angles his body and his shoulders shut out the sight of the sun, the dawn skies, the horizon, the city in the distance, the rustle of the grass, the trees, the rustle of the leaves. All of it fades and leaves just me and him. Us. *Run.*

"Five." He jerks his chin, straightens the cuffs of his sleeves.

My knees wobble.

"Four."

My pulse rate spikes. I should go. Leave. But my feet are planted in this earth. This piece of land where we first met. What am I, but a speck in the larger scheme of things? To be hurt. To be forgotten. To be taken without an ounce of retribution. To be punished... by him.

"Three." He thrusts out his chest, widens his stance, every muscle in his body relaxed. "Two."

I swallow. The pulse beats at my temples. My blood thrums.

"One."

Michael

"Go."

She pivots and races down the slope. Her dark hair streams behind her. Her scent, sexy femininity and silver moonflowers, clings to my nose, then recedes. It's so familiar, that scent.

I had smelled it before, had reveled in it. Had drawn in it into my lungs as she had peeked up at me from under her thick eyelashes. Her green gaze had fixed on mine, her lips parted as she welcomed my kiss. As she had wound her arms about my neck, pushed up those sweet breasts and flattened them against my chest. As she had parted her legs when I had planted my thigh between them. I had seen her before... in my dreams. I stiffen. She can't be the same girl, though, can she?

I reach forward, thrust out my chin and sniff the air, but there's only the damp scent of dawn, mixed with the foul tang of exhaust fumes, as she races away from me.

She stumbles and I jump forward, pause when she straightens. Wait. Wait. Give her a lead. Let her think she has almost escaped, that she's gotten the better of me... As if.

I clench my fists at my sides, force myself to relax. Wait. Wait. She reaches the bottom of the incline, turns. I surge forward. One foot in front of the other. My heels dig into the grassy surface and mud flies up, clings to the hem of my £4000 Italian pants. Like I care? Plenty more where that came from. An entire walk-in closet, full of clothes made to measure, to suit every occasion, with every possible accessory needed by a man in my position to impress...

Everything... Except the one thing that I had coveted from the moment I had laid eyes on her. Sitting there on the grassy slope, unshed tears in her eyes, and reciting... Byron? For hell's sake. Of all the poets in the world, she had to choose the Lord of Darkness.

I huff. All a ploy. Clearly, she knew I was sitting next to her... No, not possible. I had walked toward her and she hadn't stirred. Hadn't been aware. Yeah, I am that good. I've been known to slit a man's throat from ear-to-ear while he was awake and in his full senses. Alive one second, dead the next. That's how it is in my world. You want it, you take it. And I... I want her.

I increase my pace, eat up the distance between myself and the girl... That's all she is. A slip of a thing, a slim blur of motion. Beauty in hiding. A diamond, waiting for me to get my hands on her, polish her, show her what it means to be...

Dead. She is dead. That's why I am here.

A flash of skin, a creamy length of thigh. My groin hardens and my legs wobble. I lurch over a bump in the ground. The hell? I right myself, leap forward, inching closer, closer. She reaches a curve in the path, disappears out of sight.

My heart hammers in my chest. I will not lose her, will not. *Here, Beauty, come to Daddy.* The wind whistles past my ears. I pump my legs, lengthen my strides, turn the corner. There's no one there. Huh?

My heart hammers and the blood pounds at my wrists, my temples; adrenaline thrums in my veins. I slow down, come to a stop. Scan the clearing.

The hairs on my forearms prickle. She's here. Not far, but where? Where is she? I prowl across to the edge of the clearing, under the tree with its spreading branches.

When I get my hands on you, Beauty, I'll spread your legs like the pages of a poem. Dip into your honeyed sweetness, like a quill pen in ink. Drag my aching shaft across that melting, weeping entrance. My balls throb. My groin tightens. The crack of a branch above shivers across my stretched nerve endings. I swoop forward, hold out my arms, and close my grasp around the trembling, squirming mass of precious humanity. I cradle her close to my chest, heart beating thud-thud-thud, overwhelming any other thought.

Mine. All mine. The hell is wrong with me? She wriggles her little body, and her curves slide across my forearms. My shoulders bunch and my fingers tingle. She kicks out with her legs and arches her back, thrusting her breasts up so her nipples are outlined against the fabric of her sports bra. She dared to come out dressed like that? In that scrap of fabric that barely covers her luscious flesh?

"Let me go." She whips her head toward me and her hair flows around her shoulders, across her face. She blows it out of the way. "You monster, get away from me."

Anger drums at the backs of my eyes and desire tugs at my groin. The scent of her is sheer torture, something I had dreamed of in the wee hours of twilight when dusk turned into night.

She's not real. She's not the woman I think she is. She is my downfall. My sweet poison. The bitter medicine I must partake of to cure the ills that plague my company.

"Fine." I lower my arms and she tumbles to the grass, hits the ground butt first.

"How dare you." She huffs out a breath, her hair messily arranged across her face.

I shove my hands into the pockets of my fitted pants, knees slightly bent, legs apart. Tip my chin down and watch her as she sprawls at my feet.

"You… dropped me?" She makes a sound deep in her throat.

So damn adorable.

"Your wish is my command." I quirk my lips.

"You don't mean it."

"You're right." I lean my weight forward on the balls of my feet and she flinches.

"What… what do you want?"

"You."

She pales. "You want to… to rob me? I have nothing of consequence.

"Oh, but you do, Beauty."

I lean in and every muscle in her body tenses. Good. She's wary. She should be. She should have been alert enough to have run as soon as she sensed my presence. But she hadn't.

I should spare her because she's the woman from my dreams... but I won't. She's a debt I intend to collect. She owes me, and I've delayed what was meant to happen long enough.

I pull the gun from my holster, point it at her.

Her gaze widens and her breath hitches. I expect her to plead with me for her life, but she doesn't. She stares back at me with her huge dilated pupils. She licks her lips and the blood drains to my groin. *Che cazzo!* Why does her lack of fear turn me on so?

"Your phone," I murmur, "take out your phone."

She draws in a breath, then reaches into her pocket and pulls out her phone.

"Call your sister."

"What?"

"Dial your sister, Beauty. Tell her you are going away on a long trip to Sicily with your new male friend."

"What?"

"You heard me." I curl my lips. "Do it, now!'

She blinks, looks like she is about to protest, then her fingers fly over the phone.

Damn, and I had been looking forward to coaxing her into doing my bidding.

She holds her phone to her ear. I can hear the phone ring on the other side, before it goes to voicemail. She glances at me and I jerk my chin. She looks away, takes a deep breath, then speaks in a cheerful voice, "Hi Summer, it's me, Karma. I, ah, have to go away for a bit. This new... ah, friend of mine... He has an extra ticket and he has invited me to Sicily to spend some time with him. I... ah, I don't know when, exactly, I'll be back, but I'll message you and let you know. Take care. Love ya sis, I—"

I snatch the phone from her, disconnect the call, then hold the gun to her temple, "Goodbye, Beauty."

To find out what happens next read *Michael and Karma's* forced marriage story hereRead *JJ* and *Lena's* ex-boyfriend's father, age-gap romance here

Read *Knight* and *Penny's*, best friend's brother romance in *The Wrong Wife* here

Read *Dr. Weston Kincaid* and *Amelie's* forced proximity, one-bed Christmas Romance in *The Billionaire's Fake Wife* HERE

Download your exclusive *L. Steele* reading order bingo card HERE

Did you know all the characters you read about in *The Ice Kiss* have their own book? Cross off their stories as you read and share your bingo card in *L. Steele's* reader group here

Want to be the first to find out when *L. Steele's* next book is out? Sign up for her newsletter here

FROM THE AUTHOR

Hello, I'm L. Steele. I write romance stories with strong powerful men who meet their match in sassy, curvy, spitfire women.

I love to push myself with each book on both the spice and the angst so I can deliver well rounded, multidimensional characters.

I enjoy trading trivia with my filmmaker husband, watching lots and lots of movies, and walking nature trails. I live in London.

CLAIM YOUR FREE BOOK
FOLLOW ME:
ON AMAZON
ON BOOKBUB
ON GOODREADS
ON AUDIBLE
ON TIKTOK
ON THREADS
ON PINTEREST
MY YOUTUBE CHANNEL
JOIN MY SECRET FACEBOOK READER GROUP
READ ALL MY BOOKS

LONDON ICE KINGS

Team roster with 'call signs'

Captain, Center: Rick 'Stone' Mitchell #13
(He's ice-cold, stony, controlled on the ice and off.)

Goalie: Finn 'Hand' Kilmer #8
(He has a Big D.)

Alternate Captain: Caspian 'Prick' Slayer #15
(He's always in a surly mood.)

Right Defenseman: Manning 'Odds' LeBlanc #10

(He's always hard to find.)

Left Defenseman: Enzo 'Yoda' Parker #11
(Always has wise sayings.)

Right Wing: Jagger 'Shrek' Hemsworth #21
(He's loud when sober, intolerable when drunk.)

Left Wing: Maddox 'Teflon' Jonas #18
(He's smooth with the ladies.)

Alternate Captain: Joshua 'Ghost' Rockwell #4
(You don't see him coming.)

Defenseman: Caleb 'Groot' Lee #16
(He doesn't speak much.)

Defenseman: Cole 'Nomad' Devereux #9
(He's bad with directions.)

Wing: Rocco 'Pyro' Bale #12
(Always has a matchstick in his mouth.)

Defenseman: Gideon '2Dix' Callahan #6
(Umm, self-explanatory.)

Wing: Enzo 'Elvis' Lockwood #2
(He's always missing.)

Defenseman: Dylan 'Pickle' Bennett #3
(He always gets into trouble with the ladies.)

Defenseman: Ryder 'Zen' Erickson #5
(He's calm under pressure.)

Center: Noah 'Blaze' Campbell #20
(He's fast—on and off the ice.)

Center: Brandon 'Smooth' Cooper #22

(He always charms the women.)

Defenseman: Tyler 'T-Rex' Raymond #19
(He's a predator on the ice.)

Left Wing: Malachi 'Juice' Washington #7
(He's generous with money.)

Right Wing: Daniel 'Balls' Peterson #4
(He has big balls.)

Defenseman: Bruce 'Robin' Anderson #14
(His name's Bruce so, of course, he's called Robin.)

Goalie: Deacon 'Doors' Morrison #15
(You know why.)

Coaches
Head Coach: Noah 'AF' Johnson #16
(He's annoying as F)

Assistant Coach: Jillian 'Scully' Duchovny #9
(X-Files anyone?)

Physical therapist: Nathan 'Bones' Pitt
(Remember Star Trek?)

PR and Marketing Manager: Giorgina 'Mac' Kazinsky
(Call sign inspired by Kelly McGillis,
the heroine of the original Top Gun.)

General Manager: Edward 'Priest' Chase
(He used to be a man of the cloth;
now, he's trying to find a focus in the life after.)

Owner: Knight 'Midnight' Warren
(Knight – Midnight. Get it?)

BONUS EPILOGUE WITH RICK & GIO

FOR YOUR EXCLUSIVE BONUS EPILOGUE OF THE ICE KISS – FEATURING RICK, GIO, EDWARD AS WELL AS SINCLAIR AND MICHAEL, CLICK HERE

MARRIAGE OF CONVENIENCE BILLIONAIRE ROMANCE FROM L. STEELE

The Billionaire's Fake Wife - Sinclair and Summer's story that started this universe... with a plot twist you won't see coming!

The Billionaire's Secret - Victoria and Saint's story. Saint is maybe the most alphahole of them all!

Marrying the Billionaire Single Dad - Damian and Julia's story, watch out for the plot twist!

The Proposal - Liam and Isla's story. What's a wedding planner to do when you tell the bride not to go through with the wedding and the groom demands you take her place and give him a heir? And yes plot twist!

CHRISTMAS ROMANCE BOOKS BY L. STEELE FOR YOU

Want to find out how Dr. Weston Kincaid and Amelie met? Read The Billionaire's Christmas Bride HERE

Want even more Christmas Romance books? *Read A very Mafia Christmas, Christian and Aurora's story HERE*

Read a marriage of convenience billionaire Christmas romance, Hunter and Zara's story - *The Christmas One Night Stand HERE*

FORBIDDEN BILLIONAIRE ROMANCE BY L. STEELE FOR YOU

Read Daddy JJ's, age-gap romance in Mafia Lust HERE

Read Edward, Baron and Ava's story starting with Billionaire's Sins HERE

FREE BOOKS

Claim your *FREE copy of Mafia Heir* the prequel to *Mafia King*

Claim your FREE copy of *Vicious Billionaire* the prequel to *The Billionaire's Fake Wife* HERE

Claim your free very spicy romance from Laxmi (L. Steele's penance)

ABOUT THE AUTHOR

Hello, I'm L. Steele.

I write romance stories with strong powerful men who meet their match in sassy, curvy, spitfire women.

I love to push myself with each book on both the spice and the angst so I can deliver well rounded, multidimensional characters.

I enjoy trading trivia with my filmmaker husband, watching lots and lots of movies, and walking nature trails. I live in London.

CLAIM YOUR FREE BOOK

FOLLOW ME:

ON AMAZON

ON BOOKBUB

ON GOODREADS

ON AUDIBLE

ON TIKTOK

ON THREADS

ON PINTEREST

MY YOUTUBE CHANNEL

JOIN MY SECRET FACEBOOK READER GROUP

READ ALL MY BOOKS

facebook.com/AuthorLSteele

twitter.com/Author_L_Steele

instagram.com/authorl.steele

ACKNOWLEDGMENTS

Edited by: Elizabeth Connor
Cover Design: Jacqueline Sweet

Huge shout out to my Giorgina Meduri, Rachel Kroeplien, Karen Barton, Rosario India and Nancy Haggerty. You gals are my very own personal cheerleaders and I couldn't do this without you!

And to everyone in L. Steele's Team Facebook reader group, you guys are awesome!

 Created with Vellum

Made in the USA
Monee, IL
30 September 2023

43735973R00227